Recent Borzoi Novels

THE SHROUDED WOMAN by *Maria Louisa Bombal*

NOBODY LIVES FOREVER by *W. R. Burnett*

THE LORD IS A MAN OF WAR by *Stanley F. Donath*

THE LANDSLIDE by *Stephen Gilbert*

THE HUNTED by *Albert J. Guerard*

THE GOLDEN FLEECE by *Norah Lofts*

WORK AND PLAY (The tenth volume of MEN OF GOOD WILL)
by *Jules Romains*

REUNION ON STRAWBERRY HILL by *Berenice Thorpe*

Published by Alfred A. Knopf

THE BAY OF SILENCE

THE BAY OF SILENCE

BY

EDUARDO MALLEA

TRANSLATED FROM THE SPANISH BY

STUART EDGAR GRUMMON

New York ALFRED A KNOPF 1944

FIRST AMERICAN EDITION

PUBLISHED SIMULTANEOUSLY IN CANADA
BY THE RYERSON PRESS
MANUFACTURED IN THE UNITED STATES
OF AMERICA

I DEDICATE THIS BOOK TO THE YOUNG MEN AND WOMEN
LIVING IN THE SUBTERRANEAN ZONES OF MY COUNTRY FROM WHICH
ALL SPRINGS ARE FED, WHO CHERISH AN IDEA OF THE CLEAN GRAN-
DEUR OF THEIR NATIVE LAND AND WHO HAVE OFTEN BEEN FILLED
WITH INDIGNATION AT THOSE WHO DECEIVE AND TRAFFIC IN IT.

+-O+-O+-O+-O+-O+-O+-O+-O+-O+-O+-O+-O+-O+-O+-O+-O+-O+-O+-O+

Oh yet we trust that somehow good
  Will be the final goal of ill,
  To pangs of nature, sins of will,
Defects of doubt, and taints of blood;

That nothing walks with aimless feet;
  That not one life shall be destroy'd,
  Or cast as rubbish to the void,
When God hath made the pile complete;

That not a worm is cloven in vain;
  That not a moth with vain desire
  Is shrivell'd in a fruitless fire,
Or but subserves another's gain.

Behold, we know not anything;
  I can but trust that good shall fall
  At last — far off — at last, to all,
And every winter change to spring.

So runs my dream: but what am I?
  An infant crying in the night:
  An infant crying for the light:
And with no language but a cry.

LORD TENNYSON: *In Memoriam*

CONTENTS

THE BAY OF SILENCE

BOOK I

Youth

◊►◊►◊►◊►◊►◊►◊►◊►◊►◊◄◊◄◊◄◊◄◊◄◊◄◊◄◊◄◊◄◊

I

H AVEN'T the new begonias arrived yet?"

This was the thousandth time that I had seen you. You had never seen me, except vaguely. You did not see me now until you raised your eyes in a distant way, realized that the florist was busy attending to me, and smiled at your own discourtesy. There was a harsh and blighted look in your eyes, even in your smile.

I had seen you three times that year; the first time you were wearing a black, tailored suit with a blue blouse and a narrow white collar; the second time — it was raining — a glossy, transparent raincoat; and the third time, a blue suit, like the one that you were now wearing.

God, how many years have passed, how many years — at least thirteen — since our first meeting!

Looking at you, I thought: "Yes, that way she has of holding her head, that trim line of her body, that nervous vitality of her whole being are beautiful, but they are not the most beautiful thing about her."

The most beautiful, I knew, was deep down within you.

There I was looking at you after so many years, as disturbed and confused as any callow youth. But we were still strangers;

3

we did not even utter a single word, in spite of all that linked us to each other.

This was the thousandth time that I had seen you, perhaps the thousand and third.

2

I DO not recall when the first time was. You entered my life timelessly. My first impression of you was once when you were coming down Charcas Street, skirting San Martín Plaza. It was a foggy day, probably in August or September. You were walking along hurriedly, deep in thought, wearing an open sports jacket. I confess that I remained rooted to the spot like a simpleton, all the blood drawn from the surface of my body.

Later I realized that the situation was like the common print of Dante Alighieri picturing him catching sight of Beatrice for the first time as she was crossing one of the bridges over the Arno. I know of no middle-class home without that picture of the poet, in his bonnet, with its flowing ear-pieces, and long sweeping garment, one hand held against his chest. It was like that. You passed by and I unconsciously walked after you. I do not remember how I went home that day, but I recollect every detail of the many times that I saw you subsequently.

I could not know from what part of the city you were coming, nor where you were going. I was a poor law student. My parents, who sent me very little money, lived in Río Negro. My father had a modest position as an engineer; my mother was anemic. He had always been absorbed in his own thoughts and was strongly determined to stand on his own feet. He would accept favors from no one and had gone directly from the university to the interior of the country, where he found an opening in his profession.

He and my pale, placid mother, also a retiring person, lived many years of ideal happiness together, although they had scarcely money to pay for their rent and food. At length, when I was two or three years old, my father bought a small sawmill, which, because of its clamorous saws and great lofty main shed, to me seemed gigantic. I walked with him from the house to the mill every morning at daybreak — it was still dark during the winter months. It was a long walk. We trudged along in silence; he with his tireless stride, I trying hard to keep up with him — stumbling at times, falling behind, then running to catch up with him again. We crossed an intersecting road from which there was a view of the bank of a stream, between thick green willows, its clear waters revealing the tender vegetation growing from the bottom. Sometimes my father would send me to climb to the top of a tree. He would watch me, smiling, but not slackening his pace, as I performed daring gymnastic feats without encouragement. Sometimes on a February evening, in summer, we stopped to bathe in the clear stream on the way home from the mill. That was heaven to me! My nostrils worked at the scent of the water, the twilight air, and the warm, pungent odors of the leaves. This was my childhood passion. Thus I grew, a happy fruit attached to the parent trunk. When I left my parents, I felt that I was removing a moral prop from their tottering house. Events shortly proved that I was right, for my father began to lose money and my mother's condition became steadily worse. But I could not leave Buenos Aires. I had modest but steady employment as a translator, which paid my examination fees and room rent. My student life depended on meeting these obligations.

I never knew where you were going, nor where you were coming from. During the early evening hours, returning home along Florida Street from the law school, I often saw you walking northward. I remember how you looked, the hair loose on your proudly held head, your hat folded between your slender fingers, and your left arm pressing some books tightly against your side. You seemed wholly detached from your surroundings — from the noise of Buenos Aires, from the rush-hour traffic, from the crowds streaming out of the stores and banks. You seemed to be aware of nothing, attentive only to the inner voice of some dream, some aspiration, some love or hatred. Your expression was not happy. But there was about you a certain reserve, an aristocratic pride that drew me mightily.

One day I learned your name, the name of one of the oldest colonial families. Your husband — a slight, glowering, jaundiced-looking man, who was once casually pointed out to me — bore a name still more ancient and resounding. The day that I learned your name — to think that I found it out so easily as you were leaving Mitchell's English bookstore! — I felt that I was nearer to your world and that something strong and definite linked me to you forever. At the very least I would read in the newspapers about any important function that you attended.

Thus the thread of Ariadne remained in my hands. The dark currents and surprises of life could no longer snatch you away from Buenos Aires without my knowledge and without a trace. I felt much better.

I was living then in a boarding-house in Twenty-fifth of May Street, at the corner of Tucumán. It occupied the fifth floor of an enormous apartment house, with wide, gloomy halls. Diagonally opposite was an old British mansion — a club or association of some sort. Directly opposite was a bar of evil repute. On both sides of Twenty-fifth of May Street, like the old streets in any South American city, there were buildings of the most heterogeneous and contradictory architecture. They revealed the mad rush of their builders to turn their money into durable, tangible substance. Tucumán Street, which lay parallel to our front door, ran in squalor down to the river — a hundred feet of sharp descent. I was much attached to all these streets in spite of their dubious appearance. I could occasionally escape to them for a little while from the monotony of the city.

The proprietress of the boarding-house, Señora Ana, was a

corpulent woman with heavy, sleepy eyelids. She was said to be a native of one of the bordering countries and the widow of a piano-tuner. She had a squalid, washed-out-looking servant, who obeyed her like a dog and did the rooms in sullen silence.

The other boarders were a bed-springs salesman named Johnson, who looked like an Anglican bishop, and two young men, Jiménez and Anselmi, of exactly my own age. Jiménez worked in one of the ministries, and Anselmi was a law student. We were very different. Jiménez had an insufferably pretentious appearance, wore rimless glasses, and brushed his straight, pomaded hair to an aggressive point. He was a timid soul, however, and his aggressive air was merely a form of defense. His manner was hard and sarcastic, but I knew that he had an almost femininely fragile and sensitive nature. Anselmi, on the other hand, was corpulent, with a large, peasant frame and coarse hands, his personality impulsive and frank. He was constantly restless, and always seemed ready to go out and seize life by the forelock. One might think from this that the intellectual and spiritual advantage lay with Jiménez. On the contrary, Anselmi's strength, impetuosity, and courage were of better stuff. They came from a strong vitality. He was intelligent and assured and had an enormous capacity for learning. I admired him greatly for these striking assets. Jiménez was jealous of this preference, but never alluded to it.

There was also a girl. She looked tired and faded and her life was rather enigmatic. There was an air of distinction about her, however, and she was always smartly dressed. We seldom saw her and had never exchanged a word with her.

As a matter of fact, Anselmi, Jiménez, and I were not to be trusted with women. We were all three quite prepared to take advantage of them and then discuss them slyly and jovially.

Finally, there was an old Bohemian doctor named Dervil, who had given up his profession years before because of a philosophical disappointment in science. He lived as a dreamer, poor as a church mouse, but rich in ideas, experience, and anecdotes. We enjoyed his conversation. Men like him, who have come to no other conclusion in life than to be honest with themselves, are commonly called parasites, loafers, or fools. Society is prone to classify rather smugly those whom it rejects.

My room was quite large, and Jiménez and Anselmi lived in it more than in their own miserable inside rooms. Mine had two balconies, one overlooking Tucumán Street. From it you could clearly see the river, the steamships being slowly towed up the Plata Canal, the tracks of the coastal railroad — in short all of that region, so temporary and so spacious, which is exactly like the general aspect of our country — an endless, desolate plain. There were few things in my room: a bed, some books in a pine bookcase, several portraits of authors that I was reading at the time, two fine French engravings, and an enormous wardrobe which served as both bureau and filing-cabinet for newspaper clippings. The best feature of my room was an old fireplace that had a wonderful draft. On Saturdays they brought me a great pile of firewood from the corner coal-dealer's. This was the good news of the week. The chap who brought it was a blue-eyed open-handed Italian, an anarchist, and a great reader of Lermontov. Before leaving, he would glance scornfully at my books and remark that he had read but one book in Spanish, *Socialist Dogma*, by the Argentine writer Estéban Echeverría.

Buenos Aires is not a very amusing city. If you study its plan you will observe that to the northeast it is shaped like a child's profile. This is no chance resemblance. The city, which wears such an ancient aspect despite its newness, has the heart-beat of a timid adolescent. It is full of violence toward strangers. Far from pampering and amusing them as other cities of the world do, it distrusts them when they first arrive and abuses them as a woman married in anger does the husband who caresses her. We, however, knew it well. From its mud flats in lower Belgrano to the frank licentiousness of the coastal area within the con-

8

fines of Avellaneda, we knew our unconfessable topography. But as happens to men who have had a sad and lonely childhood, the lure of sin troubled us little — our inclination was to search for souls. Our catch also — and it was plentiful — was ideas and inspirations. We were constantly looking for a place in which to stimulate our own enthusiasm or to join in the enthusiasm of others. Our headquarters were in a small beer-hall in Lavalle Street. Before and after our dinner we used to go there to listen to the Swiss orchestra play the old waltzes and tangos that seemed the older for being played over and over by those decrepit musicians.

The beer-hall was a curious spot. It is worth describing. The room was a large rectangle composed of two planes: the upper one, occupying a fourth of its area, was bounded by a long balustrade. A stairway at its open end communicated with the lower floor. The downstairs portion was full of tables between diminutive colonnades supporting green plants. To the right there was a low platform where the four Swiss who composed the orchestra accommodated themselves as best they could. Some days the proprietor himself, a thickset Swiss who lacked an eye, felt inspired to animate the musty company assembled there and mounted the platform to quicken the rhythm of the lagging musicians by his energetic gesticulations. A large garland of paper orchids adorned the side opposite the orchestra, where a show-case stood. From the wall hung back numbers of the *Berliner Tageblatt*, the current issue of the *Deutsche La Plata Zeitung*, and various periodicals written in the most unexpected languages. Along a wide molding that ran around the room on both the upper and the lower levels was the inevitable profusion of German beer-mugs, grotesque vases, and hunting trophies picked up at auction. The most motley assortment of customers rubbed elbows in the beer-hall with girls of doubtful antecedents and ruddy-faced couples with noses showing prominent veins. We used to repair to that place as though going into voluntary exile — to conspire actively or passively. Our type of instigation was to clarify our thinking and intensify our own ideas of rebellion. The important thing was to accumulate within us a capital of nonconformity, a credit of available opposition.

About the table, with its bocks and pretzels, arose the most ambitious arguments, the most spirited debates as to how to mend a twisted world in which we found it uncomfortable to live. There were about a dozen of us. The lean, emphatic, dignified Letesón, who edited a modest literary review; Gómez, an ultra-modernist amateur painter; Stigmann, a short, scatter-brained Jew, loquacious, slanderous, cynical, dirty, and greasy-looking, with a magnificent head and an unhealthy combativeness; Gali, a medical student, always accompanied by his friend, a hungry-looking girl of twenty with hunted eyes; and a bare-headed, vociferous, hulking brute, a specialist in theoretical *coups d'état*, a constitutional conspirator. . . . Frequently new faces joined the group for a time. Villegas, Anselmi, and I were the specialists in general ideas; the others — with the exception of Jiménez — were somewhat muddle-headed.

At that time I was already beginning to have ideas of my own about life. I had grown up surrounded by the enigmatical, mysterious, and profound Argentine landscape. From the soil I had learned lessons that seemed essential if I was to walk upright in an environment where so many things were demoralizing. I soon saw that these lessons were generally unknown to the soft, confused world that moved, traded, and loved in Buenos Aires. The whole country, nevertheless, was striving more and more to resemble the capital. It was therefore a country lying on the ground, asleep. It had to be pulled to its feet. Undoubtedly there were already some men and women who stood erect. I had to seek them out. These needs began to be the hope to which I awakened every morning in the room in that old building in Twenty-fifth of May Street.

What joy the feeling of the future gave me then! Breathing the future was my whole salvation. I felt a boundless happiness. I breathed in unison with the slow, sure march of the planet's exhilaration. Sometimes when I returned to the house, I wanted to embrace the boarding-house mistress, to ask senseless questions of the young lady in the neighboring room, with whom I had never exchanged anything but the customary laconic salutations, and to invite the philosophical doctor to share my slender funds and enjoy a jovial but fleeting prosperity with me. I threw myself down on the bed, with the light on, my legs crossed, my hands folded under my head, and let time pass and smiled. "It's so easy," I thought, "to master the world and make my mark in literature, and in cultivated society. So easy!"

Suddenly Anselmi entered, enormous and exulting, brandishing a package. "Cheese from Catamarca!" he cried. I sat up on the bed instantly and looked at him. We were silent for a moment, our eyes gleaming; then suddenly, with a yell, rushed off like savages to the dining-room, leaving the doors open and the lamps a-tremble.

We were joyous, strong, and ambitious.

Nevertheless, I was restless.

I was in the habit of sipping my glass of beer while waiting for the boys. Listening to a badly played symphony, I watched the more dignified customers enter. I dreamed of writing two or three good books and seeing my country unite and stand on its feet. For this, for both these things, I had to sweep away first my own inertia, and then the collective inertia about me. How could I help to bring about the triumph of those two objectives? Many a quarter of an hour I spent pondering this. People came and went. From time to time a face or a gesture caught my attention. Then Anselmi or Jiménez arrived. They related trivial incidents of the outside world, and again I had to adjust myself to reality. Do not think that my illusion was fatuous or selfish. It was rather a need to share a certain abundance, to share it in order to make it more common about me, and to raise the tone of a blunted, monotonous environment.

Anselmi was devouring great chunks of black bread and butter. He said that this made up to him for the abominable fare at the boarding-house. In fact, however, his appetite was no less ravenous at Señora Ana's. When Julian Villegas and his girl arrived, she kept eying the black bread and butter hungrily. But Villegas would allow nobody to buy her a drink or a sandwich. "She is dieting," he asserted authoritatively. The girl smiled like a timid animal, with stupid, inexpressive eyes.

In the matter of love I was a casual hunter, satisfied with the easy prey that I picked up on my path. That meant girls of varying beauty, not always either discreet or well advised. I ran into them here or there in the course of my long evening walks through the northern part of the city. They were shop-girls or students. Generally they aroused my ardent and not entirely confessable illusions, and in a few days cloyed completely. At a time when I was only looking for exciting discoveries, those silent girls did not greatly stir my enthusiasm. The prettiest was a slender Irish girl of twenty-two who walked gracefully and had rosy cheeks and very bright eyes. I thought that I would be able to practice my English with her, but she refused, with that recalcitrant spirit of some second-generation Argentines who are determined to pass at all costs as coming from colonial stock. Her skin was too white to be temperamentally interesting. We met in a sinister-looking house in Lavalle Street. The proprietress rented us reasonably, for two hours, the room of a fat, nondescript merchant. It was about two yards square. One evening when Gladys and I were there together, we were startled to hear someone opening the door from the outside. The plump and ruddy face of the legitimate tenant appeared before our eyes. He stood, stupefied, holding a little bunch of violets in his left hand and the key in the other. He mumbled a few words and departed.

It was not long before it became impossible for me to endure Gladys's silences, her purely carnal ardor, her inner coldness, her essential mediocrity. We spent some sad Sundays walking about without a word to say to each other. The sex act alone attracted her, and that carried out in silence, as with animals. I then began to realize that in human relations only one thing was important to me, communication — intimate communion with beings of my own spiritual family. Where there was no fundamental communication, there could be no real affinity. When I said that to Gladys in the Blas Mango tearoom, she said nothing, shrugged her shoulders, and continued to munch chocolate candies. The jacarandas had begun to bloom along the sidewalks.

After that affair I began to be more discriminating. Which does not mean that a charming head, a certain expression, or a striking pair of eyes did not make me break my vows of caution for a few weeks.

On Sundays we used to go out to Palermo with some girls, to the gorges of Belgrano or to Tigre, in trains packed with week-end excursionists. We watched the river from the car windows during the journey — the motionless river, its vast, silent surface, like the dream of the adolescent country. What holidays and what nights at the entrance to the canals of the Delta, lying in the boats with our hands under our heads, watching the lofty, nocturnal sky, the summer calm, a sudden shooting star, the timid twinkling of the cosmic dust!

You cannot imagine how young and happy we were. Nothing disturbed our rhythm, nothing altered the illusive feeling of a great destiny within us. Our life was like an aspiration that might be realized at any moment, but which remained a pleasant indolence.

3

It is not easy to isolate his cardinal passions from the story of a youth. At this period of life a theory is as important as an emotion, or as a spontaneous act of will. All probabilities then seem equally possible, and a young man seldom knows what in life is truly his. He accepts and rejects a great deal and his choices are seldom permanent. But gradually he comes to a proper knowledge of himself. It was at this time that I began to realize that a life of selfish pleasure-seeking was not for me, that I needed to share my thoughts, my passions, everything with my fellow human creatures. I was a moody and variable youth during those days of late adolescence, but my journey toward my own country had commenced.

I had begun to write some rather affected and specious short novels and poetic fragments, but which Jiménez and Anselmi approved enthusiastically. We were in the habit of going down Viamonte Street to the port to read or revise them in one of the cafés from which we could sniff the salt air and tar. I was in doubt whether they liked my work because it was intrinsically good or merely because their reading had been scanty and scattered. I drew my inspiration from modern European models, and my fresh, violent rhythms must have seemed the very invention of literature to my two friends. They asked me all sorts of questions. Was my imagination intuitively rich or was it due to a diligently cultivated reasoning that slowly accumulated the materials of fantasy?

I tried to convince them that my imagination was poor and that it had hard work to hold up its end in those first exercises.

After our literary conversations we would walk until midnight along the river bank. From the foreshore we saw the compact mass of giant buildings behind us: first the great granaries, then the banks, the apartment houses, and the private dwellings. Seen from the river, the buildings rose like a solid hill. Buenos

14

Aires — a vast, silent expanse of new white stone and human souls.

Often after midnight, during the long summer nights — sweet nights in October and dawns in January — Jiménez and I sat in my room correcting manuscript or reading aloud revised paragraphs, filled with a passion for perfection. After working seriously for two or three hours, we would throw the papers on the table, walk out on the balcony, and laugh at ourselves like people playing on earth who had a credit of pomp and glory awaiting them in heaven.

One night Dr. Dervil came to my room to smoke a big black cigar. It was February and very hot. He sat down opposite me and looked at me silently for a while. At length he asked me where Jiménez and Anselmi were. I told him that I had seen them only that afternoon. He pulled on his cigar and expelled a large mouthful of reeking smoke.

"This is a country that cannot be cured," he said. "It is a lost country." He remained pensive. "At most it would make a good colony. And there is nothing inferior, stupider, or more sticky than the colonial spirit. A long submission dressed up in prosperity."

"No," I replied. "You are wrong. It's natural for a man of your age to think that, because you belong to the worst generation of this country — I mean the unhappiest generation. Because you have witnessed the decline of the political dignity of our country, and its social torpor after a full meal. But our case is quite different. We belong to the subsoil of the nation. We are like the heart of an athlete, and the doctor never knows as well as the heart itself does whether it is functioning normally or badly."

"The heart knows nothing," he said. "The heart is a viscus."

"The heart does know, doctor. The heart knows so well that when it is ill, the man to whom it belongs is upset, but when it functions properly he looks at things with courage. Maybe that sounds a bit puerile; nevertheless, it is true that our generation has magnificent motive force, and you have difficulty in understanding that."

"*Qui vivra verra*," said the doctor. "Your generation has not yet had any bribes offered to it."

"That is a vicious remark," I answered, "and one that is unworthy of you, doctor. The men of my generation have clean hands, and many will be buried with them still uncontaminated. What is important for each generation is that its faith be great enough to produce a few martyrs. Your generation has not produced one. That is why you are skeptical and cold in your thinking."

He looked at me intently. "It is not a matter of a generation but of years. You will see how pessimistic and tired you feel when you are dragging about old bones like mine."

"I hope that they will bury some of us before that, and then we shall at least have fertilized the soil instead of living to witness our own corruption."

Dr. Dervil smoked, silently. I realized that I had been unkind. I stood up, went over to where he sat, and laid my hand on his shoulder.

"Never mind," I said cheerfully, "at bottom there is something sound in both of us. I pin my hope to that."

He sat smoking pensively, his heavy, freckled hands on his knees and his old figure erect against the back of the chair. At that moment I believe that he felt a fundamental warmth, and perhaps an illusion that he, who had never had children of his own, might yet live on, not in a youth of his own flesh and blood, but in the tender offspring of his national and moral family.

I suggested that we go out for a walk. We went up Twenty-fifth of May Street as far as Córdoba, and I showed him that small segment of the city, that block in which the most heterogeneous elements of architecture are jumbled together. There was one house looking like a medieval palace; on the corner was an old residence, half-hidden behind a balcony covered with panes of blue and white glass; there was a boarding-house with its foundation below the level of the sidewalk, and a small garden in front; there was a gloomy Yugoslav inn. "Some time," I said, "we shall have to make this look like something homogeneous, genuine, and solid. Something of our own. The city is losing its character more and more. Its deformers must be killed without delay."

The doctor smiled, patted me good-humoredly, and invited me to have a glass of beer with him. We went into one of those cheap cafés with an upright piano and nasal singers.

4

ONE fine day Anselmi and I did not return to the law school. We did not even talk it over beforehand. We simply stopped attending classes, disgusted with methods of instruction that were pragmatic, unscientific, and spiritless. We knew that one day truth would clear a path for itself and that this would be the first day of deep satisfaction for the youth of Argentina. We thought of resuming our studies later if the political horizon showed any signs of clearing. In truth what we were pursuing was not merely a professional career but something much more general and abstract, and wider in scope — a higher state of justice and morality in the Republic. But how to progress in that direction? How? How? For the moment we had at any cost to defend our own attitude and protect its seed against all attack.

That year my mother died. It was a terrible blow to me. For months I was filled with grief. Then I gradually recovered my spirits in a sort of convalescence of the soul, unshackled my hands, and again timidly caressed the substance of life.

17

5

It was then, I believe, that I saw you for the first time.

The experience was dazzling: your dignified bearing and aristocratic features competing for noble supremacy with the afternoon air! You must have been exactly my own age — twenty-five years old. You were turning northward up Florida Street near Charcas, opposite San Martín Plaza, a beautiful gulf of shade that September afternoon.

To me you represented the ideal woman — all that it was possible to dream of and most impossible to find. Your body was delicate and slender; your legs long, and your feet small, in graceful black, suède shoes, with plain nickel buckles; your sports blouse was open at your soft throat; your dark, slightly opaque hair, with one long, fluffy lock loose, your fine black eyebrows at a slight angle, and your mouth — may God help me! — with lips somewhat parted (just as I was always to see you), as if you were taking nourishment from the air to repair some youthful anxiety.

I followed you. Suddenly a private motor-car picked you up. I had very little money in my pocket — a few centavos I think — and I could not take a taxicab to follow you. I returned home deeply stirred,went directly to my room and out on the balcony, where I breathed in the night air and looked with new eyes at the city which I now knew contained you. It seemed to me a different and strange Buenos Aires, enriched and magnified. I, who had sought an expression of dignity in faces and souls, had just found your face and expression. I was loath to stir, for fear of putting your marvelous image out of focus.

I did not say a word about you. I dined late, arriving while the others were eating their dessert. There was always a comfortable atmosphere about that modest dining-room, with its old hunting pictures and ancient buffet and serving-table.

Anselmi and Dr. Dervil were deep in a heated discussion about the old and the new in philosophy. As was to be expected, the old doctor was playing the role of a dogmatic disciple of Descartes, and Anselmi, to be contradictory, was supporting Pascal's theology.

I ate my modest lettuce salad and plate of cold meat in silence. Anselmi had the lion's share of the argument, and Dervil that of the wise tiger who parries by skillful attacks, without wasting energy or exposing its own body. Señora Ana, Jiménez — careful, proud, and well groomed — and the lean salesman, Johnson, were devouring their customary pastry in boredom. The sound of the discussion provided them a harmless accompaniment. The other inhabitant of the house, the somewhat mysterious young lady, rarely left her room, where her meals were served to her.

At that hour there was not a sound in the house.

"I don't care a rap about your reasoning, your cold, critical, mechanical reasoning," Anselmi was saying. "You may be an excellent dialectitian and still leave me completely cold. The only thing that matters to me is the amount of fire with which a spirit is warmed. Reason burns a little in that fire, but so do other things — quickness of perception, temperament, and conscience. To me the 'raison' of the French is specious logic petulantly offered as a cold, omnipotent tool. When I was a small boy, in my quarter of the city, San José de Flores, a band of us boys used to have our headquarters near the church. One of them was our infallible priest. When we had any doubts or qualms of conscience, we gathered around him and put the question to him. He reflected seriously and delivered a solemn judgment. We all knew that he was right, but never followed his advice. But we had adventures, pranks, and surprises to tell about at night. From that time on I began to consider reason a clumsy fraud against life. Reason is the dress uniform of stupidity."

"My dear fellow," said Dr. Dervil, settling down to a calm argument, "reason is what helps you to erect such a logical scaffold. The 'cogito' of Descartes. You have lived this free life of yours only because you have thought it out. Had you not thought it out, you would not have developed that essential rational faculty and would have remained only a stupid vegetable."

"That's not what I am saying," said Anselmi. "Don't put a complete absurdity into my mouth. What I am saying is that the specific for the better life is the very living of it and not a matter of taking thought; not your *raison d'être*. What I am getting at is that living has other exits, entirely different from those that reason proposes, which are always false exits."

"Give me an example," said Dr. Dervil. "I don't understand you."

"Exits by passion, heroism, absurdity, asceticism, or self-destruction. Compared with such emotions, the exits that reason offers are stupid and mediocre. Rational exits! Rot!"

He laughed long.

"You are a child," said the doctor. "You have set out on a juvenile adventure, but have not yet returned. It is the returns that involve reason."

"I prefer not to return. Why return?"

"One always returns. That is the terrible part of it. Whether you like it or not, reason will be there at the turn of the road, inflexible and insurmountable. Because reason is the measure of man, and in the end all mistakes are rectified by that sole axis on which we revolve. All the rest is romanticism or abstraction. They lie out of our hands and do not belong to us. Pity the man who does not live rationally! Pity the man buffeted by other winds, however strong and alluring they may appear!"

Anselmi was silent. Then he said: "Reason has left you in a fine fix!"

It was a rude remark and the doctor felt it keenly, but he

made no retort and went on imperturbably playing with the box of matches.

"Don't you see?" insisted Anselmi. "You have nothing to say. You make no protest. You neither insult me nor get angry with me. You take refuge behind the 'dictates of reason.' How trivial!"

The doctor raised his eyes from his match-box and looked at Anselmi calmly and pityingly.

From the little church down the street the bells could be heard striking ten. Jiménez ironically pointed his fork at Anselmi.

"There sits the man who is always making literature. You must never have a discussion with him, doctor, without bearing that in mind."

"What a fool!" said Anselmi. "When the only hundred-per-cent literary man is he." He put on a ridiculously mannered tone: "The exquisite, delicate . . ."

"He's always making literature," continued Jiménez, feigning not to hear him. "He is one of those people who speak so well of God that they feel the need to rub up against the devil just in case they have exaggerated."

Señora Ana and the salesman Johnson applauded the sally. Jiménez suddenly ducked to avoid a roll that Anselmi had shied at him.

"Poor fellow!" said Anselmi. "He's irritated and angry."

We all laughed.

"I've been a classmate of his and I know him," said Jiménez.

"If it weren't for the fact that knowledge is a faculty you lack," retorted Anselmi.

Thus the after-dinner conversation went on for a while that night. I recall it because it fell like rain on your image, but like firm soil your image withstood it without absorbing it. At length we all left the dining-room and went out to the various balconies to enjoy the quiet of the evening. Along Twenty-fifth of May Street seafaring people, immigrants, loose women, youths bent on indulgence, and foreigners were passing.

Anselmi and Jiménez were still verbally cuffing each other like quarrelsome cubs, saying the most outrageous things.

What difference did all this make to me? The city had another dimension. You were its added dimension. Both of them suddenly turned on me. "What are you thinking about?" They knew me too well and were surprised that I did not enter into their fun. Jiménez turned to Anselmi. "Give him an injection of infused science," he said sarcastically. I laughed but did not answer. "What a bore!" said Anselmi. He was staring into space, disappointed that I had not joined in their banter.

A boy ran past the house shouting the latest edition of one of the evening papers.

6

WE became more and more deeply attached to our condition of noisy young animals living in the present. There was hardly a day during which we did not manifest our enthusiasm, restlessness, disorder, or curiosity along the central boulevards of the city. Reciting poetry, we jumbled chaotically the old verses of the modest, Argentine, classical period with the stanzas of Fray Luís, Whitman's "Paumanok," or the "Alastor," of solitary vein. Anselmi, a descendant of the Romans, recited a sonnet of Petrarch, with exaggerated emphasis, and we chanted a hoarse accompaniment as we passed between the tables of a suburban café, where the middle-aged burghers looked at us with puzzled disapproval.

> *Piangete, donne, e con voi pianga Amore;*
> *Piangete, amanti, per ciascun paese;*
> *poi ch'è morte colui che tutto intese*
> *In farvi, mentre visse al mondo, onore. . . .*

The modest residential and student quarter wept at his simple song and so too did the southern district, still colonial in atmosphere, with its simple balustrades, its old-fashioned entrance halls too wide for present-day uses, its faded, reddish flagstones, and its vast, low-ceilinged rooms with their mahogany furniture and musty smell. The newer sections, near the center of the city, laughed long and heartily. The aristocratic quarter to the north, sad and inarticulate, like wealth itself arrogantly closed its mouth to grief and laughter.

However . . .

The metropolis was not the whole country. The city that we beheld was not the country that we loved, nor the one that we hoped for. Beneath the purple we wanted to see the coarse sackcloth. Sackcloth is worn next to the skin, and the skin is close to the blood. In our country the purple lied.

We went out into the street and observed the purple. We went to plays, lectures, and concerts where the purple was in evidence. We became acquainted with many men and women in that world and touched the purple. It was in the government, in the street, and everywhere. Words and deeds were purple.

But a new country, we kept recalling, should not become attached to the purple. A new country is a condition of fervent revolt. A new country should be sober, frank, trustworthy, self-respecting, and as fundamentally loyal as youth itself. A young country that becomes attached to the purple is soon degraded.

In the small hours of the night, as we lay awake before dawn, we were obsessed by the thought of our country choked by that purple; by the thought of its neglected interior; the suffering country that raises its hopeful eyes uncomplainingly to the noble southern skies; that bides its time in the depths of our national being like ripe grain in the granary.

Night and day the same thought, the same preoccupation recurred to us.

Suddenly in the midst of our laughter, conversation, and

shouting, one of us would fall silent. Then under this influence a hush fell on the others too. It was as if all three of us were uttering the same thought and repeating the same silent prayer:

"When will the submerged, healthy country that exists because we believe in it come to the surface? When will *that* country make itself visible?"

We had some wealthy friends, the Gómezes, who sometimes invited us to come and spend the evening with them. They lived in an austere, aristocratic-looking house of "purple" aspect. Everything in it was solemn. The head of the house, a dried-up, dogmatic, dyspeptic man, had been a minister of state. Tall, stoop-shouldered, and heavy, he moved deliberately, and devoted himself to writing pages of dull, academic history that no one read. Every thirty pages, more or less, yielded him a special distinction — either a foreign decoration or another appointment as corresponding member of some academy. In his children he encouraged vanity, arrogance, and hatred of foreigners. That was his conception of patriotism.

To us he represented something rotten in our national life, and we detested him cordially. Among ourselves we called him the "wearer of the purple." We went to his house occasionally only in order not to offend his sons, former schoolmates of ours, who were not to blame for being dull and half-educated. In their hearts, despite all of their family's efforts, a vague kindness shone unquenched.

In the somber, Italian-Renaissance hall — where the most curious assemblage of dusty, colonial pieces covered the massive tables: portraits, silver spurs, strings of dried fruit, and the family's coat of arms — the old man held forth on his conception of history between cups of coffee. We listened unblinkingly to his lecture on the family's usury: We must be severe, conservative benefactors, "guardians of tradition, with naked sword in hand," and must show our teeth right and left. "Beware of the foreigner!" was his motto.

I, who had eight generations of Argentine forebears behind me, smiled inwardly but listened to him without batting an eye. Anselmi and Jiménez exchanged glances. Neither of them could quite believe that such an apostle of holy fury had built his house by defending foreigners' lawsuits and being amiable to them at so much an ounce of fine gold. I looked at them smiling inwardly and knew what they were thinking: "We must fight against this."

7

On one of Anselmi's solitary, unexplained trips, he had become acquainted with an unusual man, about whom he talked little to us until one day, having learned that we might receive an extraordinary proposal from him, he introduced us.

His home was in the southeastern section of Buenos Aires, in an old colonial house with a garden behind it, filled with wistaria, and a great stone well. When Jiménez and I first saw César Acevedo with his dark, ascetic appearance, angular face, white hair, and quiet, keen black eyes, he seemed to us rather like a foreigner. No man, however, could show roots in his native soil older or knottier. What visibly predominated in his subtle nature was refinement, quiet discretion, and a habit of concealing the marks of battle. One felt that death itself would hold no terrors for him. But he was deeply stirred by a constant and delicate flame.

I don't know where Anselmi got the money for the party that night. It was during an unusually cold spell in October. At nine o'clock Jiménez and I sat waiting for him in one of the most luxurious hotels in the city, scarcely twenty blocks from our own quarter, with a glass of cheap domestic champagne in front of us. The doors opened from time to time to admit people of prominence — diplomats, indolent aristocrats, wealthy artists, well-known attorneys, and heavily powdered and bejeweled young ladies in low-cut gowns. I was telling Jiménez the names of some of these proud creatures while he smoked slowly, unimpressed by their monotonous vanity. A tall lady entered, with four orchids fastened at her bosom; her partly paralyzed husband followed. With them was a provincial politician chiefly distinguished for having named his stud horses after the expressionist painters represented in his valuable, private collection.

An orchestra of mediocre but spectacular musicians had begun a labored interpretation of Brahms's Academic Festival Overture.

Near the hotel rose the belfry of a modest colonial church, surrounded by the resting-places of the dead.

Precisely at ten o'clock Anselmi appeared in the lustrous glass door at the far end of the great room, accompanied by his new friend.

I was surprised by his soberly distinguished companion. They crossed the room and came slowly toward us, as though the place belonged to them — the aristocrat and the slow rustic.

"Man and beast," commented Jiménez gravely.

The "beast" was very carefully dressed that night. Doubtless he wished to appear to Señor Acevedo as a man of refined manners and tact.

We were introduced as intellectuals, and César Acevedo asked us in a friendly way about everything that we were doing and planning. There was some conversation about a long prose poem that I had written. I explained that it was at the printer's and would shortly appear. Then Acevedo wanted to know what we thought about politics and social conditions in general.

"These lads are deep," said Anselmi, taking a generous swallow of wine. "You will have to dig down to know what they are thinking."

"That is the way we all are," said César Acevedo. "One must dig deep in us."

His smile was frank and intelligent, and his face was etched deep with tired lines. At close range the modeling of his head showed even more refinement and breeding. He was conservatively dressed in blue, wore a white collar and a black silk cravat, and seemed altogether a person accustomed to distinguished company.

During a pause in the music the bells of the neighboring church could be heard, clear, metallic, and melancholy.

"Let's have some of this Paraná River mackerel," said Acevedo, putting down the menu. "It's a good augury for a new friendship. And instead of a white wine, I recommend what Enrique Ferri called *il vino rosso di l'amicizia*, the frank red wine of friendship. White wine has the refined perfidy of certain malefactors of noble appearance, whom you take at first for princes, but who turn out to be villains that poison you."

The clamor of the orchestra scarcely allowed us to hear each other. It continued to play with obstinate flourishes. Anselmi was watching the director and laughing at his excess of energy.

Acevedo was forthright in his speech, called things by their proper names, and talked straight to the point. I liked this. He had the evils of our incipient national organization catalogued.

"The phenomenon of regression that has taken place in Argentina is strange," said Acevedo, as he slowly ate his fish, its golden tints sprinkled with lemon juice. "It is the phenomenon of an inspiration cut short. In the beginning — our whole history proves it — Argentines, to a man, seemed inspired by active zeal, and the builders of the nation appeared on the scene one after another like persons taking their places in a directed march. A spirit, a slow, prescient dignity, operated behind this movement. Then suddenly, when the century was well advanced, the original motive force, the spirit of the march, broke down — or evaporated — and on the public boards there remained only a procession of solemn, mediocre administrators. It is as if we were to imagine an enormous factory in which, at a given moment, all the workers were suddenly to operate mechanically, producing objects *without object,* deprived of conscious will-power, not knowing how long or for whom, or why, or to what end they were laboring."

Jiménez set down his empty cup on the table.

"Exactly," he said, as if Acevedo had taken the words out of his mouth. "And to cap this, the unhappy lack of spirit of the directors is spreading to the rest of the people. The directors are lulling the people into their own image with the refrain that everything is going very well and there is no need to worry."

Acevedo went on without paying much heed to the interruption:

"It could be called the treason of bread. They have begun to say to the people: 'What on earth are you looking for so restlessly? Merely bread. Well, here it is. We give it to you. Stop your worrying now that you have it and you will sleep soundly again.' The word goes about: 'Bread is everything; we have bread!' and the people are appeased. But as it is a lie, as bread is not everything, the great treason pitches its camp on the soil of this lethargy. And the people, deprived of moral inspiration, abandon themselves more and more to bodily ease, to trafficking and to pacts, and forget their most serious and important objective — their own destiny. That is why I call what is taking place in this land of ours: 'the treason of bread.' "

His eyes were fixed on the tablecloth, his head bowed thoughtfully.

"But that is the politician's bread," he went on quickly. "In the remotest corners of Argentina another bread is eaten, one which does not betray. The bread of the men who are building on what has come from their own souls, the bread with which they stay their hunger for fundamentally moral aspirations, not political or pecuniary — fundamentally moral. On this honorable bread, on this inspired bread, this bread of reflection, expectation, and restlessness, the forgotten parts of our land are at this very hour being nourished; and thus, in its protecting

28

shadow, a symphony is forming, its crescendo shaped like an inverted cone. From a point it extends to the whole; from a rich seed it becomes the nuclear tree of an entire forest. In who knows how many remote *estancias*, poor, city rooms, Andean camps, northern forests, southern plains, and sparsely inhabited pampas, nothing is eaten today but this good bread — this bread that does not betray!"

I do not know which instrument of the orchestra lifted up his words under its mantle, mingled with them our own silent agreement, raised them, incorporeal, into space, and turned the whole into a wave of music suddenly alive, then disintegrated, disappeared.

What Acevedo had said kindled our fires of enthusiasm, and we talked eagerly on the same theme, modifying it, turning it over, and bringing it back once more to its original shape, as though we held in our hands a sphere pleasing to caress. We talked about the geography of the country, in whose rich, diversified song Argentina speaks a language which few people know — as varied, full, and resonant as the sonorous chanting of its birds on the first morning of creation. We talked of its other geography, the geography of the spirit. And all as if we were discussing not an abstraction but an absent, living, feeling, beloved person.

Jiménez was talking too eloquently and loquaciously, and the ends of some of his phrases hung floating in the air, passed over by us in silence. Anselmi feeling sobered, wanted to get on to the reason for our meeting. He told us that Acevedo proposed to organize a modest journal of criticism, and that he counted on us to join him and to bring in other like-minded people. Acevedo described his project in detail. He had thought of it for years as a remote possibility, but now felt that its realization was nearer and more urgent.

The maître d'hôtel, a short, stout man in evening clothes with a black waistcoat, little disturbed by the traditional bustle of his profession, stood aside, apparently absorbed in his own thoughts, as though calmly surveying a concert of affairs that harmonized perfectly.

"I inherited a small printing-press from my father," said Acevedo, "which turns out ordinary printed matter modestly and regularly. It is a mean activity, however, and I have always hoped that I might some day be able to give it a somewhat worthier destiny. What better opportunity than the suggestion which Anselmi made to me when he talked about you, about what you are doing, and what you stand for? I, for my part, know a rather eccentric, taciturn, and intractable man, but a singularly valuable one on account of the depth of his thought. His name is Blagoda. He has an adolescent nature in the crooked body of a pawnbroker. You will make his acquaintance. He is a violent, combative critic and a redoubtable adversary."

"I don't think," said Jiménez, "that we could justify a purely combative purpose. That is always ephemeral. We are living on a vacant tract of land. We must put up a building on it. The first thing that strikes me as necessary is to find adequate materials, stones of a shape suited to the structure that we have in mind."

"That's an old fogy's notion!" shouted Anselmi, moderating his shout in mid-phrase. "What do you mean by 'vacant space'? I don't see it. There's a building already standing on it. It's the one we live in. But it has been thrown together hastily; its elements are ill assorted and its foundation shaky. Well, what has been badly built must be razed; then will come the next step."

I laughed at his naïve formula. Jiménez slipped in an inoffensive joke while Acevedo kept on eating slowly, not caring to demur.

"The two points of view are just," he observed, "as Señor Jiménez says."

"Jiménez, please."

Acevedo smiled. ". . . As Jiménez well says, the positive part, that of simple, straightforward construction, is here not only the most important one but also the most difficult. That being so, and as we are not improvising — since to improvise would be to build again with the inadequate stones — our first step, it seems to me, is to act as critical observers, which, in effect, is the role of reconnoitering the terrain, the time, and the space in which we are to move, both as individuals and as a nation."

"Yes," protested Anselmi, "but no old fogy's notions! Old men are constantly looking for compromises in order to gain time for sleep. None of your old men's ideas!"

"None!"

We talked little more about those vague preliminaries. Each of us discussed briefly what he could contribute to our fruitful collaboration from the store of his own experience, and what he felt might come from the collaboration of the two realities, the individual and the group. These biographical digressions rang for a long time in the restaurant air, somewhat disordered — at moments candid, at others obscure. But we gained something by these confessions. We established our personal positions.

Anselmi called the waiter. He pointed a categorical finger at the fruit salad covered with thick cream.

"This is infamous!" he cried. "The fruit is soft and beginning to spoil, and the cream sour. You spend too much money on lights and slaves, but very little on the things that you should! Take this away before it rots completely and bring me something more like a fruit salad!"

"There, you see! That's what we need on the journal," observed Jiménez sarcastically; "anger and the spirit of justice."

"And a good jester for the backdrop," replied the other.

"Do they always fight this way?" Acevedo asked me.

"It's their way of keeping awake," I replied. "They are very wise."

"No, no," interposed Anselmi, "not both very wise. Only one of us; the other is a complete fool."

With cold solemnity Jiménez raised his glass to Anselmi in a long, silent toast. Then he drained its contents in one draught.

At that moment Acevedo was carefully peeling a small, bright-colored orange. He paid the same scrupulous attention to material things as to things of the spirit.

"We must be on our guard against national mystics," he said. "We must let no one be carried away by enthusiasm without knowing very definitely what he wants and why he wants it. One of the greatest dangers of certain statesmen, of certain men in any group, is that they listen to their own natural vehemence as if it were an end justified by its own internal force. In a nation like ours, for example, certain vociferous and fundamentally selfish raptures and certain primitive enthusiasms can mobilize youth against its own basic, historical spirit, although youth may itself be unaware of it or even feel that the movement subserves that spirit. I believe that the most important thing is for us to draw up a minute plan of everything essential to us as a nation, of everything that basically distinguishes us from the rest of the world. Political violence in a country without such data is like the mad careering of a blind man — it may take him either to the mountain or to the abyss.

He talked at some length on this theme with sustained warmth. Then he spoke again about Blagoda and the possible significance of the journal — if we should be able to organize it. We were immediately caught up by his enthusiasm and declared ourselves firmly ready to publish the journal. We shouted. But for some moments we were forced to restrain our enthusiasm as the orchestra was attacking the most thunderous part of its noisy repertoire — an extremely poor, synthetic arrangement of Molossov, I believe.

Jiménez proposed a name for the journal. We did not like it and each in turn suggested others. The choice was difficult. It had to be an expressive, energetic name as well as one easy to remember. *New Action?* No. *The Cause of Argentina?* No. *Mission?* We hesitated at this last suggestion and did not entirely reject it. It was not bad. But it, too, lacked something that we wanted. What we were looking for was a still more expressive and perhaps more concrete name. As we were unable to find one quickly that suited us, we decided to put off the decision for another day.

8

MERCEDES MIRÓ was holding a glass of whisky and a cigarette in her hand. A plain wide silver wrist-watch was strapped to her wrist. Her long, slender body and beautiful back, a little broad-shouldered, like those of some of the consorts of the Pharaohs, narrowed gradually to her waist. A cruel vivacity in her somewhat snake-like eyes alternated with moments of offensive indifference. Constantly smoking, she seemed tired and restless. I was immediately interested in her. The nature of my interest was at once obvious. It was a feeling of curiosity, a merely masculine desire to disarm the deliberate indifference of a matter-of-fact and beautiful woman. I tried to catch her eyes and hold them. But she was distracted at the moment, and neither of us heard the unattractive girl at Lucrecia's left gravely questioning her friend about Piero della Francesca, Orcagna, and Gian Bellini — Lucrecia had invited me that afternoon.

The hotel bar and grill-room, decorated in questionable modern style, were packed with people. Lucrecia, releasing her metaphysical evil genius, was for the moment making fun of a Pre-Raphaelite scene of an eighteenth-century romantic adventure on the wall. It gave her physical pleasure to talk about the primitives.

Like a long melody constantly interrupted by inopportune and ingenuous comments, exclamations, and assertions, the tone of the conversation rose and fell. In a single flight of garrulousness Freud and the *Phantasy of the Unconscious* were discussed, as were the generally ridiculous state of our literature, European politics, Mr. Glick the fortune-teller, a doctor living in Belgrano who wrought cures by autosuggestion, Lawrence of Arabia, and the heavenly colonial skies in Figari's pictures. Enthusiastic comments on the photographs of Cecil Beaton — in which Lady Falkland's smile bursts forth through an aureole of cakes of Pear's soap — bestrode sophisticated opinions about the little colonial houses in the San Telmo district — all pronounced in a very nasal Argentine accent, amid lively sallies of sarcasm and smiles of typically Argentine satisfaction.

I began to talk to Mercedes Miró, who was really a splendid creature, strikingly aristocratic in appearance. I asked her what sort of life she led in Buenos Aires and about her tastes and family.

She fixed her eyes defensively on me before replying.

"Do you know what it is to be awake ninety per cent of the time?"

"Almost total insomnia," I murmured.

"A deep need to live, and to live all the time," she said. "That's what it is. A sort of horror of the void, of becoming set in one's ways, of regulations and inactivity."

After a moment she added:

"I can't bear the idea of these moonlight meditations. To me they are horrible betrayals of life. Horrible if they weren't silly. Just as it would be treason to live in the country and not to enjoy the fragrance of the fields, the hemp brakes, the alfalfa, and the lavender." As she talked about the country, her eyes opened wider and her nostrils flared. I was pleased to see that her senses were alert. "As life never stops, I live inexorably determined not to stop. And I am more or less successful."

The bar-tender poured another two fingers of whisky into her glass and added some ice. He was about to pour the soda when she stopped him.

34

"Straight," she said in English.

"What annoys me about our worldly conversations," she went on, "is that they are made up entirely of allusions and references, and none of the words used seem to have any relation to reality. When politics, art, or literature is discussed, the conversation is nothing but empty, fleshless commentaries. By contrast, how much I enjoy the solid conversation of people who speak from living experience! I believe that living is a skilled trade. One must learn how to live, and live deliberately. I like to listen to cobblers' conversation because the hub about which it turns is the trade that they have learned" — she glanced about her — "but all this — " Her mouth twisted wryly and she burst out laughing. She was really beautiful in her black moiré dress and small close-fitting hat, somewhat turned up at the brim, which gracefully exposed the outline of the hair over her left ear. I looked at the smooth, delicate skin of her hands, at her long fingernails, and at the fingers themselves, which held her glass firmly, unlike the majority of human hands, which seem never to have learned to grasp things securely. I have always taken an interest in people's hands and voices as indexes that reveal breeding and spiritual qualities much more than the features of the face. Mercedes Miró's voice and hands seemed to revive the shadow of an old aristocracy.

Some of them were talking about my book and I turned to answer a question. Mercedes stood up, and from where I sat I could see her beautiful, erect body and the full, graceful sweep of her hips. I got up too and told her that I should like to see her again. She said that she would send me an interesting book within a few days and departed. A gentleman named Marcus with a voluminous paunch and a white vest began to talk contemptuously about modern art. The young ladies of the elegant chorus were outraged, and interrupted with corrections and protests.

It was late. I got up and took my leave. As I was crossing the

35

corridor to go to the cloakroom, I stopped short. You had just
come in. You walked over quickly to the men's section of the
bar, undoubtedly to meet your husband. As I continued on my
way, I saw you approach the bar and stop to acknowledge a
greeting.

I went upstairs and out into the street restless, depressed, and
disturbed, as if I had just spent two hours in a world of pygmies
and had turned out to be the smallest pygmy of them all.

9

WITHIN three days I was knocking at Mercedes's door. She lived
alone five flights up in Arroyo Street. At that point the quiet,
unfrequented street curves gently until it faces the avenue.

The quietness of the street pervaded the white apartment.
The large living-room contained only an enormous piano, a
light-green sofa, two bookcases, a mahogany table, and a profusion of flowers in many kinds of vases. The mid-afternoon sun
was declining. On the piano stood a picture of a middle-aged
man in a light-colored suit, a Cape jasmine in his buttonhole.

As I entered, a wave of fragrance greeted me. On the piano
music-rack were an open score by Bach and some exercises by
Scarlatti. I was looking them over when Mercedes came in. Her
face was softly mellow. There was something deliciously impulsive about her that reminded me of the beautiful *improvisatrice*
who inspired the famous portrait by Sebastiano del Piombo,
later attributed to Giorgione. She held out both her hands to
greet me.

"Music to throw people off the scent!" she said, drawing me
away from the piano. "I never sit down at the piano."

She laughed. To tell the truth, she never sat down anywhere.
We talked for nearly an hour and all the while she remained
standing, lighting one cigarette after another, and talking with
such constant animation that she seemed scarcely to note what
was going on about her, as though she were listening only to her

own words and to their return echo. After a whirlwind of conversation she suggested that we go out. An old English mystery film — she liked such pictures — was showing at one of the suburban theaters. Our taxi went down Pueyrredón Street from the gardens of the Recoleta to Once Square, then turned into the equally broad and smooth Rivadavia. She talked about many things; a trip that she had made to the southern lakes the year before, and the gigantic trees, petrified forest, Indian graveyards, and the Swiss hotels on the Chilean side, where delicious breakfasts of black bread and crystal-clear honey were served. She talked, too, about "Mr. Freud," whom Gide has dubbed a "brilliant idiot." She deplored the deformation of the spirit widely imposed by the views of this deluded Viennese, a negative character, whom people have turned into a demon. We entered the cinema after a good-natured dispute, because, with the enthusiasm of a student who has just received his monthly stipend, she insisted on paying for the tickets. In the gloom of the theater I enjoyed talking about things suggested by the film, until I saw that it bothered her. She followed the development of the picture seriously, fidgeting a little in her seat like a street urchin. Her comments about the film, which was too poor to sit through, were to the point. We had tea in one of the near-by sweet-shops which aped the luxurious atmosphere of the suburban confectioneries: elaborate equipment in excruciating taste, an excess of metal and marble, and a wide, oak frieze. They served us abominable tea and sandwiches. Mercedes ate with ravenous appetite, drank a second cup of tea, and lighted a cigarette. We talked about the incredible crudeness and the technique of noise and shouting of the German films — Prussian in character and lacking in nuances. She said that she would like to direct an Argentine film depicting the life of our provincial cities, with their colonial atmosphere, indolent and Creole, but full of human worth. As she wanted to walk some more, we went down Rivadavia, past its succession of small shops, cheap

37

jewelry stores, cigarette and chocolate stands, and plain one- and two-story houses, so ill assorted, ugly, and cold that one felt appalled at the architectural taste that they revealed.

Mercedes's vitality began to interest me strangely. She was always alert and on the move. She looked at things eagerly and her senses seemed to operate spontaneously. She was like life itself. Perhaps when one observed her carefully, she was not very intelligent, although at first blush she seemed so. When her features were analyzed, she was not so beautiful as she appeared at first glance. Perhaps too she did not really understand things as well as she gave the impression of doing when one talked to her first. All of the strong early impressions that she produced were the result of her great vitality and its very even distribution.

I left her at nightfall, but saw her again many other evenings. She was like no one else. Her influence over me touched no profound springs. For instance, I did not picture her in my imagination when I was away from her. It was merely that I enjoyed being with her. With all her vivacity, health, and quick, outgiving qualities she attracted me like a stupendous spectacle. In a few days she became necessary to me. The desire to go and see her became an obsession. I was like a small boy hankering after a toy. Nevertheless, absorbed in other things — her external life, the streets, plants, the world, books, news, and spectacles — she held herself aloof from any gallantry. It was quite impossible to draw her into an exchange of relatively intimate ideas, however appropriate they might be. Nothing but objects interested her. Persons — I wasn't so sure. She never alluded to her past life. She lived entirely in the present and the future. At most, some recollection of her adolescence crept into her conversation. It was always linked with impressions: gardens, fragrances, and colors. All of this heightened my interest in her. We began to go out every day after we had known each other only five or six days. I sought her eyes, tried to watch her mouth and to make her conscious of it. From time to time, as though returning from a circular trajectory to her point of departure, she at last allowed her eyes to rest, but only for a moment. Immediately she escaped.

It was that escape, that flight, more than her own personality that at once thrust itself into my life. Echoes from my book, compliments, and praises of it were of secondary importance to me. I answered none of the letters, not even opening some of them. Nor could I fix my attention on the project in which Anselmi, Jiménez, and I were engaged. A feeling of inadequacy possessed me. Something eluded my grasp. Finally it was as if my own ego could not follow its appointed course. I ate little, went about and lay down to sleep obsessed by her, becoming quite insufferable.

I could not bring Mercedes out of herself. She was too strongly held by the rest of her environment and sometimes disconcerted me by laughing at my efforts in that direction. What curiosity and what impotence!

She did not care to gather anything from life but its daily fruits, and attached no importance to correlating them. Certain that it was futile to attempt to change her strongly rooted attitude, I gradually became reconciled to her chronic restlessness. Within the span of a few days we went to a succession of concerts, lectures, parks, plays, and motion pictures. Suddenly, while listening to chamber music, a fantastic analogy would occur to her, a fragment of the music giving her a longing for the scent of cedar or to see the form of the needle clusters of some conifer. Nothing would do but that we must immediately visit one of Buenos Aires's botanical gardens. She knew them all by heart. We were always on the go.

For two days the gentle October rain fell unceasingly. On the third afternoon I arrived at Mercedes's house about six o'clock. Only a disturbed melancholy light filtered into her living-room from the heavily clouded sky. It was the first time that I had found her lying down. She was stretched out on the sofa, reading. In repose, her long, relaxed body seemed more beautiful and remote than ever. Under her light house-coat I could make out her pink silk slip and the soft swelling of her bosom. Her thighs stretched her skirt tautly to where her round knees were marked under it. There the dress parted over sheer stockings that revealed the fine texture of her skin. On the small white table beside her were scattered books, cigarettes, a glass, and a current periodical.

"Sit down here," she said, removing the glass ash-tray from the armchair beside her.

She held out the novel that she was reading. I glanced at the title-page and returned it to her. It was by an unknown author. She rang. Carmen appeared, and Mercedes asked her to bring me some sherry. The servant disappeared. She returned and phlegmatically set down the tray with the sherry and glasses on it. I stood up and closed the door after her.

"A cautious move . . ." commented Mercedes.

"Let's talk a little about you and me," I said to her.

She made a wry face.

"No, please, let's not spoil an afternoon made for conversation about remote and unexpected things. Let's not return to that stupid, besieged fortress that one always becomes when one so narrows the subject of conversation. You are one of those restricted people hemmed in by their doubts, their ideas, their small island of culture, their caprices, manias, and habits. How little you like to venture forth!"

I looked at her without comment. She continued talking, her head resting on the cushion.

"You insist on spoiling our comradeship," she protested. "What friendship brings in depth and richness of feeling, love, with its accursed sameness, destroys. Even the dullest merchant has an individual soul, but when he unites it with that of his casual mate in what is conventionally called love, the fruit of their approximation, instead of being a distinct entity, becomes the most monotonous, monstrous, and boring compound of two different products in the same wretched, shapeless dough. Have no illusion. Love is a common loss of all originality. What is important in life is not to associate, but to dissociate. The spendthrift's lot is happy; that of the miser, who merely associates, is so stupid. Do you know about Koheler's experiments with monkeys? Monkey intelligence can achieve the most surprising things when it is a matter of associating rudimentary ideas, but when they must be dissociated, it fails. Monkeys can retrieve a banana hanging from a tree by piling boxes one on top of another until they are able to reach it, but if the banana is put behind a box that has first to be removed, and the obstacle dissociated, they are completely baffled."

I moved closer to her.

"Have you never for a moment felt the need of fusing with someone?"

"Of course not. Of course not."

She said it energetically.

"Of course not. What do you mean by the word 'fuse'? It is all right for tin or other metals, but for human beings! Besides, it's too antiquated, too conventional, too awkward. It's abominable!"

She made a wry gesture of disgust, as though unceremoniously brushing aside something that annoyed her, and shifted her position on the sofa.

"Let's talk about something else. Let's talk about novels, about this one, written by an exceedingly cultivated person, who unquestionably knows how to write, and writes fluently and correctly. Each paragraph of the book is a delicate individual creation, and yet the book as a whole is a failure. Why? Can wisdom and learning joined suddenly lead to nothing?"

"That is a matter for discussion."

"It is the eternal conflict between reason and life. There are men who spend their lives reconstructing a culture, a spirit of the past, or a conception of history and society. Then they discover that they have no longer time to assemble their ideas — what they have been unable to infuse into that culture is life. The books that seem most perfect are the least vivid, the great leaden pieces like the famous *Mireille* of Mistral — that depressing monument! — books to which the erudite are at once attracted, and they alone — that is, the passive, classifying, judicious souls, the dullest creatures in the world."

"For a moment," she said with an infernally mocking air, "I thought that you were one of them."

"I?" I was shocked. "I? Thank God that in my order there is a certain disorder! Don't talk to me about systematic souls. They are the driest people I know of, although sometimes they can be very brilliant."

"A certain disorder! Are you sure that you are not boasting?"

Her smiling face was close to mine, and her fresh, damp lips and shining eyes, and that body of hers, cold or warm — I did not know which. She looked at me and laughed. I bent closer, took her by the shoulders, and impetuously kissed her astonished, half-open mouth.

"What a useless thing!" she said faintly. "What a useless thing!" she was saying. "What a useless thing! . . ."

It was raining outside and night had shut in. Only the message of time was to be heard in the silent dusk.

That was a night of liberation for me.

I O

A Buenos Aires November had arrived, with its changes of weather, its sticky dampness, and its first hot spells. People went out cheerfully, however, after the nasty winter. The small, deep-blue blossoms of the jacaranda seemed the capricious fruit of health in the mouth of the capital. We were much pleased with the preparations for the appearance of the review. I returned to my room every night laden with many unusual publications of a similar nature and spent hours studying their make-up and point of view. Anselmi too was busy day and night soliciting advertisements. He had relatives in industry in some of the small towns near the capital and would disappear in the mornings to look them up and invite them to contribute advertisements of their products. Smilovich, Jiménez's tearful tailor, was the first contributor. His poorly paid advertisement was written by Anselmi in skillful and resounding phrases that might have advertised the most famous cutter in Old Burlington Street.

Mr. Johnson also gave us an advertisement for his bed-springs. But he talked to us pessimistically about the financial position of his firm, and we immediately gave him a substantial discount. These were our first weapons in the commercial field.

One noon we met again with Acevedo at luncheon, and out of this further meeting came a name for the review. We decided to call it the *Ship* so that our masthead would have a less polemical air and appeal to a wider public by covering not only political but also literary and ethical subjects, and give our staff the semblance of a crew under sail. At coffee Blagoda joined us. He was to be the assistant editor of the review. He was a suspicious, truculent, slovenly little man with a greasy olive skin. He extended a moist hand that slipped elusively out of my clasp. His lips almost always wore a sneer. When he heard something that displeased him, his whole face twisted into a disagreeable expression. His fingers were crooked and yellow, ending in nails rough from being bitten. On the collar of his faded suit dirt from his shirt had made a heavy, grayish smudge. He surprised us therefore when he said: "I'll have a glass of champagne. I always drink one after dinner." Acevedo smiled as he ordered domestic champagne. Blagoda threw me a glance from under his overhanging eyebrows. "We are not much of a crew for the

Ship," he said, addressing Acevedo and not concealing his scorn, "and green hands, too," he added.

"And where do you come from?" Anselmi asked him bluntly.

Blagoda surveyed him angrily from the height of his self-sufficiency. He said nothing for a moment. Then he replied very calmly and with Olympian disdain:

"I have made my living by journalism. The trouble is that I have been sold to newspapers that never allowed me to tell the truth — ignominiously sold like a public woman. I couldn't stand being gagged like that any longer."

He began to curse the proprietor of the newspaper that he had worked on, as well as his family and friends. He had a prodigious fund of scurrilous data with which he could have broken up whole families, and he related them with an angry relish, looking for all the world like some insidious animal with his head sunk between his shoulders and his elbows propped up on the arms of the chair.

"They are people who believe in the sins of the flesh!" he said. "They don't realize that the only sins are those of the spirit." He sipped his champagne, with the slightly sibilant noise of a reptile. "They don't know that the only sins are those of the spirit. The proprietor looked at the women employees with the circumspect eyes of a monk, but he lied to them and tried to persuade them not to ask for higher wages or shorter hours, as that would only tie their souls to material things. He had sold his own mother, leaving her literally on the street, to prevent her from becoming attached to material things."

I did not like the little man, but Acevedo seemed to have a marked weakness for him. He listened to him and encouraged his condemnation of the sins of the spirit. As we discussed the review and the criticism of the country that we had in mind, my conviction strengthened that Blagoda was a man with a grievance. I began to hope, however, that I might be able to help him out of the pit into which he had fallen.

44

Blagoda developed feverish activity during the days preceding the appearance of the review. His brain was in a constant state of ferment, apparently needing neither rest nor sleep. At six o'clock in the morning he would suddenly knock at my door to tell me about a subject that had occurred to him for an editorial, or telephone three or four times between eleven at night and two in the morning, harried and nervous.

There were times when a mystical flame glowed in him and filled his unhappy body with an idealism that in our eyes redeemed him of his inveterate and concentrated hatred. Anselmi distrusted him, and made fun of him behind his back. One day he asked Acevedo why he had forced a co-worker on us who was more like a poisonous reptile than a rational human being. Acevedo replied cautiously: "You will see later what a useful collaborator he will prove to be."

In order to centralize our preliminary activities, Acevedo asked us to give all our manuscripts to Blagoda and to tell him any ideas that occurred to us. Blagoda never commented on our manuscripts or suggestions. His features wore an habitual air of displeasure, as if he felt that comment would be superfluous and was in a hurry to get on at once to something else.

We set up our improvised editorial office in an inner room of Acevedo's old house, which stood in one of the streets near the Paseo Colón. The room assigned for our work overlooked the patio, with the wistaria and the old well.

It was the end of winter, and the leaves in the patio had come out sufficiently to cast a shadow. Already the heavy blue panicles of wistaria were fragrant. We covered the walls of the room with Argentine engravings of all periods, depicting rural scenes and peaceful, provincial streets.

Almost every afternoon after conferring in the editorial room we went out for a walk along the broad southern street in the poor industrial section of the city, where here and there the picturesque decrepitude of an old wall dating from the colonial period or a fine balustrade still survived. Frequently we stopped to have the Argentine dish *bife a caballo*, a steak with eggs on it, in one of the bars with exotic-sounding names, where blond, tight-lipped merchant-marine officers sat smoking their pipes in the company of some wretched women. Anselmi, stirred by an obscure spirit of comradeship, always talked with these women. At first they answered him with cold hostility, but presently made him the most disconcerting confessions. The name of one of these bars, Lunamoon, situated on a corner of the Paseo Colón, combined the English and Spanish words in all their silvery significance. It was kept by a corpulent, loquacious fellow who had been a sergeant in the territorial *gendarmerie* and told innumerable tales of his life in those untamed latitudes.

Blagoda brought a journalist named Tauste to our nightly gatherings at Lunamoon. They were intimate friends, but as different as day is from night. They complemented each other. Tauste was a sort of regulator. He reminded me of one of Baudelaire's characters, Samuel Cramer, because he never had any but half-ideas. So his life was a melancholy, incomplete journey, a constant going out to meet ideas, with never a hope of encountering them. I brought a friend, too, whom I had formerly seen frequently. He was not very intelligent, but had great intellectual probity and solid attainments and wrote accurately. Lorrié was his name. He was of French extraction, ambitious, and sober. He was measure and order personified. As we temperamental wasters are impatient at the silent vigilance of a puritan at our elbow, our relations did not prosper. They were correct and friendly, based upon mutual respect, but never intimate. Nevertheless, when casting about for people suitable for the *Ship*, I immediately thought of him as a person who would be, in a certain sense, irreplaceable. He was a tower of strength in our group of subtle and somewhat weak collaborators. Hector Lorrié could well resist shocks. With the addition of Tauste's melancholy brain and Lorrié's solid mind, we felt that our editorial staff was firmly established as far as its permanent personnel was concerned. The rest would be francs-tireurs selected from among the most brilliant minds available.

"This will end in a fiasco," Blagoda kept saying.

Lorrié, who took even the most trivial things seriously, became indignant:

"I don't see the point of this senseless defeatism."

"You chaps are asleep in a fog," insisted Blagoda. "You have no energy. We ought to be tough shock troops, and instead what are we? — a lot of prosy professors discussing whether or not it is opportune to criticize the influx of foreign capital."

Acevedo rightly insisted that we must first of all set our own house in order, and that we should begin by pillorying whatever was rotten at home.

"As gently as a bevy of young ladies," muttered Blagoda malevolently. And he burst out laughing loudly.

Anselmi laughed at him and cried: "Listen to the disillusioned Hercules!"

Blagoda pretended not to hear and continued to laugh loudly. While he was laughing, Anselmi called to one of the girls eating at a neighboring table. She wore a little black hat with a white flower in it. Her hair was blond and her eyelids were tinted a dark lavender.

"Have you ever seen a person possessed of the devil?" Anselmi asked her when she came over.

The girl looked at him without expression and said nothing.

Within a few weeks we had prepared volumes of written material. In the editorial room we enjoyed handling the mass of copy, the three solid piles of manuscript that stood on the great table between the shears and the paste pot and seemed to ripen in the smoke of Virginia tobacco. The review was to have four fields of combat, four targets on the horizon of our national reality: politics in the service of the politicians, the first

47

evil; nationalism in the service of gentlemen who had fattened on the fees of foreign enterprise, second evil; the decline of the civil conscience, the third evil; and the violation and hopeless bankruptcy of the legitimate government services, the fourth and most serious and widespread evil of them all, since it made possible and gave impunity to all the others. Acevedo and I were gathering ammunition for this last objective. We were greatly pleased with some excellent straightforward articles that we had requested rather fearing that they might turn out to be pale, conciliatory, or conventional. We had selected a sober, strikingly simple style and clear, round type in harmony with the journal's objectives. The headline type resembled that of a small, well-designed Swiss daily. The letters were tall and solid, and the only embellishment was a small black lateen sail below the title.

The afternoons were beginning to get hot. At times the sky took on so white a color that it could scarcely be distinguished from the top stories of the newest buildings. But there was a glorious gamut of greens in the gardens and squares. I knew nothing about trees, and at that beautiful season of the year it made me vaguely ashamed. Beside this magnificent vegetable dignity I felt myself an outcast. I looked at them with a strong sense of my own shortcoming. Every afternoon between three and four I went out for a walk with Mercedes. As we walked through San Martín Plaza she told me the name of every tree. She showed me the aguaribay, the tipa, the araucaria, and the ceibo. They were Argentine trees, and so magnificent and noble in their bearing that I was proud to learn to recognize them. I wanted our country to be like those trees. Acevedo, Jiménez, Anselmi, Blagoda, Tauste, Lorrié, and I wanted it to be like them. We had scarcely any other ambition. We wanted moral, human, and spiritual Argentina to be essentially like those trees.

They were great, strong, worthy, imperturbable, and proud without vanity, as if the exceptional character of their growth

48

had left them no room for complacency. Great, strong, worthy, and imperturbable! I studied them with emotion that late spring afternoon. Mercedes laughed. She did not want to stop there. She wanted to be off — to leave the square behind. She wanted to go on and leave everything behind. We went on walking.

But in the uttermost recesses of that last small chamber of the soul where we are at last completely alone with ourselves, it was your picture, you who lived there. You who had gone far. You who resembled those trees.

I I

THAT year the Christmas gaiety attracted us little. I had fresh in memory the loss of my mother, and on the 24th of December Anselmi and I dined in an ordinary restaurant as usual. We did not join in the merry-making outside. Mercedes Miró was in the country. Jiménez had disappeared early that morning to visit some absurd relatives of his, who watched him arrive as if he were a nobleman and kept silent while he carefully wiped his intellectual-looking pince-nez with his handkerchief. Jiménez knew what to expect. On holidays they kept their best dishes, their few good liqueurs, and special cigars for him. Anselmi and I were the orphans of that feast day.

In the afternoon I sent a telegram of greeting to my father and returned from the Post Office feeling lonely and depressed. I picked up Anselmi at the Jousten Hotel where he was discussing foreign policy with a Prussian youth, and together we walked across the street to a restaurant where food was cheaper than at the hotel. A Christmas tree was set up inside. Many young men and a few other people sat indolently at the tables. We ordered cold turkey and a bottle of good Rhine wine. A young lawyer whom we both knew came in, stopped for a while at our table, and told us that the past year had been bad for him, but that he hoped the new one would be better. We wished him a merry Christmas, and he left us and sat down to eat alone

in a corner of the dining-room. The waiter brought the tall
slender bottle in a metal bucket, opened it, and served us. We
toasted merrily and began to talk about the review and Blagoda.
Anselmi was convinced that sooner or later Blagoda would betray us. I was not so much afraid of that as annoyed by his hostile attitude. Anselmi insisted that time would prove him right.
He lifted the bottle out of the ice-bucket and refilled our glasses.
Then we had another serving of white meat. The restaurant
was beginning to fill and the waiters were busy attending to the
diners. The cashier was impatient and surly.

Anselmi insisted that we take a bottle of Pommery or Moët-
Chandon home to drink at midnight. I tried to dissuade him,
but his unanswerable argument was that he had received a
check the night before. When we finished eating we stopped
at a store and Anselmi bought the more expensive — Pommery.
But he told the proprietor and his clerk that he could not help
protesting at the price, on principle, and that, likewise on principle, he found himself obliged to tell them that they were
robbers. The proprietor, whose freckled bald spot shone as if it
had been carefully polished, flushed with anger. The delicate
network of blood vessels on his nose turned that member an
indignant red. He shouted and sputtered that no one was more
honest than he and challenged us to name a place where French
champagne was sold any cheaper. I took Anselmi by the arm
and pushed him out. He left protesting strongly, the thick bottle clutched to his side. "It's the government that's to blame
for this," he asserted. The government was his scapegoat. "If I
were the government," he said, "I would establish fixed prices
and clap everyone in jail who didn't respect them." He was in a
carping frame of mind and commented on the ugliness of the
women that we passed. After grumbling for a while, however,
his bad humor passed away and he began to joke.

It was a very hot night. Crowds were returning from the
beaches and still swarming toward them. We went up Leandro

Alem Street, a beehive of activity at that hour on Christmas Eve. Sailors, tourists, and rascals were in the throng. A thick yellow light seemed to be imprisoned under its arches.

We cut diagonally across Lavalle Street, then Tucumán, and climbed to the familiar floor. The servants and children were on the balconies, and the interior of the house was almost deserted. The occupants of the apartments had all scattered for the night. At this hour the wealthy people would be drinking in the great hotels, while those in modest circumstances would be at the cheaper river bathing-resorts. But it would be hot in all those places and we were in a privileged situation in my room with its balconies overlooking two streets.

I lighted the little stove and heated some coffee, but had forgotten to buy sugar. I was always forgetting something. I rang for the servant to bring us a few lumps on a plate. The poor girl looked hungry and did not seem to care to join in the holiday festivities. "Merry Christmas!" she said to us. Anselmi stood up and embraced her. His unaccustomed familiarity embarrassed her, then suddenly made her laugh. "Oh, Señor Anselmi! Now, Señor Anselmi!" Outside we could hear the noise of the wooden rattles, the hiss of the skyrockets, and the shouts of merry-makers perched on dilapidated automobiles.

"I am fed up with these holidays," said Anselmi. "They bring me face to face with myself, which annoys me because I don't like my own image. There are animals that like to look at themselves! What a parcel of unpleasantness, shortcomings, and lies they must have to shut their eyes to!"

"I can't understand your reluctance to contemplate yourself," I replied. "You have an uncouth charm about you that is worth exploring."

"Yes," he said, "a petrified forest. Let's look at other people."

Midnight was about to strike. I cleared the cups away and sat down opposite Anselmi. Between us was the round table with its faded tablecloth, lamp, books, papers, and a dish filled with ripe apples. The fragrance of the apples was in the air. I took one and bit into it.

Anselmi remarked:

"Perhaps my father was right to bring us up not to be introspective. He was a strong, direct, somewhat limited person, whom life had treated well. But the ruins that so-called sensitive men pile up about them opened his eyes to the dangers of introspection for certain temperaments. He taught my sister and me to look outward and forget about ourselves. In my own case the teaching has been salutary. Without it I should have found about me only invitations to suicide. As it is, since I don't bring myself into them, things don't stir me too deeply."

I told him that he was only talking literature, and went on munching my apple. It was hot and close.

"The champagne will get warm," I said. "Why not open it?"

"Let's set the ceremony ahead," agreed Anselmi. His corpulent shadow projected against the walls was split in two. He began to struggle with the cork. It came out with a loud pop and struck the ceiling. A little foam fell on the carpet. Anselmi filled my glass, the one that I ordinarily used for water, then filled his own.

"We are like Blagoda," he said. "Down to plain champagne."

"Except that he would never lower himself to drink his out of anything but a crystal goblet. He's an exquisite."

We both thought at the same moment of his chewed fingernails, dirty hands, and sticky slander, and burst out laughing.

"Here's health!" said Anselmi.

"To you, old boy!" I said.

Noisy midnight burst forth, God's midnight, and we listened in silence to the wail of sirens, the bursting of skyrockets, and the shouts of the crowds released for a moment from their cares and disappointments.

I stood up and put out the chandelier light, leaving only the light from the table lamp. The warm, sultry air of Buenos Aires blew into the room across the balconies. Christmas Eve was being feted as though merely an occasion for collective gaiety, unrestraint, and relaxation for head and muscle. Only the cries of the children, their shouts of alarm and childish hysteria as they scampered away after lighting their skyrockets, seemed to harmonize with the condition of their souls on that Christmas Eve. They were completely natural and made no attempt to pass for better or worse than they were. Only their souls were tied to their infinite biological misfortune, to their blind destiny to kill or be killed, and to their heritage of anger and joy.

Below us on the street the barbarous howling of an urchin and the tooting of a thousand automobile horns burst out simultaneously.

For a brief second, I wanted to cry, but caught myself immediately, took another drink, and forgot the gloomy pictures that had slipped into my mind.

Suddenly you gently touched the door of my spirit and entered. I wondered what you were doing at that moment and where you would celebrate your Christmas Eve.

Anselmi stepped in from the balcony.

"Next year," I said, "perhaps we shall have accomplished something more than this year, which has been a complete failure. Next year, at least, we shall have said what we have on our minds. We shall have fought constructively and discharged our human obligations more effectively."

"I don't know," he said; "perhaps there is no salvation even for us. I can't forget the lesson of my father. He had no conscientious complexes. He was an honest workman. He did his material work and didn't worry about the spiritual side of things. In that way, at least, he was certain not to complicate further the affairs of the world."

"You are just the opposite from most people. Instead of going about justifying your mistakes, you spend your life looking for the evil side of your impulses. But it brings you to a contradic-

53

tion. Because if you find that your father's whole-hearted devotion to his work was admirable, why don't you find your own equally good? Instead of simplifying matters, you complicate them."

"I have no real vocation," said Anselmi, his rough, virile voice somewhat embittered. "All I have is vague worries, like a sick man lying in bed who suddenly feels that he should get up and arrange some things in the next room; but the room is far away, and he will first have to get up and take some steps. So in the end he stays in bed and continues his vague longing for order."

We filled our glasses again and drank.

There was a great hubbub in the street, and we stepped out on the balcony to see what it was about. A small boy on the fifth floor was lowering an enormous paper bird by a string until it was almost within reach of some people standing in the street below. They were all shouting and trying to catch it.

"Do you know," said Anselmi looking down at the scene, "none of this amuses me? I lack simplicity. I had no childhood."

His expression at that moment showed that he really regretted the loss. I tapped him affectionately on the shoulder, for he seemed to me a great child who had not yet the years of assurance of the rest of us. But then he caught a glimpse of himself in that light and reacted defensively.

"I don't know which of us is worse," he said; "you are inconsistent, easily led, and lacking in strength. In a country of cynics we would make a fine pair of invalids. . . ."

He dragged me into the room with his iron arm, emptied the rest of the bottle into the two glasses, kissed it, and, without further ado, pitched it into the street. I heard the sound of glass crashing on the pavement, followed by a shout of protest and profanity.

Steps sounded in the hall. The door opened and Jiménez entered. He stood there, paler than usual, with his slightly affected manner and eye-glasses and impeccable pearl-gray suit.

"You are late," said Anselmi. "But we have toasted your health."

"There is some cognac," I suggested.

"Too strong for him," said Anselmi. "He's too sensitive!"

Jiménez appeared to pay no attention to our conversation. He waited patiently until we had stopped talking, then said: "I'm going to bring Señora Inés Boll in." It was the first time that we had heard her called Señora. "She has been a neighbor of ours for a long time and you have never exchanged a word with her. I want you to know her. I'll tell you something about her later. She's all alone and it will do her good to have someone to talk to."

He disappeared. Anselmi looked at me, puzzled and suspicious. We had no time for words. Inés Boll entered, followed by Jiménez.

She was tall, slender, and very well dressed. I think she must have been about twenty-eight. There was a worn expression about her eyes and in the two lines that ran from her very slightly curved nose to her somewhat full lips. She could not be called exactly pretty, but she had an indefinable simple charm. She was one of those inoffensive, docile, and somewhat nondescript young women of the lower middle class who have substituted a dull collection of minor virtues for the bolder ones. There was nothing cheap about her, however.

Anselmi suggested sending for a bottle of champagne from the store across the street. Señora Boll objected, but he stepped out for a moment to find the servant and returned smiling.

When we asked Señora Boll what sort of holidays she had had, she looked at Jiménez significantly.

"I have scarcely stirred out of the house," she said.

Then she told us about her modiste shop and her busy Christmas trade. She also told us that her father had been a surgeon in Germany before coming to the Argentine. He had been very poor and for fifteen years had received a starvation salary in a

Buenos Aires hospital. Finally he had gone into the bathroom one night and shot himself. She was an only child, eighteen years old at the time. While living with a German family that had helped her after her father's death, she had met the man she had married, from whom she had subsequently separated. The family kept a clandestine gambling-establishment near the ravines of Belgrano.

The two bottles arrived already chilled, and this time I served. I put out two clean glasses for them. Something forewarned me that we ought to get used to referring to them as "they." Señora Boll examined my room and timidly praised a portrait of a writer that hung above the bed, commenting on the strength of his face.

"As writers are the greatest egotists," I replied, "it is not surprising that most of their strength should concentrate in their heads."

Inés Boll did not appear to notice the remark. Instead she answered a question put by Anselmi, saying that her shop was in Charcas Street and that she designed the clothes herself. Times were difficult, however, and she often had to work very late.

I noticed her skin, as taut and smooth as a piece of polished plaster. She saw that I was observing her and smiled at me with her large, sluggish eyes, not opening her lips.

"Do you think that I look like someone that you know?"

"No," I said, "you don't."

"Well," she said presently, "I must be going."

"I hope that we shall be friends," I said.

"Yes," she said, "of course."

It was as if she had said: "I'll take the road that you suggest; what difference does it make to me which I take?"

Before leaving she added, with a certain archness:

"As my trade is sewing on buttons, I hope that you are at least happy to have met someone who will sew some on for you."

Jiménez went out with her. "I'll be right back," he said.

Out in the hall the telephone began to ring loudly. We heard Jiménez answer it. He appeared again at my door. "It's for you, Martín." "The mistress of your insomnia," Anselmi felt called upon to add by way of comment. I went out into the dark corridor and took the telephone. It was Mercedes Miró, saying: "Merry Christmas!" She was talking from the country while the lines with Buenos Aires were free. She asked me what I was thinking and doing and how I was, where I had been, whom I had seen, whether it had been hot in the city, and what I was reading, what was the political news and whether the *Travel Diary of a Philosopher* did not strike me as a very good book. I answered as best I could: yes, no, yes, yes, yes, no, yes. She confessed that she preferred nights in the open to the *Travel Diary of a Philosopher*. I agreed. She asked whether I was doing anything amusing, whether I was writing, going out, or reading, and whether I had been to the French theater. She told me that she had written me a letter; then she said good-by. We had talked for five minutes.

In my room Jiménez was talking to Anselmi in a low voice. When I came in, Jiménez closed the door himself and joined us around the table with a certain air of mystery.

"I talked to Inés Boll for the first time this afternoon, under the most extraordinary circumstances. I had returned from Palermo at eight o'clock, and as I was very thirsty I asked Señora Ana to make me a little lemonade. I sat down to finish some notes, thinking that I was alone in the house except for her. I had been working for half an hour when I heard the sound of voices in the hall and the angry slamming of a door. The voices grew louder. I got up once, opened the door, and listened for a few minutes. I gathered only that a man and a woman were talking in Señora Boll's room. I had never said a word to her, except a few casual 'Good mornings,' any more than you. She has always attracted me, but has seemed a little strange. I went back to my writing and opened the balcony window to see whether that wouldn't somewhat neutralize the noise. Suddenly a terrific outcry came from her room. I heard someone fall and a cry of horror from her. I rushed into the hall — Señora Ana was standing there fearfully — and opened Señora Boll's door. She had fallen across a sofa, and a man dressed in black like a widower stood over her, glaring at me angrily and not attempting to disguise the fact that he had just struck her. He was a strapping man, with a Roman nose and thick, bitter lips. She sat up and, instead of making any explanation to us, faced him and threatened to have him put out if he did not leave. I have never seen a face look like hers — it was the face of a corpse, drawn, angry, and frightened. I was about to ask him for some sort of explanation — not even knowing what I would say — when he said: 'Mind your own affairs, sir,' and I struck him. My glasses fell off and I couldn't see distinctly. He turned again to Señora Boll, threatened her with something that I didn't hear, and left the room. She dropped trembling to the sofa, with her eyes full of tears and a handkerchief in her hand, staring up at the roofs that could be seen through the window. Señora Ana, who was standing at the door, asked her timidly whether she would not like a glass of water. But Señora Boll stood up and came toward us to shut the door as if to ask us to leave. She must have seen my genuine interest in her situation, however, for she changed her mind, closed the door after Señora Ana, returned to the center of the room, and said to me: 'These are things that happen in life. He is my husband, and there have been frequent scenes like this since our separation. There is no need to be alarmed.'

" 'Why not?' I asked. 'Of course there is.' There in the darkness she told me this episode."

Jiménez continued to tell us the story of the girl and her husband, a drunkard and professional gambler who had pawned all her jewelry two days after their wedding and reduced her to ignominious servitude. Now that she had the modiste shop, he wanted to exploit her again. Jiménez had taken a deep interest in her situation and, as it was then late, had invited her to have dinner with him. She had accepted and told him all about her situation.

"Her story is a commonplace one," said Anselmi.

Jiménez continued to talk to me vehemently about the girl and about the generally sad situation of women without men in their families to protect them. Señora Boll's only relatives — poor watch-makers, whom she had never seen — lived in Stuttgart, outside the walls. Jiménez said that she must be helped. He was pale and began to clean his glasses with his enormous batiste handkerchief.

"What do you suppose Dr. Dervil is doing?" asked Anselmi.

The noises outside had quieted down. A few sounds were still to be heard, but they had receded into the distance. I suggested that we see whether the doctor was in his room. We all had a sudden feeling of tenderness for the old man. There was no light in Señora Boll's room as we passed her door. We knocked on the old doctor's door, and as there was no answer, I turned the knob. It was not locked and I opened the door.

Dr. Dervil, in shirt sleeves, was lying face down on his bed, asleep, in the midst of a confusion of papers, receptacles, books, and furniture. We looked at him affectionately. He lay snoring, his arms spread out as if to embrace the bed, the only object which life gave him to cling to on that Christmas Eve.

I 2

ONE fresh, pleasant morning, I received a call from Acevedo. We were to meet that night in the restaurant of the Jousten Hotel. It was to be the last meeting before the *Ship* weighed anchor. He had called to remind me to tell Jiménez and Anselmi to be on hand promptly, as they often arrived very late. I promised to bring them promptly. Then I opened my papers and began to work on an article urging the necessity of contact with the land before attempting to invigorate our contemporary life. I did not like what I had written; although the idea was good, the article lacked balance.

I bathed, dressed, and went outdoors. The sun was high. I needed time to think and to put some ideas in order, and decided to lunch alone somewhere. I carried with me Darwin's *Voyage of the Beagle*, which I had recently bought. While eating luncheon, I read the account of his arrival in the southern part of Argentina. The restaurant had great square windows overlooking the boulevard. On the other side was an advertisement in enormous letters of a new brand of cigarettes. The boulevard was very wide, and dark lanes of motor cars were moving in both directions.

Acevedo, who was presiding at the table, raised his hand for silence.

"The worst thing that could happen before beginning our work," he said, "would be for us to confuse the terrain that each of us has been allotted. On that point I must be adamant. Otherwise we shall be in a devil of a mess. Tauste will write what we have agreed on for him, 'The Oceanography of the Creole Politicians'; Anselmi will do his sarcastic medallions, and Lorrié will draw up his careful balance-sheet of the democracies of the present century. I don't agree with Anselmi's view. I think that his enthusiasm is too great when he deliberately invades Lorrié's field, which is much more technical and scientific, and therefore calls for less temperament and greater precision. . . ."

Anselmi protested. He did not want to poach on anyone's territory. He noted regretfully that now, to judge by the plan that had just been discussed, large and important parts of the subject with which Lorrié had been entrusted would remain outside his field. He did not insist, however, and continued to eat and smoke in silence, withdrawing into his own rough shell.

"I am glad that we are observing order from the very beginning," said Acevedo.

"*Our* order," corrected Blagoda.

Anselmi did not raise his eyes. He removed the shell of an enormous crawfish with his fork, preparatory to daubing it with mayonnaise.

"Anselmi has a large appetite," said Blagoda.

"Yes, and I satisfy it by eating. Others appease theirs differently."

"My!" said Blagoda. "Anyone would say that he is irritated."

"I am irritated when I am pricked. You may have studied zoology. The secretion of certain creatures produces a local irritation. Only skin-deep of course. . . ."

Blagoda laughed heartily. He looked at Anselmi shaking with mirth.

Anselmi turned to Tauste, who was sitting on his left.

"This mixing of lobster with pork — " he said.

Tauste remained serious, but Blagoda continued to laugh loudly.

"That's a good one," he said. "What a good one!"

"Enough joking," said Acevedo. "Let's talk about what we came here to discuss."

Acevedo told us what he intended to put into a twenty-line editorial. It was to be set up in fourteen-point type, with a wide margin, directly under the paper's name. It was a concise, bold statement of motives. He changed the final sentence himself as we sat there, saying that he wanted it blunter and less literary. He asked whether anyone had any further suggestions to make. Nobody had. He took a sheet of paper out of his pocket, made a notation on it, and put it away again. Then he said that it had fallen to Blagoda, as assistant editor, to write an important editorial paragraph, and that since it was already written, he

61

would ask him to read it to us. Blagoda said that it contained very general considerations, which were not yet complete.

"We move to approve," said Anselmi sarcastically.

There was a moment of embarrassment and general disapproval.

"We are talking about this seriously, Anselmi," I said to him.

He smiled and excused himself. He was very humorous about it, and the rest laughed too.

"I'll read it after we finish eating," said Blagoda.

"The food is atrocious here," declared Jiménez.

As none of those present was exactly a gourmet, Jiménez's assertion seemed out of place.

"Don't be surprised," observed Anselmi; "he's neither an exquisite nor an epicure nor a great chef, just a professional grumbler. If the crawfish had been first on the menu, he would have ordered it instead of the cold roast beef that he is eating."

"You're just envious!"

When the fruit had been brought, Blagoda took out his grimy-looking draft, written in lead pencil. Before reading it he devoured two flattish, juicy white peaches. Then he said:

"I shall begin." He read rapidly.

"*Enough*. That is a word. *Enough*. It is more than a word: it is a decision. An expression of will, an expression of energy in action. *Assez*. That will do. It is too much. Young people who are listening to us, we want no more. *Enough*. We want to nail this word here, to our prow. This single word. *Enough*. It is not a word for capitalists. It is not a word for speculators. It is not a word for people who accumulate money, interests, *bibelots*, honors, titles, or filth. It is not a word for people who want nice comfortable things. It is not a word for ladies, actors, or intriguers. It is not a word for those who are witnessing the farce, digesting, enjoying, and applauding it. Nor is it a word for the

62

ambitious of any sort. For all such people this is no word. It is
not a word for politicians of any stripe, nor for dukes, charlatans,
orators, pious persons, hypocrites, or fools. This is no word for
these groups. There is another word for them — a very different
word. For all of them the word is: *More.*

"*Enough* is the word for us. *Enough* is the word that we
want. *Enough* is the word that we inscribe here, at the top of
our journal, which is no journal for those people. *Enough* is a
word for young, intransigent, honorable people, for people with
clean consciences. They are the ones who are waiting for it, and
it is for them that we inscribe it here. We and they are united
by this word.

"*Enough* is therefore our voice, our watchword. That is why
we do not begin, as new journals usually do, with a sea of words.
We begin with a single word. Not with a sea: a single word. For
the moment we need only a single word. We do not need to
live in the usual Babel, in a chaotic confusion of terms, in a
melting pot of rotten words, in the common caldron of the
silver-tongued, the insincere, and the mystical. We need only
a single word to sweep away the evil, conventional, fraudulent
words and to oppose equivocal expressions categorically. We
need only one unequivocal word: *enough.*

"That is also enough for us. It is enough to say what is enough.
To say: 'thus far and no farther.' To say: '*Quosque tandem?*'
Enough!

"Enough.

"Enough of many things. Enough of all the things which we
shall enumerate in our forthcoming numbers. Enough of abuse,
of enthroned stupidity, of criminal pacts, of small personal
states within the great State; of politicians, exploiters, cynics
in power, and powerful men who are cynical; enough of infamous men on top and of genuine people at the bottom.
Enough of public decomposition. Enough of people in political

63

command who are ignorant of morality. Enough of bastard sons of our spiritual country who have a voice in our material country. Enough of all this!

"Enough of many other things, of all that belittles and vilifies us as a nation. Enough of those who reduce us to their own insignificant stature; to their health, which is diseased; to their morality, which is abominable; to their power, based upon the party caucus; to their money, derived from evil manipulations; to their coarse temperaments; to their leaden-footed culture; to their stupid vocabulary and their general style which proclaim great unworthiness of conscience.

"Enough of all these!

"We are going to use that word and to brandish it. We are going to have it at the tip of our tongues, in our hands and consciences. We are going to keep it in our minds and hearts, and even in our dreams, which will be the dreams of men to whom it is important to devote their waking hours to helping others to progress, men who are unable to sleep — although they deserve it — because of injustice. We are going to carry this word within us. We are going to fetch it out whenever it is necessary. We are going to keep it clean and bright, like the sword of steel that guards the soldier's quick sleep. We are going to care for it as for something sacred. As a thing which shall never be misused. As a thing which deserves faith and sacrifice and not mere lip-service. We are going to guard it as our own lives; no sheltered lives, but lives exposed to danger and to all weather.

"This is the way — young people who are listening to us — we shall think, pray, exclaim, and shout the word *enough*."

He read these last sentences in a low voice. When he ceased speaking, he dropped his eyes and put the paper away. It was the first time that I had seen him silent and reflective. It was the first time that he had appeared to me sincere.

64

I looked at Anselmi and saw that he was getting ready to attack. I waited. There was a general exchange of glances such as occurs when everyone has something to say but each is waiting for someone else to say the first word.

Acevedo too was waiting.

Jiménez drank the last red drop from his glass, looked at Anselmi, and said:

"It's not bad, but what is the defect?"

"It has no defect," asserted Tauste. "It's splendid."

"It has a defect," contradicted Jiménez. "What is it?"

"I find it good," I said. "It is a prelude — sufficiently accurate and energetic in tone — to what will come later, instead of intonation, definition of detail, or adaptation."

"No," insisted Jiménez. "It's too oratorical. *Ça tourne à l'éloquence.* Let's avoid that danger: eloquence."

Acevedo intervened.

"No," he said. "That's not fair. It has a tone of combat and challenge that can only be put that way."

I asked Anselmi and Lorrié what they thought. Blagoda was looking around, the palms of his yellowed hands resting on the edge of the table.

"I approve," said Lorrié.

"It's good," said Anselmi with unexpected vehemence.

We all wanted a fight, and away down within us the challenging note of Blagoda's piece pleased us.

The couples at the neighboring tables stared at us in surprise.

From across the table, Tauste made expressive gestures of approval and support to Blagoda. He raised his eyebrows as if to say: "But it's quite evident. It stands on its own legs. It needs no support."

Jiménez said: "Well, let's drink to the health of our word."

"I am going to say something else," said Acevedo, pausing with his glass raised and looking at us before continuing. "I am going to make a proposal. Why not use that word as the name of our journal? The *Ship* is too academic, too trite. Why not call it simply and forthrightly *Enough?*"

Yes, it was a good idea. We all approved it.

"The suggestion seems a very good one to me," said Blagoda. Then we drank.

"It's true, as has been well said," he went on, "that this is just a general and vague introduction. You will all put the dots on the *i's*. You will say what it is that is *enough.*"

"Of course."

"Yes, certainly."

"Well, enough of this," said Acevedo. "Let's get on to other things."

He talked to us about the kind of type — italic — that he had found for the medallions that Anselmi was going to write.

"Italics are a weak type," said Anselmi; "they are type for small gazettes with weak voices."

"He prefers bold-face," put in Jiménez, "a virile type."

"For God's sake," said Acevedo, "let's not make a problem out of the type we are going to use. If there is one thing that I understand something about — "

"Enough!" said Blagoda.

Twelve o'clock struck. We stood up with the word on our tongues. "Enough!" we said with an air of sarcastic irony to the people who rode in the elevator with us. They looked at us as if we were mad or drunk. We took the elevator to the main floor and then walked down to the bar in the basement. "Enough," someone let drop while passing between the tables.

A little man with a small, blond mustache became ruffled because Anselmi said the word too strongly to him. The man set down his stein and bounced up angrily like a rubber ball.

"You lack civilization!" he said in rather dubious Spanish. "You lack civilization!"

"But, sir," Anselmi said to him, stopping at his table, "we have just found a watchword, a war cry, and now that we are

66

about to perform a great service for our country, you become indignant."

"You lack civilization!" sputtered the man. His face was flushed and his eyes were popping out of his head as he stood teetering on tiptoe like a fighting cock.

Anselmi continued on his way laughing. So did Blagoda and all the others.

13

At heart I was lonely. What I was doing seemed to me too little and too mediocre. A young country on the down grade requires new men who will climb. I was not one of them. Moreover I was a literary man — a skein of thread spun so fine as to be practically useless.

Some days, sitting with my writing-pad before me, I worked tirelessly from dawn to midnight. I felt such exaltation and such a need for someone to share it with! I kept on working. But at the end of the day, when I reread the pages that I had written, they seemed pointless. I felt sure that their spontaneous, vigorous rhythm would win applause, but could that take the place of the basic requirement of communicating ideas, and to what extent was it not all merely a means of discharging an excess of personal restlessness? Our fighting journal as yet gave only a small hope of action. I sought comfort in metaphysical reflections, but at twenty-five metaphysical compensations are not very solid. Real satisfaction comes to us only as the direct result of action and experience. As we were not politicians and had no confidence in the results of party action, with the parties rotten to the core, we were perforce limited to specifically intellectual action.

During those days I dreamed of seeing you. To see you gave me a mysterious feeling of completeness, a sense of grace, although the mysterious part of this benefit was that it was neither abstract nor gratuitous, but a solid presence, as if I felt that I would have to find in you the elements lacking in my own make-up. Mornings and afternoons I often revisited the places where I had seen you, the last few blocks of Florida Street in the neighborhood of San Martín Plaza. In vain. I did not even know whether you were still in Buenos Aires.

Most people interested me little or not at all. My search was for thoughtful persons climbing with only the joy and strength of their own indefatigable resistance to dissolution and to external obstacles. . . . How few yet how indispensable were such people!

In seven days of close application I wrote a long story. It was the story of a couple living in the snowy isolation of a high mountain valley, whom years of solitude turned against each other and at last separated. The birth of this fungus of hatred and its slow development produced a corresponding bitterness and despair in me as I described it. I needed warmth of affection as never before.

What was Mercedes Miró thinking meanwhile, and what place did I occupy in her mind? I turned my back on these questions. The reply was too obvious.

Blagoda's writing changed our attitude toward him. Although we did not like him any better as a person, we came to the salutary realization that he had a sincere side to his character worthy of our trust. However, a few days after reading his editorial piece, he proposed another article, and in this we could not help seeing a touch of personal bitterness that greatly detracted from it. Anselmi seized the opportunity to attack him in Lunamoon when the article was being discussed. Jiménez puckered up his lips in a gesture which we well knew was intended to signify: "Beware of him."

Reform movements, however, are not carried out by petulant or proud men. Such people start false, aristocratic movements, caste reactions that are always ephemeral because selfish. True reform movements are led by men with a passionate will for justice. Such a will Blagoda had too. In fact, that will was the only thing that the members of our group had in common.

One evening, as I was on my way to the press, I met Blagoda in Lezama Park. We walked on together, leaving behind us the immense tree trunks, the peaceful marble statues, the cold, backless benches, the thick, fragrant foliage, and the synagogue over the entrance of which we had seen the dusty orthodox frescoes a thousand times.

"You are against me," said Blagoda point-blank, referring to Anselmi, Jiménez, and me. "You distrust me."

"No," I replied. "The fact is that you are a harsh, sarcastic person whom it is difficult to make out clearly."

"How are we going to work together, then?" he asked.

"We are all working together. We know our duty. What difference do personal peculiarities make? We have not been made to the measure of our own preferences."

"Those are my sentiments too," he said.

"What counts is the point at which our objectives meet."

"Naturally," he said.

He tore a leaf off one of the lower branches of a plane tree. "Naturally."

14

DURING her siesta Mercedes Miró pulled down the large Nile-green, silk curtains. A cool white shadow remained in the living-room. With its naked plaster, practical adornments, and severe furniture, it was like one of those colonial rooms used by Indian magistrates. Everything was simply and comfortably arranged in excellent taste. Near the little table that stood beside the sofa upholstered in white wool, Mercedes was sitting on the carpet. We had drunk our coffee. During the past three days we had seen a lot of each other, but had not spoken a word about ourselves — we had talked about everything else. All my questions were in vain; they broke against a smiling, elastic, voluble resistance. I feigned the most normal of resignations in order not to disturb her — a precision machine geared to external events. But there were moments that disconcerted and astonished her when I became annoyed and indignant at her. She was so sincere that my irritation quickly dissolved. Then I remained silent, watching her move and listening to her speak. I was enchanted by the combination of her gray eyes and very dark skin. I liked the lithe elegance with which her whole body moved. I liked her head, her legs, her hands — her hands, which often missed the mark, so swiftly did she use them.

"I should like to write a book about you and me," I said to her. "I would call it 'A History of Two,' or 'Futility.' "

"Again?" she said. Her eyes were turned toward the white book-stand on her left.

"Or 'A History of the Futility of Two in Company.' "

"I don't understand certain ways of using words. For example, I don't know what you really mean by the word *futility*. In the first place, who can believe in the utility of lives or of the relationship between lives? They may be anything but useful."

"I mean fertility."

"Fertility is something else," she agreed. "Fertility is *doing* something, giving something material and concrete. Performing a task, building a tunnel, or having a child. That is fertility. But if I like your mouth and you like the way that I say insipid things, that creates a relationship which is rather unsuitable for fertility; and there is nothing to be done about it. Why demand more from things than they can naturally give?"

"No," I replied. "Fertility has to do not only with the production of concrete fruits. It is also a part of any relationship between two people strong enough to lift it out of the ruin of our everyday solitude."

She disagreed.

"No, no. That is the eternal tendency that people have of talking about things in the abstract. 'Fertility' is an abstraction. What a boring and mistaken abstraction! You have that tendency too, and it does you more harm than you realize. Life is no abstraction and is not full of abstractions. Life is full of men and women, fruit, vegetables, animals, minerals, and other things. When I say that I like to touch an elephant's skin, I am not speaking abstractly. I am saying merely that I like to touch the elephant's skin. Neither more nor less. So many people go astray because of those accursed abstractions! Why don't you come close and touch me? You like the abstraction of my skin — your Platonic idea of my skin — more than my skin itself. Isn't that an absurdity?"

I sat down beside her on the heavy carpet and kissed her on the lips, amused.

". . . and an extravagance?"

She was sincere in not wanting to give any more of herself, but not in her method of arguing. I told her so. She became more surprised, and recalcitrant.

"How boring!" she said. "How boring!"

Her hand, with its painted fingernails, closed my mouth. She stood up quickly, went to the white bookcase on the left, and opened it.

"I'm going to tell you something," she said. "You need stories to distract you."

"No, come and sit down. There is nothing that distracts me as much as looking at you."

"No, no. I know what I am talking about. I am going to tell you something."

"Come."

She came back with a statuette of lead-colored stone and a large book. She put them both down on the carpet.

"This contains a story about Paris," she said. "And this, one about the Netherlands."

"I'm not interested in the story about Paris, nor in the Dutch story. Come closer to me."

"I shall begin with the Paris story. I had lived in Paris with Papa for ten years. We were constantly traveling for his health between Cannes, Normandy, the Landes, and Bordeaux. Papa had bought a villa in Versailles. It was a charming old house with parks and flower-gardens. One summer he fell very ill and we had to move to a hotel in Paris. Our apartment had a terrace that overlooked neighboring roofs and attics. I never went outside the hotel, as I could not leave my father's sick-bed. At twilight and after nightfall I used to go out on the terrace and look at the neighboring roofs, and the towers of the Trocadéro outlined against the city sky. I was so lonely and sad! One day, on a neighboring terrace, about twenty feet from ours, I saw a man, dressed in dark trousers and a sports jacket. He stood looking at me and continued to gaze at me for a long time. I looked at him too, and that night I remembered how we had looked at each other. From that time on, at the same hour we went out on our terraces and looked at each other in the gathering dusk until we could hardly see each other. We did not exchange a gesture — merely looked at each other. My father became worse. There were two days when I could only look at that man through the curtains, by way of consolation; and he could not see me at all, but stood there patiently just the same. There was an improvement. Days of greater heat came. Sometimes, like an intruder, a woman approached the man. Then he went into the house with her, and later returned alone. Thus many days passed. Once he must have noticed my terrible loneliness and depression, for he took an object out of his pocket, showed it to me, and made a sign that he was going to throw it to me. He threw it and I caught it. It was this early Egyptian stone image. He signaled to me to return it to him. He caught it, gazed at it

72

for a long time, and held it in his hands as if he were telling it all his thoughts. Many weeks passed and we limited ourselves to that single rite. Not another gesture. Not a letter. Each night one of us kept the little statue until the following day. One night while it was in my possession, my father died. Relatives came to the hotel, whisked me away, and put me on a boat. I thought for a long time about the man who had done me so much good without any real contact or any tangible bond except this stone object."

She put it into my hands. It was a small, lead-colored statue of the consistency and lightness of pumice-stone.

"A pure abstraction," I said to her.

"I am coming to that!" she replied. "Now comes the Dutch story. At the beginning of a six months' visit, during which I lived alone in Amsterdam, I bought this book in a street in the Jewish quarter. I read it greedily. It was the story of a very strange woman who had succeeded in educating herself in such a way that at length she seemed to live outside of the real world, in an atmosphere neither religious nor contemplative, but of almost complete personal detachment from external events. A state akin to the mystical, but without mysticism. In short, an unusual, complicated condition, difficult to describe. The book had such an enormous effect on me that I began to want to be like that woman myself. It was stupid, if you like, but fascinating. Of course I fell into a soft lethargy entirely out of keeping with my character. It was as if I had become addicted to a drug and had entangled myself in a disgusting syrup, on the very verge of hysteria, which then seemed to me very beautiful and worth while. With what remained of my will-power I wrenched myself away from the self-deformation that I had brought about. I had to leave Holland to cure myself of it."

I looked at the title-page of the book, which was in English. It was *The Life of Mona van Amstel*. I set it down. Mercedes picked up both the image and the book and put them away.

"Those are the only two times in my life," she said, "when out of sheer stupidity I have been ill to the point of distraction. The two times when I have hoped that fertility would rain down upon me from heaven. I have told you about them so that you will see that I know what frustration is. I prefer to avoid it forever, and live! Live simply and without complications."

She planted herself squarely in front of me, a cigarette in a corner of her mouth, her eyes averted in order to avoid the smoke.

"Voilà, monsieur le soupirant."

"Of the two possible varieties of madness, one is dangerous, the other not. A fool's madness is harmless, but the madness of an intelligent person is the most dangerous thing in the world. One of the latter forms consists in explaining everything by excellent arguments that stand on their own feet, only they are completely beside the question."

"Don't you see? 'The question!' What question, what question is there between us? . . . Idiot! . . ."

She dropped to the carpet beside me and, running her fingers through my hair, thoroughly tousled it. She kissed me quickly, then suddenly sat up again, thinking about something else. Her gaze was fixed on one of the living-room tables.

"There are no yellow flowers on it."

She went to the hall door, opened it, and called loudly for the servant, who shuffled in, fat and phlegmatic.

"I have told you to bring me yellow flowers for that vase every day! You are inattentive and forgetful these days! I shan't answer for what will happen if those flowers are not in the vase by tomorrow!"

The servant departed grumbling.

"I don't like the way this room is arranged," said Mercedes, glancing about her with disapproval. "I don't like any of it. I'm going to shift all the furniture around."

I went over to her, kissed her again, and stroked her fine,

beautiful hair. She sat quietly at first, like a cat, but when I saw that she was not responsive, I stopped caressing her and sat in the armchair. She lighted another cigarette, went to the table on which she had ordered the yellow flowers to be put, and laid some magazines on it. She walked away to observe the effect from a distance, then came back to where I sat, stood in front of me again, and asked:

"Does it matter to you?"

"What?"

"That I am this way or that."

"Yes, it matters."

She reflected, then said:

"It is my characteristics that matter to you, not I."

"No, that's not true," I replied.

"Yes, yes, it is true."

"No, it's not."

She took a few steps.

"How terrible!" she said. "Nobody will accept anybody as he is. That proves how strongly human nature is given to egotism and subjectivity. And there is no help for it. The man with one eye wants his deaf neighbor to have only one eye; the deaf neighbor wants his near-sighted neighbor to be deaf. And so it goes."

I kept silent.

"You don't even care to answer," she said.

"Why should I?"

"All right."

Then, changing the subject, she told me about what she had done and wanted to do that morning, and recounted very waggishly the absurdities of an old Hungarian woman whom she had met the previous summer with a mania for subjecting people to inquisitions, who had made everybody very uncomfortable by asking them the bluntest questions with a perfectly innocent air. I laughed. I liked to look at her. In fact, I could not take my eyes off her.

"You keep looking at me as if I were demented."

"Aren't you, a little?"

"Yes, but with a madness that is unfortunately normal. Don't I spend my life trying to achieve sanity, not lunacy?" She laughed a short, pointed laugh. "I am an odd fish."

She asked me whether I loved her, as if she were inquiring about the speed of clouds in summertime. I told her that I did, and she jumped up from the sofa and went off to look for ice water and fruit.

She bit into two plums, put them both down, went to wash her hands, came back, and told me gaily an idea that she had had about some friends of ours who were living a somewhat equivocal life.

So we talked for an hour or two.

"Well, let's go somewhere," she said at length. It was after five.

She disappeared, to return in a few minutes with her hat on, dressed for the street. She had a cigarette in her mouth, and her eyes were turned up in the way that she had when she wanted to think out something personal.

I looked at her and said:

"I am thinking at this moment that it would be better for you to be alone and for me to be a thousand miles away and for us never to have met."

"Don't be an idiot!"

She put an arm in mine and with her free hand rang for the elevator. The elevator came up with the characteristic click of its spring at each floor. We went down and took a taxi to Palermo. It was hot and there was little relief even in the shade of the wood. We took a couple of turns around the lake and the palm-bordered avenue, then told the chauffeur to drive us to Belgrano. The Dietze garden was full of tables, and the ground had recently been watered, which made the atmosphere a little fresher. I had some beer, and Mercedes sipped her light

76

tea. People were coming and going. Some went straight for the covered pavilion.

We sat for a while without talking. I was smoking, watching the people, and looking at Mercedes. Before long, as I had expected, she wanted to go. We walked a little in the neighboring streets and down by Echeverría to the green ravines, from which the station, the railroad crossing, and the heavy traffic could be seen. A crowd of children was playing, and here and there an adult was strolling. Neither Mercedes nor I said anything.

We returned to her house. Night had fallen over the city. The capital was sleeping off its lethargy. Not the slightest breeze stirred. The curtains hung heavily. Mercedes lighted a candle and we were soon visited by a swarm of tiny moths and stinging insects.

"It's not going to rain," she said. "This hell will continue."

I did not answer her remark, but instead said brusquely:

"Mercedes, let's stop seeing each other for a time."

She showed no surprise and I felt no regret at what I had said. I repeated it.

"I do you no good. You are caught in a galling noose. I am beyond my depth, convinced that I am only in your way and that I shall end by becoming something of an amiable outsider who is merely tolerated."

Her reaction was impatient and discouraged. She said that she could not convince me of the truth of the situation; that I was dissatisfied with our relations and with her because I was dissatisfied with myself. I admitted that perhaps that was true, but that, if so, a separation was even more strongly indicated.

"You will get over it in a few days," she said. "And come back. The air will have cleared, and perhaps it will be better that way."

She was strong. What did the world matter to her?

"Yes," I said, "it will be better that way."

She laughed and bantered with me affectionately. But I knew

77

that in some indeterminate place a rift was opening between us.

I walked back to my house, depressed and tired and with more of a feeling of futility than ever.

That was a bitter night for me.

15

SOME days passed. One night I was working in my room. I opened the door to the balcony and reduced the amount of light by opening my notebook wide. After brushing my teeth, I took out my portfolio and began to write. I wanted to finish the short novel. I reread the pages that I had written the previous day, did not like them, tore them up, and set myself to rewrite slowly and laboriously the whole scene that I wanted to describe. The noblest part of literary work and what dignifies it beyond other callings is the severe pruning it entails and the immensity of what it must deny in order to assert itself.

At about eleven I heard steps in the corridor and the voices of Jiménez and Señora Boll. I waited for them to subside.

Jiménez knocked at my door and came in. He was dressed more impeccably than ever, in a blue suit and a white silk shirt with a fine red stripe.

"Hello," he said.

"Hello," I answered.

"In full creative fever," he said as though he had just discovered some contraband.

"Working as slowly as an ox. Where've you been?"

"I've been out with Inés."

"Acevedo told me this afternoon that you have not yet handed in any of your articles."

"That's true. I haven't given him any of them."

"Why not? That doesn't seem right to me."

"I couldn't. I haven't written them."

"It would be well worth tempering amusement with a little

work. Fun becomes insufferably boring otherwise. As exhausting as work itself."

"Mr. Moralist, I have gone out a lot recently, but by way of exception."

"Inés?"

"Yes," he said.

"Good."

"Of course it's good. She's an exceptional woman."

"She is very pleasant."

"She's an exceptional woman."

"She is, is she?"

"Yes. Such frankness! Such femininity! Really most unusual."

"I'm glad. Do you like her very much?"

"Yes," he said. He was looking at one of the photographs on the wall.

"In love?"

"I don't know what that is." He turned his eyes and looked at me calmly. "I like her very much. We understand each other."

"Ah!" I said.

"It has rarely happened to me. I have been accustomed to furniture-women — women of inferior understanding, incapable of conversation or expression. Inés is different."

"Congratulations," I said.

"And refined and even-tempered. I have dined with her all these nights, but her modest nature does not prevent her from being new and different every time."

"That's a great quality," I said.

"But there is something that disturbs me," he interrupted. "Something that worries me a good deal."

"The other man?"

"What will happen? I must help her get rid of him and stop him from pestering her."

"You will have to step very cautiously."

79

"I'm afraid for her. It is very complicated. I don't know what will happen."

"If I can be of any help to you . . ."

"No," he said. "We can't do anything to help her. We can only wait. But I don't know how it will end."

We were silent for a while. Jiménez went over to the table, put on his reading-glasses, and looked at the papers piled on it. He was different — visibly different. Much more concentrated and reserved. Almost short in his manner. I could see that he had expressed himself badly, but that it had to come out. Some details of the manuscript caught his interest. I had told him the plot before and he wanted to know how some of the technical problems had turned out. I told him about my solutions.

"Tomorrow I'm going to write," he said. "I hope to be able to hand in two of the articles on Monday. But there's still lots of time."

"Acevedo wants to send everything to the press right away," I said. "He wants to prepare three complete numbers before the first appears. It seems a very prudent plan to me."

"Yes, it is," he agreed.

He was silent, his mind on something else.

"I am happy," he said after a bit; "man, I am happy."

"First rate, I'm delighted to hear it."

"Do you know, it's as if now at the end of each day I were sure of rest. Whatever happens, there she is, there is her living, feminine nearness and response. I needed her. I suddenly realize how fagged out I was and how much I needed her."

"I understand it very well. I know exactly how you feel."

"Yes," he said. "It's as if I had lived for a long time only in profile and had suddenly discovered that my corporeal volume was incomplete. Then miraculously it has been completed and I feel more solid, rich, and sensitive."

"Yes," I said.

It was completely quiet indoors and out. Jiménez was about

to leave when we heard Anselmi's heavy tread and the song that he always hummed when he saw a crack of light under our doors at this hour of the night. It was an aria from *The Barber of Seville*. He opened the door and held it open with a droll theatrical gesture.

"My dear sirs, good evening!"

Then he approached Jiménez.

"What does the dear absent member have to say? At last we see him. What a pleasure!"

He looked him up and down as if measuring the effect of a change.

"Well, well, well."

"What's the matter, brute?" said Jiménez.

"Well, well, well. Fine conduct, I must say. Absent every night. Every night mysteriously absent. Where? The mystery stands revealed. With Señora Inés Boll. *La très belle. La très, très belle!*"

"What are you playing the fool for?"

"We shall have to make an investigation. Where do the two mysterious and daring guests of the honorable boarding-house go every night? To what door do their stealthy exits lead them?"

Jiménez looked at him with his eyes half-closed as he played with my dark, tortoise-shell paper-cutter with a magnifying glass at one end. He viewed Anselmi through the glass.

"Looking at you enlarged, you look still more of an imbecile."

"Irritable Señor Jiménez, a little moderation in your language."

He changed his tone and became serious. Going up to Jiménez, he confronted him.

"What do you mean by getting yourself into a scrape?"

Jiménez glanced from him to me in astonishment and burst out:

"Did you ever see such an idiot! . . ."

81

"You will end by becoming a drawing-room demoiselle, playing bridge and sighing."

"You certainly have a buffalo's head," said Jiménez; "appearances do not deceive."

"You are going to turn into a drawing-room miss. Taking Señora Boll out for walks! Or the director of a cutting and fitting academy."

Jiménez put the paper-cutter down on the table and raised his eyes to meet Anselmi's.

"You have no right to make certain kinds of jokes, and I won't allow it."

"The lady" — Anselmi pronounced the word with studied care — "is going to turn your head, and we are working at something else."

Jiménez laughed loudly.

"Simpleton," he said.

"It is easy to distract you. That's why I say it to you."

"Simpleton!"

I stood up.

"All right!" I said. "I've got to work! You can't go on like this. This room is no club! Out with you!"

I pushed them out.

"Let Don Juan go out first," said Anselmi. He made a bow and showed Jiménez the door.

"Idiot," said the other. "Idiot!"

"Come along, Don Juan. *Est-ce que Don Juan était une demoiselle?*"

I remained alone.

I thought about those two boys — those two friends of mine. I was very fond of them and I wanted things to turn out well for them. I thought about Señora Boll. I knew nothing about her. Was it possible that Jiménez was right? What would her husband do? I tried to concentrate. I wrote a few lines, then struck them out. It was no use. I could not concentrate or write a thing. I was off my subject. I stood up and went out on the balcony.

As I lay in bed with the light out, I thought of none of that. I did not think about the future review, or about myself, or about Mercedes Miró. I lay thinking of you.

"Some day," I thought, "I shall know you. Some day I shall hear your voice speaking to me. Your ears will be listening to what I am saying and your eyes will rest on the distance, where they always seem to be. Some day I shall be near your half-parted lips. Some day I shall deserve that. I don't want it to happen before that time. I don't want your eyes to drop; if they are to turn from the contemplation of those distant spaces, let them look out on a level, no lower. Let them look straight ahead at the man in front of them. I don't want your eyes to drop."

I went to sleep turning that phrase over in my mind: "I don't want your eyes to drop when that day comes."

16

FEBRUARY and March passed rapidly. The shorter days and morning freshness announced the arrival of autumn. The city began to lose its color and became bleaker; and the men returned to it to prepare themselves for the intense labor of the year.

Jiménez remained invisible, abducted by Señora Boll.

In April came the event — delayed by so many contretemps — the appearance of the journal. One afternoon at the beginning of the month, while we were gathered in Acevedo's old house, we received the first sheet of close printing, headed by the heavy, black title *Enough* and by the fine lateen sail as an emblem. Smelling of greasy ink, those four pages of paper charged with assertions, protests, accusations, and exclamations seemed even more virulent. Lorrié said that it was like Benito

Mussolini's *Avanti*. The rest of us made no comment, as we had none of us seen a copy of *Avanti*. In his brown, workman's cap, standing near the press, the printer enthusiastically showed us the first copy, which could not be run off, as the advertisements had yet to be set up. The odor of wet ink was like the fragrance of the first bread in a bakery. We all felt a thrill to be the proprietors of that living organ — all, that is, except Blagoda, who characteristically showed no elation at the results of his own efforts. The journal was trim and neat in appearance. We soon had a pile on Acevedo's table, all printed. That night we celebrated with Moselle wine at Lunamoon and distributed copies to the wondering customers there, to the melancholy drinkers, the homesick sailors, the dejected young ladies, and the proprietor. A terrific hubbub started and we paid for a large number of drinks. Acevedo presided over it all genially but quietly, smiling indulgently, his aristocratic, intellectual head a little careworn, as if he had walked long with life.

"Let's not sing victory yet," he kept saying cautiously, leaning against one of the columns. "Yes," we shouted, "we must sing victory!" The Lunamoon clients willingly echoed our assertion. Like the fateful classical choruses, they were willing to repeat anything. A spectacled man, dressed in black, who looked like a retired professor, scolded them because they would not let him read the new publication in peace. He seemed to have difficulty in associating the journal — written with restrained good taste — with this hilarious scene. It was a memorable night.

At two o'clock in the morning Anselmi, Jiménez, and I took copies home with us. We waked Dr. Dervil and, before he had time to rub his eyes, declaimed the first paragraph of the opening editorial. Anselmi read it in a stentorian voice, emphasizing it in the wrong places, as if he were reading it to the very people against whom it was directed and telling them in rude counterpoint: "Take the consequences!" The doctor wanted to hold the journal in his own hands and examine it carefully and seriously.

"I wish you good luck with it," he said, putting the copy on his night table.

I went out early the next morning with a few copies of *Enough*. I wanted to send them to friends in the provinces and to my father. It was a cold, damp morning. The sidewalks and streets were as wet as though they had recently been watered. Automobiles were feeling their way cautiously along the downtown streets, spattering the unwary with thin mud. Through the windows of the cafés people could be seen breakfasting on coffee and bread and butter. The windows of the high office buildings sparkled; perched on improbable-looking ladders, window-cleaners, busy at their painstaking task since dawn, were still washing them. Omnibuses were rattling up and down the Paseo. Two young ladies were soliciting funds for charity, discreetly jingling the coins in their little earthen bowls at passing pedestrians.

I walked across Lavalle Street to Corrientes and entered the old Post Office. The ancient, dusty interior was swarming with white-dustered employees with typical Argentine faces. I posted the journals for the provinces, went out again, and started to walk down-town by way of Bartolomé Mitre Street. The daily crowds that throng the cafés in the banking quarter had not yet arrived. Between the stone walls of the buildings there was an almost wintry dreariness. The autumn threatened to be a severe one.

I wanted to leave some copies of the review at an address in the Avenida de Mayo. On the way I would be able to inquire at a bookstore in Maipú Street whether some books that I had ordered had arrived. When I reached the Bank of Boston, I stopped before crossing the wide, busy canyon of the Diagonal to wait for traffic to thin out. On both sides rose the massive buildings of the great corporations. It made me dizzy, in the early morning, to crane my neck to look up at the top stories of the tallest buildings.

Then something remarkable happened. As I stepped down

from the sidewalk, I felt a violent rush of air in my face and was brutally knocked over backward. The copies of the journal flew out of my hands and I fell almost on the curb. Someone hastened to my assistance. The driver whose car had struck me jammed on his brakes and hurried out. He ran to take my arm to pull me to my feet. I was getting up by myself when I saw another face before me.

It was you.

I stood rooted to the spot, gazing at you.

You were much more alarmed than the case required. You wanted to help, but as you could do nothing, you expressed your alarm in one phrase. You looked at me and murmured: "God bless you, God bless you," as though gratefully addressing an acquaintance whom you had recognized.

"Thank you," I said impersonally. "Thank you." And with my right hand I brushed my sleeve. I smiled and said that I was not hurt. Then you smiled too — but quite seriously — again said: "God bless you," and walked on.

It was a timid phrase, undoubtedly a familiar one to you. I picked up my scattered papers, replied evasively to questions from curious people who had gathered solicitously, nodded good-by to the chauffeur, whose first confusion was turning to hostility, and continued on my way. My mind was filled with the picture of that beautiful, troubled, and hopeful face; those great eyes and slightly parted lips. . . .

I reached the bookstore completely absorbed, forgetting what had brought me there, and walked slowly past the crowded shelves and tables laden with books.

"God bless you" . . . "God bless you." . . .

The three following days were days of expectation and surprise for the members of our group. People talked to us and overwhelmed us with questions. A large number of letters poured into the editorial office. Most of them came from young people or from mature men who no longer hoped for any reaction in our political scene and who now, delighted with our vigorous words, felt their faith revive. Blagoda exhibited a telegram from someone considered by him to be an exceptional authority, a distinguished mathematics scholar and professor from the interior of Argentina, who had been a friend — of sorts — of Lugones and favorite of Einstein.

As we were leaving a club one night, Acevedo and I had an argument with two young politicians, a difference of opinion that resolved itself smoothly. "What you are is aspirant politicians, and you are attacking the very positions that you hope some day to capture," they said. We told them that actual politics, appointments, and parties were completely indifferent to us. We were blunt and they felt our contempt. Aside from this trivial incident, we were surrounded by a particularly pleasant atmosphere. The echo raised by the appearance of the journal braced us and made us eager to multiply our efforts.

Spontaneously and naturally the members of that submerged group that normally lives out its life as a lost contingent for want of a common voice came to join us. They were for the most part scattered people of intelligence, who ordinarily live their lives apart, disliked, or held in suspicion by the common mass.

The second number of *Enough* was ready and went out triumphantly to conquer the streets. In a short essay Acevedo set out his thoughts on the subject of mystic nationalists and declared that it was indispensable to harmonize a people's emotional expressions with its historical characteristics, pointing out, for example, that the mystical idea of aggressive imperialism has no place in a traditionally commercial country or among a people of dreamy, lyrical tendencies. It is not impossible to create such an ideal; a political leader of genius can do it, but to what end, and how long will it last? I also contributed an article written to give precise definition to some of the constant, valuable, moral characteristics of our people. We left the destructive criticism to the others better fitted for polemical writing, particularly to Blagoda and Anselmi.

"We are like the wild, hungry dogs that visit the settlements at night," said Anselmi.

We were encouraged by our initial step to put a little brass plate with the name of the review and the auspicious lateen sail on the wall outside the door of Acevedo's house. The metal plaque seemed new and proud, set in the old wall. After the appearance of the second number three new people joined us who asserted that they were inspired by ideas similar to our own. From the beginning this did not seem self-evident.

These three young men belonged to the scattered intelligentsia. Two of them were very similar physically. They had hothouse temperaments. These we soon distinguished — or rather failed to distinguish from each other — by the designation of "the youths." The third, Victor Lavestein, had a stronger, more serious face and much that was affirmative and even challenging in his general appearance.

"The youths" came from old families of long, oligarchical tradition. They affected a princely simplicity in their attire and dressed their minds in ideas currently in fashion. Having read Maurras, they incorporated only the prosiest and most superficial part of his ideology. Doubtless had they ever approached the reactionary old writer in person, the reek of his tobacco, his sharp tongue and rude proletarian aspect would have strongly repelled them. They secretly envied intellectuals while pretending to scorn them. From the beginning they regarded Anselmi, Jiménez, and me with aversion.

One afternoon Anselmi and I were returning from a public library. We had been leading an almost monastic life for some time. "A disgraceful life of impossible old bachelors," said Anselmi. It was a time, indeed, of chastity and purely intellectual pleasures for us. However difficult for persons of strong passions or for intermittent voluptuaries to understand, periods of chastity are quite characteristic of normal, well-balanced temperaments. We got along very well without even a thought for our past prolific successes. From time to time Anselmi had tender looks for young ladies that he passed whom he deemed worthy of a fleeting desire. "Some of them," he remarked at other times, "not even with a pickle thrown in. . . ."

We entered the editorial room. It had changed since the days before the publication of the journal. A black dish with white daisies in it now stood on the ancient table. Two wood-block prints by Masereel hung on either side of the table. In one corner a sleek grayish cat slept the bourgeois sleep of a retired hunter.

At that moment Blagoda was sitting at the director's table, his revolving chair tilted back and his head, with its prominent, olive-skinned forehead, resting against the wall. Tauste was reading proof on his left. "The youths" were seated opposite, serious and aloof. With his accustomed mocking irony Blagoda insisted on quizzing all the aspirant staff writers in the same way. It was like a challenge to give the proper password.

"Now, you two in particular, what exactly do you want to say 'enough' to?" he asked them.

His attitude was that of an attorney before the bar, and his face was as cunning as a sharp-eyed fox's. On either side of his head hung the two Masereel prints — a figure of Death running with disheveled hair down a deserted street, and a splendid, foreshortened landscape featuring three pine trees of diminishing sizes. They suggested two gloomy horns accidentally conferred upon him by his position, like the barbaric adornments on the forehead of an ancient Gallic warrior.

"Hello, Vercingetorix," was Anselmi's greeting.

Blagoda raised his eyes without changing the half-sarcastic, half-courteous smile with which he was putting his question.

"Let's see what sort of things you would want to say 'enough' to."

One of "the youths" shifted in his chair with a little smile of intelligence, intended to indicate how obvious and unnecessary this question appeared to him, a smile such as he must have put on as an infant to let his nurse know how stupid and obvious her rules of deportment seemed to him.

"Good God! What a question!" He made a characteristic exquisite movement of his body. "To so many things! Encina and I" (Encina was the other youth) "favor a reaction. We are traditionalists and absolute monarchists. Why have we fallen into this ridiculous liberal and protectionist democracy, severing our state from the trunk of the Spanish Empire? What folly! Yes, we are traditionalists and monarchists! Absolute monarchists. 'America' is a vulgar term. So is 'democracy.' Coarse, plebeian expressions. Political synonyms for the sprawling, commercial bazaar, where everything is beaten down to the level of the common auction. 'God,' 'Monarchy,' and 'the Sword,' on the other hand, are noble, hierarchical terms. What we want is a state restored to its original hierarchical condition. We want this in life and in politics and in art. We favor a state with an inquisition and the stake."

"Yes," added Encina enthusiastically, as though it were a matter for immediate action, "that's what we want."

Anselmi was about to speak, but Blagoda waved to him to be still. Anselmi spoke, however:

"Are these gentlemen foreigners?"

The youth who had spoken first, whose name was Plon Vivar, continued to address Blagoda more and more heatedly, ignoring Anselmi, Tauste, and me. On his pale, beardless face the hard, bony angles seemed to be trying to escape from their skin. He threw his chest out. His flaccid hands extended from silk cuffs that looked like ruffles.

"We are really a cultured people, but guilty of letting ourselves be vulgarized from within, like a tree rotten at heart while its foliage is still turned brightly to the sun. So day by day we are strangling our vocation for greatness. Our origin is Catholicism and the union of Ferdinand with Isabel of Castile. Our present deformity is the fault of the foreigners that we are nourishing. We are spawning children to corrupt us, who have set us on a road that is more and more problematical and confused, masked behind the riches of Crœsus. Can one take a more plebeian journey?"

He then enthusiastically set forth his conclusions. Encina gave his approval as if it were all obvious. Blagoda asked them for precise points of view, but Plon Vivar answered only in very general terms.

"In short," said Blagoda, summing up, "our past as an independent country is a matter of indifference to you. You want something else — to begin again at the beginning."

"They want to suppress the May Revolution," said Anselmi bluntly.

"It was an unpopular revolution," said Encina.

"Which according to your views should constitute its greatest claim to glory," insisted Anselmi, "its proof of quality."

"Of course!" said Tauste.

"The truth is that aristocrats are willing to have plebiscites provided they can manipulate them," said Anselmi.

Plon Vivar gave his companion a look of discreet patience.

Blagoda wanted to end the meeting. He tilted his chair forward, and when he got to his feet, the dark Masereel prints seemed to come down to rest on his shoulders. "The youths" exchanged a few words in low tones between themselves, consulted their watches, and announced that they would have to leave. "Well," said Blagoda, "we'll talk about this some more and discuss it with Acevedo." Encina and Plon Vivar took leave coldly and solemnly. The gray cat stretched itself in its corner.

Anselmi took a few paces about the room. He could not conceal his indignation.

"They have nothing in common with us! Nothing! Nothing at all!" He stepped up, face to face with Blagoda as if he were about to strike him. "How can you let them come around here with their ridiculous aristocratic drivel?"

"Your liberalism, my dear friend, falls short of being liberal," said Blagoda in a voice that was scarcely audible.

"I am no liberal!" cried Anselmi. "I am no sleek, well-fed dog of a liberal. I am a man of goodwill."

"Then?"

"Goodwill begins where bad ends. Those chaps are defeatists and traitors!"

I protested. Anselmi insisted. Blagoda and Tauste tried to reconcile the two points of view. In complete disagreement, we walked across to Lunamoon to eat. Blagoda and Anselmi were arguing heatedly. Anselmi was intransigent. He wanted nothing to do with "reactionary individuals." He shouted that he needed to know nothing about dukes and gentlemen, and that every great, broadly based movement was essentially popular; that no arrogant nobleman had ever turned prophet; and that every genuinely national inspiration springs from a humble source, not from the exquisite mouths of the privileged few. Blagoda objected; he mentioned Byron, Pushkin, and d'Annunzio and maintained that the original inspiration for a great popular movement can come from any class whatever.

The dispute seemed to me to be getting childish, and I said so. The important thing, I said, was not the possible errors of opinion or the solutions proposed, but the amount of sincerity and intelligence shown by everyone who approached us and asked to be allowed to collaborate in our work. How could our function be any but to unite, and to co-ordinate possible differences into one positive force? How could we begin by disjoining and opening gulfs?

It was a mistake to say that. Anselmi abandoned his beefsteak and gave free vent to his wrath.

"What you want to introduce," he bawled, "is the germ of

confusion, the principle of dissolution! You will all of you bear your share of the blame!"

The discussion dragged on monotonously for hours. Finally I tired and lapsed into silence, watching the waiters at their work, the various attitudes of the people in the rear of the restaurant, and the pains that the proprietor took to attend to the various things that claimed his attention, oscillating between irascibility and smiles, depending on whether he was addressing his employees or his customers. Blagoda gibed at Anselmi and called him an idle rebel. "As a matter of fact," said Anselmi at length, "the whole subject bores me. Go to the devil, all of you," and he blew his nose loudly as though that settled the matter. "To the devil with you all." He called to a newsboy passing in the street, bought a late paper, and began to read it. Blagoda, Tauste, and I were talking about the first number of *Enough*; we must be giving thought to modifying some details. About midnight, I stood up and said: "I'm going." I said good-night and Anselmi followed me. Tauste also came with us, as he had to go uptown too. A fresh breeze was blowing up the Paseo Colón from the river. The night was pleasant for walking. We took the sidewalk that parallels the smaller plazas. Lighted street-cars were constantly passing one another in the central part of the Paseo, some going in the direction of Constitución and Barracas, others headed toward the Retiro.

Anselmi was silent and moody. I looked at him and laughed. Vanity! For something to complain about he began to inveigh against Blagoda and "the youths" and to repeat: "It's not right, it's not right!" I continued to laugh at him.

At intervals small, milky-yellow rectangles of light fell across the sidewalk from the doors of the bars, the only places open at that hour. Few stars were out. Once past Victoria Street, we crossed to the central sidewalk of the Paseo. We passed the cosmopolitan night-clubs, and the posters of the new show at the

Molino Negro caught our attention as we went past. Tauste had never been to one of those places and wanted to go in. Anselmi looked at me inquiringly and said: "Let's go in and have a cognac." We went in.

It was in a cellar and we went down a stairway covered with a brown velvet carpet. The air was revolting. The enormous damp room was packed with people to the limit. On the small stage a fat, almost nude singer was bellowing her songs. The audience at the tables — dry-goods clerks, butchers in Sunday best, young aristocrats, wealthy ladies incognito, professional drunkards, and adolescents with a taste for Greek love — were continually egging the singer on, offering her improbable inducements if she would remove her very brief dancing-skirt adorned with gold spangles. The woman kept on singing undaunted, her two eyes, like poached eggs, fixed on the flat ceiling as if she were repeating to some invisible force suspended from it: "Support me and I will not be dismayed." Ironically the posters called the singer the "Kansas Butterfly." Tauste was a little terrified, and we, who were familiar with such performances, kept observing him as though he were the curiosity. The spectators at the tables shouted themselves hoarse. Harsh, drunken voices rent the atmosphere, which was heavy with smoke and cheap cosmetics. As the "Kansas Butterfly" could not make up her mind to dispense with her already scanty costume, the public became furious and shouted: "Take her off, take her off!" She lowered her eyes two or three times, looking about desperately, then again raised them, never ceasing to screech: "Neither I nor thou will dare again, neither I nor thou." Neither the public nor she was willing to yield. The shouting became so deafening that not a word of her singing could be heard, only the shouts of the anonymous instigators of the disturbance. At length a stout man came from off-stage, took the "Kansas Butterfly" by the arm, and dragged her away still singing and gazing up at the ceiling. The public began noisily to demand something else. A magician appeared, but he was hissed off the stage. An intermission of insults followed, during which the stage remained empty. The audience continued to hoot. Many spectators were standing, others thumping the wooden tables with the bottoms of their bottles.

Finally a girl appeared with a sensual expression on her face, winking guiltily. She winked some more, showed her teeth, made some lewd remarks about her own body as she moved it slowly and lasciviously, and laughed coarsely. The shouts suddenly subsided. An "Ah!" circulated around the tables. In place of the cries, only a slavering sound could be heard.

I felt that the young woman must be laughing scornfully at the public; that the audience was being led on by her like a pack of idiots, while her blood was probably sluggish, nauseated, and embittered.

The public gorged itself on this dancer and then on another of the same sort, called la Manzanares. There were shouts and delirious applause.

"There is your public for you, Tauste," said Anselmi. "You think and worry about such people."

Tauste looked about the place without a word.

After a while we got up and left. Tauste said good-night when we reached the first, small plaza. His mind still seemed to be trying to straighten out the confusion of his thoughts.

I kept watching Anselmi's massive shadow on the sidewalk, much bulkier than my own. He began to comment on Tauste's astonishment, the ignominious spectacle in the hall, and the surreptitious presence of people of prominence. He was as simple as a child and quite as clean at heart. He was carried away by himself, and his anger increased by bounds. "I would like to punch some people," he said. When his imagination could not adequately express itself, he always did the same thing, he fell back on his reserve of strength. I wondered again at the incredible presence of certain people at the Molino Negro.

95

But I was no longer thinking about that, nor about what Anselmi was saying to me. I was thinking about the tall, beautiful woman standing before me in the early morning street. I was thinking about her words that still echoed in my heart. Anselmi's assertive voice, the voices of the chilly night, of the wide, deserted Paseo, and those that came from every side — houses, theaters, people, and cafés — said only: "God bless you. God bless you."

17

I HAVE told you how my life was lived. I should not say either that it was interesting or that it was lacking in color. Its intensity lay in that part of my nature which is most difficult to express, unfolding gradually without sufficiently perceptible modification to be able to relate chronologically or even logically.

The most extraordinary part about a man's soul is its lack of logical sequence, its untrammeled changeability, and its instantaneous leap from dawn to midnight and from midnight to dawn. What enthusiasm, what discouragement, what swiftness of imagination! Sometimes I returned home with a plan for a strikingly beautiful book. I sat down and outlined it completely. I lived hours of happy gestation, my mind so overflowing with generosity that all the sympathy at my command seemed but a trifle to share with other people. I began the hard struggle of writing the book; then the dissolvent invasion slowly entered my room: the dissatisfaction, feeling of failure, and disgust with which every author is relentlessly faced when confronted by the creatures of his imagination. It seemed inglorious to me to be working there in my room at something which in reality had only a personal significance; that this was no time for literature, and that we were all conspiring to do nothing. I felt compelled, therefore, to continue my search in the vague depths of the city for the spiritual, intellectual, and heroic imagination. I roamed the streets and enjoyed talking to engineers and men just in from the country; to architects, foremen, and all that were happily and anonymously engaged in elaborating some material.

It was at this period that I became acquainted with Señora de Estalión.

She was a quick, mannish woman living in a venerable mansion in the eastern quarter of the city, the traditional architecture of which had not prevented her from decorating it with an alarming originality of contents. The house had no two pieces of furniture of the same style. Within it everything was carefully studied diversity. Señora de Estalión directed and advised various artistic and charitable institutions. Her husband, a cripple, with whom she had contracted a marriage of interest, had died early, leaving her the fortune which enabled her to bestow annual rewards upon virtue. She was a friend to artists, politicians, and foreign diplomats and kept the sacred fires of these connections alive by a table which was always set for prominent guests. Her dishes, too, harmonized with her principles of sumptuous and dangerous diversity. To get indigestion at her house was a title of distinction, like acquiring it at the palace of the Shah of Persia. The mistress of the house professed ideas of a liberal character — although not too liberal. She liked to talk, impromptu and at length on every subject, and was determined at all costs to banish banality from conversation at her house — whereby she frequently caused her guests moments of cruel embarrassment, as when she shot point-blank at a gentleman who was taking off his raincoat in the vestibule the question: "What do you think of birth-control in the Dutch colonies?" or "Why, in the matter of religion, do you favor the Catholic faith instead of the Protestant?"

But one spent pleasant hours in her house. Its active confusion was in a certain sense pleasant. To step out of an ordered, routine existence and enter her palace of logical discord was an experience not to be disdained. I seldom dined at her house — the dullest and most genteel people were generally at her dinner table — but used to drop in sometimes of an afternoon and stay on to listen. Someone would sit down at the piano and play things by Scriabin or Ravel. At times an ambassador would arrive, and conversation would turn about the latest and most solemn stupidities — documentary data worth listening to from time to time. Señora de Estalión listened to all the conversation as though she felt that the destiny of contemporary society were being decided in her house. She had a special predilection for prophets.

At a reception at her house one afternoon she introduced me to an ill-assorted young couple named Guerrero: he was tall, solemn, pompously dressed and given to short bows and sententious assertions; she was short, brisk, talkative, and strikingly dressed. Whenever he made a solemn statement, she would burst out in shrill, interminable comment. He would look down at her with an air of cold patience, if not of reproof. Jazmín Guerrero had an aquiline, somewhat aggressive face and wore horn-rimmed spectacles. His speech was deliberate and circumspect. He looked down upon the world from above, judging and reproving it.

Señora de Estalión commended us to each other. Standing between us she joined our hands and raising her eyes exclaimed: "I know you will get along famously together! Two intelligent, conscientious people!"

I was embarrassed and smiled as best I could. Dr. Guerrero took my hand coldly without betraying the slightest concern about the future of our acquaintance.

"Are you a journalist?" he asked glacially.

His lady launched into exclamations of transparent enchantment and fondness for journalists, saying with a hysterical little cry: "Like Beaverbrook!"

"No," I said, "I write books. I am only accidentally doing some journalism these days."

The diminutive Señora de Guerrero was somewhat crest-fallen.

"Journalism in our day," asserted Jazmín Guerrero, "is a sink of iniquity."

He said it with a thoughtful air and every appearance of sincerity. "I am an attorney," he went on, "another profession not distinguished for its decency in these times."

He seemed to have an Olympian scorn for literature. His wife asked me what sort of books I wrote, which was very difficult for me to explain. I attempted a rapid definition, which only confused the matter hopelessly.

"Oh," she said, "psychological."

It seemed idle to attempt to disabuse her of the idea.

Jazmín Guerrero examined me from the height of his own importance. He asserted quickly, as though wishing to leave no room for doubt: "My conception of life is eminently aristocratic and spiritual." He paused to underline his statement. "I am convinced," he declared with the solid moderation of a sound thinker, "that the cause of all the intellectual and scientific deformation of our times lies in the present crisis of religion. When I am told that we are exploring unknown lands in the individual and social worlds, I see only the moral tumor of our deprivation of God, grown to gigantic proportions. The modern world is a congeries of tumors. Psychoanalysis, collective cynicism, duplicity, communism, democracy, and the motion pictures are only different names for the same collective delusion. Man, hard pressed by the evils of an overpopulated, overwrought world, needs more than ever to avail himself of the great metaphysical remedies, but as religious metaphysics requires too great an effort, recourse has been had to gigantic substitutes."

I asked him how he reconciled the existence of a strong religion with a religious crisis. He took off his spectacles and wiped them conscientiously to give himself time to answer.

"The means employed by Providence are inscrutable," he said, replacing his heavy black tortoise-shell glasses on the red mark made on his nose by the bow. The French Revolution, the most inhuman and baleful movement in the world, was the first to assert the infallibility of the most fallible substance that there is — the word of man, reason — fallible and arbitrary by definition. When the river leaves its bed and its original energy slackens, the flood may spread to tremendous proportions. The spiritual energy of Western man has been disorganized at its source. The great crusade of our time must be the restoration of man to his traditional orientation.

"All Utopias are specious," he went on, "but they are beautiful and attractive. Faith, on the other hand, is rough and humble, hence our disbelief, which lies at the root of our present difficulties.

"Why do some communities on this planet so stubbornly refuse to heed the most vigorous principle of energy in all history, Catholicism? . . . It is no longer even a matter of faith, but of logic and common sense. I believe that the chief defect of our century can be accurately diagnosed as a total lack of historical sense. This defect has been increasing sharply for over three centuries. I might almost say since the sixteenth century in Spain, when the marked historical decline of the Spanish peoples was accentuated by the bankruptcy of the ideal of reestablishing the Christian unity of Europe. And if we were to go back to the initial cause of the ruin, the Reformation, we would see how far the cleavage, then suddenly opened in that principle of unity, sweeps down the mountainsides of history in the most catastrophic of avalanches. . . ."

Conversation drifted to Acevedo's group, to my own work on the new journal, and to the benefits that might be expected from the undertaking. Guerrero expressed a desire to meet the other members of *Enough's* staff.

Señora de Estalión called to me and led me away to meet

some people. Port and biscuits were brought. From a distance I could see the Guerreros doing them full honor. Señora Guerrero was talking animatedly. Her husband was giving himself a complete rest after his pontification. The buzz of conversation rose and fell, interspersed with noisy bursts of laughter. A clock, of old Delft ware, pointed to eight o'clock. I decided to leave. The Guerreros stood up at the same time and our hostess walked with us to the door. The street was black and misty as we said good-by.

18

THE LAST peaceful days of autumn had come, and at night we liked to go to the end of the wharves in the old port.

One night, at the end of June, a large group of us had gone there for a chat. The two Gómezes were there and Acevedo and some others whom I forget. We installed ourselves on two benches. A chilly wind was blowing off the river.

As we were sitting there, I heard someone mention your name. I was listening to some joke of Anselmi's at the moment, and immediately turned my ear toward where Cosme Gómez sat at the end of the bench. He was telling the story of your marriage. I listened tensely. But he was praising you. I relaxed and hung on his every word.

Yours was one of those fine colonial families of noble lineage, of which there are few left today — a sad loss for our country not only in the sources of its spiritual strength, but, what is even worse, in its tradition and essence. Those old family trees are its final defense against a mongrel intermixture of races. Your father was a typical Argentine aristocrat of an earlier generation, a proud, virile man with a white beard and clear eyes. He had been a university professor, but had early abandoned his career to administer and increase the family estate. He spoke fluent French and German, and although his reading was of a restricted sort — arid treatises on economics and historical chronicles in the heavy old-fashioned manner — he had a breadth of culture that books alone cannot impart. He was the son and grandson of such colonial gentlemen as we see in Pellegrini's and Rawson's portraits, in open standing collars, wide silk ties, and luxurious shirts with flowing edges.

From early girlhood you had lived on your father's property in the heart of the Córdoba Mountains, and there learned to ride horseback and to talk to the men — little gentlemen of your own age wearing trousers cut in London — without fearing them or feeling the slightest trace of inferiority. With some of these friends you read your first books in English, dreamed of the dashing Steerforth and lived in the overworldly atmosphere of Thackeray's novels; there you had struck your governess and felt too ashamed to show yourself proud in front of her, but too proud to acknowledge your fault. Miss Glowston, however, had been indulgent and pardoned you one afternoon in the park, when she read to you one of the most resounding of poems, "There was a sound of revelry by night," to which you listened in transport, more for the legendary aura that Miss Glowston had cast about Lord Byron than for its intrinsic excellence.

You did not belong to those upstart families that suddenly burst into the aristocracy. You were born accustomed to things of quality, sure of your own inclinations, tastes, preferences, and aversions. At fifteen you could distinguish at a glance and explain the difference between a Gros and a Delacroix, or the gulf that separated a coarse German artist from an Ingres. When confronted with manners and attitudes of other people that displeased you, you were content to pass them by without acknowledging them, indifferent to bad taste, insolence, brash speech, and vulgarity, as if an opinion regarding them would have been superfluous and degrading. Even as a child you took endless, solitary walks, stopping to gaze long and reflectively at plants, unusual flowers, and distinguishing landmarks. It was as if you were enjoying a friendly, silent conversation with these inhabitants of your own soil. Whenever you found yourself in the presence of the genuinely beautiful, noble, and true you seemed, not to discover, but to re-encounter it, as if you had lived with it for a long time in some former life.

Always your strength lay in your ability to recognize the genuine, and your immediate rejection of everything that contained even a trace of adulteration. Thus you grew like the magnificent tuberoses, orchids, and Alpine flowers, outstanding in your own right, assured and proud, yet without vanity. The great is great wherever it is, in empire or in simplicity, and if life led you along no easy path, it left you intact and mistress of your magnificent person.

We had all seen a striking portrait of you in jodhpurs and riding-coat, a costume that revealed your beautifully slender figure. We had all seen that portrait, and all hoped that fate had something better in store for you than what Cosme Gómez now told us had befallen you. But what makes for the ultimate greatness of certain characters is their share of defeat, not their portion of triumph; even in the animal kingdom the world is harsh only to the weakest. That young woman therefore, whose entrance into a drawing-room, they said, changed the entire atmosphere, and who was greeted with that expectation and silence reserved for none but the pre-eminent, passed by all the men of her own position without words for any of them, looking at them all with an elegant irony that sometimes provoked their ill will.

You could not permit other values than those you had always relied upon to filter into your life or to have weight with you. Therefore as a young girl you were made literally ill by the attentions of the men of your circle; by the machinery of ambitious interest, of a stock-exchange play for matrimony that seemed to beckon you into its meshes. You were repelled and nauseated by it, and the day that you made up your mind to marry, you did so out of pity and as an act of rebellion against that system of bargaining. You wanted to marry that poor man entangled in insoluble problems like a child abandoned in the night. For he had an open, sympathetic nature although no great intellectual capacity; and he was without that background of false virility and vapid, jocular *cameraderie* that made you loathe the men of your generation. You married the most defenseless and vulnerable man that you could find, out of opposition to so much pedantry and so many polished but desperately empty souls. You had no real love for him, however. You told him so good-humoredly and frankly when you agreed to accompany him through life. He had at least a proper respect for your tastes, and listened to you and to the thoughts that you expressed with almost childlike deference. You told him very plainly, however, that you would not allow him to think you superior to himself. You were aware of the falseness and harmful effect of such an attitude on two people called upon to live together in peace. But he, being young and simple, insisted upon looking up to you. The marriage took place with the splendor customary in the world to which you both belonged. For two years you lived in the country on one of your *estancias* that had been done over specially for you. Then you returned to the capital, as Cárdenas wanted to resume his practice of the law. You were twenty-one at the time, born in the same year as I.

Your premonition soon had an unhappy confirmation. Only the purest, rarest, and most intelligent characters can endure the superiority of another being, either in this man's world or in marriage. Cárdenas was not one of those. Exceedingly well disposed at first, before long he became resentful. He brooded over his own inferiority, and the solitary country life aggravated this unbearable grievance. He began to yearn for the city, for the company of other people, and for the press of society in which to forget the shame that gnawed at him.

In Buenos Aires you and your husband lived a very active social life as you had before your marriage. But if your influence over him had previously been strong, it was now broken. Cárdenas drank heavily and threw himself into a hectic life. This offended and disgusted you unutterably, although neither offense nor disgust ever showed in your serene face.

At one of the most important balls of the season there was a scandal, which was immediately hushed up by the kind offices of your friends. It happened in a luxurious mansion, the residence of a family of parvenus. The guests were dancing in the large, tasteless ballroom. "There was a sound of revelry by night." The exclamations, jokes, and jealousies of a large throng mingled with the brilliance of the lustrous waxed floors, in a fantastic display of electric lights, candles, and plants. The garden was purposely left almost in darkness except for small lanterns with discreet parchment shades. There, with a lady he had just met, a newcomer in Buenos Aires society, your husband carried his daring to the point of obscenity. The lady escaped indignant, confused, and flushed with anger. There was a whispering of husbands.

Cárdenas entered the drawing-room quite calmly. The story, passed surreptitiously around from person to person and reached you. You showed not the slightest indication of anger and continued talking with complete poise, smiling and greeting those who approached you, despite their obvious confusion. You walked slowly out that night, the same quiet person who had entered, your beautiful bare shoulders protected against the night air by a light shawl.

Some months afterward you bore your first child. He grew up weak and sickly, plagued by an extraordinarily keen sensitiveness.

That is what Cosme Gómez told us as we sat looking out over the river that night.

19

I WAS again deeply absorbed in thoughts of you, in a great underlying sympathy. Your remote presence was already directing and encouraging me during the pauses after my fatiguing labors, as I lay awake at night, and in the solitude of my room, with its balconies overlooking the hard, deserted street.

A period of concentrated work followed. I read, thought, and wrote shut up in my room in order to avoid the eternal afternoon gatherings, with their endless conversations and smart banter. I began to look so thin and exhausted that Señora Ana and Dr. Dervil became worried. The doctor kept recommending tonics to me so old that they were no longer to be found in the pharmacies. I also had to submit to a cross-examination as to whether or not I had taken his prescription. He complained, resentfully, at our lack of faith in his experience with things and life. The old doctor would cock his heavy head toward his left shoulder in a way that he had and exclaim: "What a generation! I am like an old elephant who has been slowly accommodating himself for two centuries to live on this earth, and you young people are living, as it were, at a way station waiting to catch a train that is about to depart. It seems to me that each new generation lives more rapidly and more transitorily. Life may soon be boiled down to a matter of only a few days. . . . A little intensity, and good-by."

It was then that a new inmate came to live in our boarding-house. He was a timid, smiling, courteous little old man with bent shoulders, and hands folded across his chest like a Methodist pastor, who seemed grateful just to be allowed to live free from persecution. In the street he wore a black top-hat and was constantly rubbing his hands as though expressing his gratitude for every word spoken to him, which gave him the sensation of being suddenly and unworthily lifted out of the confused general mass. This modest man suffered countless torments while we were at table. Dr. Dervil would call upon him occasionally to support his opinions and we did the same for the opposition. The timid newcomer never knew which side to take and generally showed himself ready to say that both sides were right.

He was a former professor of the humanities. We learned that many days after he came to live in our house. Ira Borescu, a native of Rumania, had been born near the mouth of the Danube. He had been a chemist in a laboratory at Galatz until compelled to emigrate to the United States, where he had dragged out a miserable existence, giving German lessons in the Jewish quarters. He spoke Greek and Latin correctly, English and German discreetly, French and Italian passably, and Spanish and Portuguese execrably. But his knowledge of the civilization of the Mediterranean and of the old Etruscan and Roman cultures was remarkable.

I considered Ira Borescu a gift from heaven and began to treat him like a king. I invited him to my room and gave him voluminous paper cornets of his favorite morsels, raisins and pots of clotted milk, as well as Greek cigarettes, and art books showing examples of the most ancient human skills, beginning with the red hand painted on the roof of the cave at Altamira. I listened to him with religious deference. It delighted me to hear him talk ingeniously and with solid learning on many recondite branches of human knowledge. I deeply regretted my financial inability to help him lavishly, by setting up a comfortable study for him where he could devote his entire time to enlarging his knowledge of the origins of society, a fascinating subject when revealed by his mind.

I spent many days walking about the city with the old man. He would stop to study recent stone porches and doorways of new rubble construction. Because of the broad base of his nose and the two deep furrows around his mouth, his carefully shaved face had something simian about it. But when he talked, he became positively handsome, although his voice always kept its monotonous quality of plainsong, deliberate and unvarying in its hoarse sonorousness.

He answered me with hopeful arguments when I talked to him about the obtuseness of our country to the things of the spirit.

"Of course," he said, "a country where expressions of art are not produced naturally must be a country where people are not living, because once they begin to live, that mechanism called sensitiveness begins to operate, and then occurs the discharge of the soul — art in its various forms. It is when a country begins to know how to tell what it has lived and what it is living that it begins to create. Think of Portugal in *Os Lusiadas*. Think of the position that Florence occupies in the *Divine Comedy*. As long as one does not know how one is living, it is as though one were not alive at all. It is childhood — and you Argentines, as actuating organisms, are still in the animal stage of childhood. So long as we are unaware of how we live, we are still living an animal life, and the animal type of life is certainly not one intended for our race. That he lives most who lives with his body, is an idea which it is important to give to porters — they need it badly enough for their own consolation! An attempt has been made to found a philosophy of elementary life based upon the spirit of some paintings found in tombs of the Etruscans, a people who in the matter of architecture had even learned to handle the *opus quadratum* skillfully. But these are mere inventions. If I have one dream for humanity, it is that it will emerge from the primitivism that clogs its genius. The only decisive reason is historical reason; every cycle of historical life has its own rules, so different from past and subsequent cycles that at practically every step life is forced to reinvent its instrumentation. Peoples do not generally invent opportunely the instruments which their hour of history requires; the great peoples are those that do invent them as needed. Two forms of art bear upon this adaptation: the prophetic and the elegiac. The prophetic art is the one that anticipates such an accommodation of peoples to their historical circumstances; the elegiac, that which laments their failure to do so. It is futile to attempt to imitate: imitation is always an indication of some lack of harmony between man and reality."

It very obviously pleased him to follow the oscillation of his thought-pattern as it swung from one concept to its opposite.

"The genius of peoples consists in having the originality and strength to discover at a given minute the instrument which they need in order to explore for themselves the mountain of contemporary circumstance. The chaos of our time lies in the fact that some wish to imitate the Etruscans and others the Chinese; some, one imperialism, others another, unaware that at a given moment the imperial greatness of a people may consist precisely in not wishing to be an empire. It is incredible what a dose of fatal fatuousness some peoples are capable of! It is also unbelievable how difficult it is to hit upon the instrument best suited to the hour. . . . And what is it, when all is said and done, that history invents, however sublime it may appear in the textbooks? Just stop and consider the present state of super-civilization on our beautiful, prosperous world: the planet is constantly becoming more and more overpopulated, and we do not know what will be our social condition tomorrow. How can we bring order out of this chaos upon which men are piling more and more Pelions every day? Sometimes I think that we shall return to anarchy, and to a predatory, individual existence. . . . Alas! What does humanity know about itself? History is nothing but the lesson of how humanity has unleashed its own anti-human passions. Nothing more. And if the spirit of history has been mistaken? What would have happened if, instead of encouraging the dispersion of peoples, humanity had aimed from the first centuries of its consciousness at organizing a single tremendous confederation? I cannot give you the answer, nor can anyone else. We find things so when we are born, and we die leaving them in the same situation. The span of human life is so brief to learn anything!"

He stood up in front of me, small and perplexed, his forehead furrowed in a thousand wrinkles and his eyebrows arched interrogatively. "If I dream of one possibility," he repeated, "it is this: the possibility that we shall break at last, socially, with our poor infatuated primitivism. If, some time, we could do something great, something really great. . . . But the theories that seem to be communal serve as yet merely to divide."

This brought him to touch upon the meaning of the primitive civilizations, which revealed his intimate knowledge of some of the least-known and curious of contemporaneous civilizations, such as the Arabic. With surprising skill he brought home the lesson that some primitive practices are superior to modern ones. And his voice issued from the most diminutive and insignificant body in the world.

I cannot say enough about how greatly my friendship with this modest professor of the humanities, whose personality was indifferent to so many other people, contributed to my own intellectual enrichment. It is discouraging at times to thoughtful persons to reflect how superfluous to the world at large are persons so important to their own mental development. There is one thing, however, for which neither philosophy nor our technical achievements nor our millions of years of progress have been of any avail — for men really to know one another. Even though one knows the most intimate details of a person's life, when one finds oneself suddenly face to face with him without the mitigating presence of a third person, one remains as totally ignorant of him and as alien to him as the rock to the sap of the fern that clings to it.

What incomparable adventures those which the innermost precincts of another person's soul can give us! It is enough for him to let down his bars for a few minutes and agree to accompany us, forgetting everything that he knows of himself and attentive only to discovering himself with us.

The little man from Galatz was less a dweller in modern Buenos Aires than in some corner of the fifteenth-century world. He looked at modern phenomena in millennial perspective, through his penetrating little eyes stored with ancient wealth. A man proclaims his own frontiers when he talks, even in the most trivial conversation. Talkative men therefore are apt to have the narrowest frontiers. Professor Borescu's frontiers were similar to those of some shrewd appraiser of his years born in an Italian town of the Renaissance. When I approached him, I touched those frontiers and extended my own world into the past. At the same time — and this was the most curious and valuable part of it — without anything anachronistic about it, and with a modernity that came from afar, a sense of reality whose roots were fed by a remote period. Only America seemed to him a great *terra incognita*, a land irreducible to his theory of life.

We read the old texts together. He seemed a devout anchorite. From time to time, however, his philosophic serenity got the better of strict logic and he would say on one occasion, quoting Samuel Butler: "For truth is precious and divine, too rich a pearl for carnal swine," and on another, citing Farquhar, the contrary: "Truth is only falsehood well disguised." At eight o'clock, as the day faded, I would take him to some of the little-frequented places under the monotonous mantle of the city. He generally looked with indifference at new stone. He had a way of raising his eyes to look at you as if he were suffering inwardly. At such times I tried to find new things to distract him. I showed him the thousand facets of our city — its teeming, diagonal streets. From the highest balconies I pointed out to him below us the immense narrow canyon, the seething abyss, the wave of humanity that crept in from the interior of the country. From the wharves, I showed him the river, the mighty Río de la Plata, for him to reflect upon its austere nobility and rich serenity, which resembled the very essence of our country. Professor Borescu contemplated the vast stretch of water uncomprehendingly. This new form of dignified and expectant beauty, converted into landscape, and from landscape into destiny, did not penetrate the secular system of his spirit.

20

I HAD not seen Acevedo during the past few days. The circulation of *Enough* had by this time become stationary at five thousand copies. The first numbers printed had been quickly sold out; then the demand had fallen to the faithful "unhappy few" — some three thousand devotees. If its readers did not increase as fast as they should have, the number of people who visited the editorial office was steadily growing. The number of anonymous insulting letters had also increased, a very favorable indication in this type of undertaking. Moreover, Acevedo found one night upon returning home three deep-blue orchids with thick white edges, accompanied by a card on which was written in the most nervous of feminine hands: "To the new intelligentsia." Blagoda commented sarcastically on it. That did not prevent him, however, from laying the card and the orchids on the editorial-room table for the edification of our new collaborators, as if such a tribute were one of those revealing, worldly signs that always accompany success.

I spoke to Acevedo on the telephone, and he mentioned that he had two orchestra seats for the French theater. He suggested that we dine together that night and go on to the Odéon. During the afternoon the mist became heavier. At nine o'clock we met at a restaurant near the theater where the more intelligent gentlemen and the less well-behaved ladies were in the habit of allowing themselves friendly relaxation. Both were chatting with that superior scorn characteristic of people who know the world too well and feel that they have it in their pockets. The tables were arranged in groups separated by black balustrades, and the room blazed with extravagant illumination entirely out of proportion to the modest size of the establishment. We ate quickly and went to the theater. The repertoire oscillated without embarrassment between the ultra-modern and the classical. The leading actress was a young Frenchwoman with reddish hair, very pale skin, and the stiff angularity of those Englishwomen of uncertain age who have popularized international tourist travel. Her voice had a slight twang, annoying at first, which became quite agreeable, however, on better acquaintance. She was the best of the cast, the rest of the comediennes being merely her obscure satellites. A girl who looked like a normal-school student in a blue dress with white piqué cuffs was sitting next to me. "*Tiens, c'est assez drole,*" she said to her escort, referring to the leading actress; "*elle semble aimer cette autre femme.*" Although it was true that during the pauses she did not take her eyes off the other actress — fleeting Panope — the judgment turned out to be over-hasty. But popular justice does not always have the best of foundations.

The performance was so good that our attention had time to relax only during the intermissions. Seeing Hippolyte honorably extend his rejecting arm reminded me of Guérin and I could almost see the noble dynastic greyhound beside the young actor. Again Phèdre's reply touched our blood:

Quand vous me haïriez, je ne m'en plaindrois pas.
Seigneur, vous m'avez vu attachée à vous nuire;
Dans le fond de mon cœur vous ne pouviez pas lire.
A votre inimitié j'ai pris soin de m'offrir.
Aux bords que j'habitois je n'ai pu vous souffrir.
En public, en secret, contre vous declarée,
J'ai voulu par les mers en être séparée;
J'ai même défendu, par une expresse loi,

113

Qu'on osât prononcer votre nom devant moi.
Si pourtant à l'offense on mesure la peine,
Si la haine peut seule attirer votre haine,
Jamais femme ne fut plus digne de pitié,
Et moins digne, Seigneur, de votre inimitié.

We watched the royal agony of the mortal stepmother, the return of Theseus, and the modesty of delicate, noble Aricia. The wonderful rhythm took us completely out of ourselves, and for a few moments we became the docile instruments of the tragedy. With the reconciliation of Theseus to his son's memory — *allons de ce cher fils embrasser ce qui reste* — we left the theater after midnight.

All the theaters were disgorging their public at this hour. Men and women in evening dress were streaming into the busy street. The early editions of the morning newspapers were displaying the decoy of their black headlines: THE "BUENOS AIRES" DEPARTED YESTERDAY AT EIGHT FROM PARAMARIBO. — POINCARÉ ANALYZES THE PRESENT SITUATION IN MOROCCO — PILSUDSKI IS MASTER OF THE SITUATION IN POLAND. We walked toward Corrientes Street.

"It is strange," said Acevedo, "how a superficial glance at this enchanting world would leave a passing visitor from another planet the grievous impression of a formidable and hateful circus in which every man vies with his fellows in playing the chief role in a gigantic anarchy; and yet the only absolute objective for which men on this earth fight unceasingly is peace. How great that aspiration must be when even war is waged in its name! And the only genuine, moving trait that redeems humanity from its savage ferocity is that poor, modest will to peace hiding behind its most threatening gestures and bloody struggles. From her terrible conflicts blood-thirsty Phèdre, *la fille de Minos et de Pasiphaé*, sought nothing but a little peace — a level plain at last dimly seen through burning brambles. The greatest passions are those that accumulate the most tyrannical thirst for

114

final fulfillment. That poor old Spanish philosopher Unamuno, who wanted glory and not peace, refused to recognize what lay behind his incessant vigil. He thought he was born for anguish, but his anguish was only a harsh and grievous awareness of his need for peace. For this reason I sometimes think of despots with irresistible benevolence. For the same reason ideologists and falsifiers will always be repugnant to me, until I see them convinced of their aberration. The men that I find most admirable and illustrious are those who fight without self-deception and bear arms not because they worship a Dionysian heroism, but because they know that to fight is a part of their human condition and that they must do so without hope of reward. From every point of view, professional bravos give me a disgust that nearly turns my stomach. . . ."

The whitish lamps were veiled by the mist, and the sidewalks glistened with moisture. Representatives of every nation were strolling along the broad street under the illuminated signs, past cafés, restaurants, and amusement places.

"Perhaps the best part of our destiny," I said to Acevedo, "is the strength and vitality of a movement under way, of a march with eyes front, fixed on the space that remains to be traversed. Look at this street. Everything static is disorder; disorder itself on the other hand — people walking, the intense, ephemeral lights, the forms of materialized time — assumes a sort of order and rhythm. What is static is our architecture, built with a horrible lack of foresight, with neither intelligence, science, nor inspiration behind it. The Londoner, Parisian, or Amsterdamer is attuned to the ancestral rhythm of material structures that resemble him and that are the solid expression of his racial and national spirit. We, on the other hand, were born to contemplate the shapeless attempts of those who have preceded us. In our turn we must try to improvise and aim at a harmony in which our spirit will crystallize into its true form. The only thing that has meaning and dramatic quality, therefore, is the adventure of our march, all these people, and all that they are building out of nothing by the mere act of living."

"It is for this very reason that our solitary labors are melancholy instead of happy; that they are melancholy today, but will be happy tomorrow. As we lack patterns and essential prototypes upon which to model our labor, our work is both difficult and blind. It is as if we were to quarry stones for a cathedral not yet designed. As we are working in the wilderness the effort is that much greater and the will must be correspondingly stronger."

We walked a few steps in silence, then Acevedo went on reflectively:

"For days I have been asking myself whether our journal can survive; whether we shall not have to come to some compromise even within our own organization. In other words, whether we shall not have to have recourse to that essentially political thing, a pact, and allow our words to be adulterated by certain ambitious, lawless upstarts. Because what is perhaps of chief value in any one of us is what he has amassed in solitude, and perhaps it is precisely that which is useless for our purpose, because it cannot be transmitted, having validity for only a limited number of people. On the other hand, it may be that collectively only the voice of the demagogue is effective, for his language — and consequently his soul — is the language that the people understand, that exploits but at the same time serves them, it being undeniable that the exploiter is the slave of the people that he exploits."

"I don't think it is as bad as that," I said, "I am not as pessimistic as you are. I think that the only thing that can purify men is the cause to which they devote their energies. Man needs to invent realms of absolute well-being outside of himself. His obvious intent is to build externally, in some place unencumbered by poisonous plants, the kingdoms that he cannot found within himself. If we succeed in turning our absorbing interest into a strong, clean, worthy movement, I think that those who approach it may acquire a measure of its dignity. Some more, others less. But all will get something out of it."

"Yes, yes, or they will degrade it to their own measure."

Acevedo smiled and presently said: "We shall see."

We passed the typically French façade of the Circulo de Armas and stopped on the corner of Florida Street. The British Ambassador, who was leaving the club, passed us in his noisy old Austin. An absent-minded letter-carrier suddenly stepped in front of it, and the automobile veered sharply to avoid him. We crossed the street and continued toward the Paseo Alem. There the traffic was lighter. An occasional well-dressed person was returning from a visit to the lower depths, which were neither so deep nor so low, merely dirty marginal streets. Some men, however, lead such boring lives that it is enough for them to visit a tavern called the Maid of Boston to feel themselves actors in an exotic, mysterious, and gallant adventure.

"I don't know," said Acevedo, continuing the conversation; "I hate to admit it, but the more I deal with our countrymen, the more pessimistic I become regarding them. Remember Phèdre and Boileau's remark about her tragic passion. He said that her grief was virtuous. As a country we lack virtuous grief. We have never incubated our ideas in an atmosphere calculated to strengthen and temper them; we have always conceived them in too comfortable and easy-going terms, and in harmony with our natures have directed them toward obtaining still more comfort. Even the most advanced ideas, which in other countries are held by poor radicals, in our country are proclaimed by complacent people, who express by their radicalism only their desire for power. This is a country without heroes and without moral suffering. It is an enormous country sunk in a gigantic orgy of colossal self-complacency. Therefore we who want a better country suffer for it and are considered disruptive elements, unwelcome guests who arrive when the meal is half over."

He was walking with his hands half-thrust into his side pockets, the two free fingers of one hand holding a smoking cigarette. The light from some street lamps fell upon us where we had halted under the arcades. Far ahead of us were some deserted benches in a small square.

"For a country to achieve a great destiny it must have suffered intensely. Only tenors are trained while listening complacently to their own singing. . . ."

We separated and I walked home slowly in the cool June night. As I reached the house, I passed an irate-looking man whom I had seen going in and out many times. I went up to my room and resumed work on some notes that I had been writing. At dawn I woke up, startled; I had fallen asleep, my head resting on my arm. As I got into bed, I could hear the rumbling of the cart-wheels of the early delivery men.

2 1

As I was entering the house one rainy evening, I found Jiménez and Anselmi in the living-room. A fire was burning on the hearth. It was cold outside and the warmth of the room was grateful. Gaily dressed in a gray sports jacket, Anselmi was belaboring the keys of an ancient upright piano, trying to decipher Mozart's Concerto in A major, number 23. Jiménez, leaning forward on the high-armed sofa, seemed to be following intently the movement of Anselmi's hands. "Of all the methods of assassination," he said, significantly indicating the pianist with a gesture of his chin, "I know of none that is more typical." Anselmi swung around on his stool as I entered. "Childhood reminiscences," he said, and added apologetically: "but I can't read music any more."

Dr. Dervil in spectacles, an old smoking-jacket, and black cloth shoes, appeared in the doorway — like a man coming from calm to tumult. "He looks like the figure of avenging justice," said Jiménez, "about to put an end to all this frivolity."

"No," said the doctor, "I am merely a just, kindly man, installed in the exact center of all things and all classes. . . ."

"Like this — " indicated Anselmi, demonstrating by striking a few solemn chords.

"Yes," said the doctor, "like that."

"A sweet state of honorable mediocrity," commented Anselmi, "bliss."

The doctor stopped in the middle of the room. On his left a pair of stag antlers projected aggressively from the wall, left behind by an American misogynist together with a framed facsimile of the Gettysburg Address.

"Nietzsche forgot," he said, sinking into one of the old leather-covered armchairs, "that between the Olympian heights of the Dionysium and the sublime plane of the Apolloneum an intermediary region exists, where one is quite well off, without fear either of being summoned one fair morning to the altar, or of being dragged off to the bonfire. A region where one can dream moderately about the most splendid adventures with the assistance of a medium-sized cup of middling Burgundy wine."

We talked until dinner time, when we gathered around the great dining-table covered with a checkered tablecloth, to do honor to a rice dish whose weekly advent Señora Ana always announced with special flourishes. After the rice, appeared a chicken *en casserole* with mushrooms and a sauce, the fragrance of which we had caught the moment we sat down at the table. Professor Borescu and Dr. Dervil decided to maintain a deferential silence in the presence of such a respectable proof of Señora Ana's prodigality. They evidently feared that mere words might convey the impression that they took it all for granted and result in an increase in their monthly board bill.

Anselmi and I were glad to have Jiménez and Señora Boll with us again; they had eaten out frequently. Both were silent and circumspect. There was something sad about them. She was paler than ever. Jiménez scarcely looked at her during the meal and talked more than usual. The light from the lamp above the table was reflected in his glasses. We discussed the latest issue of the journal, and Professor Borescu asked two or three questions about the political situation.

After dinner Anselmi went out to see a film, while Jiménez accompanied me upstairs to my room. He wanted to look up a passage in *The Prince,* having no copy of it among his own books. I set about making a fire. The chimney drew beautifully. Jiménez sat down in an armchair. I do not say dropped into it, for no such abandonment ever disturbed his slow, somewhat affected movements.

He copied the passage that interested him while I arranged my papers on the table and contemplated with satisfaction a completed manuscript whose terse rhythm rather pleased me. Jiménez came over and turned its pages with genuine interest. He asked me to read it to him, but I was not in a mood for reading and told him that I would another time. We began to talk about books.

I was standing behind the table. The room was quiet and cozy. We talked about many things.

I walked over to the fireplace and put a stick of wood on the fire. Jiménez looked at me, smiling.

"How is Señora Boll?" I asked him.

For a few moments he did not reply. His two hands were joined reflectively at the height of his lips.

"That is an opportune question," he replied. "I cling like the ivy to the wall to the bit of life that Inés represents. I like her much better than I can rationalize my motives for doing so. The understanding between a man and a woman is the most baffling thing in the world. It depends upon harmonies too subtle and obscure to be intelligible. But by the same token, when an intense compatibility exists between two people, it is as strong, compact, and mysterious as a tubercle. . . ."

He crossed over to the fireplace and we both stood looking

into the fire. The kindling wood was igniting the logs, which surrendered, crackling.

"But I am not happy in this union," said Jiménez. "Or rather I am happy, but in a region obscured by heavy fog, as if I were already defeated. It is very curious that in the last analysis our union with women, who complement us in so many ways, has a harsh background of suffering and strife. I believe that if I were to live with Inés in some other way I should be much happier."

"You have probably not been together long enough. You have to look out for the rifts that absence opens in the mind. They can be fatal if you are not on your guard."

"We see each other every day, but that may not be enough. Perhaps it is necessary actually to live together."

"But you can't do that now."

"Why not?" he replied combatively. "Why not? What sense does the life I am living make?"

"We have a job ahead of us," I reminded him.

"Yes, but something so unreal, so completely idealistic and remote! What does it amount to actually? A new youth and a new conscience. The optimistic part of a circle that will finally close in disappointment and a definitive accommodation to the *status quo*."

I realized that circumstances had latterly called his whole being to a carnal compromise and that he was reacting from this plane to other less material responsibilities.

"There are passions that raise a man and make him something different and vital, and others that defeat him and make him a coward. Look out for the latter type!"

Jiménez burst out laughing. "But what sort of moralizing is this? What trite schoolboy arguments! Look. . . ."

He took me to the window and drew aside the curtain. The cold July night had left the sidewalks deserted. The lights from the corner store seemed paler than ever and the letters on the bar sign across the street were winking singly.

"That cold air and everything out there are controlled by no theoretical foresight. Their strength is their freedom to endure and resist at the proper time, governed only by the principle of being true to themselves. I don't hide from life. I gather all of its fruits and reject or assimilate them according to my nature. Whether they do me good or harm depends on the robustness of my constitution. Theoretical precautions are miserable hiding-places for cautious, prudish people. Why shouldn't we go out free and naked to meet events?"

"It seems all right to me," I said, "only that is the theory of the means — the theory that the means justify the end. And I don't think that is a philosophy consistent with Machiavellian ideas. . . ."

"I laugh at consistency," he replied. "I laugh at everything that does not serve me for living. I laugh at people who govern themselves by catechisms. Even Christ himself was not troubled by pity when it was necessary to grasp the whip."

"That is taking things too seriously."

"I take them that way. I sink into things up to my ankles and would rather come out covered with swamp mud and know at least how I stand with respect to swamps."

I smiled. "Help me put some more wood on."

He went to the basket, handed me a log, and wiped his hands on a cotton handkerchief. He did it carefully and with great seriousness. His self-control was as solid as his own assertions.

It was an agreeable planting season.

2 2

THAT July, Jazmín Guerrero joined our review.

Every nature bears within itself its own law and verdict. On this principle, no person is defined except by his visible creations. Thus it is not the professed philologist nor the bandit that is to be so considered, but the person who actually discharges those offices. In the limbos of the "intelligentsia" that surround artistic genius in every country, mere amateurs crop up whose chief virtue is their quick disdain; but as disdain also needs its incentive and as those who are most contemptuous generally do the least creative work, these terrible parlor angels finally die in the broth of their own inadequacy. There are probably nowhere in the world more numerous examples of this type of intelligence than in Buenos Aires, for here to dress well is accepted as more than enough distinction: all the rest can be dismissed without further examination. Jazmín Guerrero had made himself a reputation on this basis: his spiritual apparel rested upon a theoretical framework. For example, it seemed to him that to be a Thomist in philosophy and a reactionary in politics were attitudes that harmonized sufficiently to enable him to hold up his head two thousand feet above the level of the rest of humanity.

Standing upon these rigid theories, he looked at the world fearlessly. He was isolated by this dogmatic *cordon sanitaire*, and nobody could trample him underfoot or take him by surprise. He was like a bronze statue dressed in a plain blue business suit.

When I introduced him at the editorial office one peaceful July afternoon, he immediately came to an understanding with Blagoda, because Blagoda was a snob and he liked the young lawyer's aristocratic background and Olympian manner; also, being boastful and slovenly himself, he was charmed by Guerrero's heavy, well-fitting silk cravats, of deep sea-blue color, which looked as though they had just come from "Brighton's" shelves.

Blagoda offered him a cup of coffee with seeming carelessness. Guerrero refused it with scant courtesy.

"I am sober and strict in my habits," he said. "I like austere men and customs. I put nothing into my mouth except at meal times, and very little then."

Blagoda would have liked to offer him the champagne which — although not exactly from Reims — he sometimes drank in the bars. He felt embarrassed at having been able to offer the visitor only the cheap coffee that Acevedo drank, fearing that Guerrero would look down upon us on that account.

"It is a necessary stimulant when you are suddenly called upon to bring something into sharp focus," he said by way of excuse. He remembered how his father had said to him in the back room of their modest store: "Learn to make good coffee. That's the way men born servants can make themselves the masters of their masters." In his cheeks he felt a glow of resentment. Suddenly on the defensive, he reverted to irony, which was like the antidote secreted by the skin of certain toads: "Probably the way you live, you don't need this sort of artificial lash."

"I don't like any whips but those that I wield," replied Jazmín Guerrero quickly. "Mine is the caste that uses them, not feels them. I hope that all of you belong to my family. *Enough*, as I understand it, is a whip."

Acevedo leaned forward, making the arms of his chair creak against the table. He studied Guerrero before speaking.

"Yes," he said, "it is a whip; not in our hands, however, but in those of a principle. Tomorrow it may be turned against us if we betray it. I don't think that I was born with a whip in my hand, although I confess that I have often thought that I deserved one. But what attracts me most in the exercise of criticism is the opportunity that it affords to take oneself to task."

"Well, that is thoroughly apostolic!" said Guerrero with slight sarcasm. "Apostolic! That is very interesting and quite all right, but it has its own danger in the practice of politics and the manipulation of ideas: the capacity to awaken harmful doubts. Doubt is weakness. In the field of politics and ideas we have no right to be weak. By raising weakness to the rank of a virtue, one may enter the kingdom of heaven but fail to conquer power. Power belongs to those who are born strong, to the powerful caste; the strong man is the Brahmin of politics. The strong man is born with a whip in his hand and lays it down only on the day of judgment."

He was talking sardonically.

"That is the A B C of ambition. I don't think," said Acevedo, smiling and looking in turn at Blagoda, Anselmi, Lorrié, Jiménez, and me, "that we are a group of ambitious people. Ambition is a form of candor from which our lack of saintliness has so far spared us. . . . No. What differentiates us from politicians and political groups is precisely the fact that interest does not weigh in our scales. At least the interest of public position, known as *power*."

Guerrero shrugged his shoulders as if to say: "That is your nature."

"I have a political head," he continued. "I see the situation and its remedy as urgent; in order to apply the remedy we must seize power, and the sooner the better."

"We are no political party. You keep forgetting that," said Acevedo.

"No matter. You are not yet, but you can become one. Without such an eventual purpose I fail to see your objective. Do you or do you not want influence?"

We all entered the conversation in confusion at that moment. The point was to define what sort of influence we wanted. Political or moral? I told him vehemently that the will of the intellectual groups engaged in our type of journalism varies enormously from country to country. In countries where the political, moral, and social structure is strong, such journalism has no point unless it applies itself to some definite and immediate objective. In a formative country in transition like ours, however, there is need for the progressive awakening of every sleeping member of society, just as one might rouse a giant of delicate constitution and prickly temperament. Although it may seem strange, we need much more caution and precision in speaking to a young country than in addressing a country of long-established culture. For it is a flagrant historical error to ask countries during their formative period for something not in harmony with that stage of development. Our work, therefore, could only be a means to attract the attention of unreflecting people, who will later mobilize in intelligent groups on their own account.

Jazmín Guerrero listened impassively, tapping the arm of the sofa with his gold cigarette-case, the corners of which were skillfully and conspicuously adorned in black enamel with his family crest. He did not seem at all convinced. Natures like his have no time to waste. They hunger and thirst for pre-eminence and demand action. Therefore he came at once to the point of his visit. He wanted to write some articles. Acevedo leaned back patiently in his armchair and smiled courteously. But what would he write about? He immediately set forth his subject. The theory of the *coup d'état*. He wanted to comment on Curzio Malaparte, to go back to the days of the Florentine Republic and attempt an interpretation of Dante Alighieri.

He stood up, walked over to one of the bookcases, and rested his right arm on its carved upper surface in an attitude of imperial ease. He did not wear a monocle, but his whole bearing called for that glistening symbol of civil pride.

From the pinnacle of his rigid excellence he expounded phrase by phrase, for our benefit, his theory of autocracy. Like a concert singer's piano, his voice seemed to obey his two hands: one didactic and pontificating; the other indolent and supercilious. ". . . But I only half believe in *De Monarchia*. In my opinion the Church and the Empire cannot oppose each other as they are a conjoint power, they are two supreme hands that stem from the same ideal body. . . ."

It must have been nine o'clock in the evening when we left the office. Blagoda was talking at the moment. He wanted to surprise Guerrero with his grasp of the technique of the *coup d'état*. Two groups of us walked on ahead, Blagoda and Guerrero followed, halting on the avenue from time to time to disagree. A passer-by stopped for a moment to stare at them.

In a picture that I had cut out of one of the Sunday papers, you were sitting in a voile dress, splendid and remote, on the dark, waxed floor in one of the rooms of your house. Your bare head rose gloriously above a broad, stiff shawl collar. All around you were white gardenias, begonias, and Cape jasmines. Your great serious eyes were fixed inscrutably on the distance.

I showed the picture to Professor Borescu.

"Isn't she proud and beautiful?" I said.

"She is," he replied, and he launched forth on an erudite dissertation upon the various types of beauty since the time of Shem and Japheth: the occult, elegiac basis of the beauty of the women of the Bible; Eleonora di Toledo's delicate face in the portrait by Agnolo di Cosimo, *il Bronzino*; Saint Augustine and his feeling of unity as the form of beauty; Klemptgen's interpretation of human beauty as an element of pleasure; and the identity of the mental and physical traits of woman, a point on which he felt one could perfectly well erect a theory of woman's place in history.

I looked at your picture and smiled at his dissertation.

An immense multitude of people moved in the capital. Their ambition was a wave; their furious activity, a rushing river. Eager, hurrying crowds surged back and forth like billows of migration weaving through the vast network of automobiles and trolleycars.

Here was the Argentine citizen in external activity. When would his soul be stimulated a little and the precipitance of his bodily activity be slowed down?

I reflected that until this happened we should not know what we are. The captain's courage is futile if he does not know where his spirit is taking him. Where were this courage, speed, interest, and ambition leading us Argentines? Where were we going?

These men that we saw were Argentines only superficially. In business and politics and during their relaxation after the day's strife was over, what were they? What were these prosperous prodigals basically? Cruel, soft, ferocious, intelligent, venal, or illustrious, or did they oscillate between them all?

Yes. It was essential to bring out into the daylight the basic merits of a people who surrender without counting the cost. It was necessary to bring its dream stuff and the hidden marrow of its genius to the surface, to protect them from being stifled by treason, chance circumstance, and the accumulation of material things.

I was deeply troubled by this stifling of the spirit of our people. Occasionally, in some action or other, I could see it surge up, only to sink again beneath the surface.

Beneath this furious activity I was aware of an undercurrent of grief, of a silent, unhappy spring in which the river of a people prepares for its liberation and greatness.

Our man, Juan Argentino, I said to myself, is being exploited. What is important is for us to look resolutely everywhere for Juan Argentino; to distinguish him from his despoiler and give him the chance that his worthy misfortune deserves. Juan Argentino is the unknown, ignored man; on the other hand John Englishman, Giovanni Italiano, and Johann Deutscher — all those other Johns — are his masters. Juan Argentino is a child; we must therefore make a man of him.

Juan Argentino, I said to myself, languishes despondently in the city, waits and suffers in the country. He is to be found in every part of his native land. We must give meaning to his life and sufferings.

I sketched out a literary project: to reveal Juan Argentino in a series of pictures showing the various aspects of his life — Juan Argentino so profoundly and intimately our own, and so neglected. I spent many days thinking about his character. The book was to be called *The Forty Nights of Juan Argentino*. The forty vigils, the forty trials of his conscience, to be set in motion and prepared for his march through time. They were to be forty tales of as many human processes.

23

AT the beginning of August we had a disappointment. I had noticed that Acevedo was becoming thoughtful and somewhat reticent. I observed him in the editorial office and at Lunamoon, where we had forgathered for several successive days to discuss the affairs of the journal over coffee and cognac.

As we were leaving Lunamoon, Acevedo took me by the arm. "This is going to end," he said, "I am beginning to tire of it." I expressed my astonishment and tried to dissuade him. "We will talk about it tomorrow," he said. I walked home with Anselmi. The next afternoon Acevedo called me on the telephone.

"There will be only two more numbers," he said, referring to the journal. "My mind is made up. That is, unless the rest of you care to undertake continuing its publication on your own account. In any event I shall withdraw from it."

When he talked that way it was idle to insist.

"I'm going to tell the others next Tuesday at Lunamoon."

That Tuesday our full complement was there. In the large amber-colored room there was an odor of wine and fried fish. Jiménez was dressed in sports clothes; on the following morning he was to go away for a week to a little town up the river. "Honeymoon," smiled Anselmi pointedly. At ten o'clock Acevedo had not yet arrived. Some who had come before their habitual dinner hour had ordered "beefsteak on horseback," with fried potatoes. Jazmín Guerrero was warming his second glass of cognac in the hollow of his hand. Blagoda was talking loudly with Lorrié. As usual, Tauste was nodding approval of Blagoda's assertions. I gazed at Tauste and realized what a melancholy soul he was. Undoubtedly Blagoda had already told him of Acevedo's decision about the forthcoming disappearance of *Enough*. He was a simple lad and I had a great deal of affection for him.

A vender of lottery tickets approached our table, his tenths and fifths displayed in a cascade of blue paper hung from his neck.

"This man is offering us the best instrument of salvation," said Blagoda.

"More efficacious than a bishop," maintained Lorrié.

"At least these tickets can lead one to the practice of frequent, fair, and wholesome simony . . ." added Blagoda. "Countries where there are lotteries are countries where Simon Magus thrives."

"I don't know who Simon Magus was," said Lorrié.

"A sort of wealthy Argentine bourgeois," explained Blagoda adequately, "born by chance in Samaria, and founder of the Gnostic philosophy, who wanted to buy from Paul and Peter the power of conferring the Holy Spirit."

Acevedo came in through the corner door. He sat down, greeting everyone quietly. He said that he had been working all afternoon and was tired. Then he indicated that what he had to say would not be pleasant: it had become necessary for him to suspend the publication of *Enough*. The public was increasingly apathetic. All attempts to induce people of wealth to support it financially had failed. "In this country," he said, "ideas have a sudden vogue. They are applauded sympathetically as the death-defying leap of a circus acrobat is applauded, and his emotion shared. As long as the ordeal lasts, that state of intense sympathy lasts too; but as soon as the public leaves the circus, it has no desire to wait for the acrobat at the actors' exit to congratulate him on his performance. We have been followed similarly with apparent applause but with real indifference. Our people are absorbed in other things. They are asleep and inert. They know only the states of deglutition and digestion. I had thought that they could be awakened by a serious enterprise. I now see that it was a vain hope. Life awakens from such sleep, but the awakening cannot be induced. It comes as the result of a sudden shock or convulsion. There is something immature about the sleep, and I believe therefore that our effort is premature. That is my view, at least."

He insisted on his comparison: ". . . the state of deglutition and the state of digestion. The other hours of a noble organism are unknown to it."

From various places at the table protests were raised. No, we could not run away like that. We must struggle obstinately until results could be seen. Acevedo was playing skeptically with his teaspoon, tapping his saucer with it. "No," was all he said, "no." Jazmín Guerrero smiled as though saying to himself: "Such lack of guts could lead to nothing else. It had to end in this shameful spectacle of flight and resignation."

"Perhaps our first mission in this society," said Acevedo, "is personal; then collective action will follow. We are still too heterogeneous, and our attitude toward the problems of a new world is not yet firmly established. We suddenly confuse a lack of selfish interest with ambition and are unable to say which we have in us."

Some of us undoubtedly got the point. But no one insisted any longer, except to record regret and disappointment. We were about twenty at the table. Blagoda suggested that even if the journal ceased publication, the group should at least keep together. We might meet two or three times each month. He looked at Jazmín Guerrero for support. Anselmi threw him a white jasmine from a glass of half-faded flowers. "Very good," he said. Guerrero declared that the supremacy of the élite must be brought about at any cost, "by fire and sword," and he spoke scornfully of de Tocqueville as "that French count who discovered democracy." Anselmi burst out laughing, creating some embarrassment. "De Tocqueville was a great fellow," he said. Guerrero replied with a ferocious look and a scornful little smile.

The conversation became more involved. Freed now from their one common bond, the paper, the latent individual and ideological animosities within the group came to the surface.

131

After an hour and a half things grew bitter. Emphatic and sweeping generalizations were bandied across the table. Remarks became offensively personal. Acevedo looked significantly at me to draw my attention to the real meaning of that disharmony. I realized that he was trying to say: "This spectacle proves how artificial our collaboration has been and what results we could have expected from its continuation."

Soon we all got up. Anselmi, Jiménez, Blagoda, Tauste, and I accompanied Acevedo to his house. Guerrero signaled a taxicab and took one or two of our collaborators with him. They would stop at his apartment in Guido Street and drink a real Napoleon brandy to make up for the bad cognac at Lunamoon. Also, Havana cigar in hand, he would show them his pseudo-Chaldean statuettes, his paper-cutters bought in second-hand stores in Europe, and his replica of the death mask of Oliver Cromwell, picked up for a few shillings in an obscure shop in Maiden Lane.

"We are returning to our personal isolation," said Acevedo to Anselmi and me, staring pensively ahead of him into the darkness. "Ever since the appearance of the second number of the journal I have been convinced that ours were voices crying in the wilderness. More recently our undertaking has been hindered by ambitious and self-seeking people. I fear nothing more than the rot that begins inside the fruit. It would only have been worth excluding the undesirables from our enterprise if the response to it had been different. It has been small, and is steadily diminishing. But if Argentina has its indifference, I have my pride. Another day will dawn. Meanwhile the initial movement has been valuable, the first numbers of *Enough* are a solid accomplishment. To have continued would have been to weaken the significance of the document that we are now leaving."

The moon was overhead. Its milky cascade fell gloriously across the unfolding length of the broad, asphalted Paseo, which contrasted with the dark leafy mass of the park beside it. The façades of the old houses, the simple balustrades, and the rusty iron gratings made a rich pattern of light and shadow. I had, almost physically, the impression of a sudden void. Youth is a voice about to assert itself, an early tumult pressing through a too narrow gate, a voice that is not yet a voice. Youth insistently demands self-assertion. Young people who for various reasons are unable to have their word, or to assert themselves in one way or another, become frustrated. Something was being torn away from us: the possibility that the little journal gave us, for a short time, of injecting a fever, a nonconformity, and a series of violent forecasts into common reality. It had been a small bridge, but nevertheless a bridge, and it was broken.

As we walked toward Acevedo's house, all three of us were surely thinking the same thing, but it would not have done to insist, since it was Acevedo who had defrayed the entire expense of the publication. We held our peace and took leave of him at his door.

24

"You see how very young I was then, so young that I was full of hope. So young that on the long walks down by the port the chill dampness of the August nights and the inclemency of that season of year did not bother me. Yes, I was very young then."

"You were, too."

At that time many people must have wondered at you and how you came through every obstacle more solitary and more beautiful. Many people in your world talked about you. At times, I entered that world, where I too had friends and a few enemies, and where I heard exaggerated talk about my work, then in its early stages. From time to time, at lectures and concerts and in hotel lobbies, I suddenly heard your name mentioned, and listened without appearing to. They knew you superficially; some spoke in pleasant terms of you, others ill; but people have a special way of speaking ill of someone whose excellence wounds them. The men of your world in Buenos Aires are curiously unintelligent. They touch everything, but superficially. The women are more intelligent, but they detest each other, and their vision is always emotionally distorted.

Through all this I could already see in what mould you were setting. Every day, while walking in the streets, I hoped to catch sight of you. My hope was calm and unhurried, but you went out less and less. You kept to your house, reading, and receiving some of the more intelligent people in your world. You were interested in everything; but one enigma tormented you: the reason for certain constant misfortunes in the world. I don't know whether you had then read the question that Marivaux had put to his contemporaries. "Why is it that we, who are so limited in every other way, have such an unlimited capacity for suffering?" I knew that not long before, you had had another child, probably your last on account of the bitter rift that had opened between you and Cárdenas.

You would have liked to see in your two sons strong natures escaped from the shadow. But that weakness which showed in their eyes revealed that they had not entirely escaped the vulnerable part of their mother's nature. Those who saw you and talked with you said that your spirit was still fresh, that you played with your two sad children as though they were well-integrated human beings, and that you laughed with them and confided in them. But whenever I saw you pass by alone, with never a suspicion on your part that anyone was observing you, your glance did not deceive me. It was as if your eyes no longer looked except to inquire the reason for it all. That troubled question was your whole being.

The most artificial sort of ostentation increased about you. Cárdenas consulted you on some of his affairs, then forgot your advice and did whatever he pleased. You nodded your head and smiled.

During those August days they told me what you had said to a friend about Desdemona: that Shakespeare's heroine was a docile, insipid creature who repelled you. You rebelled against any kind of softness. Yet you yourself were made of material as vulnerable and sensitive as a leaf that can be torn by a fingernail — vulnerable and sensitive, but far from soft. Intolerant of your own sensitiveness and vulnerability, you were like the strong-willed men who stand erect, silent, and watchful during a battle, refusing sleep.

Once someone offered to introduce me to you. I looked straight at him and thought myself insignificant and still unworthy. I was waiting. I had faith. I refused.

I left the Museum, where there were a few things worth seeing and much that was indifferent or bad. Édouard Manet's *The Nymph* was meditating her eternal afflictions there, after her woodland bath. A pretty, grieving head was sobbing. *The Funeral Cortège of Jane the Mad* was resting after the bitter tragedy.

How I loved this city! How I loved the whole country and how much I enjoyed the illusion of imagining intelligent, worthy stone-cutters! Just as from the very back of the orchestra we recognize the final note of the oboe, I perceived distinctly the sound of steps, still isolated, subterranean, and unsure of their direction, but which would be comforting steps when they came to the surface and at last trod the sensible territory of the nation.

Perhaps I was already in communication with some of them. My first book, like a fishing net, had taken a catch of souls. But the great majority of them were unknown to me. I did not know how much water they drew or where they were bound.

That night I went to my old school library to consult some books. The reading-room was silent; from time to time, students raised their heads absent-mindedly, and presently returned to their reading. In the margin of the texts that I had asked for were anonymous notes, written by hand, some insulting, others containing comments upon professors, current events, or politics.

One of them asserted that, in our country, politics is a latrine that swallows up everything filthy. "People here are measured by their material ambitions," said another note. "What good will all these books do us? The worthiest man here seems to be the one who covets the greatest domestic luxury." There were intelligent observations, sincere protests, and outrageous outbursts. Who had written them all and where were they now? Life is a regiment of dispersed soldiers, but when some of these soldiers meet for a common purpose, history begins. Upon them it depends whether or not that word is written with a capital letter.

The next day was cloudy and murky. I went out for a walk after breakfast. In front of a little book store, in Tucumán Street, I ran into Mercedes Miró. She was coming out with her arms laden with books, beautiful in her straight-cut black coat, with black gloves, and a white orchid on her lapel. The book store — La Boutique des Livres — was served by two French girls, both excessively plain, but well posted on books. With explosions of enthusiasm, Mercedes showed me the books that she had just bought. Poems by Claudel and a book by Cocteau illustrated by Lhote. "Firewood for a white night between trips." She had just arrived from Valparaiso and was on her way south. Her car stood in front of the door, large, black, and sleek. "I'll ring you up when I get back," she shouted after me. The chauffeur tipped his hat and closed the door. The product of three writers' inspiration was there, clutched to Mercedes's side.

I had been working for four hours on *The Forty Nights* when the maid ran in with frightened eyes and called me to the telephone. The call came from the near-by village of Las Barrancas. Inés Boll told me in an anguished voice through a flood of tears about a bloody accident to Jiménez and how to find the house where he was. I hammered on Anselmi's door. Fortunately he had just arrived. We set out on the run for the Retiro station.

2 5

I REMEMBER that incident as neither so absurd nor so vulgar as it then seemed. It is hard to describe. It was terrific and had its importance at the time. After half an hour of conjectures and regrets in the slow-moving train, we arrived at Las Barrancas. Anselmi kept saying that Jiménez should have heeded his warnings. Near the station the river runs past swampy banks that rise in vertical ravines. There is a twilight desolation of parks at their top. Below, the railroad tracks cross the wet land, cultivated here and there in brief squares. Above, on open terraces along unpaved streets and hidden behind climbing vines, stand aging villas and chalets with old-fashioned bay-windows, balustrades, and porches. From below you can see run-down parks and ruined belvederes dripping water.

We made inquiries at the station. There they pointed out to us, some two hundred and fifty feet away, the house we were looking for. In the late dusk only its dark roof and the balcony running lengthwise along the upper part of its whitewashed façade could be seen. We went up the lonely street bordered on the left by the ravines, which here seemed less steep. Everything was deserted and neglected.

We had to cut across a side street to climb the slope. Near at hand the house could no longer be seen — only the garden and the green terraces that surrounded it. The door, made of a single piece of varnished wood, gave on to the upper slope. It opened, and against a light we saw Inés Boll, weeping incessantly and unable to speak for hiccuping. She came running to meet us in complete disarray, putting her handkerchief to her face. "It had to happen!" she sobbed, and repeated it without troubling to explain herself. Greatly alarmed, we entered the large hall of the house, which upstairs contained in addition only a bedroom and a bath.

Jiménez was sitting in an armchair with his head almost completely swathed in bandages. Even his eyes were covered. We rushed toward him. He greeted us with a smiling voice. "You see what a wreck I am! I look like a Moor with a turban on." His voice attempted to show courage, but it sounded strangely broken and had an impressive, almost tragic note in it. We stood motionless, hesitating for a moment. Then both of us put our hands on his shoulders at the same time. "But what has happened?" We felt that Jiménez was holding something back. His chin and hands were cold and he looked like a wounded soldier sitting there in his chair. We asked him everything at once, glancing about the room before sitting down. Inés explained between spasms of despair, that her husband had learned of this place, where they had spent some week-ends. He had come at night in order to have it all end in scandal. There had been a terrible scene. "Prostitute!" he had shouted. "Prostitute! You have got to put an end to your affair with this man." Jiménez started to throw him out. He attacked him, but Boll, holding his ground, had beaten him on the head with his cane. Jiménez's glasses had been broken in his eyes. Inés saw blood stream from his mouth and nose. Before Jiménez, covered with blood and blinded by the blows, could stop him, the husband left, still mouthing insults. Inés cried out to have him stopped, and hung on his coat until she stumbled against the gutter and fell. She nearly went out of her mind as she bathed Jiménez's eyes in the bathroom and removed pieces of glass. She was crying and her tears mingled with his blood. The washbowl was red with it. She tied a handkerchief about his eyes and ran out to summon a doctor. Near by she found a gardener, who brought a doctor from the villa opposite. The doctor had treated him and bandaged his eyes again. That was all. Jiménez would have to remain under observation until it could be ascertained whether there was still any glass in his eyes. The doctor said he must be taken to the city to see a surgeon.

Inés Boll fell silent. She was trembling and weeping. She

turned her back on us, her face in her hands, then literally threw herself, still sobbing, on Jiménez. I looked at her blue dress, her Irish lace collar, and her silk stockings all stained and soiled — so much coquetry suddenly annihilated. I pressed Jiménez's hand, and Anselmi and I warned him that he must rest very patiently and not think about what had happened — not think about it at all. There is always time for despair. Better wait as long as possible before giving up hope. But naturally we would bring him home. Anselmi stood up. He was livid.

"Where are you going?" I asked. He replied hoarsely, almost without opening his lips: "For the police. I am going for the police." Jiménez was gloomy and silent. Again he spoke in a voice that faltered in spite of himself: "The worst would be if I were to go blind." His hands gripped the arms of his chair like two claws. Señora Boll was standing now, crying. I said that I was going for an automobile and started out with Anselmi. "Good-by. It's all over," said Jiménez. "Blind, blind." "No," I told him, "who can say? It's impossible yet to say anything." "Blind, blind." Inés remained on the terrace, weeping in the darkness.

When we reached the door, we heard a shrill cry: "He is still there! He is still there!"

A man was standing on the street corner a hundred paces away. He wore a black felt hat with the brim turned down on one side and held a cane in his hand. Inés Boll's cry penetrated the still night air. When the man heard it, he hurried down the slope. Anselmi and I ran after him. At the bottom he turned into another street. The solitary lamp at the crossing enabled us to get a good look at him, but when we got there, he was nowhere to be seen. Several roads intersected at the next crossing, which was unlighted. Anselmi was off on the side toward the track and waved to me to look on the other. I went down a short distance and found the streets dark and closed by wire fences or trees. I returned in the direction that Anselmi had taken.

We went out together to the asphalted avenue, caught sight

of the lonely station, and in the light of the station lamps made out the figure of a man crossing a high bridge over the tracks. He stopped in the middle of the bridge and turned back, walking quickly. At full run we went through the station and the stationmaster's rose-garden. Hens and chickens fled. The pebbled walk crunched underfoot. We left the station grounds. For a few seconds we saw nothing. "Where is he?" asked Anselmi. I could see only the marshland, the dark surface of the river, the lights of the city forming a great reef in the distance, and to our right the road and the ravines. In their somber skirts, among the reeds, tangled foliage, and climbing vines, rose the manacled form of a nineteenth-century Aphrodite, a partially ruined belvedere, and old, neglected villas, swallowed up by trees and choked by the furtive, possessive swamp grass.

We floundered into a muddy spot, but scrambled out by grasping an old, wire boundary fence. Presently we entered a wider street that climbed toward the upper part of the ravine. The man reappeared, a dark mass, walking some distance ahead, in the middle of the pavement. As the lamplight fell on his back, I noticed that he was carrying his cane in his right hand, in reverse, as one might carry a mauser. Anselmi rushed after him. The man turned his head and veered a little toward the narrow sidewalk, hemmed in by iron railings. Anselmi shouted to him to stop. His shouts rang out sharp and strident in the deserted night. The man stopped and turned to wait for him to come up. I followed as fast as I could. The man came out to the center of the street.

Anselmi grappled with him, then broke away and struck him four sharp blows. The thud of the impacts resounded in the still air. I started to join the fight, but Anselmi shouted to me to let him do it alone. The man's hat and cane fell to the asphalt. His hair sprawled over his wild, bitter face. Anselmi struck him in the stomach and Boll backed off and lunged a savage blow at him. Anselmi struck him again on the chin, then on the head.

Each impact struck home solidly. They backed up toward the sidewalk and both stumbled. The lamp above illuminated them. The whistle of an express train sounded from the embankment, then it rushed past us with a roar. "You will pay for it," said Anselmi, each syllable forced out through his clenched teeth, as he battered the man's chest, face, and body. His opponent fell twice, sprang up like a tiger, and fell again. He said nothing. He was panting and striking out in a clumsy, frustrated way. By the light of the street lamp I could see his terrible, purple face and Anselmi's eyebrow bleeding profusely, which hampered and infuriated him. He rushed at his opponent like a bull; the man reeled and both fell. I saw Anselmi's left hand at Boll's throat as his right rose and fell like a flail. He seized him by the coat collar and struck him three times against the pavement. The man opened his mouth and gasped out a formless complaint in spite of his effort to suppress it. Anselmi loosed him, stood up, grasped the cane, and as Boll was about to rise, struck him a blow in the mouth. Anselmi ground his teeth together to restrain himself from cracking his skull. His chest was heaving and he gasped out to me: "Telephone the police from the station. Let them come now."

I ran to the station and talked with the commissariat. The station-master and the ticket agent closed the wicket and followed me. From a distance I saw Anselmi and the man struggling again, standing, but Anselmi was now belaboring him ferociously with the cane. When we arrived, we surrounded the man and held his arms. Their tongues were both lolling out. Anselmi threatened him, as he rearranged his clothes, and the man reviled him in bitter, insolent language.

We took Jiménez and Inés Boll to Buenos Aires in an automobile. It was a very painful experience. Jiménez had lost all control over himself and kept complaining that his life was over and that he would have to drag out his days, blind, sitting in a chair like an invalid. His eyes were hurting him horribly. At times he shrieked with pain. Señora Boll was sobbing again.

I felt that Anselmi, true to his character, had conducted himself valiantly, and that his courage and integrity had let a breath of fresh air into the atmosphere, surcharged with theories, in which we had been living for so many months.

26

THUS, at the end of the winter, I entered a chamber of silence. Life outside touched me with only an occasional faint reflection and stirred remote echoes in me that were to end in meditation. I became a recluse in my own house. Jiménez's family took him away, and occasionally from his village came meager, depressing, monotonous letters, dictated to his brother. Professor Borescu's lessons kept him busy from morning until evening, but after supper he never failed to give me a fruitful hour of study and examination of the Latin texts. Those sessions were extremely beneficial. They greatly stimulated my imagination and my own creative work. Dr. Dervil seemed more and more infirm and resigned to the limits of his own world. From time to time, transient boarders came to Señora Ana's house. Conversation in the dining-room oscillated between stirring peaks and dreary depths. Inés Boll moved away one day, having made us witnesses of her unhappy and humiliating plight and her hope of eventually being of use to Jiménez. There was a trial. Anselmi temporarily took Jiménez's place at the ministry. Every day he became more and more unconventional. When he left his office at night, he was like a jaguar released from its cage, and commented with insolent, savage bluntness on various aspects of Argentine affairs.

At the beginning of summer I paid a visit to my father. I found him lonely and embittered by the atmosphere in which he was forced to carry on his work. He seemed cold and skeptical about everything. I spent three days with him. In the evenings I had intended to be loquacious and to tell him a great many things, hoping to bring about an improvement in his attitude. But when we went out together for a walk under the great trees and inspected his work, I felt a barrier of silence rising between us, an inhibition so strong that it seemed fated by our very natures. Nevertheless he told me that although not wealthy, he had somehow been able to save a little money and that perhaps his small capital would help me since it could not help him. The idea of money had never tempted me. It worried me. I may have had a presentiment that it would never be of any use to me, either.

I returned to Buenos Aires sad at heart, gave up my evening work, and began to avoid going out alone. I could not accustom myself to Jiménez's absence. A futile feeling of protest seized me every time that I thought of his accident.

There were days of progress on my book, *The Forty Nights*. I made notes for possible new episodes. Sometimes I read chapters to Anselmi, who found them good. When I was alone again, however, I revised my pages, as I was not satisfied with them. I tore them up and once more entered a sterile period.

I traveled through many parts of Argentina, becoming acquainted with almost all of the north, the coastal region, and parts of the south. I gave literary talks to groups of young people and met with an enthusiastic response that revealed their clearly felt need for something other than the farce of contemporary Argentina, with its beflagged mediocrity. I spent days in the interior cities, talking with our young people about what they and I wanted for our country, about its dangers and unhappy blunders. They glowed with an eagerness no spark of which had yet been quenched. They went to endless pains, too, to show me the local sights — people, buildings, and places. I left their young faces behind me at the railroad station waiting for something, for so much — poor, lonely, anonymous hearts!

They made me long to do something for them, but what could I do? A poor writer, by fits and starts expressing his personal enthusiasms, I could only bring them into my writing from time to time and let them share my own exaltation. I wrote with their assistance an episode of Juan Argentino as an adolescent seeking to discover his own features and looking sadly at himself in a mirror in which the images he saw were those of malformed, grotesque persons who did not resemble him.

But my friends and other well-disposed people in Buenos Aires were constantly inviting me to their gatherings. They began to complain of my absence, casualness, and reluctance to see them. They said I was proud, cold, and pedantic. When I ran into them from time to time, they would try to touch me on a sore spot or make ironic comments. Sometimes they fell into uncomfortable silences.

"This is a country of destiny," Professor Borescu kept telling me, "a country of destiny. Some day they will see it, but they will have to fight like Jacob with the angel, never stopping until they have achieved blessedness."

When I was very tired I went to a little village by the sea on the south coast of the Atlantic. I watched the fishermen at their work and enjoyed looking out over the ocean, so much like eternity, and like our own struggles, each wave advancing obstinately, and mutely protesting its reflux. From an offhand remark in a letter from a woman who knew you quite well, I learned what was then happening to you. From that fishing hamlet, almost isolated from the land, I witnessed your distant tragedy.

You were watching your sad eldest son growing to reason and to the dawn of consciousness. You stayed by him all day long, watching over him and listening for him to protest at being alive and blame you for having brought him unprotected into a world full of mocking laughter and deceit. It hurt you even more that as time passed he did not complain. You did not want to be away from him when he uttered his cry of protest. When you renewed contact with people after hours of vigil, you seemed to come from some shadow world and to have lost the ability that this world demands to summon a smile to your face.

But life leaves no loose ends. It picks them up and knots them in passing.

You were returning to the world. I was coming to my work, paying my way by hard night labor.

One day I received a letter from my father expressing his wish to deed me his small capital during his lifetime. Why should he continue, he said, to be the depositary of what belonged to another by the rights of life itself? I accepted his decision without any feeling other than satisfaction at the security that it afforded my writing.

I continued tied to a table covered with pencils, well-thumbed books, and ink, but ceremoniously visited by the most incredible guests that one could invite. Aside from this, everything that happens to man, as a man, happened to me. I had my subterfuges, tumbles, disappointments, doubts, passing states resembling love, quickly dissolved enthusiasms, and a constantly growing hatred for those who are betraying this country.

Thus passed eight years.

BOOK II

The Islands

27

ONE night in the spring of 1934 I arrived at the little English village of Wimbledon in search of lodgings.

The broad street extended beyond the gloomy building occupied by the local branch of Barclay's Bank. An anachronistic being came out to open the door for me that night, a nineteenth-century man, his lamp held high, his nose red from wine, and his speech harsh and guttural. It was the house of one of the good villagers of Surrey, and I knew at once that I had found just the quiet isolated spot that I was looking for in order to observe English customs. I installed myself there, with light bags, intending to stay only a short time. I had left all my heavy luggage in Paris. The owner of the house turned out to be an excellent companion for my nights of idleness or insomnia. Although the baneful effect of peace on human morality, and his personal recollections of the Boer War, were his favorite topics, he related many amusing and picturesque episodes in his difficult but voluble speech. His wife soon informed me — feigning one of those typical despairs of a zealous and economical housewife — that she would never be able to cure her husband of his habit of drinking a bottle of Scotch whisky a day. Mr. Jibbonings scorned economy. He was a devotee of Bacchus. It is most useful to meet up with a talkative drunkard in a place where everything is new to us. Night after night, therefore, as Mr. Jibbonings told me interesting anecdotes about London, I encouraged him, stimulated his memory, and applauded his strokes of genius. I spent my days in London and at night returned to the peaceful atmosphere of the little village. Mrs. Jibbonings brought me apples every morning; Mr. Jibbonings appeared in my room shortly thereafter, setting an example of early rising, freshness, and rotundity, in order to appropriate one of them, which he ate with calm relish or prudent haste, depending upon whether his intolerant consort was far or near. He brought me the *Daily Mirror* and ascribed all its news to the flabbiness of mankind and the consequent necessity of such round stimulants as wars or floods.

Mr. and Mrs. Jibbonings were certain that I was a representative of the Argentine Foreign Office. Despite my tentative and not very insistent attempts to disabuse them of this notion, they were persuaded that no one would venture from such rude and distant parts as I hailed from except on an important diplomatic mission.

From time to time I spent several days in London, leaving behind at Wimbledon — an hour's ride by bus — all the English literature that I had recently been reading, and stopped at a modest hotel in a little-frequented street: the Craven Hotel in Craven Street.

To the left, a few hundred feet away, was the Thames Embankment. Leaving Craven Street in the other direction, one ran abruptly into the last block of the Strand — represented at that point by an economical Lyons's and a small ale-room — and into a remote, astral Nelson, guarded by four sleeping lions, who watches in his turn over the destinies of the National Gallery. Every day I crossed that district to lunch in Regent Street at the Café Royal or at a Spanish restaurant up an obscure alley. It was spring and London was warm, sunny, and smiling. As I threaded my way every day through the maze of double-decker omnibuses,

I developed an activity no less important than the missions of the befogged politicians alighting from the railroad coaches at Victoria Station, the diamond experts setting out for Amsterdam, or the bustling morning speculators in Threadneedle Street. My activity had a splendid, poetic scope between Bloomsbury, with the Pharaohs slumbering eternally beside the manuscripts of the British Museum, the concert halls, from the boards of which came the nasal voices of actors in *Back to Methuselah*, and the restful, evening verdure of Kensington Gardens.

One of the greatest adventures in life is to extend or reconstruct the richest, human trails. I was keenly interested, therefore, on arriving in this rarefied, northern atmosphere from the homogeneity of Argentina, to find in the restaurants and streets of London such a diversity of types, tones, gestures, and conversation. It was like passing from a quiet rural panorama to a strenuous, teeming city.

For three months I sought out and followed promising trails in London. In Burgrave's Inn one can still converse with the shade of Bunyan's pilgrim. In Charing Cross, as Dr. Johnson assured Boswell, one can still find the tide of human existence. In the stones that form the Latin cross on Saint Paul's can be found traces of Ethelbert, King of Kent, converted by the Roman monk Augustine in the sixth century. It may also happen — alas, inhabitants of the Americas! — that none of these things are found.

With the keenest relish I steeped myself for days in the springs of Milton's inspiration, whose poetry reminded Samuel Butler of that moment when the Fleet Street bridge shrouds the cupola of Saint Paul's with capricious clouds of smoke. I became acquainted with many intellectuals and with a very agreeable young doctor from Brussels, named Ferrier, with whom I had many conversations about men and saints. For weeks on end, however, I spoke no word to anyone except for a few polite phrases with the hotel servants. I looked, saw, and thought —

and nothing more. It was enough. It was too much. In spite of everything, London's face was too arid. The Seine, with its Latin shades, was beckoning to me.

I arrived at Dover one noon. That evening I was dining at Fouquet's in the delightful heart of Paris. The night was followed by many others. It was life in the clear air of the intellect. As it is the country of intelligence — that is, of imagination — everything seems astir. How long did I live in the rue d'Amsterdam and in the rue de l'Échelle? Not long, but I made the days longer, as I rose early and retired late. Each day then seemed to me an age. The walls of the rue du faubourg Saint-Honoré still exuded something of the spirit of Balzac. It was thrilling to find it so. I went out also to meet the material fruits, because in that city they have a spiritual flavor too. To eat croissants in the rue Royale had the savor of the spiritual; so did the long loaves that pedestrians carried under their arms; and the meat cooked in Chablis; even the people who entered and left the city by the Lion of Belfort had a spiritual flavor.

But I wanted to uncover the deeper strata, just as in summer we prefer the fruit from the shady side of the tree, cool and heavy with dew. I entered the human forest of those who aspired to arrive and those who had already arrived. That is always the warmest and least vulgarly human world, as it contains the elements of superhuman nonconformity.

Life in the Americas has this that is immediate and rude: it is purely a relation between man and material. Nothing operates to soften the meeting of those extremes. In the relations of European life another factor enters, the spiritual offspring of this meeting: tradition and the fruit of reflection. This has a living substance. It is something that we Americans encounter as a solid fact. Soon we relish it.

My leisure permitted me to discover that for myself. Sometimes standing before some place or building of interest, I thought how much I should have liked to see it with you. At times, when I thought about you in the dim light of a church interior, with its mysterious windows, or beside a spring, or in the impressive atmosphere of a thousand-year-old street, I surprised my own lips moving. I laughed at myself and walked on, happy and pensive. I dropped into a café, asked for something to drink, and studied the characters about me, upon whom their nationality had placed a strong stamp.

I talked with many intellectuals, artists, and women of the street — all people with personal philosophies, because nothing has protected them and because they get nothing except in exchange for their own blood. They are the diversity and the salt of the earth. They are good company too — when they refrain from talking about other people. They are stirring, and sometimes great when their dreams are destroyed or when they talk about the things they had hoped for and forget to curse what they have got.

I had not touched my writing for more than six months. Sometimes I would jot down an impression. Generally, however, I refrained, allowing shapes to accumulate within me without putting them into words.

Across the street from my window the letters of the sign: "M. Loubiot, Upholsterer," danced grotesquely in the afternoon breeze.

28

ONE morning I left Paris, on the "Blue Train" for Milan.

After another three hours of travel I left the train at Como. The idea of shutting myself up completely and writing had returned to plague me. It was a cloudy afternoon; the hotel omnibus was waiting for me at the station, which lay in a hollow. The moist air intensified the deep greens on the mountain skirts. A heavy torpor hung over the station. The omnibus-driver was arguing heatedly about something with the porter, who was stowing the baggage on the roof of the vehicle. Then the driver threw the car into noisy motion as if to vent his spleen on the gears and accelerator. On sunny days the Italian mountains have an air of garish cheerfulness, but when it is stormy they take on a grave and imposing aspect; their colors fade, their vegetation seems to shrink, and their outlines become hard and sharp like a blade of blue steel against the sky. The green is a supersaturated monochrome. The roads disappear up the leafy slope.

We reached Cernobbio at nightfall. It is a tiny village on the floor of the valley, overlooking the lake, with an immense, beautiful hotel surrounded by gardens and sheltered by the matted, dark-green vegetation. The enormous blue lake stretched out between the high mountains in front of the hotel, and little white houses climbed the hillside, like flights of steps.

I crossed the gardens and entered the hotel. Its corridors were arranged like a cross, and at the rear, overlooking the lake, across which came the roar of airplane motors, was a terrace where many couples were dancing. While I was talking to the manager, the infernal racket of the planes prevented him from hearing me. "The airplanes," he said, with an unctuous smile.

I walked around the hotel grounds for a half-hour before returning. The terrace had emptied. The dining-room and lobbies were full, and buzzing with conversation. I went in, asked the maître d'hôtel for a table, and ate frugally. To my right, an elderly, British gentleman was eating, accompanied by his two daughters; on my left, a solitary lady in mourning was slowly sipping milk and reading a book. The room was so large that I could not see all the people that filled it. The men were all in dinner-jackets except me; I wore a blue suit. Many waiters — pomp for the first day — filed past my table, offering me specialties of the hotel. I asked for a strong, dry, white vintage wine. The British gentleman never took his eyes off me. The orchestra played hackneyed pieces, including of course the *Blue Danube*. The lady in mourning raised her eyes, fixed them on me, then lowered them to her book. When I had finished eating, I retired almost immediately, as I was tired after the long journey.

I awoke very early the next morning to the noise of the motors reverberating in the hollow sounding-box formed by the lake and the mountains. I shaved, bathed, and went out into the morning air. Three or four young people in sports clothes were walking on the terrace; sitting on the wooden wharf, with her legs dangling over the water, a girl of about twenty was laughingly signaling to the crew members of one of the noisy little boats. As I approached her, she looked up and said in French: "Good morning." She had a slender, white, young body. I asked her about the temperature of the water and she told me, smiling and kicking her legs rapidly, that it was as cold as ice. The launch, with her friends aboard, reached the wharf, and one of the young men, in flannel trousers and a crisp shirt open at the neck, jumped to the wharf and laughingly pressed her hand. I watched them depart, then walked toward the hotel gardens. It was a deliciously cold morning. I walked for more than a half-hour along the narrow main street of Cernobbio, past many beautiful houses and the usual swarm of souvenir-shops. Then I returned to the hotel and sat down before my typewriter.

Almost every morning I went out to walk in the foothills. The early hours were fresh and bright and the earth cool and damp despite the brilliant southern sun. There were steep, narrow paths in the high ravines. I kept close to the valley floor, however, walking on the lower roads and observing the barns, surrounded by low brick walls, and the rough stone dwelling-houses. The skin of the local inhabitants was so burned that their faces looked like sculptured masks of dark copper. The men worked in their shirt sleeves and great hats, and the chestnut-colored legs of the girls gleamed in the sun. For a great distance the hills succeeded one another, opening out into level valleys which communicated with one another by green gorges.

Thus passed five days. My work was progressing. I relaxed by

153

making expeditions in the neighborhood as far as Como. I had exchanged a few words only with a laconic merchant from Riga, convalescing from a bronchial affection.

One morning a very agreeable couple from the United States, named Bartlett, arrived by auto. I had met them at a gathering at our Embassy in Paris. They were young and always laughing. They took life as a jest and lived in a perfect equilibrium between loquacity and intoxication. They were always ready for anything that turned up, and would just as readily have gone with me to a religious service as to scale the Harz Mountains or conquer Abyssinia. His name was Ernest, hers Brett. When they drank more than usual — that is, a dozen cocktails in a day — they became serious and stiff. But they were amusing companions and I would have been glad had they stayed on at the Hotel Villa d'Este. After two days, however, they were called to Bern and departed like a summer zephyr, happy and somewhat in a haze. Almost immediately I received a postal card from them containing the briefest of messages and two signatures.

One night when I reached the hotel, the manager approached me in the hall and said that Baron Morgen had asked him to introduce me. I asked him who Baron Morgen was and he replied that he was a Czech citizen who had something to do with diplomacy. I consented and followed the manager to the bar, in front of which there were many people sitting on high stools, under a dazzling display of light. The hollow thud of dice and the comments of the players could be heard. The bar was attractively built of natural wood, trimmed with nickel. When I entered, I espied the Czech baron with a tall woman in black, sitting, not at the bar, but at a table at one end of the room. He stood up and without waiting for an introduction put out his hand.

"How are you?" he said. "Madame Lascaboya, Señor Tra — "

"Tregua," I said.

"Tregua," he repeated. "I am Baron Morgen, whom you do

not remember, but who was at dinner with you at Albert Lenain's one night, about two months ago."

"Ah, yes, quite right," I said.

I did not remember. I had dined twice with Lenain, on both occasions with many other guests. But I repeated: "Yes, quite right."

Madame Lascaboya was indeed very beautiful. She wore a dress of black silk, open at an angle over a small, high bosom. The skin of her throat was soft, and about her neck were two strings of pearls. She looked at me with a coldly courteous smile, not moving her eyes or lips. The baron gestured heavily with his short, puffy hand, on which glistened a ring designed like a serpent, with two small sapphires for eyes.

"I know you so well through Lenain," continued the baron, "that I did not want to let the opportunity slip of rounding out our acquaintance by a few minutes of conversation."

I thanked him by bowing, without saying anything. The baron nailed his cold, smiling eyes on me.

"Martini, Bronx, or Bacardi?" he asked.

"Bronx," I said directly to the waiter. Baron Morgen's abdomen, festooned by a chain of white gold, had overflowed its bed and made him breathe with difficulty. Madame Lascaboya looked on silently, smoking. The moment was cold and uncomfortable. Baron Morgen raised his glass, toasted Madame Lascaboya, and then turned his shrewd eyes full on me. Madame Lascaboya opened her cigarette-case and found it empty. I offered her one of mine, which she accepted with thanks. I asked her whether she was Czech or Slovak.

"No," she answered, "I am from somewhere else."

I asked the baron whether they were to be long in Italy.

"Madame and I are merely friends. We have met here by accident," he replied. "She is leaving for the north the day after tomorrow, and I shall stay here some time longer; then, before returning to Prague, I shall spend a few days at my house in

Lugano. It is a primitive place, but there are pines, a pretty little wood, and water."

He spoke with a peculiar intonation, at once emphatic and ingratiating, as if each word carried with it a hidden meaning which he wished to underline. The silence again became strained. The baron began to talk in a slow, monotonous, insinuating voice. He knew exactly when I had arrived, where I had come from, and what manner of life I had led in Paris — among artistic people and wealthy amateurs. Immediately, as though not to give me time for more questions, he referred to the still unsettled European problem. His long monologue abounded in common sense. Madame Lascaboya, slowly smoking her cigarette, continued to watch us and the men perched on high stools in front of the bar.

When the baron, puffing with fatigue, had finished speaking, she asked me bluntly:

"Are you an American?"

"Yes, from South America, from Argentina."

"You must know the Barheims there."

"No," I replied, "I don't know any Barheims."

"That's strange," she said, fixing her large, immovable eyes on me.

"Why does it seem strange to you that I should not know the Barheims?"

"Because they are South Americans," she replied.

I laughed and she remained immutable. Was she shrewd or stupid? Naturally or intentionally glacial? Her long, white arms lay passively on the arms of the sofa. I did not know what to talk about to the baron. When I asked him about Karel Čapek he shrugged his shoulders contemptuously.

"Do you believe in literature today?" he asked me.

"No," I replied.

"What do you believe in?"

The question made me laugh.

"What do you believe in?" insisted the baron.

"I believe," I said, "in a progress for mankind beginning with the destruction of his own rational resistance to that progress as if nothing else mattered. I believe in a few other things."

"What rational resistances do you refer to?"

"Those which generally stand in the way of one's believing and living naturally."

"I do not believe in any progress for humanity," he said.

Madame Lascaboya looked at him from the depths of her elegant passivity.

"I do not believe in any progress for humanity," he repeated. "It has reached its culmination. Man has only fire and death ahead of him. His 'progress' lies in those two directions. It remains therefore only to assist him to gain his ends — to reach fire and war."

Then, enigmatically:

"I am one of those who are hastening to help man attain those goals he has set up for himself."

"What do you mean?"

"You will perhaps learn some day," replied the baron. "It is necessary to help man put an end to himself. Perversity must be given its nourishment. . . ."

Touching up her lips with a stick of very dark rouge from her gold case, Madame Lascaboya said slowly:

"What a footless objective! It is precisely you who will be helped to meet fire and death. You will end by being a warlike animal, Baron Morgen."

"No," he smiled cynically, "but one of the men who leads the way to war."

Brusquely changing the subject, he asked me if I would care to join them at dinner. I said that I should be glad to. We went into the dining-room and the baron asked the maître d'hôtel to set another place at their table near one of the large windows. Then he quickly ordered a flask of red Barbera wine and a plate of noodles.

"I have no doubt that you are a man who takes an interest in general world problems. You are young and intelligent, and even if you had no other qualities, those two would suffice. I will outline some of my country's problems to you, and you will tell me whether the attitude of other nations toward it has been fair. Hungary intends to recover three million Hungarians from Yugoslavia, Rumania, and Czechoslovakia, to say nothing of demanding a revision of its frontiers. If carried out, this would amount to the annexation of the left bank of the Danube, resulting in our practical exclusion from that river. Moreover, the Slovaks want to separate from the Czechs and become autonomous. The divergence therefore could not be greater, and the problem of the Danube has become very threatening for us. A general conflagration, this time frightful, might start from this local problem. I am not interested in reuniting the members of the Holy Roman Empire, but I am in trying to assure my country by every possible means, excluding peaceful ones, which are always illusory, such strength as will guarantee her respect abroad and the possibility of the best alliances. At this moment the question of who will go to war, supported by whom, is fundamental for every country in Europe."

As he talked, the baron kept tracing invisible lines on the tablecloth with the fingers in which he held his cigar. His manner was authoritative; his voice low. What was he getting at with all his oratorical reasoning? I told him that my knowledge of the point was inadequate, that I had only read a few declarations by Count Bethlen about the problem of Hungary's frontiers.

"Count Bethlen never opens his mouth except to contradict himself!" replied the baron angrily. He paused, summoned the waiter, and looked at us interrogatively. Madame Lascaboya asked for a *fine*, and we both followed her lead.

"But let's come to the point," said the baron. "Couldn't you become interested in the fate of a small country to assure whose ultimate greatness only a small crusade is needed? In what are you interested in Europe today? As a citizen of a distant and peaceable country you have fortunately no ties that bind you to it. You don't know the anguish of constant worry over the destiny of your own nationality. But you have a critical attitude, perspicacity, integrity, and an active mind. Well, my country needs men like you. The services which its own citizens are performing abroad are woefully inadequate. Yet they enjoy considerable favors from the government. Their work is paid for in gold, to say nothing of the prestige that they acquire when they return to our country. Would you not care to come to an understanding with our government in order to be entrusted with interesting missions abroad which are discreet, attractive in themselves, and would perhaps occupy some of your leisure and give you in addition, the — how shall I say it — practical, and positive confidence and favor of a state?"

I looked at him and laughed without saying a word. The baron's hand was extended in a gesture of explanation and expectation, his palm upward. His thin eyebrows were raised questioningly.

"Why do you laugh?" he asked.

I continued to laugh without speaking. Madame Lascaboya leaned back in her chair and for the first time allowed her erect bosom to rest.

"Why do you laugh?" repeated Baron Morgen.

"It seems to me a — what shall I say? — a comical proposal."

"There is nothing strange or devious about it. It is simply a suggestion which I make because of the high estimate I put on your personal qualities."

"Thanks," I said.

"The confidential missions are exciting, and naturally full of interest."

159

"Thanks. My preoccupations are of a different nature and, as a matter of fact, completely fill my time."

I was still smiling, because that sort of point-blank engaging of spies amused me greatly. Still enveloped in his cloud of courtesy, the baron's eyes could nevertheless not disguise his deep annoyance at my smile. His fleshy lips were still half-open. In a few minutes he had changed the subject with extreme skill. We all three stood up.

Outside, the night was very pleasant. We walked the length of the terraces, among the crowd of people in evening costume. A little before midnight I left them to go up to my room.

I took a tepid bath, lay down, opened a book, and, abandoning it, began to look over my letters. Three months before, René Ferrier had strongly pressed me to spend some time with him in Brussels. It would be agreeable to spend a few days there. What would his house be like? He had not told me in what part of that dark, cold city it was.

The weather changed and the days began to get extremely cold. Madame Lascaboya and Baron Morgen spent their days away from the hotel, in Como, where they had some acquaintances. I could not endure the hotel or its frivolous guests. I had had enough of it and decided to leave. I sent a ten-word telegram to René Ferrier. Two hours later it would be in Leopold I Street. I would take the morning train. That night I saw the baron and Madame Lascaboya. He had a contrite air when they entered the main hotel entrance, and she, with her fur jacket hung loosely over her shoulders and a little straw hat like those worn by the sailors in Nelson's navy — with a narrow brim and broad, low crown — was walking with her head high, absorbed in thought and carrying a bundle of French magazines under her arm.

"Are you leaving today?" the baron asked me.

"Tomorrow at eight," I replied. "I shall drive as far as Como and take the train from there."

"Count on me as your friend."

"Thank you. I hope we shall meet again," I said to him.

"Have you read the latest news?" he asked.

"No, only last night's. What's new?"

"The pacts. Do you think that Italy and France will hold together at the last moment?"

"It is difficult to say for sure. I wonder whether the makers of the pacts know themselves."

"One of them knows too well . . ."

"Always the same anti-Fascist," I remarked.

The baron did not reply. Madame Lascaboya was writing something with a little silver pencil on a piece of paper torn from a memorandum pad. She handed me the paper.

"If you should come through Berlin in April or May, look me up in this street."

I was about to unfold the paper to read the address.

"No," she said, "later."

29

THE INTERNATIONAL EXPRESS crosses many mountains after climbing several levels of cultivated tableland. During this part of the journey there are innumerable tunnels — dark caves that the train enters and leaves noisily. Reading becomes exasperating if not impossible. Once the train halted nearly twenty minutes for repairs in one of these caverns. The coaches were filled with the acrid smell of coal smoke, and as we were almost stifled, we began to leave the train and walk along the tunnel toward the white light that could be seen at its exit. Soon the trouble was fixed and the train rolled forward again. The stations were all incredibly alike: great gloomy buildings with glass and complicated ironwork on the roof; stalls crammed with newspapers and journals; and men peddling wine, refreshments, rolls, and dishes of cold noodles from their little hand-carts. As the train reached one of these stations, open at each end, passengers rushed to the doors and windows looking for people they were expecting. Italian soldiers were in evidence, in gray uniforms and high kepis, broader at the top, and an angle of black shirt showing below their tunics. On the kiosks the gaudy covers of the English books of the "Albatross" collection and of illustrated magazines could be made out from a distance. That morning there were many people in the stations. A group of young Tyrolese girls appeared in Alpine hats, their strong knees bare. The platforms had been sprinkled and the air that we breathed under the lofty, resounding arches was fresh. When we stopped at Chiasso, I had bought the *Corriere della Sera* and had quickly scanned the headlines. They were still commenting on Mussolini's speech to the people of Brindisi. The Duce had said: "The regime demands of us only the spirit of initiative, obedience to the laws of the State, and fidelity to the cause of the Revolution and the Fatherland." Too many capital letters for the spirit of initiative to be able to breathe freely. I had recently read the conversations of the Prime Minister with Ludwig, and they had seemed to me mediocre. Despite Mussolini's dialectical and arbitrary theorization about what his words meant, which a woman friend of mine had repeated to me, I found them beautiful and simple. "Why do you ask me whether our people are happy? Don't ask me," he had said, "don't ask me! At night, at midnight, and at dawn I wake up startled, thinking: these people, in this house, in this city, and throughout our land, will they be happy, will they be well off, will they suffer? . . ." Yes, it was beautiful and simple. I continued to read the news in the *Corriere della Sera*. Disasters in Algiers; the discovery of a plot against the chief of the Iron Guard in Rumania; loss of life at sea.

The second-class coach in which I was traveling had a door

at either end, and almost all of the compartments were empty. After Chiasso they began to fill up. At Chiasso two bare-headed men entered the train, wearing black shirts, military trousers, and black boots. They sat down opposite me in the compartment and nodded stiffly. One of them was nearly thirty; the other might have been fifteen years older. I removed the valise that I had left on the seat opposite me and put it in the baggage-rack above my head. The two men talked in rapid Italian, which was difficult to follow. On one of their brown valises, a label bore the inscription: "Under Secretary — National Fascist Party," and the name of a town.

One of the officials started a technical conversation with the other on aviation. I began to read *The Fountain*, in English, but soon had to put it aside to answer the questions of the customs officials, who took down my declarations in little notebooks. They made a military salute to the black-shirted officials. The latter then stood up and left the compartment, talking and smiling about something that had to do with their arrival at Lucerne and the people who were expecting them there.

To shorten the journey I had decided to take my luncheon at the last sitting. When I went into the dining-car, I found only one place vacant, which happened to be at the table of the two Fascist officials. They looked up and handed me the menu in a friendly manner. I thanked them. They had begun a bottle of Chianti before eating. The elder of the two had a sickly, emaciated face and talked in short, precise sentences. The other was sturdy, smiling, and loquacious. They introduced themselves after a few moments, and I told them who I was. The younger one seemed pleased to find that I was a writer and not a traveling salesman or an insurance agent and began to question me about my preference in Italian literature. With that desire to be courteous usual in such conversations, we were soon in agreement about two or three names. They told me that they were going to Lucerne for a few hours, but as neither they nor

I had been there before, our conversation could not make much progress in that direction.

One of the officials, catching sight of the headlines of the paper in my pocket, asked me whether I had read Mussolini's speech at Brindisi.

"Doesn't it seem to you a beautiful moment in Italy?" the younger official asked me.

"Yes," I said, "the country is on its feet."

The official with the drawn face continued to look at me reflectively.

"Do you have any inclination toward the Fascist theory of the State?" he asked me at length, not moving a muscle of his face.

"No," I replied.

"What political ideas, then, do you favor?" he asked me.

"Imagine a man who has just come out of the sea to dry land, looking for a place to lie down and rest. His instinct is more in play than his intelligence. What his conscience is looking for is a faith. Faith is not a matter of reason. The gravest moment for a man is when his plasticity is taking the political shape toward which he is groping. His decision on political matters, in which his conscience is involved, must be made without compulsion or false enthusiasm."

"Why so much delay? It is eminently a process of the will and the intellect, and can be decided quickly."

"Conscience cannot decide it quickly. There are consciences that are lucidity itself, that call a halt and subject things to the scrutiny of reason."

"I believe that an intellectual should feel himself closer to a spiritual conception of life than to a materialistic mirage based on interests and machines."

"An intellectual is nothing. An intellectual is a word. Let's not talk about intellectuals. Let's talk about men."

"Precisely."

"Precisely what?"

"Precisely, man cannot progress by himself, my dear fellow. Man must move forward in the mass, fused bodily with the entire social . . ."

"Which is also a Communist idea."

". . . But beginning its development in an inner, individual sphere and not in a cult of external organizations and elements. Mussolini believes in the moral progress of humanity."

"I have not much belief in a moral progress based upon the adjustment of a people to practical discipline. Let's not confuse the orders. When a man creates or believes genuinely — that is, with an ardent, religious foundation — he is in communication with forces of a superhuman nature and then no human power can matter to him or subjugate him. A cause, yes, a crusade; never a merely political organizing power."

The difference between the spiritual and the temporal interested me deeply.

The young official then spoke about the regime with deep fervor, and I listened to him, assenting unenthusiastically and a little absent-mindedly. The actions of the two men at the next table, who appeared to be Swiss, had begun to attract our attention. One of them, with a blond beard, would cut up a morsel from time to time, put it carefully on his fork, and place it lovingly in his companion's mouth. The latter thanked him, chewed it, and smiled back happily at him. They were eating fruit and ice cream. The man with the beard mentioned in a low voice to his companion that the draft from the window might do him harm.

The waiter brought a bottle of whisky, ordered by the older official. It had been opened and the official protested and told him to bring a fresh one. The waiter went away and returned with an unopened bottle. The young Fascist poured it, added a piece of ice, raised his glass, and toasted: "To the Duce!"

"To the Italian people!" I said.

"It's the same thing," he replied.

We drank.

The two Swiss were now looking at us suspiciously. The bearded man's face was serious and his mouth had a certain sharpness. "Furtive lovers," commented the young Fascist slyly. His black shirt was becoming to him. It greatly heightened the virile pallor of his face. Black shirts were used by the early Fascists as a sign of mourning for the first victims of their undertaking. That civic symbol of grief and will-power, appearing as a common costume, must have been beautiful then. It is easy to imagine how, at the time, that sober, courageous, virile mourning must have been looked up to by the people when they saw how seriously and proudly the few early Fascists wore it. Yes, a masculine type of mourning, a beautiful gesture full of solemnity, it had been at first. Afterward . . .

"During the war," said the elder of the Fascists, "I saw something really extraordinary happen to a youth of that type. Our regiment was quartered at Bolzano in a building where there had been an electric power plant months before. It was in 1918 and we were tired and discouraged. Very bad news kept coming in from the front. At meals and almost constantly it was apparent how difficult it had become to get along with one another. When word arrived that the fighting was getting nearer, the news was very bitter. The dinners at night, when nothing could give us patience any longer (not even the optimism that the sun instils into men assembled in the field), created an atmosphere at table of bloody jokes, vague resentment, and anger. We were bundles of excitement and blind rage. Only one of the thirty men at our table — the youth I speak of — escaped that bitter hectoring, although because of his character he was perhaps the one principally indicated to be victimized. He was a slender youth named Fanelli, refined but affected. Months before, when he first arrived from Rome, where he had held a privileged position in the War Ministry, he had been the butt of our sarcasm and had been persecuted unmercifully by the rest of us. But he had taken our cruel attacks with the same quiet detachment with which he habitually acted. He walked slowly about the old plant and along the white, dusty road that came down from Bolzano, with his cigarette drooping from his mouth, his glance clear and abstracted. His aloofness was cold and aristocratic. There was obviously so much of the feminine in him and so little virility that his tall, twenty-eight-year-old frame seemed the frail body of an adolescent. He bore our jests unblinkingly, as if to keep the smoke from his cigarette out of his eyes — always a fresh one, which he threw away before it was half smoked. His long, well-groomed fingers kept playing with a box of matches. He was in the habit of walking as far as the Cathedral, and the passing soldiers saw him gaze at it from a distance before entering. In the end his strange dignity naturally gave him a position and we all tired of attacking his refractory nature. Gradually, too, we came to see the unique role that he played in the regiment. As our nerves were *à bout de force*, preparations for an attack developed amid great demoralization, indescribable apathy, and a wish to end it all, that revealed itself in an almost sulphurous fear. When we were all lined up to go to the front, exasperated and terrified, Fanelli's presence assumed a special significance: we watched him and noticed his extraordinary imperturbability, his clear eyes slowly glancing about and the cigarette still held between his lips. . . . Back of this attitude lay such a scorn for death, such an indifference to life, and such serenity that his contagious attitude won and calmed us. We felt grateful to him, and when the zero hour sounded and we were running and shouting through the white flagellation, the shrill whistling, and explosions of the shells — we knew that he was there, serene. The superiority to life, death, war, and men inherent in his character has often made me realize that an external display of virility and bravery has nothing whatever to do with that infinitely more precious, rare, and mysterious quality, courage of the soul."

The Fascist youth smiled.

"Yes, but don't you go about propagating the devirilization of man," I said.

"*Prosit!*" toasted the Fascist, and he drank.

An hour later the two soldiers got off at Lucerne. We shook hands, and the elder of the two said to me: "*Addio, caro. Fortuna per lei.*" Once again on the platform he repeated: "*Addio, caro.*" There was something frank and rich in his nature that made him resemble us South Americans. I watched them as they strode along the platform and disappeared into the crowd, with their boots, black shirts, and hand luggage.

At seven o'clock in the morning I arrived at Brussels.

At that hour the station is enveloped in a blue haze. When the noise of the train resounded under the glass and iron roof, I looked out the window. The platform was deserted except for uniformed hotel employees, with the names of their establishments on their caps, who were up early to ensnare customers. Then Ferrier arrived breathlessly.

I was glad to see his pale face and graying temples again — the face and temples of a young man who has lived. Ferrier was an attractive, heavy-set man. The top of his head was darker and glossier than ever and his broad forehead had a faint furrow between the eyebrows that gave his face a sad, sensitive expression. He wore a slate-gray suit and a light-colored cravat. He embraced me and affectionately tapped my face and shoulder.

"What a strange fellow you are! Months without a word from you, then suddenly a telegram and here you are!"

"Yes," I said. "We all have to await the arrival of other messages before we can leave."

"Other messages?"

"Secret orders from God knows whom. Perhaps from as far

away as the depths of our own beings, perhaps from somewhere else. . . ." I took him affectionately by the arm.

"Pure metaphysics," he said. "If you have come to immerse yourself in an ocean of metaphysics you can put those bags back on the train and go away again. What were you doing in Como?"

"Oh, I don't know — wandering."

"Wandering?" he repeated as he watched the man stow my baggage in a large automobile. "Follow our taxi," he said, then turned to me and remarked, smiling:

"You are young and strong. A perfect animal. A metaphysical animal. Literature must be very nourishing."

"It is. Very!"

"Although sometimes indigestible."

His laugh lighted his pale face. But there were dark circles under his eyes, and a yellowish tinge in the corneas. I asked him how he was and what he had been doing.

"The same as so many people: some days a living death; others dying on my feet. . . . When I think that I have reached one place, I find that I am in a totally different one."

"That is metaphysics, too."

"No, that is life, life."

"I'm glad to see you philosophizing at last."

"It's enough for a man's liver to be out of order for him to have a philosophy of life."

He was sitting straight up in the seat.

"Don't say that so contemptuously; the liver is an organ that has discharged aristocratic and mythological functions from the time that the eagle tore at Prometheus' liver to the creation of the great systems of pessimism."

"It is a noble organ," he said. "It is insulted by alcohol. I am too gross for mine, and it never fails to kick up a rumpus and give me a bad time."

The taxi passed the Hôtel de Ville. I looked up at its highest spire and it made the same profound impression on me that it had the first time that I had seen it in a picture. The narrow neighboring streets slept in the foggy atmosphere. The sky was covered with one menacing, endless cloud. The automobile turned into a wide avenue.

Ferrier looked intently at me, smiling and friendly, leaning back in a corner of the car.

"With what percentage of good humor do you manage to live?"

"One per cent," I said.

"That is not too bad."

"No, really it is not bad."

"And the small satisfactions?"

"Which ones?"

"Fame," he said, "success."

"Two hundred million books are written every year by as many authors throughout the world. What can one aspire to?"

"Women?" he said.

"I've had enough of them." (I thought of you. Had that anything to do with it?)

"Men, books?" he said.

"The eternal return. Old things. Old books. Old friends. One always goes back to them."

"It is the moment for great simplification," he said. "I have already accomplished it. I have achieved the greatest simplification, but I am less refined. I am satisfied with human and earthy fruit. Women — wine. No sophistries, no abstract aspirations. I am sinking deeper and deeper into the earth, until I shall have several feet of it over me. Do you see? I never come back. Deeper and deeper, until I sink into the earth — that is my destiny. Never interfere with destiny; it's better not to. . . . Tell me about the most beautiful and interesting woman that you have met since I last saw you. What was she like?"

"She was from Neuilly — young, troubled, and lonely."

"Tell me about her."

"Very lovely. She trembled at everything in life and was afraid of nothing."

"Vibrant," he said. "Wasn't she?"

"Yes," I replied, "vibrant."

The automobile stopped. Ferrier's house was small and had a garden in front which it shared with the adjoining house. It had a clean façade and two large windows hung with muslin curtains. The windows were open and the ends of the white curtains were fluttering in the breeze. The contrast of the white muslin and walls with the fresh, clipped green of the lawn was very pleasant. Near the entrance door a small, scarcely visible brass plaque read: "Dr. Ferrier, Medical Clinic."

I was stretched out on the bed, smoking, when Ferrier came in after breakfast. He wore a reddish-brown smoking-jacket and had a pipe in his mouth. The cheerful room, which was soon filled with its strong, pungent aroma, overlooked the left wing of the garden and the lawn. Its only furniture was a bed without head-board, a dark, brilliantly rubbed writing-table, a sofa, and a low, gray book-shelf that ran along the entire length of one wall, rising in the center to form a chest of drawers. Above the book-shelves hung an old engraving. My typewriter was on the table by my books. Beside it the head of a young Russian intellectual, Mayakovsky, hung from one of the vertical panels of the bookcase. It caught my attention. Ferrier noticed the direction of my gaze and said:

"One of the victims."

Then he added slowly and reflectively:

"Or merely one of the heroes whose sacrifice was necessary in order to show that Russia does not offer a suitable climate today for poetry. Great poetry comes from the rebellion of a fettered soul. A new revolution is necessary in Russia. Perhaps its prophets are even now in the making on the banks of the Volga."

"Mayakovsky's poetry was quite inferior," I said.

"His written poetry," he asserted. "His written poetry was bad."

"Was there any other?"

"Of course: his life, his death. His suicide in the hotel."

"There is a bit of sentimental pornography in all that. I don't care for it," I replied.

Ferrier burst out laughing, as though I were joking. He walked over to the book-shelf and showed me a button concealed among the little carved ornaments on the chest of drawers.

"When you are bored," he said, "turn this radio on."

Then he came over and stretched out on the sofa. His feet were long and narrow, his shin-bones slender, and his legs delicate. His face was lined with extreme fatigue. He was a solitary man, as men with a capacity for strong friendship are generally fated to be. I noticed that he had aged since I had known him in London.

"Well, what would you like to do and see while you are in Brussels, and how would you like to live?" he asked.

"I am entirely in your hands," I replied. "I shall try to do a little work in the mornings."

He lay pensive a moment, sprawled out on the sofa playing with his white-gold chain.

"It will be a little depressing for you to do what I should like to do. I have told you I want only two things. I'll show you women."

"Good enough," I said. "Show me women."

"Frightening women. Women who have died but are still in the world as though they had lost their train and were waiting for the next one."

"All right. That's a human situation. It may be interesting."

"No, it's not. It's something worse — a dehumanized situation."

"It can't help being interesting and instructive, to observe people who have survived themselves."

He rang and a sallow youth in a white coat appeared. "Cognac," said Ferrier to him. The boy looked at me with preternaturally sad eyes, as if tacitly seeking help from me, then turned on his heel and disappeared.

There was a clinking of bottles in the next room, and the boy reappeared carrying a tray. The glasses were tall, as if for a long refreshment.

"Just a drop," I said, "only a drop, please."

"No," said Ferrier to the boy, "we never serve only a drop. Serve the gentleman what a guest should drink to celebrate his arrival."

"Enough," I said. The boy continued to pour, embarrassed by the contradictory orders.

"The worst would be for you to do what I like and then complain."

During the pause that followed while we raised our glasses, I could hear the sound of footsteps in the house next door. There must have been a man walking back and forth in the room alongside of us. I was astonished at the thinness of the partition and realized that even our conversation must be audible.

Presently, Ferrier was called to his office, I arranged my things, shaved, bathed, and put on a light suit and blue shirt. Out of curiosity, I switched on the radio and listened to a few German words uttered in a preaching voice. I snapped it off again and stooped down to look over the titles of the books on the shelves. It has always given me pleasure to make friends with books in a new house. There I found the three volumes of Burton's *Anatomy of Melancholy*, a volume about Gratian, and George Gronau's book on Titian. Two or three anthologies of poetry and not a novel except *Ulysses*, with its eight hundred pages of the diffuse journey, musings, and monologues of Stephen Dedalus. The last pages had not been cut. Perhaps if it had been the *Portrait of the Artist as a Young Man,* Ferrier would have cut the pages, but not of *Ulysses. Ulysses* is too chaotic for an orderly person to venture into.

Ferrier showed me his city. He liked to share its rich poetry. He made an ideal guide, as he had communed a great deal in his leisure hours with its weather-stained walls, worn flagstones, and sculptured porticos, and even with the air that seemed contemporary with them. Brussels admitted him to its deepest secrets.

I told him that I was much interested in catching its major rhythms in the movement of a carved altar, of a street, or of a system of human ideas or expression. I recalled a very true remark, that all that mattered was the fervor, *"qui ne se prend pas pour fin,"* and that the attitude of the creating mind has more to do with the religious feeling of an artistic object than the nature of the object itself.

The only echoes that reached me from Buenos Aires were weekly air-mail letters, a few bundles of newspapers, and now and again a stray item about Argentina lost on the back page of a Belgian newspaper. These scraps of news, casually inserted in the Brussels press, were generally false and gave a totally wrong impression of our country. But in one of my letters your figure appeared and moved again. It was from a person who knew what it might and did contain for me.

It was at the beginning of winter. People were accustomed to seeing you cross the parks in the northern part of the city with your two sons. You walked ahead with the eldest. Behind came the nurse with the younger boy, the one with fair hair and clear, intelligent eyes. For some months past, Cárdenas had been committing serious "errors." His political ambitions had become boundless, and acute observers soon discovered about him those typical go-betweens that wheel like slow-moving eagles over men of influence who are ready to throw their scruples to the winds and allow themselves to be bought outright. Cárdenas had been born for certain types of intoxication, and to him the idea of his own capacity for promoting alignments, combinations, and pacts was as heady as strong wine. Disgrace hovered over your house. You were afraid for the man to whom your name was tied, who wanted power and money in order to be able to toss them up triumphantly with both hands, yet your sorrow for him was even stronger than your fear or your contempt.

Many nights Cárdenas brought the vultures together in the library of your home. They had Saxon names, talked cynically, and laughed loudly. Many of them came for cognac and coffee with their modishly dressed wives. At first you were cold and polite to them.

One night you found yourself face to face with one of your husband's visitors — one of the buyers. He was the manager of a powerful foreign enterprise — a perfect European, with his expensive but affectedly austere get-up: dark clothes, black shoes, carefully shaven face, polished fingernails, unctuous manner, and slow, persuasive, measured gestures. . . . He spoke with the terseness and delicacy of a smooth ruffian. You were filled with a sudden wave of disgust and perceived behind his elaborate courtesy the scorn, which he could not altogether conceal, that he felt for the people he was buying.

Let us say it frankly; in a few months, Cárdenas, the friend of deputies, and the near deputy of one of the minor parties, was — I hesitate to utter the word to you — for sale to any foreign enterprise that came his way. This he called "using his influence." You watched the proportions of his corruption increase. So blatant and cold was the established system that you were overwhelmed with shame and nausea. One day, you said to him: "I don't want to see those people any more; I don't want to meet them." Cárdenas looked at you with that mixture of irresponsible childishness and astute suavity which had become habitual with him. He said nothing, but resented your puritanical, selfish refusal to help him with his "career." "As you like," he said carelessly. In his own childish, irresponsible way, he had thought that he could buy you too and dazzle you with his brilliance.

You withdrew into yourself, became more elusive, sterner, and more discouraged. That ostentatious, rotten atmosphere made you tremble with indignation. Your house, the city, the whole country were infected with merchants whose pockets were stuffed with equivocal propositions written on fine stationery and who scornfully commented on the "diplomatic malleability" of certain Argentines.

Cárdenas redoubled his politeness toward you and solicitously urged you to take trips to the country or to the seashore. He boasted as discreetly as possible that he had been able to build up his own income to equal yours. "Everything of yours, to the last cent, continues to be entirely your own," he said. You raised your eyes, looked at him, and could not believe that his mask of thoughtful solemnity could hide such utter callousness.

Every night you talked and laughed with your sons to cover up the grief which you kept pent up within you, too proud to talk about it even to your own father. One morning in July, on your wedding anniversary, you received a gigantic basket of royal orchids, crisp and still dripping moisture. You ordered them sent back to the shop from which they had come. At breakfast Cárdenas received you with an air of interrogation and friendly astonishment. "I don't want them. I don't want them," you repeated, and felt like shouting it. You forced yourself to be calm and went out for a walk. Ah, those walks through Buenos Aires with which you calmed your rivers of anguish! You walked, gazing with emotion at the heart of the great city, at the old houses, bridges, historic residences, and gardens. Your eyes embraced the native background of so many things Argentine. You realized that all this would be sold, that in one way or another it was all being sold.

30

In the evening we went out for a walk. Except for the boulevard du Midi, the city was badly lighted, which gave the old buildings a still gloomier and more opaque appearance. We were a long way from the somber, green, wooded section — the pride of the people of Brussels — that extends almost to the Botanical Garden. The streets which we followed were modest and unlighted. They had quaint, amusing names like Wolves Pit, Butter Street, Whoredom Street, and Mountain of Garden Herbs.

Here and there alongside of simple old houses, twelfth-century towers raised their delicate spires. The name of "Brussels of the Watchmakers" was understandable when one saw those hands pointing bleakly toward the sky. Ferrier showed me buildings and places, told me their names and some bloody or sentimental tradition connected with them. On the sidewalks we elbowed drab-looking, solitary people in threadbare attire. A tall woman suddenly crossed the street, opened a heavy door, shot us a sharp, suspicious glance, and disappeared into a dark vestibule. Not only Brussels but Ghent and Ypres and all of Flanders from the Scheldt to Brabant has a depressed, dead atmosphere in the autumn. There still clings to it something of the medieval desolation of man on earth and his fear of hell not yet redeemed by the joy of living and the natural mutation of time. Above, God, intangible; below, lingering torture. Man, in his infinite solitude lost among the houses, his fascinated gaze fixed upon illimitable space; his desolation saturating the streets and buildings with its obscure essence.

Beyond the Place de la Bourse shone the lights of a little restaurant. On a green sign I read the word: *Rumpelmonde*. From the outside we could hear music. We entered. The maître d'hôtel was a tall man, dressed in a knee-length, Nile-green. Cossack coat, with rows of cartridges on his chest and short boots on his feet. He hurried across the room to greet Ferrier, bowed, and pulled out our chairs for us.

"Hasn't Blanche Alost come?" Ferrier asked him.

The maître shook his head and smiled, showing his yellowish, tobacco-stained teeth.

"She will surely come," he said, "but later."

The room was enormous, and deserted except for the musicians and two couples at distant tables. A smell of burnt brandy floated in the air. The decorations were bizarre.

"You must meet Blanche Alost," said Ferrier.

"Who is she?" I asked him.

"Mere words are inadequate. You must know her," he said. "You have to see her."

But Blanche Alost was not there, and the maître d'hôtel returned again, bowed courteously, and had the waiter bring for our inspection a bottle lying in a straw cradle. The bottle was covered with cobwebs and on the torn label the word *Burgundy* was barely legible. Ferrier nodded; the maître beckoned to the waiter, who withdrew with the bottle. The orchestra attacked a Tchaikovsky number. The young musicians played smoothly, like a magician producing something sweet and evanescent with his bare hands.

Slowly Rumpelmonde's was filling up. The patrons obviously belonged to the wealthy middle class. Their faces reflected the vain satisfaction felt by mediocre, humdrum people at the flattery of the maître d'hôtel, the brilliance of the luxurious chandeliers, and the illusion of being for a few moments influential personages and epicureans. The heavy, parsimonious-looking gentleman who came in with his wife and daughter might have been a corporation president. His daughter glanced about languidly and his wife ravenously; the heavy gentleman looked around him with immense self-satisfaction.

At that moment, three young women burst into the room from the revolving door and suddenly stopped. They stood for a moment near the first tables, observing the room. They were nearly of the same height, very beautiful, bareheaded, and had their wraps crossed over their filmy frocks, like bandoliers. The luxurious air that certain women always possess clung to them.

Ferrier raised his arm and held it up until they noticed him. Then they advanced rapidly to our table and he introduced us. We shook hands, smiled at each other; and they sat down, filling the air with their strong perfumes. Seen near by, none of the three was really beautiful; but all were very skillful in the use of cosmetics and expertly called attention only to their most favorable features. Thus the attraction of their faces could not but be instantaneous.

Blanche Alost was one of them. She was a pale young woman of medium height, dressed in a lilac-colored gown with very black hair combed smoothly back. She laid her hand bag on the table and stretched her arms in a gesture of elegant expansiveness.

"I'm hungry," she said. "I'm dying of hunger. Ferrier, please order something for me."

Her speech was rapid and very mannered. She leaned back against the felt-covered seat that ran along the wall and looked at me steadily. I guessed the order of the questions that presented themselves to her mind, as well as the answers that she probably gave them. Ferrier was bantering another of the girls. They were both younger than Blanche Alost and their hair was tinted a reddish shade. One of them could not quite hide, even by careful make-up, a small scar along the edge of her upper lip. Blanche asked me when I had arrived. "Only this morning," I replied. There was a pause during which she continued to watch me carefully but unobtrusively.

An entertainer in full evening dress sprang into the middle of the floor. He stretched out his arms in an affected choreographic attitude and waited, before beginning the dance, for his partner to join him. Blanche smiled and waved at the partner. For a few seconds I studied her thin lips. A very fine film of rouge covered them. They were attractive. At moments of laughter they suddenly widened. About her slightly rouged cheeks her face had the color of pale ivory.

The brasses sounded vibrantly and the three violins produced a dizzy, strident combination. The entertainer held his partner in the air by her waist and one foot. In that position he pirouetted rapidly. Scattered applause was heard. The three girls at our table began to eat, and Ferrier poured a glass of white wine for Blanche. She smiled slyly and thrust forward her small well-molded bosom, on which a gardenia lay.

"What a complicated concoction!" she said, examining the steaming dish they had just brought her. "I am starving, but I would rather have a couple of fried eggs than all these fussy dishes."

"Well," said another of the girls, named Alice Bomekens, "I would soon be neurasthenic if I had to limit myself to the unbearable monotony of home cooking. I need to have something set before me every day on which the chef has lavished all his inventive genius. The reverse of simplicity is my rule."

"In such things, of course, but I suspect only in them," put in Ferrier.

"And in other things too, silly," answered the girl; "otherwise life would be too boring. . . ."

While the bottles of white wine and then of red were being emptied, I danced twice with Blanche. They were slow, syncopated dances, and I felt her body tense and then abandoned against my own. She lowered her head until it almost rested on my shoulder and allowed herself to drift, her eyes very wide open, absent-mindedly taking in the guests at the tables, who were eating, laughing, and chatting gaily. Her conversation was limited to comments on current topics, but occasionally she talked at greater length and told witty reminiscences. One could sense that basically she was warm and passionate.

By eleven o'clock we had all drunk too much. The maître d'hôtel began to spare himself the customary bows and flattery when he came to take our orders. The three girls consumed four boxes of Muratti cigarettes, and bottles of Scotch whisky. Ferrier insisted on explaining to one of them that the Soviet theories about love have not changed the masculine bias for the opposite sex one bit, and that the freedom of women in Russia has only increased jealousy and other primitive reactions. The girls protested, shaking their heads energetically. Blanche was suddenly moved to unexpected frankness and gave me a lively account of the circumstances of her marriage to a Viennese nobleman, a marriage which had later hung like a black cloud over her life.

"My husband came from an old Liége family with connections in Austria," she said. "I met him by accident one night, leaving Sacher's Café, and married him two months later because I liked his deep voice and air of authority. He was a domineering man and gave you the feeling that with his help you could conquer the world. That suited my character. We went to live in a house in the gloomiest quarter of the city. But we faced the future optimistically and the first four months of our married life passed agreeably, although we had few tastes in common. But it is the little pleasures that separate more than the big ones. My husband began to like to spend his nights at the Kursaal in the company of some Rumanian dancers. That disgusted me."

"Understandably," said Ferrier, his eyes shining ironically.

"But I was a spineless creature," continued Blanche. "My life was as inert as the water in this glass. . . . For three years that seemed a lifetime I lived like a clod of earth in an atmosphere of sterility and repugnance. I came out of it an embittered woman. My husband turned into an alcoholic and was confined to a sanatorium in a critical condition. I couldn't face it any longer and fled. For two years I lived in Zürich, returning all the letters that came from his family. But in a sense my real life was over.

It had been a failure and could not be recommenced. It is un-believable what a sudden change an event of that sort can make in our lives. The only advantage in having had such a destructive experience is, as Nietzsche said about death, that you don't have to go through it again. Out of that inertia came the determination to live only for the day and to burn life down to its ultimate livable portion, since it is obvious that a part of me no longer enters into anything and that I am living a very superficial life."

I leaned forward and studied her from a different angle. Suddenly I recalled Mercedes Miró.

"Is passion no longer possible for you?"

"Passion? How horrible! A passion would last, and that is precisely what I don't want. I want combustion — to love excessively. Do you know what it is to love to excess?"

"In Buenos Aires I knew a woman who was very much like you, but she defined it in the opposite sense."

"An Englishwoman?"

"No, an Argentine."

"Then she must have been different from me."

"Why?"

"Because she came from another country!"

"But you don't believe that geography determines temperament?"

"Of course," she said. "I have no doubt of it. On this soil nothing in us commands, everything is ordered. Geography or time or chance, whichever it is. We are much more than predestined; we are predetermined!"

Like Hamlet, I wanted to say reflectively: "Words, words, words"; but I refrained and poured some more whisky into her glass. *Ne s'interrompant que pour prier*, she drank with something that could have been called passion, except for the fact that she did not even taste what she was drinking. If someone had poured sherry into her whisky glass she would not have said a word. Her eyes shone. From time to time she nodded to acquaintances at other tables. A young man approached our table and greeted her effusively. When he withdrew, Blanche turned back to me. I knew that she had lied and that she was full of passion.

"That man," she said, "has a magnificent way of carrying his head. He has been laying siege to me for months and says that I am driving him mad. The day that I give in to him, his magnificent manner of holding his head will disappear. The best thing about men is the dignity that living alone gives them. In general, it can be said that when they are multiplied by two, they lose a great deal. Don't you think so?"

I felt very tired and wanted to go to bed, having slept badly the night before. Ferrier was looking at Blanche with his motionless, somber, heavy-lidded eyes. She kept talking, fidgeting in her chair, and gesturing with her long, bare arms. The three women never stopped talking.

Finally, when it was very late, Ferrier asked for the bill, and we all left Rumpelmonde's. Each of the girls was to be dropped at her house. We halted a taxi and Ferrier asked Blanche tartly:

"Are you still living where you were yesterday?"

"Exactly," she replied. "But first let's leave these young things at Lamont 3."

Streets, squares, and more streets. We were driving with three elegant and intoxicated women; their breath, heavy with alcohol, mingled with their perfumes — those most in vogue, Lanvin and Coty. We drove along without talking, having reached that dead point beyond which our small talk could make no further progress.

One of the girls was monotonously humming a popular foxtrot. In the back of the car Blanche had laid her head back against the seat and closed her eyes. Ferrier and I were on either side of her; the two girls sat on folding seats in front of us.

Ferrier continued to glare angrily at Blanche. Suddenly she started up.

"But what's this!" she cried. "You people are all used up. . . ."

"Used up and available," said one of the girls.

"Shame on you! How can you waste an instant of life? Let's be anything, charlatans, mad, anything you like, except a parcel of mortal bores."

3 I

On Sundays we journeyed in a merry group to the outskirts of the city. Night after night during the week we went from restaurant to restaurant, stopping occasionally at a café. The two girls seemed to be protégées of Blanche's; they had a high regard for her judgment and kept watching her out of a corner of their eye to surprise any gesture of acquiescence or disapproval. During the day, except for the hour that we went out for our lunch, Ferrier and I stayed in his house in the rue Leopold I. It was a quiet street, seldom disturbed by motor-cars.

I spent hours stretched out on the bed, reading. My room was very pleasant with all its recent books, the majority of which I knew by reputation but had not yet read. To me the literature of the present century was a sadly empty well. With the exception of Proust and Joyce — in spite of their terrible defects — and of Kafka, everything seemed to me minor literature; that is, national literature that does not rise above its peculiar limitations. I was convinced that the complexity of our world demanded a complex literature: the old system of narrative and unilateral notation of episodes is a medium that has necessarily been abolished; the preceptive and rhetorical principles of Aristotle have today ceased to rule; the present stormy, human autumn demands to be represented by a man in whom, like that complex atmosphere, a multitude of divergent and contradictory forces live, whose coexistence is recorded by

184

words forced into no synthetic formula. Today's art cannot be simple, standardized, and balanced; it must be an art like a hurricane. That is, militant explosiveness surrounding a central germ, rather than elaborate craft and nice balance. Have we, perhaps, reached the end of one rhetoric and the beginning of another? Musical snuffboxes, beautiful contrivances to enchant in small doses, Shelley's skylark, and lyrical delicacy have all reached the end of their tether. At certain historical periods the art of peoples has been apologetic about the national grandeur from which they sprang; at other times, in some early epic that intuitively revealed a national harmony, it has been prophetic. Today Hamlet's phrase has again become fitting: "the time is out of joint. . . ." All great art must now keep before it the mission of discovering how to rearticulate it. This can be called a crusade, a forced march in rough weather. Art today is militant or nothing.

At noon, Ferrier appeared in his white gown, holding a cocktail shaker in one hand and two glasses in the other. He set them on the table, opened the nickel shaker, and carefully filled the glasses. Then he came over and handed me a cocktail. This daily operation amused me.

"First Bacchic interlude," he would say.

Every day he put on a linen gown as spotless and newly ironed as if contact with illness and blood had never soiled it. His dark skin grew daily darker.

"You are not grateful to me for these attentions," he would say when we had had our cocktails.

"Of course I am," I answered with a laugh. "I appreciate them very much."

"No, you don't. Blanche is right, you are an indifferent brute."

He carefully filled his own glass. When I asked him anything about his patients, he always avoided the subject.

"I have been for hours wrapped up in a fog of fevers, aches, and complaints. I have a right to breathe a little when I am away from it. Don't ask me to tell you how I explored a lachrymal duct or what ointments I prescribed for a dorsal eczema. It would be too stupid."

Hardly pausing, and with sincere regret, he added:

"I am sorry that you are bored. Brussels is a dull, grimy city at this season. . . ."

"Don't be an idiot, I'm not bored. On the contrary, I am really enjoying seeing you and your friends. You are forthright people."

"Yes," he said, "but it's a vicious circle! Life has us surrounded, hemmed in. When we dream of escaping we find ourselves up against a stone wall or a yawning gulf."

"Doesn't everyone live that way?"

"Not people who have found themselves," objected Ferrier, "people who have given sense and unity to their lives."

"But they are the heroes of the white war that the world is now fighting. . . ."

"True, and we are the common soldiers."

"That's it."

"Cannon-fodder."

"Perhaps awaiting our moment for heroism."

"Rot!" said Ferrier. "Moment for heroism! What does that mean? Moment for heroism! Are we to fight for the Chinese?"

He continued to drink for a long while, not saying anything, sitting on the arm of the sofa with his back against the bookshelves. Having a warm feeling for his nature, in which I found a background of embitterment, I tried to discover the reason for his moral ailment. But he closed up and hid his head like an octopus. He was a genuine product of defeated Europe turning around in the circle of its own bewilderment. But back of it there was something else.

32

O<small>NE</small> night I went for a walk in the neighborhood of the Exchange. My thoughts sped back to Argentina and to my hero — Juan Argentino — caught in a morass from which he must extricate himself to keep his sanity, and even to keep alive. The true map of Argentina appeared in my mind, and across it I distinctly saw flowing in the distance a river of muddy water, the river of the pit. It meandered silently through the great capital city. On its bosom it carried the "buyers" to the offices of men of influence and power. With abominable frequency, the river came to the door of some opulent senatorial gentleman. By the time I returned that night to Ferrier's house, it had reached the home of a certain Dr. Larguirós, whose activities I was again describing:

"The honorable gentleman is leaving his office in Buenos Aires. It is seven o'clock. In the elevator three neighbors, three obscure lawyers, doff their hats diffidently. In this country everyone is docile and restrained in the presence of an 'honorable.' It is as if he were the prophet Moses. Who would dare to importune Moses when he has democratically deigned to enter an elevator? This honorable gentleman feels himself like Moses as his elevator descends the eight floors that separate him from the ground. He growls, but smilingly, as he leaves the elevator first, in deference to their unanimous invitation.

"He decides to walk. That he should walk that day is a tribute to the city. He feels in its lights, and faces, and even in its stones, that the city is grateful to him for it. The elastic, almost rigid tread with which he makes his way through the crowds that jam the sidewalk of Cathedral Square at this evening hour is a sign of the race to which he belongs — the race of the great, decisive, and eminent actors in life. As a philosopher — let the word be used this once! — has said of Mirabeau, Senator Larguirós is *par excellence* the busy man, never the preoccupied one. What is important to him is to act. There is no greatness but in action. Action, or rather realism. If he did not scorn those miserable slaves called intellectuals — worse than the proletarians and worse than the lower bourgeoisie, whose destiny they share — he would sit down and write a tract entitled *On Realism*. Not reality — realism. Reality is a hypothesis, realism a system. The strongest system is that which affords the greatest promise of survival, the most energetic source of power and leadership. He who holds the key to realism can easily dispense with reality and forget it, for realism is *more reality* than true reality. Dr. Larguirós is realistic. His whole being is realistic; his flesh is the flesh of realism, and his intellect the reason of realism. The phrase with which he opens and closes the discussions that he wishes to settle dogmatically and beyond appeal is: 'We must be realistic.' Confronted with that remark, elementary natures remain abashed, and realism scores again.

"He turns into the short, brilliant canyon, the Diagonal, luxurious with lights and colossal store windows. In life there are only two alternatives — eat or be eaten. Poor fools, those who are caught napping! 'Not at all' — a poor fool has just bumped into him and is begging his pardon, although it is the poor fool who nearly fell; that's the way one must act — say: 'Not at all,' and go on! He owes all his power, authority, and prestige in the most important circles of the nation to this categorical method of dealing with affairs. In the vaults of the bank he is passing he has sufficient stocks to make any ambitious person happy; and in that one yonder — and thanks to his influence and reputation with the government, the ten stories of that insurance company rise there, massive and imposing, their thousand windows illuminated. He also owes the distinction of his recent election as president of an exclusive club to his determination to permit no slightest vacillation, no slightest pause, no slight-

188

est delay in his progress. . . . He smiles at the reflection that there is a whole unfortunate group in society that fuddles through life. These the current drags down. Doubt is the — not a bad phrase! — doubt is the paralysis of conscience. A strong conscience never doubts. A strong conscience forges ahead, conceals its small hesitations, advances, and decides things according to its own will. And if there is one slight failure, what difference does that make when measured by so many successes?

"He walks another six blocks, opening a passage for himself through the crowds that swarm like flies over the whole width of the street without vehicles — Florida Street. The deferential greetings that he hears are the sign of what he represents nationally. Internationally, too, for many boards of directors, nobles, and gentlemen know his name as that of a good co-operator in Argentine affairs and in the greatness and progress of their own enterprises.

"What a grand emotion — power, that deep, broad influence extending in every direction, to every corner, office, and employee throughout the country! To sign a card and have it instantly swing open the heaviest doors — can one conceive of a more sovereign pleasure in a democracy? Scarcely two weeks ago he agreed with Gehens upon the details of his action as influential intermediary with the politicians. Gehens is an extraordinary man. He speaks as God would wish and takes off his hat when he passes a church. He wears patent-leather shoes, modernized by severe cloth over the instep, and his clothing is always impeccable. He expresses himself with such perfection that one is inclined to overlook the real meaning of his words and quietly accept them. He has been in Argentina for ten years and knows every man in the country like the wrinkles on his own hands — the pale, polished hands of a lay abbot or of a monarch. . . . A personality, beyond the shadow of a doubt. Above all, what a way of treating the most delicate matters, even with the humblest person, to whom he gives the feeling that he is essential to the compromise! That dropping of the phrase: 'Just say yes and I will close my ears and eyes and remain only grateful to you for your good will!' . . . Then from his strong-box issues the mythical flow of checks, the white river whose current drags along with it, at giddy speed, chiefs, deputies, and councilors. . . . What skill and kindliness of manner! He is a Mazarin who would add luster to any cabinet or to the ante-chambers of the Vatican! It is a pleasure to deal with him, especially when one is alert enough to catch oneself in time and not lose all the advantage. Which of the two was the more successful in the interview a fortnight ago? But that is ancient history! The doctor is looking at the pavement as he cuts across the narrow street. This very day he has exerted his influence by making a few simple marks on stamped paper which have been of decisive importance in settling a transaction for which he will receive from abroad — as advance payment on a magnificent gentleman's agreement — eighty thousand pesos. This will give him greater influence, and make it possible for Adela to build the summer house that he had promised her, on their property at Rosario de la Frontera. How lively she is! A jewel! He will also get one of those new Cadillac models. There is no doubt that it has the most lordly appearance of any car.

" 'Humph!' At the entrance to the club he almost ran into that highway robber Dr. Laplace, who recently sent him a bill for twenty thousand pesos for the operation on the little girl — a mere appendectomy! He should have talked instead with one of the company's surgeons, who would have asked three thousand pesos, and the girl would have been sitting up in her arm-chair within the week, reading the *Ladies' Home Journal* or one of Maurois's novels . . . By the way, now he can get her the book she wants from the library — a whole week has gone by and each time he has forgotten it. 'Hello!' Well, thank God, he did not stop to be bored by that stupid co-religionist, that blockhead who wants to purify the Conservative Party from within. To purify, if you please, when the essential characteristic of a conservative party is precisely not to change its form! What idiots reformers are!

"The library is already full. New faces. Who are they? — Ah, let's see what that German, Zubiaur, is saying. What? Prating about his ancestors? Why, bless me! Yes, of course. Ah, no, no, no! That branch of the Juan Crisóstomo Rivera family has no connection with the Rivera family that boasts of the Delfín who coined the famous phrase: 'Argentina will live above all rapacity in its conception of the continent' — Zubiaur's forebear on the maternal side. No, of course not. They are other Riveras. Riveras from Chile. Worthy people, but not brilliant.

'Well, librarian, I want something for my daughter. I don't know. Some little novel — by Maurois if you have it. No! What do you mean, Disraeli! That must be worthless trash. All that one needs to know about Disraeli can be found in Larousse. Just give me some little novel.'

" 'No, my dear Zubiaur, don't talk to me about that! Haven't you read my article on "The Role of Foreign Directors in the National Greatness"? It is all said there. That is unwillingness to understand the spirit of the question, the key to the whole affair. Such lack of realism! . . . You can't comment on the matter unless you're in the know, wait and you will see — foreign capital is the only possibility, so to speak, instrumental in the matter. We must encourage it. Then you will see what the country will gain.'

"With his carefully pomaded hair, his faultless chestnut-colored suit, and the flower in his buttonhole, Señor Larguirós, standing by the magazine table, as erect as a forty-year-old, remembered all the ancient readers who used to frequent the reading-room during his brief tenure as minister. It was a pleasure to see his rosy, shining cheeks light up as he smiled in his imperturbable, stiff, somewhat vain contentment. But as he was leaving with a book in his hand, someone mentioned something unpleasant to him about his nephew who had just graduated from the law school. He was displeased by the comment and his lips twisted with impatience and anger. 'That won't last,' he said. 'He is very young and inexperienced.'

"At the street corner he hailed a taxi and drove over the asphalted avenue, crowded with heavy traffic at this hour, to his French palace in Rodríguez Peña Street.

"While he was waiting in the library for dinner to be served, he opened two letters that lay on his desk, and felt happy. Adela had got over her brusque manner and the irrepressible weeping spells that her gastric ulcers had caused months before. The girls had a little more sense too. And there on the silk damask-covered wall, a few feet above his head, hung a parchment crowded with signatures, attesting the universal respect in which his present career as a counselor was developing and would continue to develop. What more could he wish for? And now he held in his hands an invitation to attend the Congress of Jurists at Lima, and they had informed him in confidence that, because of his 'good repute,' he was the candidate for its presiding officer.

"Soon after Adela came in, they sat down in the sumptuous Louis XVI dining-room. She and he presided at either end of the table. A brilliant group of young people occupied the remaining places. The girls had invited Jimmy Arguedas and Jorge Cavalcanti that night. They were merrily telling about an unexpected encounter that they had had, and shrieked and laughed excessively. Adela stood up and comically kissed her husband when he announced that she could order the new car. The young people applauded noisily.

"At ten o'clock his nephew arrived, late as always. He was a modest, agreeable lad. He had to begin with the larded ribs of beef. The discipline of the table forbade the previous courses' being served to him. He added his congratulations, but found the master of the house cold and silent. He was seated at Señor

Larguirós's left. In view of his uncle's attitude, he devoted himself without a word to eating.

" 'I have never liked to insist on things which seem to me obvious,' the honorable gentleman said with an air of displeasure and uneasiness, lowering his voice so that only his nephew could hear him. 'But when certain things are forgotten it is incumbent upon someone to recall them. I have heard more comments at the club about your declarations concerning a new investigation, and your attitude of rebellion against certain political and social habits which are identified with the very marrow of our family tradition. You are putting yourself, and perhaps all of us, in a situation which I can only characterize as ridiculous. What is this grotesque talk about a new order? New order indeed! Today at the club they were discussing that latest assertion of yours, in favor of a revolutionary regulation of affairs. I must say that your views seem to me not only false but much more harmful than you realize. We belong to a class of people who take pride in wearing a clean shirt. Our place is beside our own people. Any other attitude is rash, and disgraceful. Young men learn this late.'

"The youth gazed at his uncle's unsullied linen shirt, flawlessly cut by Edouard and Butler, which, together with his hoarse, solemn, senatorial manner of speech, was ineradicably associated in the young man's mind with a stream of pounds sterling, a deluge of contracts, 'gentlemen's money,' and a mire of influence. He choked on his mouthful of stuffed tomato. Could an incontestable right exist — yes, there it was under his eyes — to frown and display a moderately ruffled composure? The human face sometimes docilely masks infamous operations. . . . The young man abandoned the theme because he was truly sincere and truly ashamed."

33

I WAS allowing life to grow naturally in me at that period, not wanting to disturb the slow process of ripening that my nature needed. I let life deal out whatever it had in store for me: triviality, usefulness, good fortune or bad. My expectation, desire, and hunger were insatiable.

But there is a rapid life and a slow life. The slow life we live within ourselves, far from the swift, external one. The slow life stores up in us strange, deep cravings, fatigues, and aspirations — as the poet Whitman said — to meet the night, storm, hunger, ridicule, accidents, and rebuffs as calmly and unperturbed as the trees and the animals. "Passive, receptive, silent." That, and what it deposits within us is the foil to so much artificial agitation.

Whenever I was alone, my mind reverted to these thoughts. Nor, to tell the truth, did being with Ferrier and Blanche Alost, or going out with them to a café, bar, or night-club, modify the direction of my reflections.

"Man's struggle is more terrible today," I thought, "than ever before. Everything in the world suggests artifice, and death — not life. Life and art and the relations between things are false; and the deceptive appearance of co-operation that the world offers is likewise false. They are all figures in a confused jumble of additions and subtractions. But one is a part of this life and confusion. How is one to break one's shackles and detach oneself from it without becoming a sterile fragment of humanity, since from a human point of view isolation is sterility?"

I kept thinking this as I sipped my morning coffee, with the newspapers lying open before me on the bed. On the radio next door I heard a Negro spiritual; the music swelled, melted, and poured its fluid power of love, enrichment, delight, and surrender over everything that received it: human ear, plant, or atmosphere. Beauty, fertility, vibration, and exaltation for everything touched by that music.

I felt that I wanted this too; wanted the human phenomenon throughout the world to resemble this form of love. Every man like a song — demonstrating his worth by the intensity of his vibration, by the rich fullness of his tone, by his power to communicate and to leaven. But can all this be achieved by bringing men together, by hearing their confessions, and teaching them to mistrust only themselves?

No one is ripe for this yet. Faith is not yet ripe.

"If my mission is to write," I thought, "why do I have this deep aversion and depression when the sheets of paper are lying in front of me to be covered laboriously with symbols — symbols that will cost me blood? And if my mission is not that, what is it?"

I felt that at that hour many men must be asking themselves the same question.

I sat down at the table and sipped my coffee, slowly savoring its delicious, warm aroma. I waited, with my pen poised, for my ideas to take shape, for a force and a conviction to come that my hand could not fail to obey.

For an hour or two I sat quietly at the table, with my back against the chair, thinking. Suddenly I leaned forward while my pencil traced absurd marks on the white pages, on the first of which ten lines had been written and then scratched out. For many minutes I thought that I was going to fill a page and make some headway. I was filled with sudden joy and enthusiasm; my whole body curved over my right hand, the hand which at that moment no longer hesitated, but wrote furiously. This sudden light however was followed by an eclipse. The intrusion of a new protagonist — a skeptical cloud — on the scene unfolding in my room was enough to cause my mind to flag, my hand to stop, and my conscience to demand enlightenment and insinuate its disagreement and hesitation. This hesitation separated it from the material that it was about to dominate. Bitterness, revulsion, and keen disappointment succeeded my former joy.

The night before, as we were leaving a picture theater where we had seen an excellent Joan of Arc, Ferrier had said to me: "Tomorrow you will meet an interesting character, an Italian, anti-Fascist *émigré* named Orio Scariol. I have invited him to have lunch with us especially to meet you."

At half past twelve we met the young Italian at the restaurant. He was thirty years old, had a square jaw and keen eyes, and wore a heavy gray tweed suit and a black bow-tie. He pressed my hand firmly. Ferrier, always eager to put friends into quick rapport, did not hesitate to describe to each of us the peculiarities of the other. With a cordial nod of his head, Scariol interrupted him.

"It's very simple, I have no story. I was studying architecture in Milan thirteen years ago. I should have been killed at that time by the supporters of Signor Mussolini's *Popolo d'Italia*, but I was too young. Old enough, however, to realize shortly afterward that their adventure was sinister, and that the best thing that could be done with them would be to burn them in the public square. In June 1930, nauseated, I left Italy voluntarily, intending to work out some plan to disparage the Demagogue Maximus and his followers abroad."

"What was your plan?" I asked.

"I can't reveal it, but if you would like to know more about what we are thinking, come to the Théâtre d'Harcourt some night, where you will hear Professor Autoriello, around whom our group has been formed."

I had already heard Professor Autoriello's name mentioned; but in connection with scientific work, not with his political activity, which I now learned was important. Ferrier had ordered us a dish of *gnocchi à la romaine* and a bottle of Chianti in

196

Scariol's honor; he also called the fat proprietor and asked him jovially:

"Can any of your girls sing Italian love songs?"

"They are Walloons, sir!" replied the corpulent man, raising his eyebrows, as though to indicate the inevitability of accepting a historical fatality. Orio Scariol made a gesture of impatience and looked at Ferrier with frank annoyance.

"I beg you: forget for the moment that I am Italian. We don't need any local color."

"I was not doing it on your account only, but for myself too," said Ferrier. "I have very pleasant recollections of Italy, and among other things I am fond of your love songs. . . ."

"That's all one can have of it now: recollections. Until a new order."

"Are you from Milan?" I asked him.

"Yes," he replied, "but please don't talk to me about Stendhal: a bourgeois overcome with admiration for Bonaparte and for the chorus girls and divas of the Scala! Every time I say I am a Milanese, people remind me of that admirer of divas' bosoms."

"That was a good deal for that period," smiled Ferrier. "The first nudes. . . ."

I couldn't help thinking that it was not worth such a childish outburst — aside from the fact that I had had no intention of mentioning Stendhal. But the appearance of the steaming *gnocchi* put the subject out of our minds. They came in, like classical *gnocchi*, in a silver dish, followed by the smiling proprietor, who was as eager to note the surprise on our faces at the success of his masterpiece as if he were about to announce the birth of the King of Rome.

The luncheon proved a great success. Scariol went on to tell us about his first disagreements with the early promoters of Fascism, his definite break with them, and what he thought of the transitional period. Ferrier growled affirmatively, between swallows of Chianti. After dessert Scariol took a tobacco-pouch from his pocket and began to roll a cigarette with a calmness contrasting with his nervous manner. One could not say that his words were intelligent, nor the reverse, but everything that he said was obviously inspired by both hatred and impatience. The two fine lines that ran from the base of his aquiline nose to the corners of his mouth were constantly brought into play by those two sentiments. In spite of that, I found myself sympathetically drawn to the effervescent rebel, to his seething spirit, and his brain that now saw the phenomena of the sensible world only as exposing the political fraud against which he had taken up arms. At least he had played a dangerous part and knew what he had to contend with. He was a fixed star that followed the course traced by his own light.

One of the Walloon girls, with bright red cheeks and very full dark-green skirts approached our table to solicit a contribution, with her violin under her arm, which was bare to the elbow. We each gave her something, and before rejoining the other players she thanked us with a cold, absent-minded expression.

I refused the cigarette that Scariol had rolled and offered me, the edges of its rice paper not yet glued together, and asked him if he was a Communist.

"No," he replied, "I am not a Communist."

Then, as though he felt that he owed us some further explanation, he added:

"I'm not a Communist if what you understand by a Communist is a person affiliated with the party. I belong to no party. I'm a democrat, just as in the days of Christ I should probably have been a rebel and a Christian, but without advertising it or carrying it about on a banner, and without its having any practical extension outside of myself — merely a process of maturing and clarifying my own vision."

He talked in staccato tones, looking at us through eyelids half-closed to keep the cigarette smoke out.

Not a drop of Chianti remained in the bottle, and Ferrier ordered another, losing his patience at the waiter's slowness and glowering at him when he returned. He frowned easily.

"Have you never been to the Théâtre d'Harcourt?" Scariol asked Ferrier.

"Yes, once, two months ago."

"Would your friend like to go . . . ?" inquired Scariol, indicating me.

"Of course," said Ferrier.

"Professor Autoriello will be there at three this afternoon. Come along if you feel like it."

We agreed to go.

We left the restaurant about two thirty, walked along a short, narrow street, and soon turned into some cross-streets. A postman was carrying on a heated discussion with a servant girl at the door of an ancient house, its tiles thick with grime. I did not hide my curiosity about Scariol's life in Brussels; but he maintained his reserve, more out of indolence than from any real desire to be secretive. He said that they met almost every day at the Théâtre d'Harcourt, which was a sort of general headquarters for Italian *émigré* socialists, and malcontents of every shade, without distinction of origin. It was a center for free discussion, where any theory could be discussed if stoutly defended in militant dialectic.

Turning off one of the main thoroughfares, we went up a dark, narrow passageway between a short row of houses. A characteristic theater entrance opened on this street, through one of those abortive alleys called *cités*. Dirty old posters, with actors' heads painted in black and yellow, were rotting on boards attached to the façade. The reddish wash was scaling off the walls, their crumbling bricks well rounded with age. In the entrance the ticket office, with bars eaten by urine, the odor of dampness, the filth of the walls, the rickety condition of the doors, and the thick accumulation of mud on the marble stairs, all combined to give the place an atmosphere of neglect and squalor. Above the street, like the arm of an ancient skeleton projecting into space, iron brackets from the upper part of the balcony, supported a sign on which the words: *Théâtre d'Harcourt — Variétés*, could be made out with difficulty. In the entrance ceiling there was a great leak, the whitish margins of which had soaked the lurid old posters affixed to the side walls, representing a cancan dancer, with a feather hat, swelling bosom perversely supported by a brief black net, and thighs crossed in an impossible position. Orio Scariol quickly led the way across the entrance and opened a door that communicated directly with the theater.

The place was cold. There were rows of battered, empty orchestra chairs, two tiers of boxes in a similar state of abandonment, and beyond the hundred feet of orchestra chairs a stage. Some people were standing on the stage, and others were seated around a table. Stage scenery, partly pushed aside, showed against the characteristic unpainted brick walls in the background, ropes hanging from the flies, and a few dusty, broken pieces of stage machinery.

"We have rented this dilapidated theater for a song," Scariol explained. "Professor Autoriello lives upstairs and pays for the whole building only what he would have had to pay for any modest house in Brussels."

Many of the orchestra seats were broken and backless; in the front row two girls of ambiguous appearance sat talking. Their hair was blond and frizzy and their eyelids and lips were heavily tinted; one of them seemed to have reversed the colors — her lips were violet-colored and her eyelids a pale red. We climbed the steep stairs to the stage.

"Hello!" said several of the group about the table. They were men of varied appearance, almost all young. The tallest had an aquiline nose and an almost white face. Scariol spoke to him.

"How are you, Marchia? Hasn't Autoriello come down yet?"

"No, he hasn't."

Scariol introduced us. Curious glances were directed at us, some unfriendly. The two girls in the orchestra seats looked on with silent curiosity. Only after some moments I noticed that one of the people standing across the table from me, hidden by Marchia and two other people, was a woman. She was surprisingly masculine in figure and appearance, with high, angular cheek-bones and thin lips. I learned later that her name was Olga Beerkens; that she had been a motion-picture actress in Munich and had emigrated to Belgium following a lawsuit in Germany.

Apparently looking for someone, Scariol glanced about, then asked a man standing next to him about a person whose name I did not catch. "He was here a few minutes ago," was the reply. Scariol went over to the door between the stage and the galleries and dressing-rooms.

"Atkinson!" he shouted. "Atkinson!"

He waited a minute, listening. There was no response, and he joined us again about the table.

"This is our forum," he said at length; "a squalid enough place, but it serves our purpose well and we fill it with vigorous and stimulating expressions of hope and aspiration. Basically we are all disappointed, deeply skeptical people. Autoriello alone keeps the sacred fire of optimism alive among us. . . ."

Scariol noticed Ferrier's puzzlement about the two girls lost among the rows of empty orchestra chairs.

"A variety troupe used to play in this theater. The company failed after acting here for many years. Some of the chorus girls keep coming, through force of habit, and we have allowed them to come as often as they like. . . ."

One of the painted ladies was carefully listening to Scariol, her vacant stare indicating that anything could be said about them in their hearing without hurting their feelings.

Meanwhile, on the stage, I had exchanged a few casual words with some of the men and with Olga Beerkens. Did I write novels? Yes, I wrote novels. She had written a "socio-political" dialogue, summoning women to a new notion of freedom and outlining a plan to give them complex functions in the State mechanism. "Those eyes," I thought, "were made to see things only from an aridly logical point of view." One needed only to look at her to see how barren her nature was, and how little her lack of femininity had fitted her for warm, creative human work.

It was three o'clock.

I did not know that since morning, Cesare Autoriello had been leaning over the table in his room above, correcting proof. Two photographs stood on the plain pine table; one showed the powerful bust, broad, energetic face, and bull-like neck of Benedetto Croce; the other, the smiling young face, above an open white sport shirt, of Professor Autoriello's son, Ezio. The old professor, who fifteen years before had occupied one of the most distinguished chairs at the University of Bologna, interrupted his work only to raise his eyes, look at this picture from time to time, and then lower them again. The picture represented all that he had held most dear in the world. The son, now dead, was buried in a Brussels cemetery among so many other foreign graves. . . . When the news of Ezio's death had reached him, already an exile, Autoriello's faith in the significance of his career as a biologist, to which he had devoted forty years of strenuous labor, faltered for the first time. Graduated from Bologna, Professor Autoriello had lived in poverty, sustained by his enthusiasm for laboratory work. At forty he had attained eminence and, not satisfied with his purely technical research, had begun to write on philosophical subjects, projecting his years of specialized experience into speculations concerning the final nature of things. Thus in the autumn of his life his academic empiricism had been transformed into an intelligent, skeptical dogmatism. Later the Fascist revolution had opened his eyes to an urgent violent reality. After a short period of confusion he had decided that he must leave his native land in order to keep his integrity. Then had come Brussels, the other exiles, and the Théâtre d'Harcourt, in one of the floors of which he had set up his small biological laboratory and, with some of his friends, opened his great rebel, propagandist workshop. His son, Ezio, a writer and sociologist, had died in London of pneumonia when not yet thirty. Autoriello and his wife nearly went out of their minds. The son, whom they had educated intelligently and with passionate tenderness, had now been snatched away from them, like their own liberty a few years earlier. Scariol, their son's intimate friend, only increased their grief by his words of sympathy. Professor Autoriello was prostrated. But time, which destroys everything, sometimes enjoys games of reconstruction; slowly, like vegetables recovering from wilt, Autoriello and his wife gradually returned to an awareness of life around them. Only hatred for their country's oppressor, and their strong attachment to each other after fifty years of married life, now remained to them. Resolutely the professor began to assemble the scattered papers that his son had left behind; a "Chronicle of the Last Ten Years of Western Europe" was almost finished. It was a book written in the service of the democratic and liberal ideas which Ezio had shared with his father, but it had also a bold, youthful stamp that made it his own. Cesare Autoriello wanted to put his son's chapters together and publish them promptly; he would ask his friend Croce for a preface. The father declared that it would be a volume of capital importance, but he would allow no one, not even his son's intimate friend Scariol, to put his nose into the manuscript or the proofs until he had corrected them himself.

He had had a violent discussion with Scariol in the Café Albert Roi three days before. What had Scariol been driving at with his story that he, Cesare Autoriello, former professor of histology at Turin, former member of the Academy — titles which Scariol had enumerated sarcastically over a steaming cup of chocolate — was betraying the "Chronicle," his son's thoughts, by his corrections? Corrections which he had made merely to improve the intrinsic quality of Ezio's work as much as possible. But Scariol had rapped the table and said: "No, sir, no, sir . . . not even with the best faith in the world have you been able to avoid committing an act which, with all due respect, I cannot help calling vandalism!" Vandalism indeed! Always big words. Youthful emphasis and declamation. If the judgment of youth were not fallible it would have been unnecessary to alter a single word in Ezio's manuscript, and he had merely limited himself to cutting out unsuitable parts and modifying the spontaneous bravado of certain expressions that could only have hurt the book by revealing a lack of that cold judgment and proportion which a documented work should have. . . . Was not this respecting his dead son's memory and even dignifying it? Although Scariol had been completely unjust, the sincerity of his friendship for Ezio excused any impulsive overstepping of the bounds in the eyes of the outraged father.

A blond, elegantly dressed young man walked briskly into the theater and stepped out on the stage, the corners of a red handkerchief showing from the pocket of his gray herring-bone, tweed coat.

Scariol greeted him in English.

"Hello, Dennis! I've been hoping for a long time that you would come."

"Well, here I am, my friend, at last."

As he was introduced he shook hands heartily, with Ferrier and me. The two girls in the orchestra smiled at him, and Dennis Atkinson waved a friendly, humorous greeting to them. He radiated life. Tall, lithe, and athletic, he looked at everything generously and with an amiable smile, and people enjoyed looking at him.

"I want you to know each other," said Scariol introducing him to Ferrier and me. "Dennis is a real friend."

We expressed our pleasure.

"Are you foreigners?" he asked.

"I'm not; I'm a Belgian," replied Ferrier. "My friend here is an American, an Argentine."

"Argentine — " said Dennis. "I have read something about your country. O'Neill and Georg Keyser have visited it."

"Yes," I said, "so I have heard."

"I should like very much to see it," he continued, "a country of water, land, and sky, not like these dun-colored countries over here, where we all seem to have been cast up on the planet instead of having been born on it."

Ferrier and I smiled courteously. Scariol, who had stepped aside a little, was reading a French newspaper that displayed a prominent picture of Colonel La Rocque, the chief of the Croix de Feu.

"I don't like the smell of this," he said to Olga Beerkens. She looked the newspaper over with her cold, expressionless eyes.

At that moment, one of the side doors opened and Professor Autoriello stepped out on the stage. From his austerely lined face shone a light of calm contentment. He wore a black bowtie and carried under his arm a portfolio stuffed with papers. He waved a friendly greeting to his associates, but froze when he saw strangers conversing with Scariol and Atkinson. Scariol explained who we were. We congratulated him on his tireless activity.

"We would like to prepare an explosive pie here," Autoriello then said cordially, "but all we do is to bake harmless cakes. Happily for some gentlemen," he added immediately.

One of the men who had been standing quietly beside Olga

Beerkens drew a couple of newspapers out of his pocket and commented on some editorials that had appeared that morning, one reactionary and the other anti-Fascist; both were from Budapest. He translated haltingly one of the articles aloud.

"The reactionaries are not satisfied with Starhemberg," interrupted Scariol; "he acts too legally; what they want is a little *duce* saved from the masses like Moses from the bulrushes."

Dennis Atkinson's head was resting against the orchestra seat in which he had sat down. He was gazing at the ceiling as though listening to celestial music. A cigarette hung indolently from his lips.

A short, bald socialist from Antwerp, who looked like a bourgeois, remarked tartly: "These discussions are stupid and beside the point. We must go and burn the nest where it hangs. What's the use of all this talk?"

"What is this about burning the nest where it hangs?" asked Autoriello.

"Go and kill," replied the Antwerp socialist. "Let one, or two, or three, or a hundred fall; it matters little. This is not a question of conviction or of mass idealism, but of men. Fascism is one or two men, with a handful more to guard the rear; that's all. Fascism is an emergency created to quash the more important movement behind it — the real revolutionary ideology. We must look for someone either among ourselves or outside who will not boggle at doing what must be done."

Autoriello protested with glacial dignity:

"This is no place to come to, to say such things. That is a method that lies outside of our competence. We are here to condense and canalize the *conscience* of our truth; to propagate that conscience, and to contribute in any way — by speech or writing — to making it a *prescience* among the young people. That is our best weapon."

Scariol leaped up like a tiger.

"Yes," he said, "provided you respect the truth of youth as youth itself sees it."

"What do you mean by that?" asked Autoriello, looking at him with perplexity mingled with irritation.

"I mean to say that what you have done to your own son is neither proper nor fair."

Autoriello indignantly pounded the black portfolio that he had laid on the table.

"You are up to your old tricks and making a grievous mistake! I have here the proofs of my son's book that he left behind him. I have put his writing in order, revised it lovingly, and supplied what he was unable to sup — "

"You have put it as it *ought* to be! No, Professor Autoriello, on the contrary: you have not left it as it should have been left. You have revised it, corrected it, and *touched* it. You have read those proofs to me, and I told you what I thought. You know well my friendship for Ezio. He went further than you: he was your son, and therefore destined to have a longer projection not only in point of years, but in knowledge and ideas; because the problem which you suddenly faced when you had already reached middle life, he met in full youth. He was therefore in a better position to grasp it. His book was conscientiously written. It is as much of an outrage to whittle it down as if the forces of reaction had burned it by auto-da-fé. That is something that you refuse to recognize, Professor Autoriello."

Autoriello's hands had seized his voluminous black briefcase like two claws. His face was working, and his eyes were full of righteous grief:

"You can't do that! You can't do that! . . . That is untrue, do you hear? — untrue. . . . If Ezio had seen my corrections he would have approved them; they are retouches made in harmony with the spirit of his book. You are mistaken when you say that they betray him. . . ."

207

"No," said Scariol. "I am not mistaken. I accuse you of doing violence to the ideas of a man who was your son and my friend, and whose ideas should be published intact. I am far from making a mistake."

Everyone kept silent — an awkward silence. Dennis Atkinson alone preserved a quiet detachment. Scariol stood up and began to pace back and forth on the stage. He was nervous, lighted a cigar, and sent the smoke straight up in short, quick puffs. Professor Autoriello said no more, but leaned forward protectively over the briefcase that contained his son's book, as if he feared that the pages might be wrested from him.

"This discussion is futile," said Olga Beerkens.

"Futile?" protested Scariol ironically. "Futile? The questions of form, on which we spend our time every day, are futile. Not this serious, fundamental, symbolic question."

Autoriello raised his thin arm, allowing his knotted, nervous fingers to escape from the rumpled sleeve.

"Enough!" he said. "I put the final period to this affair. It is a matter the determination of which lies within my exclusive competence. *Exclusive!*"

The Antwerp socialist requested that some paragraphs from the Budapest editorial be read again, as he had not noted certain statistical data the first time. The man who had previously translated the papers took them out of his pocket, unfolded them amid general silence, and slowly found and read the pertinent passage.

Scariol had sat down again, and turned to Atkinson in the orchestra.

"It's useless," he murmured, with a gesture. "Everything that was living and fighting in Ezio is annihilated. And with what complete assurance!"

34

THAT night Ferrier and I were at Rumpelmonde's having an apéritif with Scariol and Dennis Atkinson while waiting for Blanche and her friends to arrive. It was the eve of a holiday and the restaurant was crowded, and lighted up to its last bulb. There were even lights among the leaves of the large potted plants around the central fountain.

I heard the young Italian's voice riding his favorite theme. His rage was monotonous. "I shall never forgive the dictator, Benito Mussolini. He has sacrificed us, and tried to kill the principle of rebellion in us, without which no human being deserves to live. He has tried to break us, and trample ignominiously on our dignity as he did with the salaried classes. He may have built us roads, but we shall never forgive him that to the end of time. He thinks he has heroically saved a people and redeemed it from moral inertia, but he began by killing the principle of rebellion in every spirit, the capacity to break with everything and fight with head up, without forever thinking about the master. I could forgive a man's wanting to make himself the master of other men, provided he left them their arms and fought it out with them face to face. . . . But to mutilate, silence, cheapen, and subjugate a people, allowing them to be strong only as servants, is revolting and ignominious. I am disgusted with myself for not having a rifle or a firebrand in my hand!"

Dennis Atkinson looked at him phlegmatically, smoking an Abdullah, his carefully combed red hair smelling faintly of lavender water. Scariol's cigarette was in the corner of his mouth as he talked. It was interesting to watch their different temperaments.

Blanche Alost and the girls entered the room noisily. One of them was limping, having hit her knee as she was getting out of the car. Blanche's long, aristocratic fingers were yellow with nicotine.

"An unavoidable delay," she said.

Introductions. Neither Scariol nor Dennis had met Blanche, but Dennis said that he had seen her eyes somewhere before. She received this compliment with a burst of laughter. Ferrier shot him a suspicious glance. The waiter came over quickly for our orders.

"Sherry," said Blanche. "Well chilled." The two other girls ordered sherry too.

"You are going to freeze your insides," said Dennis.

"I should like to," said Blanche, "but unfortunately the sherry will take my temperature, and not mine the sherry's."

"Would you really like to be as cold as that sherry?"

"Of course, cold is a marvelous anesthetic."

"I see: fear."

"Fear? No chance. Boredom with pain."

Blanche turned to me. "How are you?"

"Very well."

"Are you able to get any writing done?"

"Sometimes, a very little."

"What's the difficulty?"

"Sudden tiresome questions that come up. Always the same thing."

"I wonder whether there are many people who can work these days without being interrupted by such questions."

We had another round of sherry. More people kept coming in. The revolving doors continued to spin a little of their own momentum each time they propelled new people into the room. Blanche had a pretentious way of speaking that grated on Dennis Atkinson. Inwardly Ferrier, too, suffered when he listened to her. Scariol, on the other hand, encouraged her by laughing and showing how well he had understood her meaning. Ferrier was silent. I could not fathom his sudden moody spells.

"Quite definitely," said Scariol, pursuing Blanche with a glance, "you are a domineering woman who likes to be dominated. . . ."

"Men are so quick to reduce everything to a simple formula," she said, laughing. "Everything seems so easy that way."

"It is a need for classification, and to pin vague, illogical women down to facts."

"To tell the truth, I do not know what I am."

"Of course you do," said Ferrier quickly. "A woman of transitory emotions, but without passion, a sort of flesh-and-blood ventilator."

He continued to glare at her. Blanche made a grimace as though frightened by his manner.

"Poor Blanche," she said. "Isn't there anyone who will come to her rescue?"

Scariol leaned toward her and whispered something into her ear; she burst out laughing. The two girls protested. Intimacy was out of place there. The fun must be shared. Scariol and Blanche continued to laugh.

"You are a vile man," she said to him, and turned again to me.

I noticed that Ferrier was growing pale.

Dennis raised his glass and drank twice. Then he began talking:

"When I was about twenty, I used to get drunk alone in my room at Oxford in front of a little bust of Keats. Since then I have continued to get drunk only before other living busts, which I hasten to add have not been those of John Keats. . . . The result is the same."

"The worst of it is that you never know how far it will take you," said Blanche.

"Bah!" said Scariol, who was sober. "One can never go either too near or too far."

"Do you really believe that?" asked Blanche.

"Of course."

"I can always go far, always farther. . . ."

She laughed with an unpleasantly suggestive expression. Ferrier did not take his eyes off her.

The orchestra, near us, was softly and sentimentally playing the Overture to *Tannhäuser*. Blanche leaned back in her chair.

"It is something that should not be thought about," she insisted.

"Quite right," said Scariol, "it should not be thought about."

"Would you think about it?" said she.

"No, I wouldn't," said Scariol.

"You would simply do it."

"I would simply do it."

"Bravo, that's the way I like them," she cried. She laughed like a madwoman.

Ferrier could not restrain his anger. "Don't you laugh that way," he said to her.

"Why not?" she asked with insolent astonishment and a wry face that made him seem ridiculous.

"Very well," said Ferrier. "I am going."

He asked for his own bill. The waiter calculated a moment, scribbled the amount on a piece of paper, tore it off, and handed it to him. Ferrier took out his wallet and paid. Scariol, dumfounded, tried to persuade him to stay, but Ferrier's mind was made up.

"No. I have work to do in the morning. I'm going."

I got up to go too. Blanche was serious now, smoking a cigarette and feigning detachment from the whole scene.

"*Au revoir, mon cher,*" she said to me, and as though she detected a smile on my face, added: "Be good to him! I'm so wicked."

Ferrier and I left the restaurant. In the street we could still hear the music, loud and vibrant at first, then muted, then gone.

The automobiles were throwing up a fine dust from the pavement.

"What's up?" I asked him when we were on the street. "What has happened?"

"She's a slut!" he replied. "I can't stand her."

"All right," I said.

"She is a slut!" said Ferrier. "And there is nothing I can do about it."

35

ONE cold afternoon in the early darkness as I came in from a long walk with Dennis Atkinson, two extremely agitated men were talking and gesticulating in front of Ferrier's house. Their excitement and alarm were evident. They were carelessly dressed. One of them had on a derby hat with a dusty crown. When he saw me approach he spoke to me:

"There is a wounded man inside."

I looked at him in surprise and crossed the vestibule. What could the matter be? The consulting-room door was open and Ferrier was standing by the operating-table wearing his white gown and rubber gloves. Two other men were gazing into the white room from the vestibule door. One of them had a great Bourbon nose and shining, terrified eyes. The other was a tall, lanky young man of about thirty.

I was about to continue upstairs when Ferrier called out from the consulting-room: "Come here." The wounded man, with his chest bare and a pair of gray flannel trousers on, loosened at the belt, was lying on the table in a corpse-like coma. His face showed no pain, his lips were white, and his eyes stared out from between half-closed lids. Ferrier had applied a pad of cotton to his left side at the height of the upper ribs, apparently where the wound was. The man had brilliant black hair and a finely chiseled, carefully shaven face set in an expression of anger or icy terror. The nurse came in from the adjoining room with a chloroform mask. Ferrier looked at her hesitantly. She continued her task, putting the mask gently over the wounded man's nose. His head suddenly moved.

"He shot himself," said Ferrier.

"Who is he?"

"He was living alone in one of the apartments close by."

Then he nodded his head in the direction of the two men standing at the door of the consulting-room, who were looking on spellbound.

"Those gentlemen are his neighbors. They found him immediately after the shot and brought him here."

Ferrier was hunting for an instrument in the nickel box that he had just taken from the sterilizing unit. One of the men said in a low voice, as though communicating a secret: "Yes, we brought him."

Nervous and very agitated, Ferrier glanced at the nurse. "That must be enough now," he said.

"No, doctor," she replied. Ferrier lowered his head, picked up a wad of cotton with the pincers, gently wiped the blood away with a piece of gauze, and examined the wound again.

A grim, black, starless night looked in through the high window.

Complete silence reigned in the room. Only the uneven labored breathing of the wounded man could be heard. The nurse stopped counting the drops and nodded.

"All right," she said.

I glanced at the round clock that stood on one of the glass instrument-cases. It was exactly nine o'clock. The wounded man's arms twitched epileptically, then became still. Ferrier looked at the nurse.

"I think you can begin now, doctor."

"All right."

He still waited a little before beginning, stopping to set various scissors and scalpels in order on the small table.

"The anesthesia won't last long, doctor," said the nurse supplicatingly. "Quickly."

"It will be only a few seconds," said Ferrier. He was nervous. He put two forceps on the edges of the wound to hold it open and took another instrument from the table. His gloved hands moved deliberately.

The wounded man began to moan weakly, and a little foam appeared on his lips. Almost at once he began to talk in a loud, delirious voice. He was talking about a card game.

"They often ramble on like that," the nurse said to me.

As though praying, he kept repeating the same thing in an increasingly loud voice.

"What has won the game? What has won the game? What has won the game? The queen!"

The patient's lips paused for a moment. Ferrier continued his slow, difficult, bloody work.

"It was on the table . . . Magda has taken it. Magda has changed so much! The bow she was playing with is a ring . . . the bow is a ring . . . the wooden bow is a gold ring . . . gold. . . . Why are they taking it away from me? Why are they taking it away? . . . Stop! Let me have it! It is all I have left! Let me have it! Let me see it . . . see it. . . . Let me have it . . . I want to see . . . Magda. . . ."

He continued talking. The nurse examined the mask; then, taking his wrist, felt his pulse.

"How is he?" asked Ferrier.

"We need oxygen," said the nurse.

"We haven't any oxygen."

The nurse was silent. She had the blond hair and cold, serious face of a doll. Again she took the inert wrist between her fingers. He was still talking. His voice did not seem to come from his apparently lifeless body.

". . . to know it. . . . We couldn't lie down together any more . . . she wouldn't have it . . . thinking about him. He

215

was everywhere. . . . On Sundays we went out with him. . . . He didn't know what a beautiful body she had. . . . I knew . . . he didn't know . . . but that body was his. He didn't know it was his."

"We must have oxygen," said the nurse. "His pulse is failing."

". . . didn't know her soft body."

Without moving, but obviously addressing the men at the door, Ferrier said: "We must have oxygen. Ask the hospital to send a tank of oxygen. Quickly! Quickly!"

I showed one of the men where the telephone was. He picked up the directory and began to hunt for the number. Then he put it down and lifted the receiver off the hook. It was busy. "Give it to me," I said, taking it from him. I called the chief operator, asked to be connected immediately, and handed the receiver back to the man to ask for the oxygen. Again I took my place behind Ferrier. Small beads of perspiration covered his forehead. His face was as white as a sheet. The wounded man, stirring restlessly in his delirium, trembled and began to pray in a stentorian voice. "Thy womb . . . full of grace. The Lord be with Thee. Blessed art Thou among women. Blessed be the fruit of Thy womb . . . Jesus . . . Holy Mary . . . Mother of God . . . pray for us . . . sinners . . . now and at the hour of our death . . . amen. . . . Hail Mary . . . full of grace . . . the Lord be with Thee . . . Blessed art Thou among women . . . blessed be the fruit of Thy womb . . . Jesus . . . Holy Mary" (his voice was hurrying) ". . . Holy Mary, Mother of God . . . pray for us. . . . "

"I can't find the bullet," said Ferrier.

"Please," said the nurse. Her cold voice had a supplicating tone.

"Thy womb . . ."

"I can't find the ball. I can't find it."

"Perhaps with the other pincers, doctor."

". . . sinners . . . now and at the hour . . ."

Tense silence reigned in the room. The veins stood out on the parts of Ferrier's arms that were visible between his white, rolled-up sleeves and the tops of his gloves. On the instrument table shone the small nickel, sterilizing apparatus. Beside it stood a wide-mouthed glass jar containing cotton. Ferrier kept repeating like a monomaniac: "I can't find the ball. I can't find the ball." He repeated it either in desperate self-justification or to give himself courage and cover up his own nervousness. The wounded man continued his refrain. The hand that was probing deepest paused for a moment as Ferrier scrutinized the wound; then he put out his other hand, grasped a pair of scissors, and quickly tied another ligature. The pincers remained hanging to the flesh. Ferrier picked up another instrument and used it to assist his fingers.

"Open it more, a little more," said the nurse. "Quickly, doctor." She was watching tense, and worried for him.

Ferrier went on probing without a word. His quick, slender, nervous fingers seemed to be fighting against time, against the passing minutes.

"A reel of silk has dropped," protested Ferrier. The nurse looked. She raised her eyes again.

The room looked like a slaughter-house.

"At moments he has no pulse at all," said the nurse. Her voice had become cold again.

"I can't close it now," said Ferrier. His tone was a muffled complaint. His body was rigidly curved over the wounded man's thorax. The delirium had become labored, spasmodic, and rattling: ". . . among women." Suddenly his voice faded.

"It's too late now," said the nurse, raising her blond head. Ferrier hurriedly put out his hand and touched the still warm wrist, the stiff artery, and the forehead of the dead man.

An hour later we were looking for a restaurant. We had neither the time nor the energy to go downtown. Ferrier was sick at heart and I did everything I could to rally his spirits. In a narrow old street, next to a garage, backed up against a grimy wall from which posters were hanging in shreds, we found an eating-place that Ferrier knew. Its reputation dated from the previous century. Under a sign bearing the single word *Necker* in Gothic letters was a window displaying old bottles of wine, covered with cobwebs. There were also boxes of dates wrapped in gold paper. We both tried to conceal our grim feelings and lack of appetite.

"I can't get used to this," said Ferrier, referring to the man's death under his own hands.

"It's past," I said to console him. "There's no use in thinking about it again."

"But it haunts me, it haunts me."

"Every second contains many deaths," I said. "We must school ourselves to accept death as something familiar and always a release."

"Death is the only thing, I think, about which the mind does not change its attitude. Education scarcely helps. Bravery, considered a virtue by strong characters, is merely an artificial attitude of the mind and does not come from the depths of the conscience. In those depths there will always be terror. And with some people, as with me, doubt about what death will be like, and ignorance of eternity, have become an obsession lurking behind every act, like the gloomy background of an old painting. I do and see nothing without the picture of my own dissolution rising before my eyes."

"That's all right," I said. "It's all right to think that way. Of course, it is a part of the fundamental anarchy peculiar to our breed of unbelievers. Banishing fear is a necessary part of education; otherwise that feeling of terror would be so widespread that the world would go mad. We do not go mad, however, and cross the bridge of death well or badly according to the religious education that we have received."

"I'm not so sure. That's a type of education in which I don't believe."

"You don't believe in it because, as a matter of fact, we are little inclined to believe in transcendental truths. We are content to believe in accidental, immediate truths that cost us little, and prefer not to face the important ones."

"Philosophy!"

"Yes, of course, philosophy, since it is the essential reason back of things."

"How about a cigarette?"

"Thanks, afterward."

"They are very mild. Like grass."

"All right," I said. "I'll take one."

It was a dark hole and had a disagreeable smell of common cooking-oil. The proprietor himself served his clients in shirt sleeves, his hairy, yellowish chest showing through his dingy, gaping linen. The old lamps that projected from the walls like gargoyles showed more brass trappings and scrollwork than light.

We ate in silence and, leaving the restaurant, walked down the street without talking. The fresh temperature contrasted pleasantly with the grimy cornices, ancient walls, and buildings redolent of years and lives long past and decayed. We came to a triangular park in which a single lamp, crowned with a milky halo, faintly revealed a few ailing, ragged shrubs. Benches were arranged to face the three streets.

"Let's sit down here," said Ferrier.

We sat for a while facing the quiet street. Everything went on living. Even we, as we sat there breathing, were expending our lives.

The rhythm of universal growth was everywhere sharply perceptible that night. A drowsy gendarme was slowly walking his beat a hundred paces away. We could make out only his black kepi and the short cape about his shoulders.

Ferrier spoke, staring straight ahead of him into the night air.

"I feel terribly bitter and exhausted," he said. "I am all done in. Few people know what that is."

His voice was altered and hoarse, as if the springs from which it issued were about to overflow.

"I have cheated life. I have an almost criminal responsibility hanging over me. Like so many other medical students who have followed a few courses and done a few classroom experiments, I was given my diploma one fine day — a diploma that permitted me to prescribe, treat, and kill. I have been a doctor for years, but as for a knowledge of my remedies, or a thorough grasp of my profession — nil. I know nothing. I have never known anything. I could have shut myself up and studied, but I was desperately anxious to enjoy life, and for that, money was necessary. I shut my eyes and kept on prescribing. Sometimes I have cured, often I have killed. I have spent ghastly days and nights feeling myself a criminal. This business of tonight is nothing. The man would have died of his wound anyway. It was very serious. A dark, cold, criminal force has gained the upper hand in me and, in spite of my ignorance, I keep on diagnosing, advising, and ordering people to do this or that. I am a chaotic person in a chaotic world who has lost his bearings and can find no signpost to guide him to confidence and peace of mind. I have tried time after time to forget it all by throwing myself into a superficial life of purely physical pleasure — alcohol and women — which is only the final proof of my hopeless situation. As the days pass I have come to the gradual conviction that my total destruction would be the only suitable exit from this terrible struggle. I have been on the point of setting fire to my house and going off to settle somewhere where I would be a total stranger, but, coward that I am, I have not stirred a step."

He stopped, breathing heavily now and looking at me.

"A few nights ago you saw me leave Rumpelmonde's outraged at Blanche's attitude. . . . I can't bear her. I can't stand anything about her! She has been my mistress for nearly three months, and I am unfair. I have no right to condemn her on her manner of life, but my irrepressible anger against her is a part of my present state of mind. But I feel that mine is merely one of innumerable lies all around me. Everywhere at the present time there is the same nauseating odor from all humanity. An era of disgusting little middle-class people, with their revolting, petty resentments and reeking little gods, who want to be in the limelight. . . . What can I do? It is not enough to do away with oneself, for one individual lie to disappear. No, something new must come. From somewhere a fire must consume us, and purge us of our putrefying stench and inveterate lies! A fire of human or divine origin in which humanity will perish or be reborn! . . ."

The electric light faintly illuminated the walls in front of us. The black outlines of the trees, in their iron guards, were undernourished and deformed.

"But don't you see," I said to him, "that if sacrifice is necessary, it must begin with you?"

Ferrier looked at me intently.

I insisted:

"How is the world to be cured unless the cure starts in each one of us? It is absurd to imagine anything else."

"But what sacrifice? What sacrifice? What sacrifice can there be?" he shouted.

"I don't know. I am no professor of ethics. You must supply the answer."

There was a pause. Time passed. Minutes of life.

"I'm fed up with it all," said Ferrier, "fed to the teeth!"

His voice broke.

We stood up a few moments later and continued to walk. The sleepy gendarme eyed us mistrustfully.

36

It was a typical damp Flemish day, with dirty dark-gray clouds in the sky. The sidewalks and pavement looked as though they had been covered with metallic veins of coal; the angles of the cornices gleamed faintly white against the grimy background; and the dark façades glowered at the solitary birds that pecked monotonously at the stone. Throngs of people hurried along the streets toward their offices. Women with baskets were still coming from the northern part of the city. I sat down on the terrace of one of the central cafés and ordered *café crème* and croissants. I began to thumb a book that I had just bought. They brought me a colorless liquid, practically cold, that cost nearly a franc. I sipped it and asked for some paper to write two or three letters to Buenos Aires, to Anselmi, and to some old friends that I had almost forgotten. Nearly the entire sheet of café stationery was taken up by a picture of the establishment printed in red. I wrote my letters and left the café.

Every time I thought about Buenos Aires, an unfamiliar country arose in my mind — not the city, but the great latent, unknown, and still submerged Argentina that would take shape on the banks of the interior rivers, on the hills, and in the vast open spaces that stretch out under the heavens. An invisible country within a visible one. The visible country was thoroughly uninteresting to me, but the other was poetic and imbued with mysterious greatness like the tranquil faces of certain mystics. This inner country must be called to sentient life, helped to emerge and exalted by the voice of poetry, or tenderly stirred as one would arouse a loved person. The external country, its empty prosperity, and its men, aroused only in a purely physical and opportunistic sense, were all detestable to me.

The storm had gathered overhead. A peal of thunder dragged itself roaring across the cloudy sky followed by yet louder ones. Without hurrying, as I wanted the rain to overtake me, I walked toward the café district. It was raining when I entered a café and found Orio Scariol drinking at the bar.

He was sporting a flowing, carelessly knotted tie and looked as though he had been up very late or had not slept at all. His face was drawn.

He answered my greeting affably.

"I have just received an important letter that I have been waiting for," he said.

I looked at him questioningly, and he went on:

"Von Goritz will be here on the 17th. He's an anti-Fascist German, a very intelligent, determined man. Although I don't know him personally, I know that if there is one man the imperialists fear, it is he. I have important confirmation of that from Italy. The Nazis know him well."

"Will he join your conversations?"

"Yes."

"Will he change your original plan of action in any way? Will he be useful?"

"Probably. He's a man who has ideas of his own about strategy. But the important thing is to get his estimate of the forces of infiltration in Germany and Italy."

"I see."

"Ours is an intellectual movement. What we have to fight with is intelligence. Our strength and our fate depend upon multiplying it. Von Goritz will be a formidable addition to our group."

We were both silent for a moment. Scariol stared at his greenish apéritif. Through the plate-glass windows the rain could be seen falling on the street. I took a nut from the dish beside me, cracked it, and put the ripe kernel into my mouth. Scariol suddenly pulled a folded newspaper out of his pocket.

"Look," he said, unfolding it.

It was a Belgian morning newspaper. I saw Professor Autoriello's name below a forceful article of liberal tendency. The title was "Sophistication." He denounced the sophistry of violent acts which had brazen self-protection and self-perpetuation in office as their sole purpose, although cloaked under a guise of civil protection. I glanced quickly over the article and looked up at Scariol for an explanation. "Senility," he said scornfully. "With such ideas we shall get nowhere. The eternal, idealistic thinking. . . . It is pure romanticizing, and at the present time that is suicidal to our cause. Fancy opposing idealism to violence! No more absurd senility could be imagined! Autoriello is wasting our time." Scariol stretched out his hand, took two nuts, and cracked them against each other in his palm. After a mouthful of nuts he took another sip of his apéritif. I was absent-mindedly watching the white sleeves of the barman as he deftly mixed drinks behind the bar. After refolding the newspaper, I handed it back to Scariol and leaned my elbows on the bar.

"For the immediate future," I said, "as far as political action is concerned, you are right; but what will triumph in the long run is tenacity to an ideal — the spirit of men like Autoriello, which represents greater continuity than the most powerful political act: power in time. Autoriello's mind may reach further in its ultimate efficacy than all your activity. Violence is killed by spirit, even if the violence is the most active in the world and the spirit the most passive. Have you thought of Gandhi?"

"Yes, but such triumphs are long-term ones. Meanwhile men are suffering ignominy and death."

"Great causes are rarely won opportunely. The measure of man is the measure of his capacity to plan his triumphs timelessly. By that I mean that only men who are not afraid to work for future generations are great."

Scariol looked at me intently.

"That is the only heroism of the spirit," I continued. "It might even be made into a mathematical proposition that the nearer in point of time a man places his success, the smaller his stature."

"But let's not talk about heroism in connection with Autoriello!" said Scariol vigorously.

There was a pause, after which he went on abruptly:

"Besides, what you say is quite arguable. One could maintain the contrary with equal logic. A man is great according to whether he is willing to give his life for the man beside him. This conjuncture of history requires instant action."

"Which supports my contention."

"I believe in only one form of greatness — to walk straight toward the stake at which one is to be burned, with both eyes open and one's mind fixed upon the idea for which one is being sacrificed."

"We are getting away from the question, each talking about a different sort of efficacy. You believe in the efficacy of the sacrifice of one life for another. I believe in the efficacy of a thought that endeavors to survive by itself, through its inherent truth. Much greater effort and sacrifice are required to make an idea survive than an act. The history of human deeds is a spectacle; the history of human genius is addressed to more critical and subtler eyes."

"Shall we have another drink?" asked Scariol.

"No," I replied, "let's have lunch. It's time."

"Would you like to come to my house?"

"Good," I said, "first-rate!"

Scariol's house was in the northeastern section of the city. We went up four flights of wooden stairs. Each landing was lighted by bulbs screwed into a bracket shaped like an enormous griffin's head. The narrow stairway smelled musty, and in the semi-darkness there was danger of colliding with the griffins. The house must have been built before the turn of the century. Scariol opened the door and stepped into a large room in complete disorder. There were books carelessly thrust into bookshelves, and tables littered with pencils, papers, and more books. Everything was covered with a thick layer of dust. The room had one large window, through which a near expanse of gray slates, laid like fish-scales, was visible, and in the distance, ancient, dingy roofs and a church cupola. The table was set for one. Scariol went out to the landing, shouted upstairs, and returned. He laughed, walked over to the shelves, and picked out a book which he showed me eagerly. It was Joyce's book, minutely annotated in the margins. The annotations were so copious that they would have taken as much space in print as the text itself. I referred laughingly to the commentator's exuberance. "Yes," said Scariol, "a second volume could be made from these notes, but it would destroy the first. . . ." The maid-servant entered the room, a thin, timid, wispy-looking girl. She listened to Scariol's orders, went to the little oak cupboard, and took out another plate, which she wiped with the back of her apron before setting it on the table.

"What have we got to eat today?" asked Scariol.

"Hors d'œuvres and vegetable omelet," she replied.

Scariol invited me to sit down. The girl went out to fetch our meal from the floor above.

"No luck," said Scariol. "Sometimes we even have truffled veal!"

37

I RECONSTRUCTED the scene as Ferrier had related it to me:

Blanche Alost's beautifully proportioned body was sensually clad in a clinging, silk dressing-gown. Her eyes deliberately attentive to the exacting but trivial task of polishing her nails, her long legs crossed, and her air of total languor and boredom clearly showed what little heed she was paying to Ferrier's words that warm afternoon. Night was already gathering outside. The interior of the apartment revealed little of its occupant's character. It contained a mixture of too many colors and objects. Its deliberate, old-fashioned atmosphere contrasted strikingly with a certain up-to-the-minute manner which Blanche liked to affect. She was very proud that she could see the towers of Sainte Gudule from one of her windows while lying in bed, the triangular façade of the portico when she walked about her room, and from close to the window the beautiful, white perron as well.

She surveyed the luster of her nails with satisfaction.

"For some time past all our conversations have been futile and tiresome."

"And am I alone to blame for that?" asked Ferrier.

"I don't know which of us is to blame. I make no accusations. They put my nerves on edge. I am merely putting my finger on a fact."

"Too disagreeable."

"Of course, far too disagreeable."

"It's the beginning of the end."

"Yes," she said, "the beginning of the end." She stopped polishing and sighed.

"Instead of making our love something fruitful, we have made it the adventure of two corpses."

"Because of hesitation and mistrust."

"Because of the natural force of circumstances and the atmosphere that you have created for me — a really unhappy atmosphere."

"I? For many weeks we have scarcely opened our mouths except to criticize each other politely."

Blanche laid the nail-buffer on the satin-covered sofa.

"You need another type of a woman," she said.

"That's true," replied Ferrier.

The veins stood out on his throat as he tried to swallow a lump that had formed in it.

"We have both been poor lovers, Blanche."

A silence followed. Angrily, each avoided looking at the

other, feigning deep abstraction. Blanche stood up and went into the other room. Ferrier glanced about the room that had become so familiar to him and in which he now felt an aggressive coldness. It had formerly brought him the joy of a beautiful woman, but had now become a hostile camp from which only cold courtesy would come in the future. He was at one of those dead points from which there is no turning back.

Blanche returned to the living-room in a suit of black cashmere. Without looking at Ferrier she arranged some carnations at the head of the sofa.

The telephone began to ring loudly. Blanche took the receiver off the hook. She was tall, and the black suit made her seem more slender. She wore a wide silver bracelet on her left wrist and held the receiver in her other hand. She laughed as she talked and her laughter sounded metallic. "Ah, Scariol. How are you? . . . Very well. You don't say! Yes, I remember perfectly. . . . Of course, delighted. . . . Why, as for that, no; absolutely not." A long peal of laughter followed. "We'll see about that afterward. *Au revoir.*" She hung up the receiver and quickly resumed her seat. For the first time she looked at Ferrier.

"That was Scariol," she said. "We are going out for dinner together somewhere."

"Ah!" said Ferrier.

"A charming man. Full of life!"

"Of course, very exceptional."

"People like that seem to fill me with life."

"You should always have them very close to you."

There was a bitter note in Ferrier's voice. Blanche felt that the time had come to put an end to the conversation.

"I'm going to finish dressing," she said. "We can go down together if you don't mind waiting for me."

He did not mind waiting for her. He was in no hurry. At this time in the afternoon a great void always opened in his existence, lasting until the following morning. His only interruption was the hours of work in the consulting-room. He could wait, therefore, while Blanche finished dressing, rouged her lips, touched up her eyebrows with a black pencil, and looked into the mirror — before which he had himself so often stood to comb his disordered hair — to view the final effect as she put on her hat.

After a few minutes Blanche entered, enveloped in a wave of fragrant lotions and perfume. She had on a small close-fitting hat that gave her face a girlish appearance and heightened the contrast between her darkened eyelids and the pallor of her face. She was pulling on her gloves as she came in. Ferrier picked up his hat and she held the door open for him to pass. They walked downstairs, as the concierge only allowed the elevator to be used for going up. When they reached the street door, Blanche made a gesture of farewell, smiling courteously. Ferrier asked whether he could walk a few blocks with her. He wanted to talk, to say something that would bridge the gulf of coldness and resentment that lay between them. Blanche seemed absorbed; at times she hummed a low tune.

"With a slight effort on the part of both of us, the course of events could have been changed. Surely to our mutual advantage," said Ferrier.

Blanche remained silent. Under a yellow light in a carpenter's shop a carpenter was planing a pine board, his shoulders stooped, his head thrust forward determinedly, and his hair in disorder. Perhaps they were both thinking the same thing: equally arduous effort must also be devoted to polishing and embellishing human love! But in them that effort had not been exerted. The wood had slipped because not enough pressure had been applied to it. Blanche walked a few more steps without a word. Ferrier waited for her to speak.

"Why?" she asked. "Why?"

He did not want to insist; he wanted only to implore, but not for anything in the world would he have done so. He said nothing, thinking: "Within a few minutes she will be meeting Scariol. Anything may result from that meeting." Blanche and Scariol were not persons to hesitate when they saw clearly what they proposed to do. Within a few minutes what direction would their immediate destiny take? But — could he change events now or arrest them?

He made one more attack. What if he were to close his eyes to the events of the last few days and weeks — if they were to try to recapture in mind and spirit the previous state in which they had lived joyous and carefree? . . .

Blanche remained bitterly silent. Her mood pervaded the air beside him. They had left a small park behind them. Everything about them was pitch-dark. Ahead could be seen a zone of light, an intersection where a modest theater added its pale illumination to that of two luxurious hotels. Blanche would undoubtedly meet Scariol in the lobby of one of these fashionable hotels. Ferrier realized that the affair was past help. He took leave of her and retraced his steps in anguish.

38

THE DIM lights of the Théâtre d'Harcourt fell full upon the thoughtful faces on the tawdry stage.

Ferrier felt old, depressed, and disappointed; Scariol had a prehistoric mentality, and his youth showed only through the cracks in his tough, dogmatic exterior. Professor Autoriello was an offshoot of the nineteenth century, sadly battered by the winds of the present age; his dozen or more satellites seemed overwhelmed by their fate; and Atkinson's lyrical enthusiasm was indeed so lyrical that it bore no significant fruits. As I watched them shouting, gesticulating, and losing their tempers in the ramshackle, old theater, the curious spectacle became in my imagination the mythical manifestation of a conscience — their hoarse shouting, as it reached my chair in the deserted orchestra circle, seemed the remote complaint of Old Testament voices. They were deluding themselves into thinking that they were engaged in an activity sacred by nature. Without such a feeling they would have died heartsick and lonely in some corner of the old city, hearing as their last farewell the distant voices surviving in their own country.

Once I heard them voice the necessity of engaging an incendiary. No sooner were the words out of their mouths, however, than their timid, scrupulous consciences became affrighted at their own daring. Why, they asked themselves hurriedly, is intelligence not a sufficiently effective weapon to win out in the end by itself and overthrow the naked force of primitive despotism? For a while they rested again on this hope, but set no fixed time for its accomplishment. Then, with rare intelligence, they limited themselves to a purely dialectical and theoretical type of discussion, and everyone debated skillfully and vigorously the antagonistic fields of politics and ethics. It was easy to realize that these intelligent people were the last surviving representatives of an intellect not yet trampled upon, subjugated, and degraded into servility. They were the fragments of a Europe that was changing, traveling unexplored, incredibly rough paths.

With stooped shoulders, Professor Autoriello walked back and forth on the stage and stopped at the table where Scariol was making notes of the important points discussed.

"I am a born believer" — he raised his eyebrows in a gesture which he accentuated, as though to excuse his words — "I am a born believer in Croce's ideas. I believe that the moral idea cannot tolerate the alternatives to which the weak and fainthearted are trying to subject it with their alternative of immediate action. It is these weak people who devote themselves to urgent remedies and make our age conspicuous for its lapel emblems and certificates of membership in the most naïvely direct organizations. But the moral idea has a solid, continuous, historic lineage; it remains true to type and has the means to effect the changes necessary to its own existence undisturbed by the timid deserters. Their defection does not destroy it; it leaves it where it was, like those regions which, the more sparsely inhabited, the more conspicuously their hills and other geological features stand out. What if this century is marked by brutal, predatory action? The river leaves its bed, but it returns only the more surely to it. In reflecting on the greatness and decline of the Roman Empire I have always taken this principle into account, and without principles before taking action, humanity becomes merely an arena for ferocious and absurd ambitions. The reflecting world is not subject to passing fevers. It is the man who is subject to skin irritations, spasms, agues, and passions — conditions which, even in the individual, cannot last for more than a few years — that falls a victim to fevers.

"*Respondere, cavere, scribere* were the three functions of the jurist of the time that Augustus made the Roman aristocracy a formidable diplomatic and military power. The *respondere, cavere, scribere* that humanity must now await in the darkness that may be universally approaching is *insist, reflect, resist.*"

He stood like an old actor with his hands crossed behind his back.

Scariol watched this parliamentarian and idealist coldly. He continued to scrawl on the paper in front of him, from time to time taking a swallow of the coffee that had been poured a few minutes before from the thermos bottle.

Professor Autoriello took out tobacco and paper and rolled a cigarette deliberately.

"Force is chance," he went on. "Force cannot be anything but chance, because whatever is not chance is periodicity, stability, solidity, and the essence of the human being, and consequently of collective humanity; it is therefore neither periodicity alone nor stability, nor solidity. Force is chance, and where can it lead us except to a disaster, like that which the morbid, authoritarian Crispi loosed upon Italy in 1895? When force is let loose, liberty disappears and the spirit recoils and hibernates. Then, like cockroaches on a kitchen floor, the voracious tribe of infamous servants, careerists, mercenary lawyers, and accommodating politicians swarm out of their hiding-places. Those who suffer most are the simple ideologists who had theorized about force and called it into existence, but who realize, once they see it in power, that it can permit no tyrant but the one who brandishes his sword over everyone's head, and that he annihilates all the lesser strong men who get in his way. I have seen fine, zealous young men who supported Fascism in Italy before it came to power, arguing theoretically that it would be great and would usher in again the spirit of ancient Rome; and I have seen how, when the regime was on the march, those same young men wandered about idly with no voice or employment even for their zeal, in a country where only the dictator had the right to speak. These pure, ardent, intelligent youths were cruelly disappointed to find that their own voices had been silenced."

Several people present shouted approvingly: "Hear! Hear!" Autoriello sat down beside his wife, who held an ancient parasol in her lean hands. The professor stood up again, went to the table on the left of the stage where Scariol was sitting, and with uncertain hand helped himself to coffee from the thermos bottle.

For many weeks I listened to their conversation, meetings, and debates. I was able to reflect at leisure on this scene, more real than the imagination could picture — a small rebellion in a small world. I was able to reflect too on the springs that moved those living puppets. They were far from me, yet near. Near because of their simple goodwill and faith; far because the basis of their faith was wholly negative. Their faith was in something that was ending, not in something yet to be born. Poor shipmates on God's darkest ship; they had a cargo of faith, but faith is not made of "good faith," however much of it we may have.

I was thinking of my own country and how to encourage its worthy, thoughtful men. Some day they would rise, not like these men, but full of intelligent, constructive, combative will, and with the firm tread of a man who knows where he is going, is convinced of his strength, and has no need to shout or gesticulate. A man was marching in my country, in Argentina. He came from the deep hinterland, from the roots of that spiritual continuity that makes a nation, and was marching from all its borders. The tips of his toes in Tierra del Fuego were ready to bear the weight of the whole country. His powerful shoulders in the north formed the territories of the Andes, Jujuy, Salta, Formosa, Corrientes, and Misiones; his forehead, facing the Atlantic — Santa Cruz, Chubut, Rio Negro, La Pampa, and Buenos Aires. He became stronger as he marched in his serene unity across half the continent, from Ecuador to Cape Horn in the extreme south. Insistent, reflective, and advancing, but in his own way.

As we were leaving the theater, I tried to give those Europeans the feeling of a new country, but they grasped it only imperfectly, picturing it as something lyrical and shapeless. They clung to the skeleton of more ancient structures, in which man is a little iron screw, born and dying, in his precise, rusty little threaded hole. They looked at me as, according to Thoreau, the crickets must have looked at the birds when they said to them: "Ah, you talk impulsively like children. Nature talks through your mouth; but we speak from mature knowledge."

It was a Friday in September.

I told them that I was leaving, going home to Argentina. I had completed only a small part of my journey. It was my flesh, the roots of my flesh, my physical country that called to me. I could neither walk nor sleep nor continue until I obeyed that summons, that need to return.

At the Savoy, at lunch, Ferrier and Atkinson told me that

they sincerely regretted my departure. The wine list on which the famous Burgundies were catalogued, carried a caricature of an elegant "nighthawk," from whose mouth came the phrase: *"Je veux mourir au cabaret entre le blanc et le claret."*

That same afternoon I booked passage, put my papers in order, began to pack my luggage, and went out alone to say good-by to those streets burdened by the years. A gentle rain was falling. I was to sail from Villefranche within a few days. They wanted to give me a farewell party in grand style at Rumpelmonde's on the following Sunday.

Not all the *habitués* of the Théâtre d'Harcourt were there, but the majority were, and they were merry. They had only their goodwill, but they laughed and frolicked like children. Atkinson was the spirit of the occasion. He was both merrier and more collected and dignified than any of them, with his way of repeating the admonition of Saint Paul: *"Ambulemos non in comessationibus et ebrietatibus."*

We were seated around a long table, decorated with Dutch tulips and beautiful Belgian roses. Atkinson had contributed champagne for the occasion, and chilled bottles of Reims stood at intervals along the table. The girls had got up to dance with Ferrier, Atkinson, and Scariol. For a few moments I sat alone at one end of the table. At the other end Professor Autoriello was leaning forward conversing seriously with the Antwerp socialist. I looked at the men who were there. They were all lonely people, grateful for every second of forgetfulness. For one reason or another all had failed. But did not that failure lie in their own inner decency, in their inability to gloss over comfortably their profound truth?

Blanche wore a low-cut evening gown. One of the girls was drunk and shouted tiresomely: "Long live life!" Blanche sat down beside me and asked me endless questions about my journey. Was I going directly to Villefranche? Wouldn't I stop in Paris? Didn't I know anyone sailing on my ship? Wasn't it a long crossing? Didn't one tire of dcing nothing for so many days?

She moved on to talk to Professor Autoriello, who received her unenthusiastically. She was so impulsive and restless that she made everyone she was with conspicuous.

All night long we talked about nothing but ourselves, shouting, laughing, dancing, bantering, and drinking serious toasts to the most improbable things. Atkinson even proposed a toast to the remote elevation of Professor Autoriello to the ministry, and the latter, completely sober, smiled benevolently, confused by the excesses of such spirited youth. Standing up, Atkinson proposed to me that we found a fraternity, with branches all over the world, composed of those who come after those who try to push ahead. The "last-but-not-least," he said, a world confraternity of people opposed to money-grubbing. The women applauded heartily as though it were a brilliant idea. Atkinson sat down and immediately insisted that the idea must be baptized. He called the waiter and ordered three bottles of Bobby Burns.

I felt very much at my ease with those friends and realized that I should miss them.

Tapping the picture of Bobby Burns on a bottle, Atkinson said there was nothing like drinking with a poet and quoting Bobby Burns. He declaimed softly:

"That I for poor auld Scotland's sake
Some useful plan or book could make,
Or sing a song at least."

His mouth closed gently on the scarcely audible concluding words. One of Blanche's friends, the plainer and noisier of the two, gave a savage yell, doubtless intended to break the lack of epic inspiration of the gathering. A kettle-drum sounded stridently. Professor Autoriello, alarmed and uncomfortable, stirred in his chair. Finally, excusing himself, he withdrew, accompanied by the Antwerp socialist, who had not changed his expression of total boredom and indifference the whole evening.

Two of us had started to talk seriously. Blanche fell upon us like a typhoon to break up such disorder. She talked to me again about America, which she imagined a region of old manor-houses hidden among poetic swamps, over which swarms of gaily fluttering butterflies suddenly scatter in fright at the approach of an eagle. Her description amused me greatly and I assured her that in fact it was much like that. She opened her eyes wider, astonished at herself and seeking solid data to round out her poetic notion of the American world. From the other side of the table Scariol smiled knowingly.

We had agreed to observe the rite of waiting for the dawn. Blanche, Alice Nonnekans, and two other girls, Ferrier, Scariol, Atkinson, and I were the last to leave.

We left Rumpelmonde's as the day was faintly dawning. Through the revolving doors could be seen a picture of grim, stormy clouds. We marched along singing. Scariol and I felt sober beside our unrestrained friends. As the darkness receded, Atkinson was beating time for us in the middle of the broad street.

Old city outstretched to God, sister of Bruges, great vigilant city with silent eyes! The suburbs. Etterbeck, Ixe-Iles, Saint-Gilles, Anderlecht, Molenbeck, Saint-Jean, Lacken, Schaarbeck, Saint-Josse-ten-noode. . . . Echoes of the Count of Louvain, the Duke of Brabant, Margaret of Austria, Mary of Hungary, and the Prince of Orange Nassau. . . . What other spot is there where death so rules life? That night her reclining body must have raised itself a little to look at us. Everything that was eternal in her seemed to us as though, at its very commencement, it had already come to an end. Her wrinkled brow was returning to rest as our group of young people, strung out in a long row, walked arm in arm into the dawn.

From the train window that last afternoon, amid the tooting

of whistles, blatant advertisements, crowds, hurried arrivals, and farewells, I watched them as they stood on the platform. They were gay. Atkinson had brought me a stock of cigarettes, and each one of them some little gift. I watched them silently and thoughtfully. There they stood, useless as far as their enterprise was concerned, but for the moment sturdy, calm, and happy.

They were an unsuccessful crew, isolated islands, hopes and sorrows. When the whistle blew, and the train pulled out to the shouting of farewells, I saw them standing there, pronouncing my name, growing smaller, then lowering their arms and withdrawing — poor, beloved friends — to the region of their dreams.

BOOK III

The Defeated

○-○

39

I was thirty-five years old at this time, but my first youth seemed already far in the past. Every day of my life had carried a heavy burden. The life of reflective people is so much longer than that of men of action! For thoughtful people, every day is a populous, slow-moving, rugged landscape, and every hour an open window overlooking so many different roads.

My apartment was now in the upper part of Buenos Aires, a few blocks from the Torre de los Ingleses. The comfortable living-room showed not walls but books, and as it was very large, I had my dining-table in it, at which Ruiz, my valet, served me — taciturn, melancholy Ruiz, who padded noiselessly about on the dark brown carpet.

In the solitary twilight world that I entered when I returned from my long journey, my mind began to synthesize. It was a time for gathering in the fruits of my reading. Ah, how well I recall those rainy afternoons in Buenos Aires when I walked back and forth in that room, rejecting literary recollections no longer applicable and storing up in my mind for future reference the books of which I retained the meat, marrow, and spiritual fruit!

For a time this period of study took the place of people. Of them I was determined to see as few as possible. If I could not find as friends people with a capacity for humble, sincere, substantial, and direct functions, the others interested me little. Indirectly this brought me closer to the world than ever. I began to read aloud to myself some of the books that gave me proof of the unity of mankind.

American cities have a characteristic rhythm that makes one feel a little strange and out of place in them, returning from abroad. Everything is too new to throw out bonds of sympathy. There was a time, therefore, after my long journey when I found myself out of tune with my Buenos Aires and superfluous to its visible movement. Soon, however, I was again deeply attached to the dark, thoughtful soul of the capital. Its vast, melancholy, uniform extent seemed to me the mute triumph of its stones over the people that they contained. Divided into endless straight, intersecting streets, one could walk about it for hours without discovering, except for the letters on the signs, any variation imposed upon the stones by the human mind or will. Sometimes one ran across a variation of a purely superficial sort, a façade, portico, or balcony designed to display the smug opulence of its owner or the florid arrogance of some industrialist. Day after day new streets were opened, extending the never ending suburbs, but they were not planned for harmony or beauty. Sidewalks and pavements were laid and rows of horrible houses thrown up haphazard on either side.

I used to pass the house in the Twenty-fifth of May Street where I had lived thirteen years before, and always felt saddened by it. Of all those people, I now saw only the faithful Anselmi. I knew nothing of Dr. Dervil or of Professor Borescu. Scanty news of Jiménez reached me from his remote province. He had remained there, swallowed up in the tranquillity of his village. Only of you the wind was constantly bringing me the freshness of some sudden news.

Meanwhile the venal population of the buyers and the bought kept growing in Buenos Aires, stifling the sincere intellectuals that raised their heads a little to denounce what they saw going on. The picture was sinister. The man who refused to sell himself for an office sold himself for money. The advisers were bought; whole groups of public officials — judges, professors, office-holders, and others — were bought. Then everything, devaluated and scorned, sold very cheaply. Everything, that is, except prestige. That remained intact, strengthened rather by the price to be collected. It was infernal: to sell oneself gave prestige. Ostentation gave prestige. The gentlemen who sold themselves most frequently — haughtily coming and going from important porticos before bareheaded lackeys — were not satisfied with their physical possessions, comforts, sumptuous tables, and monotonous triumphs of entertaining; they wanted to be still greater. They pontificated about everything human and divine.

The nights that I was free, I called up Anselmi and we went out for a walk near the Recoleta. He was always ready to talk detachedly, like a jai-alai player bravely facing the wall. With him I knew exactly where I stood. He hated whatever seemed odious to him, and admired extravagantly what struck him as worthy of admiration. He did not give a tinker's damn about the moral side of a question, nor about the little gentlemen who touted absolutist doctrines of blood and iron. He was honest, and whatever he gave of himself he gave fully. He was an Argentine, and a friend, and as strongly built as a great oak. To be with him was to touch something deep and rich and primal. His pockets always bulged with newspaper clippings. When he found a table near him, he would spread them out and point scornfully at the articles that seemed to him the foam floating idly on the surface of our society. "A white foam, but just like plain white cabbage," he would say, laughing. And to season his clippings, he had always a short marked item chronicling some insignificant but illuminating episode — a resignation, or an honest, futile, anonymous protest. "This is the good white cabbage, the sound white cabbage of our soil." Anselmi laughed a great deal. He laughed at everything. He laughed at me, at my anger, at my indignation, and at my laughter that his laughter caused. But deep down within us we were both troubled.

One afternoon Anselmi and I were leaving a down-town restaurant. We walked along the sunny street that led from one of the wide avenues to the most somber, restful, beautiful plaza in Buenos Aires. Just before it reached the plaza, there was a picture gallery in front of which I had stopped almost daily for many years to look at the canvases displayed in the window. There would be a tiny sketch attributed to Vermeer, or some delightful moderns — a Utrillo, or a Vlaminck, with his tragic whites, a Braque, with his deep blues and delicate mastery of the fluid tones. Several days in succession I had stood transfixed for more than a quarter of an hour, stirred by the plastic vigor of a forehead or a mouth by Domenico Veneziano, all the color of which seemed to be absorbed by its spirituality. Anselmi and I stopped. There were two small canvases in the window by a new Argentine painter. On either side were two Chiricos, spirited white horses and amputated segments of columns. The Argentine pictures impressed me by the quality of their technique and their perfection within the scale of minor art. They revealed an admirable artistry, the acceptance of the humble part, the obscure road, the zone of sacrifice, without crossing which no art can achieve success.

Three gentlemen were standing alongside of us, also looking at the pictures. They had come from the hotel side of the plaza. All had the family look that turns the inhabitants of a whole section of Buenos Aires into a monotonously standardized army — that cut of clothing and typical, hard presumptuousness. They stood for a time looking in the window, their eyes squinting and a scornful smile on their lips, so exactly alike in manner as to seem three replicas of the same person. One of them finally gave his mouth a contemptuous twist: Yes, he was insulted by

the daring of form displayed there, and by the attempt at
originality. Anger finally loosed their tongues: "This is a shame!
What have we come to! How exaggerated!" Another in a blue
double-breasted suit and gray hat agreed with him: "Outrageous!
Outrageous!" The three gentlemen strode on disdainfully, absorbed in their denunciation of the three works of art.

I looked at the pictures. They seemed to me as insulted and
defenseless as an Ecce Homo! Anselmi looked at me as if waiting for an order.

"We are the simpletons!"

40

I SHUT myself up, worked feverishly for two unforgettable
months, and refused to see people. I went out only to eat, and
scarcely exchanged the necessary words with Ruiz. I closed my
doors even to Anselmi. At times he would come and sit reading
quietly until just before dinner, when I was in the habit of going
out for a short walk. Then he would keep me company and we
would talk about things in the city.

During the pauses in my work nothing pleased me so much
as to talk with some of the modest people in the neighborhood.
It was an incomparable tonic. I encouraged them to ask questions and to tell me about their problems.

At night I went down to the river and watched the birds at
close range, or observed the skill with which some workmen
were using their cranes.

Before lying down to sleep, I drank a glass of cold milk and
sat for a long while trying to sketch in definite outline some of
the critical scenes of my book. Of the first volume of the *Forty
Nights*, only two "nights" remained unfinished.

More than once I felt swept along by a mysterious current. I
wrote from early morning without stopping as if at the behest
of some master standing behind me who never took his eyes off
me, unable to lay my work aside. Late at night, after eighteen

hours of work, pausing only for a few mouthfuls of food, I found my nerves so excited, tense, and rebellious that they were ready to snap. I had the disagreeable sensation that my whole external body had shrunk to nothing, and that my nervous system was branching out and swelling to monstrous proportions. I would awaken Ruiz and get him to come and talk to me for a while.

I did not want to leave the book for even a day. It must be made a sea, a rich, abundant sea, with its storms, anxieties, wearisome wastes, and quiet, delicious bays. Some nights my nerves were so on edge that even the light from the lamp by which I wrote jarred them. I had to shade it with translucent paper. The large room remained in partial darkness, and as the night wore on, the noise of my pen grew louder and louder.

There were other unhappy times when I was plagued by the idea that what I was doing was useless; that the book inspired by the sufferings and hopes of my people would never stir anyone. That I was talking in a void, and that my own sitting there so persistently day after day was the height of folly — as vain and futile as the empty, useless activities of the parasites that I had the illusion of overcoming. When this idea possessed me, I had to stop. It became an obsession. I regretted my solitude, stuck away there between the smell of ink and the reproduction of Memling's Virgin that hung by my desk. What was I after? Communication? But I was alone in my senseless, sterile, selfish seclusion, a pitiful nibbler.

I remembered my friends the poor dreamers of the Théâtre d'Harcourt and compared my extravagant zeal with their congenital ineffectualness. This room was my Théâtre d'Harcourt.

Then I missed the companionship of my friends, and yearned for the warmth of a woman in my house — the house of a wastrel. Even the humblest laborer surely did more respectable and useful work than I.

They were days of boundless despair, the saddest of my life. But the torrent again commanded me and threw me headlong into the final march to the end of my book. The delicate sympathetic eyes of Memling's Virgin — smiled.

After seventy days the living *Forty Nights of Juan Argentino* were finished.

I was exhausted.

I gazed at the bulky manuscript on the table. I had nothing to do. Time and the world were mine. I was at liberty. The revision was easy compared with the struggle of writing the first draft.

Now I could bury myself again in the city as though after a long absence. I went out very early in the morning and enjoyed the freshness of the vegetables and of the white fish exposed between long cakes of ice, in the bustling market; I stuck my nose into the flower market for a while and, returning to Lezama Park, joyful at my new freedom, sat down near the large pool at the foot of the terrace where thirteen years before a group of us boys had breathed another sort of ardor.

I had no desire to go to Acevedo's house. Married for the second time to one of those women in whom the sexual complex achieves a baneful splendor, my friend was obviously fatigued by his private struggle with the dragon. As the result of such a union, the center of a man's life becomes displaced, his various preoccupations are stirred up and suddenly polarized about his conjugal struggle, more artful, overwhelming, and enervating than the worst of moral struggles. Petty, perverse, and obstinate, a woman of this type in the long run breaks down the resistance of the strongest man and undermines areas in him that no other battle could have reached. In a few years Acevedo had become an ingrown, unhappy, taciturn man. The seriousness of these defeats is that they are not lost by weakness or by lack of virility, but by discouragement at a treason to reality. It was impossible to see Acevedo in his home, for his wife, who was always present during our conversations, interrupted him with cutting, dogmatic remarks. At first he had resisted; then, when he tired of it, the dragon had remained in possession of the field. It was as though he had died.

Anselmi helped me with the task of copying and correcting proof. He arrived at seven in the morning, fresh and clean-shaven. Ruiz served him his usual fried egg and Spanish bacon. While I was dressing in my bedroom, I could hear them discussing the troubles in Europe. Ruiz agreed with Anselmi, sighing heavily.

When the book was finally copied, I had another keen disappointment. My work had taken on a mechanical quality, and its faults were more conspicuous and its hollows deeper in the clean copy, which seemed to have become an inferior version of the first draft. I set to work again feverishly recasting whole chapters, now disgusted with the book. There is no discouragement comparable to the sense of failure that comes when creative works are seen in their first finished form. Another stage will follow when, though still alien, they seem improved; but the rereading of the first clean copy leaves a bitter taste and an irrepressible feeling of disgust and satiety. "Years of labor in vain," I said to myself. People's faces also seemed to say to me: "Years of labor in vain." But it was neither notoriety nor fame that then seemed to me compromised; it was the possibility of communicating with the subterranean zones. Had I just built a broken bridge?

At times I came across vivid passages, and hope suddenly revived. Finally I took the book to my publishers. They thumbed the pages carelessly, their minds occupied with external details of the book and the best method of selling it. What difference did it all make to me? I left the voluminous manuscript in their hands and, as if I had sloughed off years of my life, crossed the little square in front of their office. With its leafless trees and lacking benches, it was bleak and wintry-looking. Unconscious of time and circumstances, the bronze head of a gentle faun smiled from its pedestal.

My life-blood returned to the house to visit me in the shape of the damp proof-sheets, fresh and vital. They pleased me. In the crisp, shining, printed letters the book took on a new life. At last I was satisfied! I telephoned immediately to Anselmi to invite him to have dinner with me in a gay restaurant. He accepted with the alacrity that I had hoped for. Sitting down to correct the proof-sheets, I let Ruiz handle them, which he did with superstitious awe.

At last everything was saved! That night the people that filled the restaurant struck me as different. I saw them once more through optimistic eyes. I could regard myself with a little more indulgence. I enjoyed Anselmi's witty sallies keenly and shared in his gaiety. We had a delicious fresh *brótola* baked to a golden brown, sprinkled with lemon juice and accompanied by two bottles of Chablis. Anselmi told me that I could be proud. I believed him.

I believed him, but my mind was not yet at rest. During those days of proof-reading, the text was so close to me that it became confused. It was difficult for me to distinguish between the good and the bad. My desire to have a bird's-eye view of the book's general structure and details as I examined it for the last time was therefore thwarted.

A work of art is such a perfect organism that its survival depends less upon the excellence of its culminating parts than upon the proper subordination and perfect interweaving with them of the more obscure and relatively minor parts. In the most luminous works shadow at times plays a principal role. A world seen in perspective such as the novel, but whose naturalness is not of this world, needs much fallow land within its compass to delimit and throw into relief the splendor of the cultivated areas. These untilled fields are difficult to execute, as the tendency of the artist is to make extensive and general use of brilliant tones. Often when studying critically El Greco's *Agony in the Garden* in the National Gallery, and Jan van Eyck's famous portrait of Arnolfini, I had been surprised at the crucial importance which the vigor and feeling of the accessory parts played in the whole picture. Thus rough terrain and seemingly superfluous events must receive painstaking but thankless attention, for they run the risk of confusing us by their minuteness.

I busied myself therefore revising the book and bringing its general structure into harmonious unity, suppressing furiously and adding patiently. The publishers kept asking me every day to return the sheaf of proofs. One night I put them into an envelope and said good-by to them.

I wandered about like a lost soul for some days. Then I received the first package of books. At last the work of so many years had taken definitive shape. It was solid and consistent. It could defend itself against time and could wait, even though ignored, until someone found it.

But, for all that, it no longer belonged to me.

4 I

THE FIRST time I saw Gloria she was standing near the desk where the old man usually sat. He was absent. Her type was strange; her eyes gray, her skin dark, and her hair very straight and black. Far from giving the vivid impression of black eyes against a pale skin, hers showed deep and pained surprise. She was tall and had slender legs. Her forehead above one of her eyebrows twitched almost imperceptibly, as if her effort to concentrate had its focal point there. She was very pretty.

The lending library was in a back street in the southern section of the city. My gray moods had just given way to an enthusiasm for reading and the enjoyment of extraordinary daily discoveries; I treated myself to the simple, lyrical *Suppliants*, to Landor's poems, or to Ovid's tale of King Midas, who was horrified at his gift of turning everything he touched into gold; or Albertus Magnus — *magnus in magia, major in philosophia, maximus in theologia* — the wonderful story of the displacements of the soul, and of winter turned into spring.

The old house occupied by the library, dating from the end of the eighteenth century, comprised a large patio, which had been transformed into a reading-room, and spacious rooms, now utilized for neatly arranged book stacks and storage space. An inscription in one of the rooms recorded the fact that General Balcarce had once lived there for a week. The old house was as still as a tomb. I was one of the very few readers and there were whole afternoons when no one else came in other than some eccentric or an occasional bewildered student.

I approached the desk inquiringly, looking about for the old man. She asked me what book I was looking for. I think that I gave her to understand that I was looking for the other employee.

"Señor Rojo was only here substituting for me while I was on vacation," she explained.

She had a quick, somewhat short way of speaking. I asked for one of Nietzsche's books. She got it for me and took down my name. When she read it, she raised her eyes and looked at me intently for a moment; then she lowered them again and went on writing.

The human face has always evoked in me, as it does in all reflective and solitary people, an infinite variety of instantaneous associations, and recollections of other faces or occasions — historical, literary, or contemporary — which it brings to mind.

I was struck by her unusual appearance, by the quiet concentration of her sun-tanned face. That day I watched her every movement. When she was not helping the few readers, she was reading herself. I must have spent my whole time looking at her. The striking look of concentration on her face seemed to come largely from the tone of her skin, a somber quality, totally without artifice. Her heavy black hair, brushed resolutely back, gave prominence to her eyebrows, a conspicuous feature of her face in spite of their fine texture. Her gestures had the decisive, dry nervousness of people who try hard not to neglect the unimportant things of life and to seize them even in their most insignificant aspects. A few minutes before eight o'clock — the hour of closing — I handed her the book. She took it without paying particular attention to me and put it back in one of the neighboring rooms. I left the library.

I returned there every day. She raised her head quickly when I came in, gave me an incurious glance, and later a cold response to my greetings upon arrival and departure.

One morning, as I was turning the pages of the catalogue on the desk, she suddenly asked me:

"Are you a writer?"

"Yes," I said to her, self-consciously.

"I read your book last night," she said.

"Which one?"

"The last one."

I asked her in a low voice whether she liked it.

"Parts of it," she replied. There was always something cutting in her tone.

We talked for a while. Her accent was no longer harsh; on the contrary, it was warm. It had a rapid, sweeping warmth. She hardly ever talked, however. She looked at you, fixing her quiet, mysterious eyes on you. She seemed to be mutely asking questions and giving herself the privilege of answering them silently.

Ten days of silence passed after her reference to my book. For almost a week I stopped going to the library. Several afternoons in succession Anselmi and I visited an exhibition of delicate Fouquets and bold, proud Chiricos in his latest manner. Ah, his majestic, stately horses! Then I returned. I read her name for the first time at the end of a list of books. Gloria; and then: Bambil. What sort of family name was that? . . . It stuck in my mind. As I had to put some ideas on paper for a future book, it was three days before I again returned to the library. I was working up some new "nights" for my hero. Ruiz kept plying me with glasses of iced orange juice.

It was a stormy afternoon when I went back to the library. The rain was falling heavily on the city, and the panes of the skylight resounded with the fury of its impacts. The library was gloomy, but it was agreeable to have a refuge there to read in greater intimacy and isolation than ever. I immersed myself in some pages of Melville, which I had started to read four days before.

Gloria was at her desk. The corners of her mouth had their characteristic slight droop. I was the only reader in the room. When I finished my book, as I had two hours left for lighter reading, I went to her desk and, when she looked up, asked for a book of Sandburg's poems. His verses about the great bustling stone city of Chicago would harmonize with the gloomy afternoon. The library did not have the book. Then I asked her to choose something that she liked. Without a word she went to one of the inner rooms, and through the doorway I saw her select a volume from the shelf. She leaned forward and her mass of black hair bent and spread out as it touched her shoulders. She brought back some plays by Synge and handed them to me. They were all very short. Among others were the *Riders to the Sea* and *Deirdre of the Sorrows*. I knew only the former.

"Do you like them?" I asked.

"Yes." She looked at me intently. "To read them is like touching something cold." Then she said: "They are written almost without words; the absolute minimum. It's like touching something cold." After a pause she added: "But a cold that is there, not merely imagined."

I realized that the book would give me an opportunity to talk to her some more. But in due time. I said nothing more for the moment and went back to my seat. The noise of the rain could be heard as it monotonously battered the skylight and dashed against the pavement. She switched off the overhead light, leaving most of the room in obscurity.

The book struck me as exceedingly beautiful. Although I read the two plays quickly, I waited for a while before returning the book. Gloria's personality interested me greatly — I don't know why; perhaps because of her expression of stern, cold sadness — and I wanted to learn more about her. Her rare, instinctive, unaccountable attraction made me very curious about her. A few seconds before eight I stopped reading and brought her the book. She had already put on her raincoat. The strong lines of her face were thrown into relief against its high raised collar and severe military cut. Her gray eyes looked at me steadily, one hand resting on the buckle of her belt. I spoke enthusiastically about the book. She put it away, called the watchman, and told him to put out the lights. We went out together and paused as we saw the dense sheet of water whipping down obliquely. I opened my umbrella and turned up my raincoat collar. The street was deserted. A taxi was out of the question. She said that she was going to take car number nine at the corner of Piedras. I was going in the same direction. We ran for the corner and took refuge there to wait. It did not seem to concern her one way or the other that I was standing with her under the awning of the closed store. She lifted her grave, clear eyes and looked up at the dark sky. We talked about the weather, how long it had been since it had rained, and the effect of the storm on the country.

The street-car arrived full of people, from the direction of Constitución on its way to Retiro. We stood in the aisle. The window panes were opaque with steam, and great drops trembled on them before plunging headlong to dissolution. We talked about the rugged characters of Synge, so elemental and profound.

"And no analysis," she said. "Analysis, so-called psychological observation, is a lie. Synge's people are people. They are that way because they are that way. They move relentlessly. No matter how nor why. Their lives have a solid destiny." She hesitated. "I think — They can't be broken down into fragments. They can't be taken apart experimentally."

It was difficult to keep our balance at the street intersections on account of the swaying of the car. We clung to the straps.

"The main events in Synge are, certainly, solid masses," I said. "They are masses that move like tides; the mass of tragedy, the mass of solitude, the mass of grief, the mass of shipwreck. . . . His events have the scope and motion of waves."

"That's why I like them," she said.

One of her hands grasped the strap. The other held the edges of her raincoat over her bosom. The small black felt hat, turned up a little at the brim, showed the straight plane of her hair, part of her thoughtful forehead, and her two calm, attractive eyebrows. I noticed that she wore no ring or adornment of any kind. Her clothes were severely simple.

The street-car passed San Juan's Church, crossed the avenue, and at Esmeralda Street left the north Diagonal and the business section behind, their shop windows as gaudy as a motley crowd at a fair.

We talked about Synge's fatalistic, fanatical old fishermen.

I asked her, without transition, something about herself.

"I live alone," she answered with quick candor. "I make this trip four times every day. When I get off the street-car, I walk exactly three blocks. I leave my door punctually twice a day and enter punctually twice more."

"That's what I would call a properly ordered existence." I smiled.

She burst out laughing. It was the first time I had seen her laugh. She laughed with her head tilted back a little and without moving her fine, high eyebrows. They moved only to form the intense expression that her face habitually wore. She had a fresh mouth and marvelous teeth. She seemed to me very beautiful and delicately bred.

The seated passengers, eager for distraction during the trip, stared at us curiously.

When the street-car reached Lavalle Street, she said good-by. She made no signal to the conductor to stop the car, just looked at him; the car stopped and I watched her stride rapidly away in her military raincoat.

The rain had lessened. I stayed on the same car. It progressed slowly between the old houses and modern façades. In the interior of the brand-new Municipal Loan Bank building, family jewels, opera-glasses, pictures by unknown artists, Irish lace, mantel clocks, cornucopias bursting with flowers and apples of gilt metal were every moment depreciating in value.

In the same street were flower-shops, dressmaking establishments, and the noble stables of the somber Paz palace. The street-car crossed the east side of San Martín Plaza almost empty.

That night I dined very happily and told Ruiz, as he was serving me at table, what sort of person Gloria Bambil was.

42

I CONTINUED to see her during the days that followed. To be with her was not easy. She was not an outgiving person. She lived silently immured within her own personality. After a brief, expansive mood she would again retire into her obstinate taciturnity. I told her, laughing, the story of a friend who asserted that orchids close up when they hear certain words supposed to have an acid reaction on them, and said that the same thing happened to her when I talked to her. But she remained silent; she never replied to remarks that might imply a compliment. Many times I went to the library without being able to exchange more than a conventional greeting with her, just as though the previous day had never taken place; there were also more readers under the sky-light. Heraclitus and Émile Zola were consulted by a crowd of poorly dressed, suspicious-looking young people; Bernard Shaw by old-fashioned socialists; Marx by a few enthusiasts; Péguy by occasional gloomy individuals. The necessity to order a book for the library by the poet Robert Frost gave me an opportunity for a long talk with her one afternoon. Gloria was a person of culture, and it shocked me to hear her talk about books wearily, as if they belonged to some remote past life with which she had parted without regret. She had learned English as a child, but as she only read it she had merely a passive knowledge of the language. At times, with a sudden sparkle of humor, she referred to things that she had learned in English; then, because of circumstances or people about her, quickly took refuge again behind her indifference. She gave the impression of being absorbed in thoughts and calculations incompatible with the world in which she was destined to live. She seemed to live somewhere else and to come here only on the wing, eager to be off again. At other times we would talk about the films that she or I had seen the day before. She always wanted to isolate herself personally from things. She was looking for something — trying to find her own terrain. I did not know what it was, or where. I, in turn, was looking for mine in her.

I found in Gloria Bambil — I had suspected it from the beginning — what was undoubtedly a virgin human field, devoid of the horrible, boring machinery of studied, trite attitudes. By not allowing herself to be observed, by turning away when she was hard pressed, by her withdrawal into herself, she showed that if she wished to admit no one to the vulnerable depths of her nature, it was not because she did not possess them. That was also the reason for her naked, intent, almost cruel gaze.

Basically, I realized that we should never have, perhaps never could have, problems in common.

One day I invited her to lunch with me. I thought that she would refuse, but she accepted quite spontaneously.

At a table in the Munich restaurant near the library — a small room in pseudo-Bavarian style — I felt in a more comfortable atmosphere to talk to her and ask her questions. The reserved tables were on one side of the room, in large wooden alcoves, open to the ceiling and on one side. The seats had their backs against the wall. They were comfortable and gave a feeling of intimacy.

After ten minutes I had asked her many things.

"Whom do you see? Who are your friends?"

"I haven't any."

"None?"

"None."

"Acquaintances? Plain acquaintances?"

"Few."

"How long has it been that way?"

She shrugged her shoulders. Her gray eyes did not blink. "I don't know! Always."

"And you live alone?"

"Alone."

"For how long?"

"For five years."

"And your family?"

"My father died five years ago."

"What did he do?"

"He was a merchant. A man of no importance. A man."

"And how long have you worked at the library?"

I did not see her gray eyes blink.

"Five years too."

"Do you enjoy solitude so much that you want to make it absolute?"

"It is no less absolute when one fills it with people. But the truth is that if I have become accustomed to being alone, it is not on principle" — she smiled — "but because I have never tried to get outside of my solitude."

"That is strange; very strange."

She shrugged her shoulders with a certain brusqueness and looked pensively out the window into the street.

"Occasionally I see someone," she said. "I go out with someone." She shrugged her shoulders again, but this time slowly and with a certain sweetness. "People. Everyone to his own caprices and tastes."

After a moment she said: "I have come to doing without anything that might make my days endurable to me. I don't even live in an agreeable room. I live in a horrible room."

"Why? I don't understand that either. I don't understand any of it."

"What need is there for self-indulgence? The worse off one is — "

She looked at me, mocking my surprise and incredulity, and began to laugh.

"And that's not the worst of it. The worst of it is that I *am* that way. I don't make myself that way. That's the way I *am*."

"But that's such a strange sort of asceticism."

"No, it's not asceticism. It's not asceticism. Asceticism is something deliberate. I don't plan things to be like that. They happen that way because they happen; perhaps because I make things turn out that way."

I remembered that she had said something like that about Synge.

"I don't mind it at all, so it involves no sacrifice."

"Really?"

"Perhaps if it required a sacrifice I wouldn't be the way I am, because I'm incapable of sacrifice."

"Then with that fatalism — " I started to say, intentionally.

"It's not fatalism either."

"What is it, then?"

257

"Nothing. Is it necessary to label oneself?"

"I think so in order to understand oneself."

"Nothing is gained by it," she replied. "With one face you are one thing, with another another."

"I meant that being as you are — without giving it any name — you would have accepted my invitation to lunch with me as you would have allowed an advertising leaflet to be thrust into your hand on the street."

"Why?" she said. "I also know how to say no. And I mean it very much when I say it!"

"That's a little more comforting."

"But there is one thing that you don't know about me and you seem to believe the opposite. To be with me is depressing."

I told her that I did not believe it and that on the contrary I found it very pleasant.

"All right, you will find out differently."

She took out a package of cigarettes, lighted one, and asked me about my work. In a few moments, and a flood of words, I told her that my history, if I had one, was the history of common moral dissatisfaction and great restlessness, but at the same time of hope. I told her that I felt the destiny of my country as keenly as if it were my own, and that because the hours that it was passing through were blind, I found that I too was leading a blind life. Wanting to fight to make it better, I could not fight alone and was even unable at that moment to get others to fight.

Gloria's eyes were fixed on mine and I read clearly the thought behind her eyes, the thought that said: "Why?" with keen, calm, cold detachment.

Her gaze seemed to come from the icy depths of despair, yet it was young, beautiful, incredulous, and terribly sure of its indifference, not a gaze of failure.

"She interests me," I said to myself. "I should like to arouse her enthusiasm and give her a faith of some sort."

She leaned an arm on the table, her face resting on her hand at a slight angle, as though to see me more distinctly. She acted as if, divining my secret thoughts, she relied on her firm conviction that nothing was worth while.

"You can't imagine what lucidity living entirely alone gives you," she said.

"Do you think I have done anything else? I live alone too," I commented.

"Perhaps you have not lived as completely alone."

She glanced out into the street again and said: "You can't have been really alone if you still believe that."

Then after a moment, extending her smoking cigarette toward me significantly, she asked:

"What would happen to a man forced to spend his whole life like an animal?"

"Who knows! He would rage like an animal."

"That's what some of us do here." (I thought she was looking at me angrily.) "Only instead of rage it's a consuming sense of futility, perhaps a deep malevolence too. Something like feeling yourself an intruder in your own house and as though you were constantly throwing yourself out of every place."

"I would never have believed you capable of such pessimism." I set my knife and fork down on the plate and leaned back against the carved back of the bench. "At first sight you seem, on the contrary, to be made of such strong stuff."

"Strong? Thank God, I am!" She tossed her head with a nervous gesture. "Thank God!" she said again.

"Then?"

"What has the one got to do with the other? My resistance is a positive quantity made up of negative quantities. That may sound like nonsense, but it is mathematically sound."

The heartiness of her laughter made the empty glasses vibrate. For a moment she seemed to have escaped from herself through laughter and become something much more docile and human.

259

She opened her handbag and took out a handkerchief, leaving the mirror in its place without even thinking of looking at herself in it. She was extraordinarily sure of herself and indifferent to the impression that she made on others. She laid the handbag on the table and settled back comfortably against the bench. Her action symbolized the distance that she always tried to keep. Except for some polite, casual question, she gave no indication of any interest in me, in what I had done or in how I had lived prior to that very moment. She was solidly there with her beautiful gray eyes and keen, sun-tanned face, without visible ties with any person or thing except the bonds that chained her to her own solitude. Her independence had the blind stoicism of a plant weathering its storms alone.

Reversing her position, I leaned forward on the table, resting my elbows on it, both hands folded over the package of cigarettes that lay on the tablecloth.

"Apparently there is nothing more desirable than to carve out one's dimensions completely on every side, breaking all points of contact as though they were points of confusion. But isn't that state of personal crystallization the worst sort of prison? Tell me the truth, don't you ever feel any temptation to break your walls and open a crevice in yourself?"

"I never feel the temptation because I would go out to others through that crack, and I am a fright."

I knew that this was a conventional phrase, and that it was my part to take it seriously and try to talk her out of it. But as though suddenly annoyed by something I had said to her, or restless or impatient at the turn that the conversation had taken, she glanced at her wrist-watch and said that it was time to return to the library. It was three o'clock. While I paid the waiter, she stood up and straightened her tweed jacket. She continued to be impatient to go, but she was smiling again; her nostrils flared a little and the corners of her mouth wore an engaging expression of polite affability. She could be by turns harsh, cold, aggressive, or again childishly soft. But all this from the remote region in which she lived, like a person who occasionally relents but never yields.

While we were walking the few blocks that separated us from the old library building she had time to laugh again with a touch of irony at my innumerable questions, and to tell me that, when asked the meaning of the word *life* at the age of four, she had immediately replied that it was "something full of people."

But the days that followed showed me the terribly sad side of her character. In the course of our many conversations she never hinted at a single relationship with anyone about her or one — even distant — effective or solicitous presence in her life. Nothing! There was a total void around her, since the multitude of faces about us means nothing unless their pallor or gaiety can be related to us in some way. But why had she sought it and how could she endure it? Almost daily, whenever her calm, somber reserve permitted, I tried to fathom her secret. Was it a failure, a disappointment, or a congenital inability to be at peace with herself and to maintain an emotional equilibrium with people? It was no less difficult than at first. She hated to talk about herself or to say anything that was self-revealing. As I soon saw, it was because she genuinely detested herself.

Her resistance could not have been stouter. The day after a friendly chat I invariably found her silent, absorbed in her work, and impossibly distant. I had to start all over again and renew the siege. It was not an amorous siege. It was rather an instinctive feeling of deep solidarity, as though someone were to tell us that we have mysterious duties toward a person we scarcely know — duties imposed upon us even before we became aware of that person's existence. When I recall her resistance, I find it difficult to believe — it always seems an exaggeration of my memory. The truth is that I see in her tortured nature only the painful series of those sudden retreats, subtle withdrawals, quick silences, and recurrent evasions.

43

MERCEDES MIRÓ had suddenly revisited my life. In that dingy, grubby little restaurant in Carabelas, as she was powdering her nose with the aid of her little mirror, she said: "Come along, you will have a good time. The most admirable fauna of Buenos Aires will be at the Luinis'. . . ." Receiving an astonishing letter from her after not seeing her for so long a time, how could I fail to invite her to dine in one of the little restaurants that enchanted her and reminded her — alas, too pallidly! — of past suppers in the Bucca di San Ruffilo, in the Covent Garden grottoes, or in the little Roman taverns in the Via dei Condotti. The poor girl insisted on finding in Buenos Aires the nearest chance equivalents of her European life. The letter that I had received from her might have been written by a bright pupil of Señor Menéndez Pidal rather than by Mercedes. She was well made up, but no longer so young. Alas, the blurring effect of thirteen years on a delicate face!

There was news also of Jiménez. Shortly after the publication of my book I received a letter from him that delighted me. His vision being so reduced, he had immediately had my book read to him and had even deciphered some paragraphs of it himself. He said that it had given him hours of happiness such as he had not known for a long time. "Our ramshackle old ship seems to be afloat again. I see it sailing staunchly from this distance, and I recognize with emotion the hum of its motors that we fashioned together." He told me which "nights" he had liked best in the panorama of my character's life.

With this agreeable impression in my mind, I left for the Luini reception in the latter part of the afternoon. The Luini house, modeled after a luxurious old French mansion, had undoubtedly weighed heavily in the mind of Giovanni Cova, Baron Luini, when he had decided to marry his Argentine wife.

I quickly mounted the broad stairway and walked through three enormous, deserted rooms before coming to the small dining-room, its walls nearly hidden by magnificent old tapestries. A crowd of people was milling around the table, reaching for orangeade and port wine.

I found Mercedes and went with her to speak to our hostess.

The nervous exclamations of the elegant, perfumed women rang out sharply, accompanied by the metallic clanking of their bracelets as they raised and lowered their arms, picking up glasses, setting them down again, and selecting tempting tidbits from the small dishes. At that moment I caught sight of Señor Somberg coming in, carefully and resplendently groomed, accompanied by his wife, who had the beautiful, languid face of a gypsy and wore a white dress with a black bolero and black hat. We exchanged a few words of greeting, and as we mentioned Borescu, I remembered the thirty pesos a month that Somberg had given him for tutoring his son. "He was a truly well-prepared man," said Somberg with the air of one who always recognizes evident things. "A truly well-prepared man." We were surrounded by various people. What a sweet, beautiful face, with its golden ocher skin, that unknown woman had who was looking at us through her half-empty glass! Beside her, with light hair and dark, pointed beard, like the gentleman in the steel gorget in El Greco's *Martyrdom of Saint Maurice*, the host's brother-in-law looked at us with questioning eyes and half-open mouth, happy to be alive, the representative of the oldest and idlest colonial stock of landed proprietors.

Luini entered with halting gait and fine, well-bred head, weighed down by tradition and years, dressed in black, with a white, old-fashioned waistcoat. He was accompanied by two ladies of abundant age, lost in a whirl of bright rouge and resplendent silk. Their entrance provoked a cross-fire of compliments, ejaculations, and greetings. From the end of one of the tables in the rear of the dining-room the senator from Salta, the very eminent and conspicuous Dr. Riveros, raised his champagne glass, directing a smile of malicious complicity at one of the recently arrived ladies, who blushed faintly and replied by arming herself in turn with a glass held out by Baron Luini.

A half-hour later I said good-by to my hostess and to Mercedes and walked slowly down the avenue toward the Recoleta, climbed the steps of the upper plaza, and crossed the street in front of the Museum, breathing the purest air in the world. The surrounding garden and fountains were in darkness, but the rectangular lake was discreetly lighted. Some children were still sailing tiny sailboats. A man, a simple, smiling person, was teaching them how to make their boats turn. The children religiously watched his hands, their tongues squeezed between their teeth, as if to help the arduous operation. The man and the children were happily absorbed in their task. I stood awhile watching them.

44

I REMEMBER going with Gloria one Sunday afternoon to a concert at the Colón. We bought cheap seats in the gallery, cheek by jowl with poverty and enthusiasm, where one breathes pure rapture when the right note is struck, but where pandemonium breaks loose if a false one is hit. What shall I say about that afternoon? We were deeply moved by a solemn Brahms symphony and by a simple Haydn canzonet.

When we left the theater, night had already closed in. We walked down Viamonte Street toward Cerrito; alone in the little square, the friendly statue of Dorrego was riding, eternally motionless. After walking a few blocks, we dropped into a confectionery for tea. Gloria chose a table near the big window. The unflattering light showed her delicate face at a moment of such sensitiveness that her quiet expression seemed full of grief. We ordered tea with lemon. When it came in steaming, I enjoyed its acrid odor, which had pleased me so much as a child.

We wondered who the person in a heavy traveling ulster at one of the center tables might be, who was studying a railroad time-table by the window overlooking the broad, newly paved avenue. With his apoplectic neck and fat, powdered face he looked like an impoverished impresario. A few melancholy, nondescript Sunday strollers were passing along the great avenue, flecked from above by the incessant blinking of the electric signs. We talked casually about the places where we had been brought up.

Gloria suddenly told me her father's history.

"I have had a false shame," she said, "about my personal affairs, as I find it difficult to talk about even the most trivial thing concerning myself. But why shouldn't I tell you about it? Perhaps my silence has been only because of mistrust. Today, at least, I feel like talking."

Why did her somber, dry, almost dour manner of telling about her father add so much to her beauty instead of detracting from it?

. . . "I was an adolescent and had the curious impression that he was sharpening his selfish isolation to a stabbing point like a pencil sharpened by a razor. He became all point, all sharpness, with scarcely any flesh left on his body. We lived alone. From the time of my mother's death he took every opportunity to wound me. His cruelty was subtle, indefatigable, and so intellectually refined that for years there were whole nights when I couldn't get a restful sleep, starting up every little while as though I saw the image of his persecution materialize out of the darkness of my room. I would go out and walk the streets, returning overwrought and exasperated. I still remembered the time when he had showed some affection for me. A suspicious, intolerant old age was closing in about him. I never ceased to wonder about life, which could shut us off so completely from all that is human and make us so intolerant and intolerable, so repugnant and selfish, as we grow old. Perhaps our lives serve only to make us aware, for a moment, that we are to live alone for all eternity and that there is no relief, oblivion, or rest except that journey toward the hardening of our arteries and our souls. . . ."

She painted a grim portrait of the old man wandering in the corridors of his canny malignity and of his particularized and general hatred. She interrupted herself to tell me what her home had been like at that period of her story, a gloomy place, even the little garden where the sun seemed to try to hide its head and shine less brightly. Her childhood had been lulled by the sound of the sea, but her adolescence in the capital had been darkened by living beside the old man who became daily more and more crabbed, sarcastic, and insulting. Old age ended by turning him into an island of hatred.

Gloria raised her teacup in her slender, ringless brown fingers.

"When you control circumstances and can mold and transform them, you force them to resemble yourself, but when you accept them as they come and give in to them, you end by resembling them completely. From those four years of living without a moment's rest, surrounded by lovelessness, monotony, sarcasm, and aversion for life, I acquired similar characteristics and a distaste for life myself.

"To economize, Father spent the last eight months of his life in a sanatorium in the suburbs. He had a small fortune in the bank, but he would not have touched it for anything. I went to the sanatorium every morning in a slow-moving street-car and stayed until nightfall, watching in silence the whole day beside that corpse, whose only remaining sign of life was a latent bitter, concentrated hostility. He needed me there to nurse him, but he hated me. I knew that that was his constant feeling; he hated my youth and the thought that I would outlive him. It made him lie sullenly for hours on end with his eyes fixed on

266

the ceiling. No one can have any idea of what that was like." Her voice became husky. "It was like a cancer with which my father had deliberately infected my morale and affection for him. When I did not feel already dead myself, I wanted to commit suicide. I would open the window — in the last hours before dawn, waiting for the light, calling for it, needing it desperately, feeling that I would go mad if it didn't come. I had neither memories nor plans for the future to steady me. Instinct alone saved me. As for any outside life, not one stimulus, not a single tie."

She made no gestures. Only her lips moved. She was all self-control and calmness.

"Then he died. He left all his money to a charity that was to bear his name. He wanted to remain here somehow after his death, even though his whole family died neglected. He recommended me to an influential friend to give me suitable employment. I have been in the library ever since. At first I walked about in a dreamless sleep, like a specter. I remember that period as one of complete alienation. One day, I don't know why or how, it all changed. I began to take an interest in things. It was like opening my eyes to the delights and richness of the material world — a sort of rebirth; but how superficial! Much of my inner being had been warped and destroyed, and little by little my renewed interest in things in turn waned, leaving in its place only this wreck that you see here. . . ." She smiled. "Do you think that anything interests me now? I look at people pass as if I were watching a parade from the sidewalk, having no share in it or interest in its purpose."

She explained that this came perhaps less from cowardice than from a strange lassitude.

I replied that I could not imagine her that way, as she gave no evidence of lassitude, but, on the contrary, of strength and of being very much alive. She did not reply; she merely looked at me.

As if continuing the same theme, she began to tell me about expressions that she had observed on people's faces at the concert.

"At times," she said, "one feels that communication is still possible, that there are people capable of reaching, touching, and treading a land where a certain nobility is breathed, a certain awareness of one's own vulnerability and of the supremacy of other sounder and gentler values."

I was overjoyed and said:

"You see. You have a determination in you to find it."

She quickly defended herself:

"No. It's only a passing fancy. I immediately become convinced that nothing is worth while."

After a few more minutes' conversation about other things, she suddenly showed again that eagerness to get away that at times possessed her.

"Tonight I have an enormous list of books to copy." She smiled as she exaggerated its length.

We crossed the avenue, entered Lavalle Street, traversed a short, dark block, passed the theater district, and again entered a gloomy section.

We were walking quickly, and I talked about one trivial thing after another. She replied smiling.

"It would be nice to go out often together," I said, "and see some shows and things."

She walked a few steps without replying. It seemed as though she were not going to.

"All right," she said at length.

"Can I come and get you tomorrow night?"

"No, not tomorrow."

"When, then?"

"Are you going to the library?"

"Yes."

"Good; then we'll make plans there."

We reached the door of her house. One of the old Lacroze street-cars passed. The night was agreeably fresh and encouraged us to continue walking. A few blocks to the east, Leandro Alem Street dipped down toward the river. I told Gloria that these were my old haunts and gaily described Anselmi and Jiménez. Then I became silent. She looked at me without saying anything, her head leaning back against the wall where it made an angle with the door. She was tall and very pretty. I said something to her again, hoping to light up her eyes with sudden curiosity, but her expression was absorbed, as if she were thinking instead of listening.

We took leave of each other until the following day.

45

WE were walking toward the revolving bridge, the throat that separates that part of the city from the mouth of the river, the narrow palate of the Costanera. Sleepy guards were halting motor-cars and inspecting them apathetically before allowing them to proceed. The great customs warehouses loomed up one after another against the cold background of the night, the number of each slip painted in black on a whitewashed rectangle. Gloria and I were both great walkers and liked to take long strolls at night. We were swinging along rapidly, saying little, breathing in the fresh night air with relish and approaching the zone appropriated by sky and water. There was the Fresh Water Sea; beyond, the Atlantic. We talked about the two bodies of water and Gloria said jestingly that it was like talking about physics and metaphysics. As we passed a sentry-box, one of the guards looked at us suspiciously. Gloria stepped down from the sidewalk and we took a bee-line along the deserted pavement. Diffused moonlight bathed the blackened freighters tied up at their moorings. Near at hand a dog howled in pain. The silence shut in again immediately. Far off, at the end of the street, the sky dipped down to the river just beyond the low wall.

I did not know what to say to her.

"Have you never been tempted to take a ship and sail away without any fixed destination?"

"Why? Why take myself on a trip?"

"To see things."

"Things?" she said, as though I had said something grotesque, and she gazed down the street ahead of her. "Food for the brute beast. . . . Besides I am poor."

She thought for a moment, then returned to her answer to emphasize it:

"But I can't let myself do anything that I like. I can't do it. You won't believe that I can't bear myself."

"That's not fair. It's an attitude."

"An attitude? Why do you say that? An attitude! I am thoroughly convinced."

"You are thoroughly convinced of what?" I asked her.

"That I annoy myself, and that I am annoying Martín Tregua."

I laughed. It seemed to me so absurd and childish!

We had come to the wide esplanade that skirts the shore.

"It's unfair of you to say that; but I am not surprised. What you need, as you yourself have let me see, is to put down roots into external reality. You make me think of those air plants that droop because they don't get proper nourishment from the soil and don't mingle with its joys and sorrows. Have you never thought of creating living problems for yourself, of putting external difficulties in your own path to overcome?"

She fixed her gray eyes suspiciously on me.

"I do nothing but that. That's what my whole life is — a process of overcoming things. Otherwise I should already have disappeared."

"No, it's not that sort of struggle. What you consider a prob-

lem is mere living, which is no problem. It's no problem to conquer the more or less strange antipathy that one may have for
living; the problem is to struggle loyally against reality instead
of allowing reality to rule your life."

She looked sharply at me.

"Do you know what the trouble is with you, Martín?" she
said. "You have had no calamities in your quiet life and you
seek in fictitious problems the accidents that you have missed.
It's the other way around with me. I have had many things
happen to me. Concrete things, not imaginary ones."

She tossed her head to shake her hair back from her forehead, and when she spoke again, her tone had changed:

"But why so many arguments? What is the use of them here
in this silent spot, and on a night like this? They have no problems. Or perhaps you think they do." She glanced at me mock-
ingly before turning her eyes again toward the darkness where
river and night mingled and only the southern constellations
were to be seen, more brilliant than ever.

"Isn't it splendid?"

It was really splendid, the vast expanse of darkness, and the
swift winging of a bird in front of us.

"What bird is that?" she asked looking up.

"I don't know. I never know the names of trees or birds."

As she laughed, her teeth flashed very white against her
delicate brown face.

"Why don't you tackle that problem and learn them?"

"I've often thought of it, but I was not born to learn them."

"That sounds as though I might have said it."

"You are right. It is something you might have said." She
smiled, gazing off at the river with an air of abstraction. Her fine
head was well set on her shoulders.

"God!" I thought. "How sad and pensive her slender figure
looks against the night and the river!"

She had a strange way of turning from a light conversation to sudden seriousness and then remaining quiet, absorbed, and impenetrable. Her moods disconcerted me. I was desperately looking for the right word to draw her out of her abyss, but, unable to find it, I too lapsed into impotent silence.

A one-horse coach passed in the darkness at a slow trot. An embracing couple could be barely distinguished inside. The coach receded along the avenue behind us.

Gloria picked up an old piece of wood from the ground, apparently driftwood. Looking at it carefully, we found that it had a large letter Y, like an initial, burned into it. We wondered what its history could be.

"Let's walk, shall we?" she said.

The poplar-bordered avenue seemed to extend endlessly along the river. The poplars were young, short, and spindly. On the west side of the boulevard were merry-go-rounds, Ferris wheels, and other contrivances to divert the summer pedestrians and catch their pennies; beyond lay a vague, uninhabited region upon which the city encroached in places. Like a small peninsula of masonry, a salient on which the bathing-establishment had been built jutted off the avenue into the water. The avenue, filled in summer with vulgarity and coarseness, had a silent, mournful reserve in winter, like the clowns who resume their solemn, dignified private lives after the circus is over.

It was undoubtedly this atmosphere that made me notice how far apart we were. Gloria was walking more slowly than a few minutes earlier and I was right beside her, but two people more remote from each other could hardly have been imagined. Touched by the same air, we were otherwise completely extraneous to each other.

She was telling me about what had happened to her while shopping that afternoon. Coming out of a store, she had seen a ragged young man standing by the window. As she was about to pass him, he withdrew a step, looked at her, his eyes flaming with anger, and insulted her. Astonished, she had tried to see what he looked like, but could see only his averted face. He continued to insult her.

"What ailed him?" I said.

"I always draw such attitudes," she replied. "I have thought about it often, but I don't know why it is. It's as though I saw my face differently from the way it appears to other people. . . . From time to time I come across that expression that I know so well, an attitude of hatred that seems to be evoked by some word written on me."

She told me of another similar incident. It had happened several years before, the offender that time being an old musician who had lived for some time in the house on Lavalle Street.

"I think that shows a great power," I said to her. "It indicates that you can attract the opposite just as violently."

"Which?" she asked. She often asked bluntly the most obvious things. When I answered with a trivial compliment, she said nothing. She did not even look at me, but continued to gaze intently into the distance as though refusing to admit that any friendly phrase could have been addressed to her. Her wide brown eyelids seemed never to blink.

Then — hypocritically — I thought it the part of strategy to take the offensive. I told her that to me she was made to please greatly, to attract, and to hold. I stopped. She must have heard my breathing and perceived that I was waiting for her reaction.

She began to talk quickly about something else, about a play that was to open the following day at one of the theaters — a translation from Gogol — that she wanted to see, and about how little was showing currently that was worth while.

I insisted on bringing her back to the subject. But she kept to her silence, and I saw that I had showed my hand and been disavowed.

I too became silent. We crossed over to the central planted area under the poplars and walked back toward the city. Gloria was rarely unaware of the invisible projection of her spirit. There was something about her of the sculptor who continues to think about his modeling, deep in abstraction as we talk to him; who approaches his work, imprints some lineaments on it, studies it thoughtfully, steps back, and again resumes his uninterrupted abstraction.

Sometimes I made her laugh and succeeded in coaxing her face to open in surrender. I was satisfied with this triumph.

46

"PLEASE don't," she said.

It was after midnight and we were again standing by the same parapet. Only now it was winter, harsh, tyrannical winter, that ruled over the meeting of the river and the shore.

"Please don't."

A movement of her tense neck drew her suffering face away from mine.

"Why not? Why not?" I heard my voice saying in the night. It seemed solitary and alien in tone, even in its intent. Having its origin in warm seed, the night chilled it. It seemed necessary for me to try to repeat the phrase with more control over my voice, but my voice persisted in breaking as it struck the atmosphere.

"Why not?"

Gloria dropped her hands. I stood in front of her. She was leaning against the parapet, the misty river behind her.

"But don't you see that it's impossible? Don't you see that it's impossible?"

I continued to ask why. There is a moment when we can no longer bear the burden of words. When our body tries to break other moorings than intelligible, verbal, argumentative ones.

"But don't you see, it's impossible?"

I repeated again what I had said five minutes, ten minutes, fifteen minutes before. I don't know what possessed me not to vary it, to break that obstinate bridge, in order that she should finally burn her boats, and the object and the obstacle dissolve.

Suddenly I took her by both arms. She stood rigid, not even trembling. I looked at her with the intensity that goes with a last appeal, to see whether it will be wrecked and sink.

"I was not made for love. I was made for solitude, and I want to keep it."

"That is not true."

"I was made for solitude. I am no good for anything else. I don't want to be different. I have a horror of being anything else."

"No, that's not true."

"Yes, it is true."

I felt the desperate appeal of her eyes, contrasting with her dark skin. Her mouth was half open, between displeasure and entreaty, her whole attitude closely akin to physical pain.

"I don't want to give that to anyone. I don't want to! Haven't I a right not to let what I am be destroyed?"

"No, that is not so. You're keeping up an attitude."

Her voice writhed, but her body was calm and serene in its rigidity.

"It's not true," I repeated.

"You know nothing about me, poor lad. You don't know what I am like, or that tied to someone I would be impossible, even more impossible."

"Only life can prove or disprove such a statement."

"What has life to do with it? One is oneself, stable. Life passes."

"Life is what forces things into their true shape. Why do you insist upon denying and pretending?"

"I'm not pretending. I want to be mistress of my own poor substance. That's all I am saying. I want to be mistress of myself."

I moved closer to her, but she wanted to walk and I gave in.

We walked. Again she was retreating. I said nothing. Far off to one side, against the darkness of the river, a tiny moving light could be seen, the faint reddish blinking of a ship in the fog.

For a moment I thought that she was merely proud, that she was acting as she did as a matter of pride, and that it was difficult for her to yield. But I realized at once that I had done her an injustice and that it was the storm within her that divided and ruled her.

"I don't understand," I said, "how you can maintain such an artificial decision, so cold and so lacking in human feeling."

"I'm not human."

"Not frank."

"I'm not frank," she said decisively. "Who is frank? What does that mean?"

Although I knew that she was telling the truth, I denied it. Again I took her by the arm and made her stop. She looked at me, shaking her head as at a child whose whim cannot be granted, and continued walking.

"Why do you insist upon an impossible thing?" she said. "Why spoil what was really pleasant and rare? This friendship of ours. You want to destroy it all, to put things on a plane where they will at once become absurd. You know so little about me that you don't even know that I have had some experiences. . . . That is why I know. That is why I know."

Her remark worried me instantly. I was dismayed. I abandoned my eagerness to argue and listened to her.

"I know myself. It is like knowing — what shall I say? — a shipwreck."

She said nothing of what I wanted to hear. Then I insisted. We stopped. The river was behind her again.

"Only for a moment," I said to her, "let's give up all prejudices for a moment."

"But what has that got to do with it? It's that I am useless, I'm no good!"

Back of her head, against the river, I saw a dark bird pass, flying toward the water just as some nights before.

She became still more determined, almost violent.

"It's like compulsion. What you are doing is to try to force me. I won't be forced. When I am forced, I rebel. I can't understand why you want to spoil things this way. Why do you want to spoil them? How ignorant you are! Would you insist on transforming something that can't be changed?"

Suddenly she changed her tone and, pleading, said: "Forget, forget that there is anything but friendship."

Her hand was resting on my forearm. It lay there asking to be heard and believed. All the blood seemed to have gone from her brown face. Her large eyes were quiet and her lips parted.

I took a step forward, drew her quickly to me, and felt the passiveness of her warm, half-open lips. Her arms had dropped to her sides and it was as if I were kissing a corpse except for the warmth of her mouth and the delicate firmness of her body. It was for a second. She raised her arms and made a quick effort to push me away. Her eyes and eyebrows had contracted in an expression of despair, almost of horror. I let her go. Her back again touched the low parapet, and she looked at me in sad anarchy.

"Please," she said wearily and without anger. "Please."

I felt that something had happened which could no longer be arrested.

47

THE DAYS that followed reflected a change in our relations.

At first we both lived in rapture. We lived exalted, devouring time in greedy gulps. My daily work pointed toward my meetings with Gloria. She would dine at my house or we would look for an obscure corner where one could take refuge at will among the clarets or the straw-covered bottles of Chianti, and where at times an indigent violinist wandered in.

She seemed to me to represent the noble, silent, somber country that I had always been looking for.

She was not carved in the large. Perhaps nothing about her was impressive, everything had rather an intimate, individual, restless quality.

She did not yield everything about her; a part of her remained out of reach, irreducible.

What sort of bond tied me to Gloria? It was impossible to determine the sentiment that lay behind our relations. In the final analysis there was something strange about it, a painful foreboding and an intuitive need to accompany a soul rather than to love. Accompany? What did that mean? Suddenly, behind these questions, behind Gloria's picture, your picture arose — and, curiously enough, you were the substance and she the shadow.

You were more flesh to me, because you incarnated my need for your visible and moral nature; while with Gloria my whole person, so carnal, felt disembodied and merely a sentiment of solidarity.

What Gloria and I gave to each other was human warmth, but as two strangers might give it, by making a unifying warmth out of everything that separated them.

There were mornings when she came to the library so strangely haggard that I asked her at once whether she had been ill. She answered that she had not slept all night and had got dressed and gone out to walk until daybreak. It was not an unusual occurrence. I realized that her conscience was constantly troubled and unhappy, fighting against itself. What remedy was there against this inveterate restlessness? That was our goal. I thought of every possible means of diverting her and holding her attention. But my own problems did not always interest her, and her mind was reluctant to admit anything that came unbidden.

Under a pretext of our both taking a rest, I persuaded her to spend a week with me in a hotel in the south. The cold air, as bracing and clear as a living crystal, greatly benefited her. The hotel was a small frame structure at the foot of a snow-capped mountain, built as an aid station, on an isolated slope leading to a dam that created the most marvelous lake in the world. I thought of the Villa d'Este at Como. This was newer, and more intimate. Gloria returned to the hotel with her dull skin chilled and tense after walking with the wind whipping her face. The only other guests were an English professor and his wife, and a naturalist of uncertain nationality. During those days we were both very happy. Waking early, we opened the window and looked out at the reflections cast by the winter sun on the ice that crowned the distant peaks. A road climbed to the summit of the nearest mountain, and the gigantic pines and proud araucarias stood like statues in the splendor of the chill north wind. We played and laughed. Gloria enjoyed the rolls, butter, and honey that we ate for breakfast in front of the open window. She seemed to be happy.

"Do you want to stay here?" I asked her.

"Yes."

"How long?"

"A thousand years."

Laughter on her beautiful, penitent face was always wonderful to me.

When she found herself before the immensity of the icy landscape, under the rugged crevices of the sharp, snowy crests that fell at last in soft syllables of water, Gloria always remembered the sea. She asked me to stop and said, looking at the tremendous distance that lay between the slightly bluish vertical peaks: "Perhaps if we had gone to the seashore — "

"What? What would have happened if we had gone to the seashore?"

"I don't know. It fascinates me and yet I am afraid of it. It's strange. I am so absurdly afraid of it that it sometimes makes me wonder. I can find no explanation for it."

"We are going to the seashore, too."

She looked down at the earth under her feet.

"No, perhaps it would be better not to go."

We went on, and after a little she again brought the subject up.

"Isn't it absurd! Such an inexplicable fear. A sort of negative science — a science of the subconscious."

"Yes," I answered. "It doesn't make sense. We'll go to the seashore and you shall get rid of your fear."

"How strange it would be to lose that fear! Shall I lose it?"

"Of course you will."

"Maybe only conscious fears can be banished."

We took exhausting excursions. Leaving the hotel well before noon, we scaled mountains and visited lakes with our Piedmont guide. We came suddenly upon beautiful, noble, awe-inspiring spots. We spent the day laughing, happy to have left our cares and occupations behind us for a few days. At times I helped her to scramble over an obstacle, and she laughed at my efforts. The guide laughed to see us laugh.

"Señores," he said, "ah, señores."

We stopped while the guide went on ahead. I kissed her on the mouth and felt her tremble, not from timidity, but from fatigue. She always looked at me with a gaze that I never knew how to interpret, a long, quiet, sad gaze. She was terribly mistress of herself, as though she were looking at me from a far-distant point.

After viewing gorges, lakes, and peaks, it was generally dusk before the old Ford, driven by our guide, reached the hotel at twilight. We went up to wash. I sat down on the edge of the bed, opposite her, as she fixed her hair before the mirror and got ready for dinner.

"I like you so much," I said to her.

"That's not enough."

"I like you to the point of being enough and more than enough."

"That passes quickly," she said.

"No, it's the only thing that never passes. Other things do."

"What do you like about me?"

"Everything."

"Everything!"

"Everything."

"I would rather you had said that you liked one thing about me."

"I don't like one thing. I like all of you."

"I would prefer it to be only one thing."

"No, it is better that it should be everything."

"No, one thing."

We burst out laughing and I kissed her and stroked her hair, which was so fine that it did not seem human. She let herself be kissed, but never took the initiative. All her gestures seemed to have been inhibited by solitude.

We went down for a cocktail before dinner. In the crudely paneled hall, furnished with rustic chairs, a fire was burning on the hearth. Through the windows the distant landscape could be seen in the chill early evening. At that time of day Gloria was silent. She withdrew into an apathy of distaste and tedium. My battle began again. Every evening at that time my war against the dark angels recommenced. It made me by turns a buffoon, a professor, a story-teller, a dialectician, a liar, and a fool — anything but a quiet man.

Gloria listened and smiled.

Heavens, how I hated to see her suffer!

48

My book had sunk into the water without a ripple. To work on the second part required a great effort. In August a brutal period of demoralization hit me again. I went about like an animal with a sore head, fierce and glowering and hardly able to tolerate my own company. "If you are no good even for this," I kept saying to myself, "what are you good for?" There is nothing for it but to get down to rock bottom and do what you have never been able to do: fight. Gloria seemed not to notice my state of mind.

"This country," I said one night when we were dining in one of the remoter suburbs, "is a giant asleep. Each of its members must be awakened until its whole body is aroused. On this Gulliver's body consciences are stirring of which it does not even feel a tickle as yet."

"There is grave danger," I went on, thinking to myself, "when culture and conscience sleep. They fall easy prey to invading evil. We live here in a system of superficial attitudes, and the giant sleeps more and more soundly."

Gloria unsympathetically watched me embroil myself in these thoughts. She had confidence neither in the people nor in any of the causes that might be taken up on their behalf.

"Let's try to improve ourselves, if improvement is possible," she said. "Why think in abstract terms about a lot of people with whom we might not even be able to find one subject of agreement if we knew them personally?"

Later I was talking to her about herself, and she was looking off into the distance with pensive, reserved eyes. We were making plans. "One day," I said, "we'll make a slow journey all over the country. We'll see the desolate crudeness and solemn beauty of southern Argentina, where the country stands with its feet planted close together, and we'll follow it up from inn to inn to the northern territories and see the tall forests, great rivers, and massive dignity of our humble laborers. One day we'll set out on a slow pilgrimage."

But Gloria was not enthusiastic about the idea. She did not like planning. She had no interest in the future, even in what the next day would bring forth. It was as if every day her anchor took hold at such depths that it was difficult for her to pull it up and move on.

"Look," she said, suddenly pointing to a street that dipped down and disappeared at a lonely crossing, brightly lighted like a deserted portico. She did not need to say anything else. The most trivial scenes and places gave us common impressions that brought us to a plane of intimacy. "If I were to paint a portrait of myself I'd make it like that — deserted."

"You'd make a bad portrait of yourself, then. We all carry about with us a self-portrait that we don't in the least resemble."

"It would be a good portrait of me."

We left the crossing behind us, but turned around for another look at its bright desolation.

"It's beautiful in spite of everything," she said.

"Yes and it's true that it resembles you a little."

"I'd rather look like things than like people."

"You are an incurable romantic. . . ."

"Things sometimes have such solidity, dignity, and quality," she said.

"Shall we keep on walking?"

"No, let's turn back."

"We can go back to the house for a while."

"That will be nice."

"I wonder whether we can find a taxi around here."

"Here is one now."

I gave the address to the driver.

49

So we went on, the whole month, happy and united, and made the acquaintance of new places, new refuges, new inns. The August cold settled down on the city. On damp days the temperature was bearable, but the dry ones brought a white, piercing cold.

Oblivious of everything, we walked about the city tirelessly, from dawn to midnight, chilled through, but light at heart.

Gloria laughed her sad laughter. We argued in fun, had our serious preoccupations, and spent another month with the deepest gratitude to life for giving us such light and serious moments.

Sometimes, a little after nine in the morning, I went to the library and we talked with the students. At lunch Gloria and I discussed the restless intelligence and rebellious spirit that I liked so much in our young people. Whenever I talked impetuously about that promising vein in the soil of our country, about that other world, that other family, that source of perfection which was the only thing that really mattered to me, she looked at me silently as if, although not wanting to cast doubt upon it, she were skeptical of my vision.

Sometimes I was provoked by her pessimism and protested strenuously. She only laughed at me.

The afternoon's work finished, we met at an appointed place and walked until dinner time. Sometimes we ate in the grill-room of the City, sometimes at Banus. I had returned part of my income to my father and enjoyed feeling poor and working harder than ever. My income now only allowed us to patronize the cheaper places, but in them we were in contact with people stirred by impulses not to be found in the more expensive restaurants, where one saw only presumptuousness and a certain superficial elegance. Only one kind of elegance mattered to me, that of the soul; dignity, scorn for the mean, predatory part of life, and noble detachment in life's struggle.

It is very difficult to find such an aristocracy. A little of it, however, seemed to me to have been fundamental in Argentine character throughout our history. I saw certain noble, open-minded, and chivalrous courage and an intelligent, unselfish strength as basic in the history of our young nation, whose highest military expression had been to call itself "a Founder of Liberty," not a conqueror or a Cæsar. Recognizing that quality as essential, I was all the more disappointed to see it vanishing from Argentina.

I begged and urged Gloria to try to rediscover that quality with me and to make it conspicuous in everything that we saw and touched and in every man that we met. Sometimes I thought that I had actually rediscovered it and said to myself: "Yes, that dignity still lies in our marrow, it still exists — it is only covered up, but it will reappear — it will be worth while to have lived among this people." But Gloria's glance always brought me back to ourselves and to the present moment as if, by way of urging me to rest and relax, she had said: "Nothing can equal a moment of communion between two people, the rest and pause between two series of misfortunes."

I was still unable to define exactly what sentiment Gloria inspired in me. Was it a great compassion, or a simple human tenderness unrelated with the idea upon which love is based, that she was the only woman for me? Something fundamental in me remained untouched by her. Something in me did not belong to her. But, seeing her so remote from life and so lonely, what tenderness seized me, what desire to help her, and what need to give her support, comfort, and faith!

I saw her, during our interminable excursions, lost in this world, wandering in its remoteness, and then it was no longer she but I who cried out. We seemed like two lost souls constantly calling to each other, who, when they see the danger of finding no meeting-ground, feel a greater need than ever for each other and redouble their tenderness. We quickly found a point of meeting, but Gloria always had her strange way of turning from laughter to depression.

There were days when she seemed more tired, more surfeited with life, and less sure of herself than ever. When I asked her about it the next morning or for any reason reminded her of it, she still remained serious, absorbed, and distant. It was useless

285

to try to arouse her. I could only wait for the day to pass. The next day she invariably looked wan and chilled as if she had arrived after an interminable journey. Her smile was frightening.

One of those August nights, a little before midnight, we left the restaurant where we had dined, walked along Florida Street, crossed San Martín Plaza, to Esmeralda and at length turned into Alem Avenue, and home. The temperature was frigid in my room. I closed the window. The long, graceful fingers of Memling's Virgin must have been frozen. I put on the light and Gloria sat down on the arm of an easy chair near the low bookshelf, picked up an apple from a plate, and sniffed it. The room was still very cold. The clock on the Torre de los Ingleses struck midnight. How remote the world was and how quickly time passed! I sat down on the sofa opposite Gloria, threw my head back, and gazed at her as I rested. She asked me how the book was progressing — the second volume of *The Forty Nights of Juan Argentino*. I said that I was writing about the adolescence of one of my characters, who as a child slipped out of his father's old house into the garden and from the top of a ravine recited to the night air poems and speeches that he had learned by heart. The child, and later the adolescent, in the novel was preparing in his permanent night the future sufferer from the stultification of his country, with its swarm of mercenary governors. I told her that in writing the childhood portion I had had Dennis Atkinson a great deal in mind.

"I want you to read it to me," she said. "Please read it to me."

"No, come over here and sit by me." She did not want to come and sit on the sofa. "Come."

"All right."

She sat down beside me.

"Tell me some more about it," she said.

I told her about another part of the book. She listened.

"More."

"No, enough."

"Why?"

"It would be better for you to read it when it is finished."

"No, it's better for you to tell me about it now." She raised her eyes. Her whole being was concentrated in her gray eyes. "Do you love me?" she asked.

"Yes," I said. I didn't know whether I loved her, whether I really loved her. I thought of you.

"Yes," I said, but it was not the whole truth.

She laid her head on my shoulder and held the lapel of my coat in her ringless hand.

"No," she said, "you only like to be with me."

"I love you," I said to her.

"No," she said.

Her eyes were fixed on the floor as she spoke, her head against my shoulder. I could feel in my chest the thoughts that were turning over in her head.

"But one day you will think of me and of the places where we have been together, and about this room, and it will seem very far away to you. You won't feel pain, only a very, very distant recollection."

"No, I shan't ever remember that way, because we aren't going to be separated."

"You'll remember this room. But do you know — ?"

"What?"

"I want you to remember then that you were the only person who had ever done me any good. The only one who had been helpful to me."

"You're a silly girl," I said, "the silliest girl I know, always dwelling on the least pleasant aspect of things."

"And you'll realize too that I was of no use to you, and remember that you insisted that I was."

"I shan't think any such thing."

"And you'll remember that one night, when this room was cold, we were both here, and that there was no one more impossible, no one more insistent upon wasting life and thinking up tragedies."

"Yes, that's true. I shall think that, but I shall also think other things."

"What other things?"

"I shall think that I was very fond of you, that I was infernally fond of you, and that when I held your breast in my hand, it was as if I had in my hand the best in the world, and the best in the world was small and full."

"How happy I shall be for you to think that! And what else?"

"I shall think that I liked your mouth, that it seemed bitter, but inside was full of living warmth, almost a happy warmth."

"Does my mouth look bitter?"

"A little."

"It has a right to look bitter. Was that why that man insulted me? That's why people like to insult me."

"No, it's a bitter mouth that is lovable."

"Nobody loves it."

"I love it."

"No."

"I love it."

The clock on the Torre de los Ingleses struck twelve thirty.

"And won't you think about anything else?"

"Yes, I'll think about other things."

"What other things?"

"I'll think — " I paused and smiled.

"You see, you don't know what else you'll think. What you imagine you'd think is so little. . . . Shame on you. You won't think of anything else."

"Yes, I shall think of other things. I shall think that I liked your fragrance. The fragrance of your skin and your hair, and that it was necessary to me. And that your soul also had its own aroma, a wild, savage aroma."

"How horrible!"

"A wild fragrance like calendulas."

"Jack-ass! Calendulas have no fragrance!"

"Yes, yes, they must have. They must have a fragrance, a fragrance like your soul."

"I haven't a wild soul. My soul is gentle and useless."

"No."

"Yes, my soul is docile and good for nothing."

"You have a soul with a wild fragrance."

"A gentle, useless soul. A soul not worth two coppers."

"Nonsense! A very dear soul! A very valuable soul!"

I squeezed her. We burst out laughing and for a moment were protected by the breath of God. We were happy. I stood up, put out the light, and kissed her. Through the window by Memling's Virgin, only the placid clarity of the August night entered.

50

IT was a baneful year — the last in the 1930's. Pessimism hung like blighted fruit from every tree. Sluice-ways running blood had been opened, irrigating the land and soaking the wheat in the furrows. The corpses lay stark and useless, for all eternity. The living too were useless except for a few who won a place for themselves in history. They burned and destroyed. Throughout the world the vibration of a gigantic resentment turned to self-vindication and mysticism. From the dead earth a fog of theory welled up. Young men facing death said: "It is not gay to die at thirty-five." And they smiled and marched until they fell. A young American astonishment looked at the red fangs of Europe. At the end of August that year there was a bitter cold spell in Buenos Aires. People even wondered whether it would snow. Down by the river the fields were covered with frost. Bounded on three sides by the river, and on all four by the three parties — under the celesti.l patronage of three saints: Justo, Martín, and Isidro — the great heptagon of the metropolis squeezed in its calloused hand its millions of merchants, petty gentlemen, politicians, and other fauna rushing for the easy exit. It was difficult to find a spot where improvisation and venality did not thrive. Everything in the city was jerry-built to save money, or sumptuously fitted out to rob. Everything seemed to have been thrown together to imitate, deceive, or grow rich. It seemed a great city built by dull-witted immigrants, escaped from the secular oppression and misery of other lands, who had gained wealth and power in Argentina. Only what had been built earlier, in the spirit of another Argentine period, kept its proportions and identity in the confused jumble, and even what was Argentine was apparent only when it was faithful to its traditions.

During that cold spell Gloria and I saw each other only at night. I worked uninterruptedly on my book from morning until it was time to meet her. We read the afternoon papers together, sitting in a café or restaurant window, and watching the people hurry by bundled up in heavy wraps. When we went out again, into the pale winter night, I remarked to Gloria that we had the appearance of furtive people hunting for a hiding-place.

"No," she replied, "we don't look like that, but like people carrying a heavy burden. You do particularly. Don't you see what a burden I am?"

I squeezed her arm, which was resting lightly on mine, and became more solicitous than ever. She walked along, her large, thoughtful eyes scarcely ever blinking.

I wanted to get home immediately to my problems and work. I felt that I was wasting time and grew impatient as I remembered the blank paper on my table and all that still remained to be written.

But I did not go. Instead I suggested that we see a show, and I stayed with her, watching over her disconsolately.

She sensed that I was staying on her account. I could not

completely hide it. Then she was even more affected by it and felt uncomfortable, but she said nothing. As soon as the performance was over, she was determined that we should go home. "You could work for another hour." But I insisted on going with her as far as the door of her house in Lavalle Street.

Then I no longer hurried. I walked back through the familiar streets, accumulating pictures, ideas, and impressions for the book. I was living with the creatures that had cost me so much effort to bring out of the subterranean depths of the country to which I owed my own origin. I felt happy. I knew that the intuitions and personal sufferings of that submerged, spiritual population would one day become articulate and important, just as it is important to put people who matter to us, who are weakened and lost, in touch with other beings who can strengthen them and help them radically to find themselves. I was swept away by sudden enthusiasm. Yes, there before me, reflected in the spirit, I saw that complex, fresh new country, a world of purer and younger people in moderate circumstances — no longer overdressed, pompously disguised off-scourings. Once that reality touched me, my vivid vision of the new world that was worth bringing into being pressed forward and made me eager to get back as quickly as possible to the blank paper that awaited me in my room. To the struggle at once!

I wrote until dawn, with a glass of cold milk standing on the table and Memling's Virgin a few steps away.

I went back, drawn by the strength of the current deep inside me, to be myself, to tie myself to the inexorable duty of remaining silent and postponing living in order to tell my message better; of allowing myself no liberties except the sober, sacred liberty of giving my personal testimony.

But something was germinating in the insidious, threatening world, causing something else to wither and die. The American hour was about to strike. Soon — immediately after the sinking of the Old World under its disastrous victories and shouts of hunger, privation, and hatred — the American hour would sound. If that hour did not strike loudly, how were we to justify our position as a small, unarmed nation, and how were we to avoid becoming a permanent colony? Nevertheless, in the new world, we were still too young, too short-sighted, and untried in our commerce and relations with each other. It would be essential for our confident progress to create a state of tension and strength and a conscience almost violent in its decisive energy.

One of those nights, when I reached the house, I found a few lines on the floor, inside my door, hastily scrawled by Acevedo. He had been to see me and asked me to meet him the next day at luncheon. I found him a little cold and very embittered. His noble head seemed to lack its former impressiveness. His hair had turned a snowy white. We lunched on noodles, a roast, and some strawberry-jam pancakes and talked politics. When I was about to order coffee, he protested that we should drink it in one of the Brazilian shops in Florida Street. All of his manias had come to the surface. Hardly anything but manias were left. He was obviously very careful not to talk about his wife.

I went to the library for Gloria at dusk.

"I was going to call you," she said. She seemed worried. "I wanted to see you." She was nervous and looked very thin in her short black coat. We walked toward the Paseo Colón. She did not talk. I told her about my meeting with Acevedo and again thought up cheerful stories to amuse her. I told her about the dinner that first night in the luxurious restaurant and Acevedo's theory of the treason of bread; and about the birth of the journal and its demise. She remained silent.

As we were approaching the customs house, she asked whether we could not go in somewhere and sit down and talk. "I'm all fagged out," she said. "I can't go on."

It was a tawdry place, with a tiled floor. The cold swept in unhindered from the street. On one of the walls hung a lithographed wine advertisement showing Napoleon on St. Helena.

She told me that she was worn out and did not know what to do, or why she went on living.

In the bar a pianola started to play. Its stammering music had something depressing about it. From the small reserved rooms above came bursts of laughter. The proprietor shouted up from below: "It's Bach!" He muttered an imprecation.

Gloria smiled, but sighed unhappily. She propped her head on her right hand, her elbow on the table. The smoke from her cigarette hung close to her face. She talked about the great irredeemable void of her life. I looked at her gray eyes and serious, lonely face. She could not take part in the game. There she sat opposite me, an isolated onlooker, as sad as the timid, unwanted youngsters who stand on the side lines watching other children play.

She seemed to come from miles away. She always gave the impression of speaking not from her natural mind, but from some point far removed from herself, from a distant, weird, intractable, moral world.

I protested. "But you have a tendency to let yourself fall into these states." My voice did not sound persuasive in the bar, which mocked the young night with its garish brilliance. "You deliberately reject all stimuli as if you wanted to end in complete demoralization."

"It's not demoralization," she objected. "It's utter exhaustion."

"That's the same thing."

I was nervous and harsh and dogmatic, and Gloria was very tired and profoundly discouraged or indifferent and did not protest. She merely corrected this or that comment on her state of mind as though anxious that her attitude and underlying condition should not be considered muddled, but rather the logical result of her inability to cope with an accumulation of factors beyond her control. Any misunderstanding of this situation increased the expression of despair and worry in her eyes.

"Besides, I am unhappy that I have talked to you this way about myself. I am not in the habit of tolerating complaints or of telling people about things which are enough to have happend to me. . . . When I first had the feeling that I could give you something and be useful to you, I searched my heart for new attitudes, to replace the hostility and dryness in which I had formerly lived, and I have succeeded only in falling into this greater weakness and uncertainty as to what to do."

"Good God," I thought to myself, "how strange life is! Here I am once more, under almost identical circumstances, using almost the same gestures in dealing with a creature ripe for disaster and ruin."

We human beings attract only people of our own obscure family, only those who have been joined to us by blood for God knows how many years. The miser, the robber, the invalid, and the lusty man each attracts his own kind; and so the world is broken up into roving, hostile tribes that will neither unite nor reach an understanding among themselves. "Good God," I thought again, "how strange life is!"

Under the gaze of that likeness of Napoleon, I laid my hand on hers, cold and tired and with its barely perceptible tremor. "Yes, it's precisely that that's unfair," I said to her. "The fear of not giving enough of oneself and the tendency to change one's character for a different one. But you are mistaken. I need your intelligence and your sensibility. I wanted you. I have wanted you for a long time. You help me, and I rely on you implicitly. You are very, very useful to me. You are already a part of me."

"No," she said, shaking her head vigorously. "It's terrible. Before, I was hard, dry, remote, and recalcitrant, but strong. I was something. I had form and shape. Now I have neither. Your contact — through no fault of yours — has made me unhappy. . . . Soft, soft, soft — something that I detest. That's why I told you before that it would be better not to come near me, not to touch me, because I knew that it would ruin me."

"Enough, this is foolishness. Your introspection is very harmful to you." There was something about the charge of introspection that always chilled and wounded her and made her turn in on herself.

"Because you deny yourself, because you hold yourself back and persecute yourself."

"That's not true," she said. "That's not true." Her voice had a hurt, bitter ring. Long afterward I was to remember exactly the tone of her voice as she said: "That's not true."

But she quickly changed her tone and in a voice that sounded more cheerful, explained the almost physical suffering that she endured daily on account of happenings in the world that she abhorred.

"And it is not once only, but many times, almost always early in the morning, that I feel a cloud hanging over me; a heavy cloud stifling me, as though my lungs were forced to breathe an unaccustomed air. . . . I begin to tremble. I seem not to belong to this earth and try to escape from my body and from thinking about things and seeing them in this or that light. What can a bit of reflecting flesh do? Of what use can it be? I am unable to sleep and I seize a book. All the worse. There, in the corner where I am, is that bit of useless thinking flesh, that intruder able only to tremble."

She looked at me and added:

"And what an interruption of the solitude that you need for your reflection, what a drag on your work!"

The proprietor shut off the music and a couple came downstairs and went out.

When I tried to convince her again that it wasn't so and to show her how mistaken she was and how together we had a mission to carry out, it was futile. Futile, like so many things. I saw against her pallid face the stubbornness of her clear, intent, determined eyes.

Finally we left the café and after crossing many squares and passing under many arches, avoiding vehicles, talking endlessly, thinking contradictory thoughts, hesitating, and recommencing so many times, we reached the Retiro station, with the radio strung from its tower and the great moon face of its clock shining over the bare trees. The hands pointed to eight o'clock.

"I never used to be troubled by my solitude," said Gloria, "and I had never given up a certain hope. Deep down within me I had confidence in life — not in people, that is different — in life; and now I see more clearly every day that natural relations are not of this world, and that when one finally meets some man who is not on his guard, one can do him no good and ought never to join him."

I pointed at the clear winter sky with its myriad luminous stars and the Southern Cross.

"In this country," I said, "I have suffered and longed for so much; in this country I have wanted only one type of soul — a soul so tender and sensitive that to approach it would be like hearing a pure cry. When I saw you I realized that you were one of them. With souls like yours something can be created. All the others are moribund, fit only for compromises, pacts, vacillation, and conformity — born compromisers. But when one comes upon a soul with a strong wrapping — warm, truthful, and full-blooded — one can hope for an eternal destiny for it, independent of circumstances. We must live and carry on in order to build something together."

"Something, but what is *something*? What something?"

There she stood boldly demanding a reply which would save her.

And I could give her no answer. Who could have given it to her? I knew what I had to do; I knew my own vocation. I ac-

cepted my part — but she? It was cruel to see her there so delicate and beautiful in her black jacket with her little hat femininely turned down over her right ear.

"For the moment, hold out," I said to her; "for the moment,
have confidence that we have been given a shape to oppose
things. Why not let the external, accidental, varied confusion
give in instead of yourself yielding? Let the cry that one has to
give when one is touched ring out as hard and clear as a crystal
in its infinite range of vibration."

And I knew that I was talking literature.

"The world is intolerable the way it is today," she said. The
street light flared up momentarily and lighted her thin brown
face. "To live is to feel oneself an accomplice in its errors. We
are all working joylessly in a sort of immobilized death. One
gets so tired of it!"

We were on the upper level of the cold, inhospitable, deserted
plaza, its trees grasping with their knotty claws at the inky
atmosphere. I guided her toward the south end of the plaza and
told her that we would go back to the house. She had no reason
to say no or yes. She went.

We climbed the stairs to my room, where we sat down and I
began to kiss her. She was cold, terribly cold, and her hands lay
still against her dark dress. They felt stiff on my arms.

"Poor girl," I said, "poor girl."

"Your house is cold, Martín," she said.

"It warms up as soon as one comes in."

"Yes," she said.

From the highest point in the sky over the river the silvery
splendor dropped so quickly to the street that it fell in fragments to its dissolution and death. Again we returned in the
direction of the Retiro, looking for a place to dine, and again
we came to the plaza. It was ten by the tower clock. We climbed
the slope to the upper plaza and saw the thousand little lights

of the Cavanagh and of the smaller Plaza building, with its recessed façade and smoking chimney. I turned up my overcoat collar.

"What a beautiful woman!" said Gloria in her suffering voice.

I turned around just as you were entering the hotel, in evening clothes, alone.

5 1

I HAD heard nothing about you during all this time. Nothing. I knew only that you were living your own life, on that lofty island of reserve and pride.

That aura of mysterious respect still clung to you. You were more and more isolated, and the name of Cárdenas loomed larger and larger in public affairs. People calculated his name in terms of considerable wealth. You came and went like a stranger from your own house and appeared less and less frequently in your city home. Even its walls were alien to you. Everything about you seemed cold as you crossed the great rooms on the lower floor with a bunch of splendid pink begonias from your garden. Cardinal Richelieu, Addison, and Carlyle must all have died of boredom in the library. When books fall into certain hands they suffer punishment for life. You arranged the flowers carefully in their vases and shut yourself up in your inner rooms.

What could you say about all the money that came into your home through the cautious channels of bribery. It nauseated you, but your sons tied you to it and induced you to put up with it as best you could. It was your burden, as any other might have been. In winter you shut yourself up in your greenhouse, spending whole days there, among the tuberoses, tall shrubs, orchids, imperial roses, jasmines, and the myriad types of begonias. You had a great fondness for begonias, with their thousands of varieties originating in the hot regions of America, Asia, and Africa. In addition to the magnificent Welton, with its gigantic stem, you admired the stately, vigorous Ascot and the unusual fuchsia-leaved and chestnut-leaved varieties. Those with the beautiful pink blossoms that bloom in the summer gardens, and the strange, stiff, Carolina variety were among your favorites.

Your sons were now adolescent. The elder and more thoughtful and solitary one, about whom you worried particularly, was nearly fifteen. The younger one was still quietly playing with his engineering toys.

You had long conversations with them both and never tired of drawing them out on all manner of subjects. You watched them for hours on end. They were your companions. For them were your intimacy, warmth, and laughter. Ah, how you made them laugh during the long evenings in the park when the three of you sat together at the edge of the pool, listening to the mad croaking of the frogs!

I bought an afternoon paper, walked for another five minutes, and returned to my house. After setting the hands of the old clock, I sat down in an easy chair with the windows open to the dusk and began to read. From the street came an interminable wrangling between some hucksters. At length the concierge intervened, and I could hear them hawking their wares as they moved on down the street. I opened the newspaper. To judge by the important news, the world was infested by robbers and criminals preying on their victims. I read until late, the quiet of the evening interrupted from time to time only by the mournful whistle of a locomotive from the near-by station or the melodious bells of the Retiro. Then I jotted down in my notebook some ideas that had occurred to me. It was a voluminous notebook, bound in flexible English leather, that had seen a great deal of the world. Its friendly, pliable covers seemed to indicate that it was conscious of its role. Prose, short original and translated poems, all went into it as they occurred to me. It was old and stained with ink like the notebook of an old campaigner.

I had been invited to dine at a hotel by some foreigners and had just taken a warm bath when there came a knock at the door. I slowly put on my dressing-gown and went to open it. On the doorstep stood the rustic-looking Anselmi. There he was, his face every day more lighted up with contentment. "Hail!" he said, and walked in.

He planted himself jovially in front of me, commented on my fresh appearance after my bath, winked, and, loquacious and happy, helped himself to a cigarette out of the mahogany box.

"You going out?"

"I've got a dinner on, but don't have to go yet. I must leave at nine."

He seemed disappointed, having undoubtedly planned on our going out together.

I went into my bedroom to continue my dressing, while he stayed in the living-room, whence he informed me that he had just discovered a nest of "brilliant eaglets." He was delighted. "Yes," his voice boomed from the other room, "there's no doubt about it. They are the new youth. They're springing up on every hand. It can't be stopped."

I continued dressing while he informed me from the other room why the young men that he had just met seemed to him both important and symptomatic.

"It's not that they are active themselves or even about to start something. No, that's not it. I don't know when that will come. The important thing is that they are active, vital fragments of a state of conscience. They're lads much more inspired to take up a clean, new, palpitating cause than absorbed in their own individual lives."

According to Anselmi, it was almost as if what they needed was a cause to die for. They scorned the old way of living and were ready for anything.

I was somewhat skeptical as always regarding Anselmi's news. I felt that he was even more ready than I — which was saying a great deal — to let himself be swept away by sudden enthusiasm where his aspirations were concerned.

"Now is the moment when we must really start creating," he said. "We've thrown many years of illusions into the street. But now the moment has arrived."

As I heard his voice and went into the bathroom and began to comb my hair, all those past years and his present effervescence flashed through my mind.

Then I heard him get up and go into the kitchen for some whisky. I called to him laughingly that it was time to spare his health and stop poisoning himself with alcohol.

"No," he shouted from the kitchen, "now we can look at things with the eyes of spectators. What the devil! There is a time for sowing, and another for reaping."

I reflected that he had never sown anything but hopes.

"Now we can go into the reserve, my dear fellow." He burst into a laugh. "We are like those colonels who have never served and who, when called up for important duty, turn out to be hopeless invalids. . . ."

"Speak for yourself, old man," I cried.

"For both of us, Martín," he said from the living-room, to which he had just returned bearing a bottle of Bobby Burns and some glasses for both of us. I came in too, putting on my coat.

"Turn down your collar," he said.

I turned it down.

"To both the invalids!" he toasted.

I hurled an insult at him. He laughed and we drank.

"No," he said, changing his tone. "Seriously speaking, those boys are really worth watching. Look here — "

He took some typewritten pages out of the inner pocket of his double-breasted coat and asked me to listen to them. He read a short political poem in a serious voice. It was very good. I told him that it had quality.

301

"It has, hasn't it?" he said.

"Yes, the verses are good."

He handed me the papers, and I read them over carefully. There were excellent pieces among them. A virile poetry with great human warmth like that of Charles Péguy. Only one of the poems was halting and vacillating.

"Who are they? I should like to know them."

He laid his index finger mysteriously against his lips to indicate that he would take it upon himself to arrange it.

"I'm on another trail," he said, "another small group that has ability. They're fine rascals!"

I had often seen him harbor similiar hopes. He always announced them with the same glow of satisfaction in his youthful eyes, though the years were now slightly thickening his lower lids.

"Good!" I replied. "I hope you're right."

I set my glass down on the table. The Bobby Burns bottle always reminded me of my friends in Brussels and of the comfortable, well-lighted dining-room at Rumpelmonde's.

We began to talk about other things. We could no longer see objects about us in the room. I switched on the light and closed the window.

Anselmi came over to the table and began to look over the papers and books. He dropped a French volume with a snort. Some strange quirk in his character always made him react strongly against literature. He must have had an idea that a literary temperament was a sign of weakness or effeminacy, though I knew, of course, that he lived steeped in books.

"Yesterday I found a perfect book for you, in a second-hand bookstore," he said. "I didn't buy it because it was an expensive edition and I was broke. . . . A history of literature and how it has deformed character, written by a contemporary of Keats. A curious book in which one could see the sort of boobies that

Shelley and Marlowe became. And how for every Jacopone da Todi there are two hundred libertines who act like ranting prophets."

He uncovered some of the manuscript of *The Forty Nights* and insisted on my reading part of it to him.

"It's too late for that, I must go."

52

GLORIA arrived at eight o'clock with a bag of hot chestnuts, bringing in a little of the cold from the street on her hands and clothes. Sometimes I read a part of my book to her, with the ink still fresh on it. She listened with close attention, her hands folded under her chin, and commented intelligently and to the point on what I had read. Then I put the paper away and we went out for supper to one of our usual restaurants. We had made friends with some patrons of the Banus.

Three students and two foremen in a metallurgical plant especially interested me. They were real people. They had the clean, wholesome attitude toward things of men who have never trafficked or done anything but devote themselves to doing better what they are destined to do in their community. Some nights when Gloria was very tired, she crossed the street to her house while I stayed behind with them in one of the neighboring cafés discussing a thousand different subjects. We talked about Argentina and the world. All had keen minds, which one realized only after penetrating several thick outer layers. They were enthusiastic readers, but their reaction to books was never literary. Their demands were substantial. They were not satisfied with the merely superficial meaning of words or with the insinuations of easy dialectics. They were very exacting, and as this was fundamental in their attitude, they were always strong and genuine. It gave me a great deal of pleasure and a feeling of well-being to be with them. We were of different ages. The students, still very young, were finishing their literary studies at the university. The two metallurgists, Orioli and Alfaro, were about thirty years old. The names of the other three were Valdés, Dupont, and Camauer. The only one of them who had unusual physical characteristics was Valdés, with his thin, ascetic face, his reflective brown eyes, almost all pupil, and very broad forehead. I enjoyed their criticism of me: that I was the worst sort of a bourgeois and that my book was the swan song of the bourgeoisie.

One night Gloria and I were crossing a well-shaded street in Belgrano where the night seemed cut off from the bright sky, pinioned under the lofty treetops. She had been happy lately. She knew it, and it gave us both satisfaction. As we passed a house with a little garden in front of it, a cheap piano struck up Mendelssohn's *Wedding March*. Gloria stopped in her tracks. I felt her arms suddenly stiffen in front of me like a barricade. After a moment we went on and she started to laugh, saying that she was stupid and that the oddest things happened to her.

I laughed too and took her arm and poked fun at her. She laughed again. I had never seen her mock herself like that before.

"What a shame!" I said to her. "What a shame! Joan of Arc caught in flagrant sensibility!"

"You see what a hopeless person I am. Completely hopeless?"

"Yes, you're right. You are hopeless!"

But I did not say what I felt. I felt that her sudden stopping had been strange, that it had had nothing to do with sentimentality, and that as usual her instantaneous reaction had been due to something less simple. I saw that her laughter was only superficial, and suddenly a fear for her gripped me.

I pressed her arm and we walked a few blocks in the cold night. The wooded regions of Golf surrounded the little railroad hut by the wide, deserted avenue. We were talking. We playfully tried to walk as fast as we could. She lengthened her stride to match mine, pretending that she was very strong, then tired and begged off. I kept laughing at her. "Joan in defeat! What a bad day for fighting Joan!"

With sudden enthusiasm I talked to her about our friends, the pleasant young people at Banus.

We entered the wood. Gloria ran ahead a few steps, climbed the grassy slope, and stood by the trunk of one of the old palm trees, touching its venerable bark and breathing in its aroma with the cold air. The grass too, as if protesting against being trodden on, exhaled its fresh fragrance. Gloria pressed her face against the cold bark.

"That's the way," I said.

She ran impulsively toward me — I waited for her in the path — and pressed against me as she threw her head back with a quick gesture to free it from her long, fine locks that hung down to her shoulders. She was breathing deeply. For some seconds she remained like that, full of a sense of deep contentment. Then she closed her mouth, and the expression of restless fatigue that I knew so well crept back into her quiet eyes.

"Martín."

"What?"

"It has been a great mistake, hasn't it?"

"What?"

"All this."

A feeling of impatience seized me.

"For God's sake, Gloria, don't talk to me any more about that! What intolerable nonsense!"

"I am useless!" she ejaculated, and her voice was both a sob and a cry. I upbraided her and repeated my remark. She was staring straight ahead of her, holding on to my arm. She seemed not to have heard or heeded what I had said. At length she said calmly:

"Isn't that star over there above the avenue beautiful?"

I raised my eyes. The broad avenue was like a sea of black asphalt. In the sky above and ahead of us there was, as she had said, a beautiful star.

Gloria continued to gaze at it. "When I was a little girl I used to run and try to get behind that star and was disappointed because it could never be done."

We passed the last of the iron cages at the Zoological Park, where so many varieties of animals were sleeping in exile.

"And after all it has been the same thing ever since." Her voice changed. "But never mind, never mind. It's just my mania."

She burst out laughing and her whole body yielded to a moment of forgetfulness, like a person shaking off caution and plunging ahead. Every impulse of hers had qualities that were both soft and violent; her gestures seemed not to come from her body; her whole being, rather, accompanied them in her changing moods. One felt her now near at hand, and again far off, escaped.

"I feel so well for the moment," she said cheerfully. "I have the feeling that the sluice-gates are opening and that all my stagnation is escaping with a rush."

"There is no stagnant water in you, Gloria. I can see very clearly inside of you." (I could not see her clearly.) "So clearly!"

"Then suddenly come days of stagnation! . . . Of such physical desolation that I see myself a woman wandering on a desert island, weeping over very ancient woes. . . ."

"Weeping over ills so young that they seem ancient to you."

"I always see myself wandering like that late at night, and alone."

"What ideas!" I said. "What ideas!" I was a poor chump and did not know what else to say to her.

"I must be so boring to you," she said.

"You are quite the opposite. You are a love."

"It seems to me as though you were playing, big as you are,

with a little girl . . . and that the little girl is always stupidly spoiling your games. . . ."

I was not strong, I was a poor chump.

"No, such a serious little girl that no one can play with her. Something incredible!"

"Yes, yes, you can play with her, can't you?" she asked.

"Sometimes. Not often."

"Don't lie! Too many times," and her eyes sparkled with unexpected roguishness. She tried to deceive me with her naïve playfulness.

I thought of her young body, so little attracted to love, brown, slender, and passive in its chaste nudity, her body that I knew so well, but had never been able thoroughly to awaken.

From the depths of my anxiety I talked to her jestingly. "You are a love, and not in the least a Joan of Arc."

"Thank God!"

"No. It's too bad. It would have been so beautiful for you to resemble Joan of Arc."

"Armed?"

"Armed and fearless."

"Wearing a suit of armor?"

"Yes. You would have been splendid, and imposing in armor!"

"No, I am a lonely woman on a desert island."

"I like the other picture better."

"I don't."

"I do."

We laughed and, chatting good-humoredly, walked on together, past the Museum, the massive hotel, and the old Palais de Glace, from which pennants and little flags still fluttered. Then I talked to her more seriously about my book, about what I had written that afternoon, about the thirty pages I had torn up and the anger that had come over me afterward. She told me the story of Coventry Patmore's poem "The Toys," which she had read in the library and liked so much. The fact that she had recently found the poem that I had thought about so often years before stirred me and made me feel still more tenderness for her. I blessed the cold that had brought us together and the night that had offered us its vast hospice. Like the character in the poem leaning over his son, I had a great need to comfort her sad heart. But as I could not find the necessary words, I limited myself to pressing her arm a little more warmly. This was slight comfort, as usual, because in the last analysis we always lack the essential words, those that have not been revealed to us. After walking some more and talking about things that did not relate to the real issue, we paused before crossing one of the narrow intersections of the Paseo, linked with the most varied sorts of arcades. Gloria looked across the street and asked me in the uncanny voice that sometimes terrified me:

"It has been a great mistake, hasn't it?"

The next day I took a holiday and, after an early breakfast, wandered about Buenos Aires. It was so long since I had faced it in a leisurely, friendly meeting. The city was oriented differently, turned toward its bustling center. It was enough to look at it to see that it was a city of words. Written words, spoken words, great public parliaments; large signs entirely covered with letters; even insults in Buenos Aires took on an air of eloquent bravado.

Oh, the great familiar city! I crossed it that afternoon from the sunny circles opposite the Post Office to Cangallo, the boulevard that cuts it vertically in two after seventeen hundred of its numbered houses.

But ah, I loved you, city! For thirty years I had had my hand on your warm body.

At seven in the evening Florida regaled its crowds with bright lights.

But I was not at rest. I was by no means at ease until I had achieved something, until I had tested my ability. . . . I smiled to myself reflectively, but was not at rest. What a long life without a flowering!

I needed to finish the book, to write the last word of it. I stopped in front of a shop window. Again I was aware of an inner restlessness, a need to hurry.

At that moment I became conscious of someone standing beside me. It was Jazmín Guerrero. He was magnificently dressed in an ample, ministerial top-coat with an English stock of black and gray silk about his throat. He looked up in surprise, smiling cordially and expansively.

"Martín Tregua!"

"Hello," I said to him.

He boomed his pleasure, to the wonderment of the passers-by, as if I had just sprung out of a cave. Across the street, a jewelry store displayed an advertising placard. He was much more jovial than years before.

"Well! Well!" he exclaimed, and he repeated: "Well! Well!"

His whole person radiated pompous amiability.

Only when I replied, and he had repeated for the third time his "Well, well," was his enormous effusive energy discharged. He asked me how I was and where I had been keeping myself; then without catching his breath, which, however, did not seem to run short, he told me that he had written three volumes on the State and the individual, that he had been made a corresponding member of two academies and had had three banquets given in his honor, that he was very busy, and that if the world was in bad shape, it would soon be mended.

"But let's step in and have a drink somewhere."

We walked northward and went down into a basement bar. It was a little room shaped like a T, wainscoted in light-colored wood. The upholstered armchairs against the walls seemed to be hugging the angles, to escape from the delirious illumination. Guerrero nodded to everybody with his characteristic expansiveness. From time to time he whispered a name to me and mentioned an office. "But it has no importance," he said. I was uncertain whether he was referring to the person, or to our meeting, or to the information itself. The waiter wiped the table with his napkin.

"What are you going to have?"

Guerrero glanced about as though looking for someone in the little room. In the rear there were some men drinking at the bar.

"Bronx," I said.

"Same for me. No, hold on! I'll have a champagne and sherry. My mixture, you know," he admonished the waiter. "Three to one."

He took off his top-coat and rubbed his hands, visibly settling down for a talk. I remarked that it had been a long time since we had seen each other, but that I had read something in the papers about his political activities, his appointment to many commissions, and his attending numerous important functions.

"Yes," he said, "everyone has his own path to follow. But without political power individual action is too pale and limited. Your wings are clipped. And you are hampered in playing your part in the larger field of affairs."

Three bareheaded girls wearing smart fur boleros came in talking gaily to a staid, white-haired, blue-eyed gentleman, who smiled as serenely as a great oak. Guerrero whispered a name into my ear.

"Oh," I said, feigning real interest.

The girls were young and attractive with their gardenias and elusive perfume like dry wood that filled the room. They sat up on high stools at the bar.

"It cuts you out of important affairs," he added, pointedly greeting the girls' companion. The gentleman came over and Guerrero stood up and introduced us. They exchanged a few

310

words in low tones. The old man said: "Good-by" and Guerrero sat down again.

"I have always thought . . ."

While the waiter was serving us, he began to tell me what he had always thought, which was that the rulers of Argentina, collectively and individually, were a lot of dull bureaucrats unhappily caught up in a maze of political and social questions, like shepherds who know neither how many sheep they have nor how to drive them.

He was pleased with the simile and turned it over to say it again in different words: "or a drover whose oxen escape because they are so large and numerous, and consequently the most important questions wander about ownerless like stray oxen." He raised his voice, to study the effect of his words, until it boomed to the farthest corner of the room like a proudly beflagged ship. "Their situation must be attributed to a wrong type of education. They have been trained in the outworn, oratorically brilliant, Gladstonian democracy and have had constitutional and legal experience, but they have not one iota of creative genius. That is because they were brought up in the old school of English politics, in which, I might say, *trop de génie tourne en danger*, and in which the slightest trace of improvising genius is not only feared but crushed as soon as it threatens to become a public menace. Raised on political principles that might be compared to an acrobatic dance between the covers of a closed book, their organs of inspiration are stunted and atrophied. But a great policy is the result of an improvising genius, a conflagration kindled by a spark that has not been put out in time by a bucket of water. It must be based above all upon the liberty of a single man and the submission of the rest, quite the reverse of democracy, where the freedom of all turns on the shackling of one man, called government. . . ."

At that moment the distinguished old gentleman came over again and, with a slight nod, left a card with a message on it beside Guerrero's glass, after which, so as not to interrupt Guerrero's exposition, he quietly returned to his seat.

"From time to time, with a great display of liberality, democracy tosses its ruler a succulent bone, with hardly any meat on it, however. Discretional powers! Discretional powers are a lot of nonsense! A clear field for the chief, or perpetual imprisonment to adminstrative red tape and the Constitution! The Constitution! Another sacred cow! The best constitution is the one that walks like a strong man. There is no other. It is like trying to teach genius by a correspondence course. None of your cantatas for me! The Magna Charta is all right when it is a little speech perched on the back of a fabulous empire. But to make that empire, virile hands must begin by scrapping prejudice with the ax of genius and setting in motion a terrible creative mechanism that blasts the dreams of the legalists, sleepers, and compromisers. Knock down and build up! Down with the guilty, pudding-headed, sentimental bourgeoisie, drugged with expedients and rotten with caution! Long live the only vital forces in continuous transformation, the people and the aristocracy!"

He made a sweeping gesture with the hand that held his glass, as though he had finished sowing his seed, and spilled some of his cocktail on the table. One of the girls, with cat's eyes and full lips, who wore a dark, calfskin jacket and a white gardenia, looked at him with open-mouthed wonderment. The other girls were talking to the elderly gentleman.

"Philip II. . . ." He impaled me with a theory in which he gloriously jumbled ultra-modern administrative practice with the creation of a holy State, somewhat at variance with his theory of improvisation.

At a modest suggestion from me that rationally one could subscribe to everything, but spiritually to very little, his polemic

fury, under the girl's eye, seemed to redouble, his added vituper-
ation of the democracies, however, being elegantly toned down
on her account.

Like a virtuoso listening to himself, he launched forth on an
imperial symphony.

"I used to be so simple as to believe," he went on, his tapering
fingers adjusting his eye-glasses to the bridge of his prominent
nose, "that affairs could be settled by metaphysical or religious
solutions. Now I believe that our internal house-cleaning must
include a superficial dusting and an energetic sweeping and
polishing. The classical economics of the eighteenth century"
—he threw a circumstantial glance at the young girls by the bar
— "the classical economics believed in the absolute idea of
liberty, and in its pragmatic principle, just as the Jacobin conception of history played with the fountains of free will in a
Versailles occupied by the rabble. Today, as those systems are
dead, only the idea of a will and a State joined together remains
standing. What the old liberalism considered as a mere tutor
and administrative co-ordinator — the State as such — dawns
today with the strength of a creative entity in its own right,
which, being also a creator of history, relegates man to his
proper place. I have learned from Burke and de Maistre that
man is nothing outside of history."

This reactionary talked like a revolutionary. Then he lowered
his voice as if to confide in me a more personal and less categorical truth.

"Wouldn't I be a dunce if I thought otherwise? The will to
power is the will to accumulate. I am accumulating. My strength
lies in pressing that button. Thinking against the bourgeoisie
brings luck with the bourgeois, while thinking with them brings
luck neither with them nor with their enemies. That is an excellent tactical principle."

He laughed more and more complacently and continued his
ogling of the young girls at the bar. None of the three was pay-

ing any attention to him now. I thought of his wife and the philanthropic rhapsodies in which she used constantly to involve herself.

"I am trying to make proselytes," he said suddenly. "I am anti-positivist, but positive (in harmony with my theories). Unfortunately, however, the number of legal cases that I have to defend takes more and more of my time. It is not the same here as in countries with an older culture. Here it is absurd to think that a political leader or an intellectual or moral apostle can spring from the thin broth of misery and privation. Our reality is shaped differently. Wealth is our atmosphere and we must constantly take that into account. Who could bring about a revolution here without the wealthy? The wealthy must be attracted to the movement by special appeals. It is difficult to talk to them about State socialism. They must be told about state aristocracy; something like an oligarchy, of course, but nobler. A theocracy of gentlemen — how shall I put it — not of plutocracy; the term has been demonetized. They would think they were losing caste. Another word would have to be invented. A crœsocracy. V*oilà!*"

I realized that it was a caricature even of his own views; that the group that he belonged to was the same worn-out, tottering one that he was pretending to oppose, and that no sane, right-thinking man could take this leader of revived deceptions seriously.

"Well," I said, "it's getting late. I must be off."

I thought of going out and wandering about the city.

He started as if he had only just realized that other people besides himself existed, and insisted that we must meet again and have another talk. He added that he would let me know when they gave him another banquet. He smiled at the girl with the fox scarf and gardenia. She made a scornful face and turned to the white-haired gentleman.

Jazmín Guerrero then realized that he had forgotten some-

314

thing, and before standing up, he asked me what I had been doing.

"Nothing," I told him. "I am not doing a thing."

He acted as though I had said that I had just built Reims Cathedral.

53

WHAT interest had I in politics of that sort? What was important to me was the human fact, the source and destiny of that living abundance from which politics springs, moral or spiritual, honest or crooked, according to its condition.

I got up early and saw the first dawn in September. Every human experience, however dark, bears in it such a power of revelation!

During the morning my book suffered a hiatus. My whole mind turned to Gloria. Her chronic listlessness did me a great deal of harm. I could not put the thought of her out of my mind for a moment. How to bring her back from her abstraction and repeated escapes, how to keep her here? I employed all my resourcefulness. It was like a doctor's vigil at the bedside of a hopeless patient. It was my sole occupation. One day I told Gloria that only our permanent union would give us a little alleviation and a little pragmatic faith — as necessary as other faiths. It only made her worse. She seemed troubled rather than frightened at the thought. It threw her into great confusion and she was visibly more nervous that day than ever.

I stayed with her whenever it was possible. We were separated only during the time that she was at her work, but it was quite obvious that this situation upset her rather than giving her peace. I do not know how much her conscience may have been troubled by the thought that she had completely disrupted the preoccupation around which my own life had shaped itself.

I exhausted my ingenuity to find ways to divert her. I tried to occupy her mind and hold her interest in a thousand different directions, ranging from plans for travel to reading together in the pleasant, restful atmosphere before the fire and discussing our reading afterward. How many afternoons we spent — from two to eight — listening to recordings of the best modern and classical music, or reading, stretched out on the carpet, the most curious and stimulating texts! Then Gloria made tea while we laughed at many quaint and amusing whimsies.

But her intelligence, which attracted me so powerfully, perhaps because of the traces of basic rawness and desolation always present in it, and her soul, which never rested from self-persecution, were harsh and unrelenting toward herself and dissatisfied with life and its daily round. At last she felt that her presence beside me was harmful to me, and that nothing mattered except to take herself so far away that she could not be recaptured.

The nature of her fears may make it seem that she was completely despondent, but it was easy to lift her spirit quickly. It was enough to touch her deeply for her to open her eyes and become tense, alert, and intelligent. After such periods of buoyancy, however, she sank back again into the twilight of the world. She became as intractable as a wounded bird. How could she have seemed strong and resilient to me in the beginning?

But what worried me most was precisely her habit of keeping her hurts to herself. She lowered the curtain in order to let no one witness her disaster, ignominy, or neurosis.

It was on one of those September days that she arrived unexpectedly as I was copying some translations on the typewriter.

"No, go on," she said. "Please."

She went into the kitchen, made two cups of coffee, and brought one to me. Her ringless hands trembled more than ever. She wore a black blouse under her suit, and suède shoes. She sat down on the sofa and tried to persuade me to keep on writing. I went over to her and looked at her closely. The clock on the

Torre de los Ingleses struck six; almost simultaneously a shrill factory whistle announced the closing hour to its workmen.

Gloria had frequent vexations in her office that brought — as she was so inclined to turn everything into humiliation — fatigue and discouragement to aggravate her moral wound. But I learned about them only by allusions that sometimes escaped her and that she tried immediately to cover up.

I pursued her in the subtler vicissitudes of her problems, trying to find facetious ways to rally her spirit, and called her by famous names symbolically suited to her mood of the moment. Joan of Arc would become Cassandra, or, again, the prodigal son's wife, or Deirdre of the Sorrows, or Cynthia (of Propertius). That afternoon, seeing her particularly low in spirit, I said: "Well, Deirdre?"

She smiled and repeated: "Deirdre!" We had talked about Synge's sad heroine a few days after our first meeting.

She told me that she was very much disturbed. "I have come for the antidote, but I always leave behind what I bring."

"I don't know what it is you leave, but I need it."

She looked at me, a trace of sarcasm mingling with the embitterment that so often came into her eyes.

"I am ready to believe anything — even that I radiate joy."

As I drew her face toward me, she shrank back suddenly like a hunted animal.

"No, that deforms me." She referred to our friendship as though it were something material standing before her. "That makes me worse. I want to be what I am, something completely apart, and poisonous like Paris green."

"Did you come to tell me that?"

"No, not for that, but because of the persistence of my error. I can't resist error when it is pleasant."

"If it is pleasant, why don't you think a little about its pleasant aspects."

"It deforms me and makes me good for nothing."

317

"But one can't be more useful than in being natural and in giving willingly and naturally. Why, why, why are you constantly looking for the sharp edges of things?"

"One can't help one's nature . . . whether it is softness or futility that dissolves on contact. . . ."

When I was about to reply, she stopped me and went on.

"But do you know what a woman is? Something valid, a valid person? Then she needs hands to clutch, resilience to soften the blows, naturalness to exist, confidence that the trivialities of daily living have some meaning behind them, a little softness, and a little possibility of joy or even — of peace."

"Agreed."

"Those things constitute the framework. They make people's faces and foreheads and their roofs and their soil. Without them what does one amount to? Nothing. That's what I wanted to show you. Nothing. Emptiness and poison. Not even mere vacuum; a void filled with poison, humors, and disasters. . . ."

I raised my voice:

"That is constantly looking at yourself in a distorting mirror. And you know what that is? It has a bad name!"

"I don't care at all," she said. "Names don't frighten me."

I insisted, then became indignant. I strode quickly over to the window, and turned around with my back to it. The Virgin of Memling was on my left. I hoped by sudden violence to bring about a reaction, to wear her down, or convince her.

Gloria held a match to her cigarette. Her hand always trembled more or less, depending upon the circumstances and to what was said to her. She replaced the matches in her handbag and laid an arm on the arm of the sofa, her close-fitting black sleeve forming an angle with her body. I was touched with pity by her cheek-bones, which showed too prominently as the light threw them into contrast with her hollow cheeks. In her cheek-bones lay the focus of her strange interest, her somewhat harsh and stubbornly distant air. Those two bony elevations, in which the skin of her whole face culminated, served to accentuate her large eyes.

I thought that she would calm down, but I was mistaken.

"I don't want to talk," she exploded. "I'm going."

She stood up, tall and very slender in her black suit, and buttoned her jacket.

"We'll go together," I said.

"No, I want to be alone."

"Why? To go on looking at yourself in the mirror?"

"To begin something."

"What?"

"To begin a new habit for you. The habit of not seeing me."

"What nonsense!"

"It's got to be that way. There must be a beginning."

I was putting on my things to go out with her when she suddenly stopped.

"I won't have it," she said emphatically. "Do you hear? I won't have it."

But I got my hat, opened the door, and pressed the button for the elevator.

"I won't say a word," I assured her.

We went out. Gloria walked toward the Retiro, and I followed her without speaking. When we had crossed the two plazas and climbed the slope between them, she stopped and wanted to turn toward her house. I dissuaded her gently, and we made for the port, entering Viamonte Street in the direction of the Avenida Costanera. Night was falling. Her depression disturbed me acutely.

She stopped again when we reached the bridge.

"No. I'm going back. I want to go home."

Then she raised her eyes, looked at me, and must have seen how deeply troubled I was by her fragile nature. My brusque coldness had passed off. She seemed to recognize that she had been unfair and said:

"Forgive me. I know how stupid and ugly it is. Ah, how I wish that you weren't so patient!"

Again I mustered reassuring arguments. I was as gentle as possible, regretting my brusqueness, and we continued to walk, she defeated and silent and ready to listen. She was like a small boy who has been punished. I remembered Coventry Patmore's little boy falling asleep sobbing, his toys having been carefully lined up on his night table in a vain effort to brighten his sad little heart.

I was obsessed by my inability to help her. I would have given up so many things — preoccupations, solitude, and work — to make her life a little more tolerable! We came to the part of the Paseo where we had been two or three times before and where our intimacy had begun. I thought that it would do her good. Those days — at least so it seemed to me now — had been days of relative happiness, of a certain tranquillity. A cold blast blew across the river.

I thought how worth while it would be to give up any problem, no matter how absorbing, in order to devote myself to the difficult care of a soul.

"I used to say that I would never be caught complaining!" Her voice broke with emotion. "But as I don't want you to think that all this is your fault, I must tell you some things; even though they will clear up nothing, because what has nothing to do with reason, or consciousness, or even with the heart cannot be explained."

She wanted to sit down on one of the benches in the Paseo. We crossed the street and sat down. It was very cold. She pulled her legs in close and we both lighted cigarettes. It was pleasant to feel the warm smoke in the body.

"You know," she said, "everyone keeps talking about freedom. It's the most frequently used word in the world. Even children use it, and when adolescents want to feel grown-up, it is freedom that they talk about. But it makes me laugh to hear a word used so positively that is so positively non-existent. It is a vague, terrible, meaningless word, so like people." She sat facing me pensively, one hand on my arm, her cigarette in the other. "What freedom is there? Where, in God's name, is the freedom that they prate about? Life is a series of rooms that have nothing to do with freedom. Some people find large rooms that seem to have no walls; others, small rooms that are decorated to look large; still others think that their room is open because it has a mirror in it. The worst rooms are those with no windows, or that open only into other rooms. The rooms may be halls so large that they dazzle everyone and give the illusion of freedom, and there are even some that look out across broad spaces or a pretty landscape. These are the best rooms. But they are all just rooms."

I listened to her, puffing occasionally on my cigarette.

"But there are many people who are privileged to pass from one room into another, from a dark, mean room into a splendid one, where they find flowers on the tables, fireplaces, books, and everything needful for their comfort and pleasure. Also these privileged people generally have a soul to match the room that they find. Finally, others can even choose a room to suit them. . . . Perhaps you, for example, one fine day entered the room of your vocation — a good room. It has windows overlooking society, windows that command a view of the whole country and of spiritual things. One day, I am sure, you will leave it for a better one. . . . Ah, what a spacious, happy, many-windowed room I wish you, Martín!"

Her voice trembled. Sitting under the budding poplars she looked at me with her great quiet eyes.

"But how I wish you would think what my rooms have been like! The first was a very small room with no windows at all and only my father in it. My mother had already gone. It was terribly sad and lonely. I thought about the rooms that lay ahead of me and wondered what they would be like. But the next one was worse. My father was in it too, and his hatred of me was growing. When he died, something in me died too. Then I entered my most solitary room. There was nobody in it but myself, and I did not need myself. You don't know what life is for a woman alone, earning her own livelihood, or what it is to depend upon the whims, coarseness, and brutality of employers.

"Then came my best room — which I was not expecting — the room in which you were living — with a window that looked out on your life. But how useless to think of passing through that window! I am limited by my own nature. I shall never be able to leave my rooms and I have things in them that would be horrible in yours. I was born for them and I am going to stay in them. You get used to the worst and sometimes the worst becomes a part of you."

"This all sounds absurd to me!" I said (although, as a matter of fact, it did not sound absurd at all). "How nonsensical and exaggerated! It will all change for the better when we have a room full of windows in which we shall both live."

I was laughing.

Gloria laughed too and her hand that still rested on my arm patted it affectionately. After a while we felt cold sitting there. We were both shivering.

"We must walk."

We climbed to the top of the dike.

"One thing that I should like," she said, "would be for us to go away together to the seashore for a few days."

She smiled. Would I agree to accept that window?

"Of course, my dear, of course," I said.

She added that she had known for a long time of a secluded hotel at a place called Monte Hermoso, and that it did not matter that the weather was still cold.

"I'll ask for a week's holiday, but you won't touch your book, will you? Not a paper!"

"Not one!"

54

THE NARROW street bordered by tamarisks and sand-dunes, its pleasing enclosure of houses built on heavy piles, led down from the cultivated slope to the seashore in a way that gave to the newcomer the illusion of being on an island. It was no island, however, but a cluster of modest dwellings belonging to the inhabitants of the bathing-resort. The cheerful cottages, painted a gay green and white, were surrounded by green grass. The unpaved street dipped down to the beach, defended against the intruder, in the vicinity of the hotel, by the heavy sand. A draft horse, dragging chains behind him, was driven back and forth, ready to pull out automobiles that stuck in the shifting sand of the dunes or in the wet surface of the beach. The coast *estancias* had left this stretch of public beach, a splendid slope lying at the foot of the lighthouse. We had the end room in the northern wing of the lonely frame hotel, with a window over-looking wild sand-dunes and the sea. At night the wind whipped the sand sharply against the faded old wooden building, its paint half blasted off the two sides from which the gales blew.

Gloria said nothing about the sea. She had wanted to see it, and here it was. On the day of our arrival she stood gazing at it for a while, from the veranda of our hotel. It was a gray day and little whirlwinds of sand skipped along the beach. The sea was leaden that day and grumbled ill-humoredly as it monotonously pastured its flock of white lambs. The wind commanded land and water.

How had the sudden change and flowering taken place in her tortured nature?

"I want to leave it all behind me," she said emphatically as we walked behind the hotel proprietor. The sweaters and gray flannel suits came out of our bags. "The days will be so few!" she said.

Night fell quickly and we ate alone in the dining-room, served by the couple who owned the hotel. The tables were covered with bright checkered cloths. There were two or three kerosene lamps, and in corners of the room stood two stoves and an ancient phonograph. The dinner, one of the beef dishes with a salad, had the appetizing, wholesome flavor of home cooking. But Gloria scarcely tasted the food as it came on. She seemed sustained by the atmosphere of the place, the solitude, and the air warmed by the stoves.

The vast beach, interrupted only by the lighthouse and the few wooden houses scattered in the distance, was enveloped in total darkness as the night closed in.

After eating we made our way cautiously along the shore, feeling the wet sand sink beneath our feet with the approach of a wave, hesitate, slither toward the sea, and again soften under a new wave.

"How do you like this new window to your room?" I asked her.

"It's wonderful!"

We had stopped after walking briskly. Gloria was breathing in the cold air and looking up at the shaft of light from the lighthouse, which disappeared and reappeared in slow rhythm. The wind buffeted us. The beam illuminated now a charge of the waves and again the steely brilliance of the sand strewn with seaweed by the receding tide.

We returned quickly to our warm room and read aloud for a while. The sand from the dunes tinkled against the wooden walls. It must have been splendid company for solitude. But now we had each other's company.

A calm docility seemed to have settled down on Gloria. She showed me a black handkerchief with white polka dots that she had used as a child and now wore knotted about her neck. Suddenly she slipped it over my neck and laughed at the effect. I took it off, carefully knotted it around her neck again, and told her that it was very becoming. It was not. It made her look more sallow and detracted from the soft brown glow of her skin. She glanced in the mirror, doubtless thinking it unbecoming too, but agreed that it suited her and left it on until bedtime.

From then on she became increasingly animated. She began to show more life than I, and a greater reserve of enthusiasm and gaiety. She would not have us stop for a moment and kept suggesting visits to the neighboring *estancias*, to the Post Office, and to the wide lagoon two miles away.

We went out in a Ford in the morning. It was an ancient model, and my poor driving amused Gloria greatly. After traveling fifteen miles among the sand-dunes, we left the hotel property and entered the broad, dusty highway, enclosed by wire fences. Clumps of trees surrounded the main buildings of the first great *estancias*, their red painted roofs conspicuous from a distance, looking like toy barns on the slightly rising ground.

It seemed to me that Gloria's restlessness, curiosity, and constant animation had caused her loss of appetite and made her look haggard. I was surprised by her sustained enthusiasm, but did not dare tell her so for fear of dampening it. When we returned to the hotel, she wanted to go right out again to the beach.

"Isn't this just as beautiful as the hills, or more so?"

She took my arm, and before returning we stepped out more quickly in the direction of the lighthouse. The proprietor of the hotel and his wife watched us from the veranda. From time to time he had to go out with his team to pull an automobile out of the sand. The wind lifted the lapels of his heavy coat and whipped his long hair out to a point on one side. At the top of a distant dune a cloud of sand twisted upward like a plume of smoke over a volcano.

We watched the winter scene beside the ocean. I asked Gloria if she felt happy.

"Yes, as never before."

325

"Really?"

"Yes, I have never been so happy."

"Outside of our rooms, aren't you, and free?"

"No," she laughed, "not outside, but with a window that I have never known before. A big one and growing bigger."

"Big enough to climb out of?"

"Big enough to climb out of."

"I'm so glad."

"Yes, so am I. Happier than ever."

"Don't you see that it had to pass?"

"Yes," replied Gloria, "it had to pass."

We liked most to walk at night along the beach to the solitary oasis of brightness beyond the lighthouse. Through the windows of a miserable wooden hut filtered a bright, yellowish light, by which we could see the heavy figure of a man moving about inside. His existence seemed the most enviable one in the world. Near the house grew a small, dried-up tamarisk hedge.

"You, who always give me names — "

"Yes."

"After this week you may call me Freedom."

"Excellent idea. From now on: Freedom."

"No, not too fast."

She began to laugh. I put my arm across her shoulder and we watched the distant beam flashing from the lighthouse.

"This ocean has its window too," I said, "which opens on another ocean and much farther away, in a straight line, on New Zealand. I wonder what the people out there on the other side of the planet are like."

"They must be like us."

"Perhaps they are, or possibly very different. Saxons. They have bronzed skins."

"But they must be somewhat like us. My skin is a little copper-colored, too."

Every day and night Gloria was a youthful companion. It was

as if we had amputated the sober years of our past.

She was so different and so exhilarated that I was constantly afraid that it might be interrupted or ended.

Only after the week was over was I sure of the permanence of the vital enthusiasm that made her romp like a child over the firm, damp beach. I laughed twice as hard as she, because my worry also laughed inside of me. How happily we scratched the beach for fresh mussels, hunting for the little telltale holes in the hardened sand; and with what sound fatigue we dropped off to sleep at night after all our excitement!

"Do you see how happy I am?" she asked me, and repeated her question.

"Yes."

"Are you always going to remember that these have been good days?"

"So good that we shall think that they were dreamed."

"But they are real. Don't you see how real they are?"

She gave me her mouth, chilled by the air, and soon her lips warmed and we raised our heads happily to breathe in the salt air.

In the train Gloria was still happy, but why was she returning so emaciated after her holidays?

"From living," she said. We were drinking soup in the crowded dining-car. It was brightly lighted and nothing could be seen outside except when we came to a station. They all looked the same, so we had to put our heads out of the window to see where we were. We heard the panting of the locomotive reverberating under the station roof, which it almost touched. There was the inevitable white fence, the standardized lamp with the name of the town or hamlet cut like a stencil through its green, iron shade, and the station-master standing at attention under the bell.

We reached Constitución at ten in the evening. Gloria dropped her valise on the platform and we both laughed at the

narrow escape it had from destruction under the wheels of the
train. In the taxi I suggested that we should not yet separate
and invited her to make some coffee at my apartment, but she
was in a hurry to get back to her house and quickly said good-by
when we reached it.

I slept heavily that night, with my conscience relieved of its
worry about Gloria, happy at last to be able to begin in peace
the most difficult part of *The Forty Nights*.

55

SOMETIMES it is not a voice that speaks in us but an ownerless
emanation as old and impersonal as the complaints of the lower
classes and the ambitious tone of the upper. It was not my voice
that spoke in me. Suddenly it became a cry: "No one influences
anybody. No; no one influences anybody!" The check boy
handed me my hat as I was leaving the restaurant. "Thanks."
No; no one influences anybody.

The September sun bathed the street, and the baroque
façade of an old residence — someone did not see it — and the
display of glassware in the show windows of a prominent store.
My mouth was tightly closed, but the voice inside broke out in
a mad burst of laughter: "To influence! To influence! What a
coarse satire life is!" Who exerts influence? There are casual
and accidental influences, but who can influence deliberately?
In a café a phonograph was monotonously playing Liszt's Concerto in E flat. To pretend that we can influence the egg that
develops and one day receives life tied to its mother's flesh, is
then severed from it, and, like a madman, goes careering down
the years, beset by obstacles, worries, manias, beliefs, and hesitations — that that virulent material can be influenced to suit
our inclinations, ideas, and tastes! Can we influence running
water? We can stop it by throwing up dikes; but the water re·
mains water until it evaporates. The concerto by Liszt fills
multitudes with emotion, but the rapture of its birth is never

repeated in any of the individuals charmed by it. What is condensed by the collective emotion is only a highly complex rhythm. In one soul the concerto stirs pure joy, while to another, alongside, it gives protracted torment. Gloria was right. No one ever influences anybody. Before birth we are in a room and afterward we live in nothing but rooms. Some people think that they are free, but they are the most shut in. My mouth was compressed and I felt a mute grief swelling inside me like a tumor.

Here is the Santa Fé Boulevard. The new church is wedged between two apartment houses; where were the sacred love and inspiration of the architect to give it the indescribable atmosphere of Santa Maria Maddalena dei Pazzi or even of the colonial Santo Domingo with the heroic balls surmounting its humble towers? I went inside. It was so long since I had been in a church. I remained standing in the gloomy nave, troubled by the liturgical rhythm that flowed spontaneously from the few pale, tapering lights burning before the titular saint. I offered not a tear nor a vocal prayer, only that pain, and desolation at our inability to influence human acts by persuasion or conviction.

I went out into the intense sunlight of the street. Alas, my friends of Brussels who were failures, here I stood like you, ardent and insufficient, full of will and incapacity! Alas, my old, disappointed friends! Young, anxious, and disheartened mariners. Sensibility and scruples. Alas, conscientious mariners waiting for their ship in the bay of silence. . . . Dazed, I sat down for a few minutes on a bench in Rodríguez Peña Plaza, then walked down Rodríguez Peña Street. To whom was I to tell all this? A man nurses his joys and angers, buries them, and weeps over them alone. Weeps over them! What tears mine were! But that great weight, that infinite, virile discouragement on reaching the end of the wharf. . . . But isn't the wharf just one more room like the others? At length the warmth in the street was suddenly chilled as the sun disappeared under a cloud. I hurried on, along the Plaza de Mayo to Rivadavia Street. Florida was full of people.

Dusk was gathering, the lights of the narrow street were pouring down from above from every window, door, and balcony. People can influence each other no more than two minerals lying beside each other. One quartz crystal beside another! I crossed an anteroom and went down to the bar. Jazmín Guerrero was not there. It was more brilliantly lighted than when I had been there with him and there were more people. I went up to the bar, asked for a drink, and noticed the girl with the fur bolero and gardenia sitting on a high stool, with a pretty little black hat on, tilted to one side. She looked at me intently, surprised and perplexed; I looked away from her and caught a glimpse of myself in the mirror behind the barman, hedged in by multiform bottles bearing the labels of famous distilleries. Who could have discovered behind that imperturbable, somewhat pale mask reflected in the mirror the ironic despair and fury that it hid? I drank and drank again. I had never done anything, but who has any influence over anybody? The elegant people were shouting and laughing; and hearing their cries, I felt like a corpse that needed some resonant, living reference. I felt a sudden warmth in my body, a delirious sense of well-being, and a repose that quieted the delirium. The girl with the white gardenia came over, bringing her glass, and sat down on the stool next to mine. She smiled timidly and charmingly.

"I know you," she said. Her voice was too soft. "The other day you were pointed out to me here and I hoped that you would come back. I know who you are." She mentioned my name.

I felt very confused, but looked around at her and let her talk to me about one of my books, trying to act naturally. She was lively and insistent; I wanted to shout at her to be still, but I behaved correctly. I heard her voice say: ". . . and do you really believe in those subterranean men? Yes, of course, you must, or how could you describe them so passionately, but . . . " Her eyes were made up skillfully, and her arm moved with a quick, insistent nervousness. Her whole body was insistent, from her eyes and the white gardenia caught in the dark fur to the azalea perfume by Guerlain or Worth.

"Don't you believe it. I have had a good education."

She sat on my right. On my left a youth was leaning against the bar, listening to her and drumming monotonously with his ring on the glass top. ". . . I like best of all the gaiety of the young characters in the first volume of *The Forty Nights*, because they play with life and don't allow themselves to be swept away by the modern philosophy of youth. I can't understand why so many young people are taken in by that Danish pastor — Kierkegaard. He's a poisoner of youth. The idea of death does not seem to me so sinister. Of course there is a young death and an old one. I like the idea of dying young. The symbolism amuses me. That's why I use this azalea perfume. The azalea yields a deadly honey. Do you remember Xenophon's ten thousand? The honey they were poisoned with came from the azalea. What do you think Kierkegaard's influence over the young people is due to?"

I felt my voice swell to violent anger.

"Influence? Kierkegaard is only a vulgar, exaggerated, thwarted man, betrayed by his adherents, as happens at one time or another to every man. Some exploit him to make up for their own inability to create, others to pander to their personal prejudices, which they reinforce by phrases of his taken out of their context. Still others sing him a soothing lullaby for his pains. Is that what is called influencing? What do you think prejudices are? Do you think that they are a bundle of outworn notions that elderly people have about new ideas and customs? No. Prejudices are all the inhuman and dogmatic attitudes at which we strike. Haven't I just been guilty of a terrible prejudice?

As I did not love a person completely, as I was not basically in love with her— for that cannot be commanded — I clung to the prejudice of pity. I thought I could convert her. Convert her to what? What presumption it is to try to convince! I should have left her as she was. When I first met her, she was like the rest of us, like herself, nothing more. I thought that something could be done, but life is completely anarchical. No sooner do we harden into one mold than we set about softening and deforming it, while still paying it lip-service. Undoubtedly the only thing that is not deformed is what lies beyond death. I have known some few people, incredibly few, who have been able to protect themselves, by tooth and nail, and prevent the best that they had in them from being deformed. It is the fiercest struggle there is. The form must be respected. Of those few people, some succumbed morally, and the last one physically. She wanted to go away and she went. . . . Perhaps she was the only one of them unwilling to witness her own deformation and slow defeat, and preferring to cut her moorings while she was still faithful to herself. Why do most sincere people have an air of defeat about them? Do you know?"

The girl in the bolero did not know. She looked at me curiously, with a baffled sympathy that had not completely understood my thought.

"I don't know why it is, either, but they do. In order to appear up to date you must always be a little insincere."

The girl agreed to this, and invited me, as an exception — as she said that she did not like literary people — to come to one of her parties.

"No," I said, "I won't go. I have other things to do."

Instead of becoming angry she laughed, and for a few seconds her strong white teeth were framed by her full, red lips.

"You would like me to go and talk to you in your house? You think that it would be amusing. It wouldn't, nor brilliant, either. Do you think that ideologies as such interest me? I take this or that political view just as I would take a bromide for my health. But nothing matters to me except that strange, delicate, troubled, free, varied human flower, a conscience. Nothing now can matter to me as much as that. The passions, griefs, and extraordinary movements of the conscience, its dawn and sunset, and the blossoming that enriches, exalts, and stirs us by its contact the more the politicians try to bully or lull us into complacency."

We each ordered another drink. I looked at her.

"Do you think that a conscience fades and disappears like a piece of paper consumed in a stove? No. Didn't I tell you that it is a flower? Only death brings it to fruit. That is why I love this country and this continent. It is vast and man struggles in the solitude in which this strange, delicate flower blossoms. . . . Do you know what these men who are alone here today will produce tomorrow?"

"What?" she asked.

I was tired and oppressed by that shadow inside me, that mute grief. I looked at her smart costume, her young face, blue eyes, and full lips, and did not answer. The youth beside me was also looking at her. He had ceased tapping with his ring, but during our silence began again, pretending not to have been listening to what we were saying.

"Yes," said the girl. "It seems to me that we shall have to wait."

"Be quiet," I said to her gently. "What thoughts can you have about this?" It struck her as funny. "A human being is something too serious, and easily destroyed. He has merely to fall out of an airplane or be crushed between the cogs of a machine or shot. But to believe that he doesn't leave his seed! To believe, unless he was born in vain, that he can be blotted out without a trace like something useless!"

I was suddenly ashamed of my vehemence. I felt unworthy, paid the bill, and said good-by. It was very cold in the street. I walked home, opened my window in the dark, and stood for a long time gazing out at the point on the river where I had so often been with Gloria.

56

You entered the flower-shop on that 25th of November, the day that this book began, and in your somewhat hoarse voice, which seemed to come from far away, with a rather troubled look in your eyes, asked for the new begonias of a rare species that you lacked in your collection, with luxuriant, stiff petals, and narrow borders slightly tinged with lilac.

Once more — it had happened seldom in more than twelve years — chance had put us beside each other. As before, you remained entirely in ignorance of who the man might be who had entered the flower-shop in the noisy Diagonal a few moments before you, to put in an ordinary order. This man, who had seen you for the first time twelve years before, was greatly altered by the experiences that he had been through. For more than two months now he had carried about with him through the streets of Buenos Aires, in which he was both an old resident and a stranger, the grief of a sudden, brutal loss. He walked only during the recess between his two cycles of daily work, which he had made heavier than ever and which had finally isolated him from all distractions and from all personal relations except with a few obscure people in various parts of the capital.

I had stopped to have some carnations sent to an old friend, and while I was giving the employee Mercedes Miró's name and address, I saw you come in. You did not find what you had come for — the employee said that the begonias were due to arrive on an early transatlantic liner — and went out again to Maipú Street, where the traffic in the direction of the Diagonal is heavy. I followed you out because I liked to think about you and because I was always stirred by the sight of you.

334

You walked quickly to the Diagonal, crossed the little plaza of Sáenz Peña, where the sculptural group daily offers its solid symbolism to indifferent crowds, and when you reached the sidewalk in front of the Bank of Boston, drove rapidly away in your automobile with the black convertible top. In that district, only a few steps away, we had met years before, and that "God bless you" which had escaped your lips — pronounced over an unknown man — had come from a much less battered, perhaps more sensitive and reserved nature than that which you now bore as unflinchingly as one bears a congenital misfortune.

A terrible misfortune was to overtake you a few days after my glimpse of you that morning at the florist's.

It is strange how apparent your infinite disgust at so much ignominy was to the observant eye. Born of a distinguished family, trained for a triumphant career, and made of exceptional human material — an exception among exceptions — fate had given you an unhappy life, tied to a world of venality, to a husband become cynical and dishonorable, and to two handsome sons — the one weak and the other an alert, handsome youth.

I would never have dared to put you into *The Forty Nights*. To me you were untouchable. You represented the culmination of my deep aspirations for our countrymen; such dignity, integrity, faith in the noble quality of an older Argentina, and scorn for the parvenus that I wanted to follow you and watch over you until I saw the new representatives of Argentina produced by you. Perhaps your sons would resemble the men of the interior, my people, those soldiers who are organizing the advance guard of a spirit called upon to infuse the pure, ancient sap of the country into new facts, into the thoughtful exile of their "forty nights" of subterranean preparation, ordeals, and obscurity.

Do you think that I was unaware of your minor activities? No. Through a thousand channels, some fortuitous, the city told me many secrets almost every day. Only solitary people know a city intimately, just as the beggars standing before the doors of a great hotel know the characters of its guests better than they do each other.

At last, after years of spiritual poverty and suppressed torment, you were finding in your adolescent sons an outlet for your somber, proud, steadfast character! You spent long, merry hours amused by their notions, their keen, varied questions and comments about the grotesque and dishonorable traits of so many people in your world. Your sons were saved, at least spiritually! The older boy read a great deal and his restless mind was awakening to essential problems. The second was more independent and you gave him a freer rein, as a more privileged child of fortune. His frank, manly, intelligent face smiled indulgently while you discussed many abstruse subjects with his elder brother. The three of you were so at one in spirit that when the father raised his crude, boastful voice at supper time you were still united in frequent silence. You seemed to shed your years when you visited your beloved sons in the morning hours, and entered into their activities and interests as though you were their own age. Whenever a visitor came to see you, especially during the months when you all lived in your summer house, you seemed to have been called away from your children's world to a very different one.

You also watched over their physical welfare, and after reading to them in the morning in your favorite corner of the park, and explaining their books to them with a charm that made the stories seem delightful living fables, you turned the younger boy over to an instructor and joined the older son on his short ride through the park, riding a beautiful white horse. The younger boy, in his long, black jodhpurs and white cotton shirt, seemed able to take care of himself, despite his weakness, and carried his head high as you held his horse's bridle. In the late afternoon you taught them curious legends about the flowers, which by their variety of form and color constantly teach the fundamental mystery and principles of creation, as well as the cause of differentiation in nature. Without severity or compulsion, you led them to think about such things and explained colors to the elder boy with a lively touch and an occasional comical mistake that greatly amused his younger brother. Night often surprised you in a frank rough-house with them.

When Cárdenas arrived from the city, it was as if the crystal had suddenly become clouded. He acted as a damper on you and the boys and kept talking and telling stories to cover up his awareness of it.

Other days, after having tea with them on an iron table in the garden, you carefully checked the condition of your delicate plants. You put on your gloves, went into the greenhouse, and skillfully tended the growing things, giving explicit directions from time to time to the gardener.

I suppose that at night you returned to the reality of your personal world, spending little time in reading — books by George Meredith or the poetry of Francis Thompson — but lay long awake, thinking. I imagine that you went to sleep with your face to the open window, lying cold and still like a person who, after turning various sides of his body to meet a driving rain, raises his face to take the punishment and lets the rain beat relentlessly upon it. . . .

On the 10th of December the news appeared in all the papers. It was given brutally, without warning. People learned of it, and remembered it for two days; then it vanished into thin air.

When the white horse slipped his bridle and ran away, throwing the child heavily, and you saw him lying inert on the ground with his head against the stone curb, and his shirt torn open at the neck, when they picked him up and carried him into the house and you saw the silent, stark tragedy before you — the newspapers reported that you were struck dumb with despair.

When I learned about it, your figure leaving the flower-shop some days earlier rose before my eyes. I walked past your city home. A row of automobiles stood beside the curb. The door was closed.

After that I heard nothing, nothing.

I laid siege to your house, stationing myself near it at nightfall after my work was done. A beautiful plaza near it showed the first of the summer luxuriance.

I caught not a glimpse of you. All the windows were closed.

One afternoon, late, I saw you go out. You were walking alone at your rapid pace, dressed in black. You passed me at the corner. Your expression was tragic, and because you had lost much weight, your face had taken on a cold, unapproachable, ethereal beauty.

Your eyes rested on me for a second and you must have been surprised, in your turn, by my expression.

God! What could I do for you? . . .

I had never been able to do anything for anybody. My own life was a wreck. The only acceptable thing about it was its strange, confident faith in the new humanity.

I saw you walking alone in the corridors of despair and was terrified at the thought of your being alone with life, lest you destroy yourself. Alas, didn't I know? . . . Didn't I know because of what had happened to Gloria?

That night, just as the year was ending and the usual merrymaking was going on in Buenos Aires, I laid aside the manuscript of *The Forty Nights* once more, almost completed, and began to write this history for you.

I wrote it quickly, feverishly, needing to confess. I had to commit it to your care. It was the only thing that I could do for you.

Here it is at last. I give it to you. It is long and labored!

When you open it and read it with surprise, think of what I have tried to tell you.

Think of what you have always represented for me; that neither you nor I are any longer alone, and that strong bonds of companionship unite us, for we have shared a common bitter experience, and have carried within us many perhaps illusory images, many desires, contradictions, rebellion and frustrations. All of this that has happened to us was perhaps fated to happen in order to constitute, in the midst of so much ignominy, deception, and death, the sacrifice without which nothing new is born.

As you read the tale of this long and arduous journey, your discerning eye will see, as Tennyson's poem says, with which my manuscript opens, that nothing is lost and nothing lives in vain; everything implies continuity and rebirth; and only what compounds with luxury, sloth, and corruption is sterile. There is a demagogy of the soul just as there is a social demagogy, one that produces nothing and ends with itself.

Do you think that Acevedo, Anselmi, Jiménez, Dennis Atkinson, Professor Autoriello, and that poor Gloria Bambil were failures? I hope that after knowing them you have become their friend. No, they may have been mistaken, inadequate, deluded, or lost, but they were not failures. Theirs were consciences that could not be bought, and what is not bought is genuine. What is sold is only the utilitarian, or the materially imposing. The genuine has a spiritual destiny.

You and all of them have reached that place at which the angry sea of persecution and adversity licks in vain.

All of you, and who knows how many others in this world, have reached the bay, that place of waiting, where their silence is concentrating and where their fruit is ripening without fear of storm or gale. How deep and beautiful is the bay! There wait those who have turned their failure into triumph. At this hour the bay of silence holds you and them. I see you all there, silent and expectant.

339

TYPE NOTE

This book is set in Electra, a Linotype face designed by W. A. Dwiggins. This type is not based on any historical model, nor does it echo any particular period or style. It avoids the extreme contrast between "thick" and "thin" elements that mark most "modern" faces, and attempts to give a feeling of fluidity, power, and speed.

The book was composed, printed, and bound by The Plimpton Press, Norwood, Massachusetts. The typography and binding design are by W. A. Dwiggins.